COLOSSUS

STONE
&
STEEL

COLOSSUS

STONE
&
STEEL

by David Blixt

Colossus: Stone & Steel

Copyright © 2012 by David Blixt

First Edition by Sordelet Ink
Cover by Rob McLean

ISBN-13: 978-0615783178
ISBN-10: 0615783171

www.davidblixt.com

Printed in U.S.A
Published by Sordelet Ink
www.sordeletink.com

FOR RICK SORDELET

Be careful what you wish for.
You may get it.

CONTENTS

Dramatis Personae

JUDEANS

JUDAH – Judah ben Matthais, apprentice mason, twin to Asher
ASHER – Asher ben Matthais, student, twin to Judah

DEBORAH – Judah's love
PHANNIUS – Phannius ben Samuel, Deborah's brother
EUODIAS – Mother to Deborah and Phannius

ANANUS – Ananus ben Ananus, High Priest of the Sanhedrin, leader of Jerusalem
JOSHUA – Joshua ben Gamala, Priest of Jerusalem
YOSEF – Yosef ben Matityahu (later Titus Flavius Josephus) Priest of Jerusalem

ELEAZAR BEN SIMON – Idumean leader of the Judean Rebellion
SIMON BAR GIORA – a leader of the Judean Rebellion, Priest of Acrabatane
YOHANAN OF GISCHALA – Yohanan Me-Gush Halav, Galilean leader of the Judean Rebellion

KING AGRIPPA – Marcus Julius Agrippa, great-grandson of Herod the Great, Rome's client king of Judea
QUEEN BERENICE – Berenice of Cilicia, Agrippa's sister
TIBERIUS – Tiberius Julius Alexander, Apostate Jew turned Roman knight, Governor of Aegypt, brother-in-law to Berenice

LEVI – Levi ben Patroclus, professional bodyguard

ROMANS

VESPASIAN – TITUS FLAVIUS VESPASIANUS SENIOR, Senator, general of the war in Judea

TITUS – TITUS FLAVIUS VESPASIANUS JUNIOR, elder son of Vespasian

CERIALIS – QUINTUS PETILLIUS CERIALUS CAESIUS RUFUS, Senator, Vespasian's son-in-law

CAENIS – ANTONIA CAENIS, mistress of Vespasian

TRAJAN – MARCUS ULPIUS TRAJANUS SENIOR, Senator, commander of the 10th Legion

SEXTUS – SEXTUS VETULLENUS CERIALIS, Senator, commander of the 5th Legion

PLACIDUS – GNAEUS TERTULLUS PLACIDUS, Senator, military tribune in Vespasian's army

BARBARUS – GAIUS SACIDIUS BARBARUS, Roman centurion of the Fifteenth Legion

THORIUS – GNAEUS THORIUS, Roman Optio of the Fifteenth Legion

CURTUS – APPIUS CURTUS, Roman legionary in the Fifteenth Legion

An appendix at the back of this novel details the organization of the Roman legions.

STONE & STEEL

PROLOGUE

AZOTUS, JUDEA
31 MAY, AD 61

"MATTHAIS? IS SHE..?"

"Your daughter is alive, my lord. Seth is following, with my sons. They have her."

Releasing a long-held breath, Symeon sagged as Abigail wrapped her arms about him. Holding her close with his right hand, his left slipped beneath his long beard to rest on his racing heart. Days of prayer had left his knees raw and aching, yet he fell to them once again to offer up his joyful thanks. Abigail joined him, and they prayed together, clutching hands.

Finished, Symeon looked back to the bearer of these glad tidings. "Matthais, thank you. I can only say..."

Abigail noted the curious look on Matthais' face. "What is it? Was she—?"

"She was not molested, my lady."

"Hurt?" asked Symeon.

"No man raised a hand to her, my lord."

Symeon did not care for the title of lord. He was a simple fisher-man, son of a fisherman, turned into a fisher of men. The joke, though old, still made him smile.

But there was no smiling now. Three days ago his daughter had been taken from him, kidnapped by a rich old man who found her beauty irresistible. First he had tried to buy her. Symeon had turned down the match, but the miser Elkanah was unused to being refused. Just as he would have stolen an excellent horse or goat, he had sent his men to abduct Symeon and Abigail's only daughter to be his bride.

There was no recourse at law. As a regular resident in the cells of Fort Mariamne and Fort Phasael in Jerusalem, Symeon had no standing. The new Kohen Gadol, Ananus ben Ananus, was a bitter foe, and the enmity of the high priest put all Jerusalem against you. If Symeon had dared bring this complaint, the Sanhedrin would like as not lock up him, not Elkanah.

And there was no turning to Roman law for Justice. Not for a Jew. So Symeon had turned to prayer. A prayer of deliverance. A prayer for salvation. A prayer for the iron hand of the Lord to reach out and protect his little girl.

His friends had more forceful solutions. Seth, loyal Seth of the Scars, insisted on bringing her back, and Matthais the Mason had offered to help. Despite his fifty years, the stonemason was strong and vigourous, with arms like clubs. He'd taken his two young sons with him. Though not yet men, their father's yard had made the twins stronger than any children Symeon had ever known.

Returned now on a lathered horse, the normally impassioned Matthais was being maddeningly reserved. "What is it, then? Is she injured? Has she gone mad? I beg you, speak!"

Matthais addressed both parents. "Your daughter – they say she prayed all the way to Elkanah's holdings. It's a day's ride. The moment they reached the walls and dragged her within, she was felled by some kind of fit. Writhing and sputtering nonsense, they said. That bastard Elkanah thought she was faking and tried to shake her, but she broke his nose with her forehead. He lost two teeth." Matthais' grin was fleeting, gone as soon as it appeared. "The fit lasted an hour, and when it was over everyone was afraid to go near her. Someone put her in a bed, and when she woke the next morning—" Matthais paused, clearly at a loss for words.

Symeon's vivid imagination usually served him well. At this moment, it was a curse. It was Abigail, brave brave Abigail, who pressed to know the worst. "What? What is it?"

Matthais' voice was like one of his stones, hard and blunt. "The left side of her face is slack. Lifeless. Looks like she's had a stroke. But what thirteen year-old girl has a stroke? They're saying, at Elkanah's hold, they're saying that she was touched. Marked, by the Lord. Elkanah, the coward, ran back to the city just an hour before we arrived. His men said something about a sacrifice, penance. When we got there, Elkanah's men were more than happy to hand her over. They're afraid. As they should be, the bastards. I hope the Lord shrivels their cocks and splits their shins. Pardon me, my lady."

Symeon tried to imagine his daughter's beautiful face as a Greek tragedian's mask, half smiling, half mourning - the face of the insane. "Be careful what you pray for, my friend. The Lord may answer you in kind." He looked to Abigail, whose eyes were swimming. Did she understand? Did she see it? "We prayed for deliverance, for salvation. For the Hand of the Lord to reach out to protect her. And He answered our prayer in every particular."

"Praise to the Lord." She understood. How could he have doubted? No wife was ever so in tune with her husband. A pity that he could not give Abigail the title of wife. "Matthais, where are they?"

"A few miles behind me. She's tired, naturally. Seth wouldn't leave her, so he sent me ahead. Said you'd want to arrange passage to wherever you're heading next."

"He was correct." They had to leave. If this story spread around Jerusalem, that would be just one more excuse to lock him up, stop his work. Perhaps even murder him. Already they had executed so many of his friends. From the old days, only Seth and Matthais were left. *And Saul,* he reminded himself. *But Saul has always traveled his own road.*

"Where will you go, my lord?"

"Where they can't touch us," answered Symeon. "We'll go to the center of the world. We'll go to Rome."

When she arrived, an hour before dawn, the girl was half-asleep in her saddle. They'd ridden all night. Seth, good Seth, suspicious Seth, he understood the danger they were all in.

Matthais' twins hopped off their mounts at once, stretching their sore legs. "Horses!" groaned one. "We would have done better to walk."

"'*Blessed is the man that walketh not in the counsel of the ungodly,*'" retorted the other. That had to be Asher, the boy prodigy. It was said he could perfectly quote any part of Scripture from memory. Which meant the other was Judah, the brawler. Always getting into fights, or so his father claimed. Of the two, Matthais was prouder of Judah.

Ignoring the twins, Symeon and Abigail raced to their daughter's side, pulling her down from horseback and enfolding her in their arms. Abigail had no words, and Symeon found himself able to say nothing but her name. "Perel! Perel! My pearl..."

Drowsily she blinked at him. "Father. I'm fine, father. Truly." And she smiled up at him.

That smile smote his heart. The right side of her face was life, joy, a flower in full bloom. But the left was a mawkish imitation, waxen, limp and lifeless.

Tears flooded Abigail's eyes as she reached out to touch her daughter's slack cheek. "Does it hurt?"

"Not at all." She was trying to sound chirpy, the way she'd always answered them. But she had to speak carefully, for her lips were only half in use. "Papa, I'm sorry for all the trouble." The *sorry* was a little slurred.

"No trouble, no trouble," murmured Symeon, pressing his lips into her hair. Over her head his gaze fixed on Seth. "No trouble?"

"Not yet." Sliding down from his saddle, Seth looked as he always did – hideous. Wounded as a youth, a shiny puckered scar ran from his nose all the way to his left ear. It made the sinister side of his face even more so, pinching the flesh under one eye and giving him a grotesque leer. Not even his neat, trim beard could help. *My friend and my daughter are now a matched pair.*

Still hugging his daughter, Symeon heard the stonemason greet his sons. "Boys. Made yourselves useful, I hope."

Seth answered. "They did. Judah got a deer with his sling. Asher kept us awake with his stories."

"Stories," sneered Matthais. "At least your brother does something useful. You're not a priestling, boy, and doubtful ever will be, no matter what they tell you at your *beth hasefer*. Seems to me you ought to learning to be a man before you give it all up for *stories*."

Red in the face, Asher was silent. It was his twin who answered, flexing his fists. "He kept our minds off our saddlesores and hunger. Pretty useful, I'd say."

Matthais owned a deep and volcanic temper, and was at the edge of eruption. "You'd best say less, boy."

Side by side, the twins faced their father. Half past eleven years, their mother had died bearing them, and they seemed the Castor and Pollux of Judea. So alike in form, so different in spirit. Yet inseparable, even in the face of their father's anger.

Symeon released his daughter and put a hand on his friend's shoulder. "Matthais, I haven't yet thanked your sons. Judah, Asher, I owe you both a debt I can never repay. It was a brave act of loving kindness."

The boys had only met him a handful of times, so his debt likely didn't matter much to them. They had gone after Perel as an adventure, as a boon for their father. The mason had never explained the bond between himself and Symeon. Doubtful he ever would. Matthais was a man of Jerusalem, and in the White City a link to Symeon meant death.

Still, he owed the boys something more. He didn't have an inkling what to do for the rough-and-tumble Judah. In Asher, however, he knew just what offer would serve. "If you ever want a teacher, Asher, come to me. I'll treat you as my own son. You can be a priest, even if it's in exile in Rome."

The boy's eyes widened. "Rome?"

Perel's eyes had similarly turned into saucers. "Is that where we're going?"

"We sail in an hour. Best we get our things aboard."

Seth moved to obey. Symeon took one more look at his daughter's face, feeling he had best say something. Softly in her ear he said, "He has marked you as His own. It is an honour."

Perel dropped her eyes, leaning her slack cheek against his bearded chin. "I *know*, father." She then followed her mother towards the ship that would take them away from their native land.

Symeon gathered the rest of his band of followers and made for one of Azotus' three quays, Nebi Yunis. Their passage was on a Greek merchantman called *The Crest Dancer,* its V-shaped hull making extra room for amphorae of oils and perfumes. It would call at Ptolmais, Tyre, Paphos on Cyprus, Rhodes, then the long run to Athens. From there the small band would have to find their own way to the City of the Seven Hills. And there were many cities, towns, and hamlets on the way to preach in and cast his net for more men.

Watching his daughter board the Dancer, Symeon was glad to be quitting this port city, which had once belonged to a dancing princess called Salome, a woman who had arranged the beheading of one of Symeon's friends. *So much death. And so much of it Jew shedding the blood of his brother's blood. Cain has much to answer for.*

Matthais and his sons helped them shift their possessions aboard, then returned to the quay. Symeon said, "You're certain you will not come?"

The mason shook his head. "Jerusalem's walls have too much of my blood in them. It'd be like leaving behind a brother. Besides, masoning is all I know. And a mason needs a city as much as the city needs him."

Symeon understood. Unlike him, Matthais was in no danger. He had never been a true convert. Only a friend. Yet if there was ever a man to be fished… "Rome is always building. There's never a shortage of work."

"Like as not I'd be carving false idols, then, and new Towers of Babel. No, thank you. I'll see you when you return."

Symeon frowned. *Return? When will that be?* He had always assumed that he would die in Judea. But now he had the strangest feeling that this was his last moment on Judean soil. *Farewell, Israel.*

Embracing Matthais and thanking the twins again, he climbed aboard. As the oarsmen shoved them off and wafted them around, he noticed his daughter looking back at the twins on the quay. One of them waved, and she waved back, her sad half-smile clear as day. He wondered which of them had become her friend until she said, "Do you think he will come and study?"

So it was Asher, the prodigy. Naturally. His daughter favoured the exceptional. "Perhaps, when he's old enough." Hugging her tight, Symeon watched his native land grow smaller and smaller. He had left it many times, but always to return. This felt more final. The last farewell. The sun crested the horizon, dazzling him. His last impression was of the handsome twins on the quay, wrestling and playing as boys will, trying to topple each other into the water. So much of Judea in them. Or rather, of Israel. Intelligence and strength. A questing mind, and a strong will. Those were the rocks of Judaism.

All at once one brother hooked the other's foot, sending him over backwards. The falling twin kept hold of the other's wrist, and they fell together into the water, much to their father's disgust. Symeon laughed, squinting at the sun glinting off the water.

When he was unable to stare into the bright sunlight any longer, Symeon escorted Abigail and Perel below, then asked the ship's captain if there was a fishing net about. "I like to be useful."

PART ONE
EAGLES AND VULTURES

I

AS IF OBEDIENT to Joshua's famous command, the moon hung over the plain of Ajalon like a lamp. A threatening lamp, close, cold – taunting, just out of reach. Full of promise. Full of menace.

The name meant *the Place of Deer*, and just now the deer and gazelles were skittishly returning after a fright. The terrible stamping thunder had shaken the earth, driving them far afield. Venturing back now, their hackles were up, their nerves jittery. So at the first sign of another influx of hunters, they fled again in silence – unlike the birds hiding in the grove of apricot trees, who screamed their outrage as they took flight. It was night, they protested. No time for hunter's games.

They needn't have feared. This night the hunters were after different prey.

Among the hunters was Judah ben Matthais. At seventeen, the mason's son was more Goliath than David, his expansive chest built by years of hewing stone. But unlike Goliath, he had an almost embarrassing comeliness – lush black hair, strong brow, and a body sculpted by years of hard work. Shirtless, barefoot, running in just his kilted cloth, his overall appearance was almost Greek – not the Greeks he rubbed elbows with every day, but the statuary, the beautiful figures of Hellenic myth and song that had invaded Judean culture. Yet his face, from the strong chin to the slight curve of his nose, was pure Hebrew.

The hard planes of his muscles moved like a wild animal. He ran with a lithe step, almost weightless, and he flew over the terrain as if he were one of the deer, barely touching the earth.

There was one difference. Deer didn't carry spears.

Judah shifted the weapon in his grip. From sawing stone to swinging a stick, he had capable hands, strong and large. He didn't have his brother's way with books or words, nor his father's sarcastic streak. He didn't have his grandfather's fabled patience, nor his dead mother's sweetness. Judah was just an angry man who was good with his hands.

Passing the grove of apricot trees, he remembered bringing Deborah here in the summer months. It had been sweet smelling then, but in the time between the fruits had all been stolen and the trees stood denuded as if by locust. These trees were lucky. The larger trees of Ajalon had all been ravaged, knocked down for the invaders' fort or made into siege engines.

Thinking of the invaders fed his anger. Thinking of Deborah made him angry, too, but not in a way that would help. Pushing thoughts of her from his mind, Judah ran on.

Past a small village, Judah and the rest arrived at the great ancient highroad, new-covered with paving stones. This same road had brought the Canaanites, Israelites, Philistines, Aegyptians, and Syrians. It was the road of pilgrimage, and the road of invasion. But unlike all other invaders, the Romans had not only used it, but made it their own, repaving it as they marched. They put their mark on everything they touched, like some hideous nation of Cain.

Breathing hard, Judah ignored the road. Instead he scrambled up the ancient goat-paths on the southern hill ridge. He'd spent countless hours among these hills with his brother, quarrying stone for their father. Normally he might fear a panther or a wolf lurking in a shallow cave. He remembered a nasty fright as a boy when he'd encountered a lone hyena. But tonight the noise from the road had driven all such beasts away.

Behind him, hundreds of men followed as fast as their feet could carry them. Others crossed the road to ascend the northern slope, racing to get ahead of their prey in the valley below.

The Valley of Beth-Horon.

It was here that another Judah, son of another Matthias, had led a revolt against foreign overlords. He had been called the Makkabi – the Hammer of the Lord. Whimsically, Judah wished he had brought one of his father's stone-working hammers. He liked symmetry.

Across the ridge ahead, Judah heard the uniform stamp of hobnail boots, the clatter of hooves, and the creak of wagons and siege machines. The sound of a Roman army on the move.

Racing and stumbling over the rocks, his free hand groping up the rest of the slope, Judah clutched the spear haft. Apart from this lone spear he'd plucked from a dead man, Judah's only weapon was a sling. Traditional, almost poetic. He didn't even have a sword, and there'd been no time to go home and take his father's. Things had happened so fast! One moment the Romans were attacking the Temple, the next they were pulling up their stakes and marching smartly back the way they'd come. And the whole city, it seemed, had given chase.

Judah was no rebel. He paid his taxes. He'd had no part in the riots, the kidnappings, the murders. Those had been the agitators, the Zelotes and Sicarii. Even when word came of the massacre in Alexandria and the death of his twin brother, Judah hadn't taken to the streets. But the anger, seething and boiling, had built. And built.

Then, this morning, the Romans had attacked the heart of his faith, the most sacred site in all the world. In answer, the common men of Jerusalem, men like Judah, had poured into the streets. No shouts, no cries. They were more fearsome for their silence. After a few brief skirmishes, the wary Romans had retreated, and the Jews had followed. As fast as the Romans ran, the Jews ran faster. Without shields, without helms, without armour of any kind. Nothing but their righteous rage.

Judah started among them, then suddenly he was ahead of them, leading them out of the city after the fleeing Roman legion. Anger gave him inexhaustible strength, his lungs filling and collapsing like the bellows under the brick-furnace in his father's yard. The spear in his grip weighed almost nothing. It was crimson, still covered in the life-blood of his neighbour Jocha. Poor Jocha, so eager, so slow. The short Roman *pilum* had pierced his throat and knocked him from the rooftop before he could loose his first slingstone. Kneeling beside him, Judah had plucked the spear forth, and a welter of blood had pulsed out behind it, speeding Jocha to his death.

"Fool," his father had said, closing the dying man's eyes. "Brave idiot. Now who'll look after your mother and son?"

"I will," said Judah, clutching the spear so hard his knuckles turned white.

His father had laughed. "Which means me, since I look after you. You're awfully free with my largesse. Now come inside before some Roman makes us pin-cushions as well. They'll be gone soon enough, then we can bury our dead."

"No." Judah had stood and headed for where the fighting was.

"Where are you going? Judah! Judah, no...!" The old man's voice had been lost to the thunder of voices crying for vengeance, the thunder of Roman boots and trumpets, the thunder hammering in Judah's ears.

Forgive me, father. I can't be anything but what I am.

Now, under the heavy and pregnant moon, he scrambled to be first to launch his weapon into the Roman ranks. But that honour went to another. The short man wore a priest's robes and looked wild as a desert jackal. His hair and beard were all disordered, and spittle was on his lips. This man had led the charge out of the city, and barely stopped for breath the whole way. Reaching the top of the ridge just three steps ahead of Judah, he screamed like a lunatic and threw his spear blindly into the disordered Romans below.

Judah took pause to aim. He'd seen them thrown, but he'd never handled a spear himself. Planting his feet wide, Judah raised his weapon to his ear. Taking a huge breath, he stepped into the throw and heaved. The spear vanished into the shadowy depths below. For a moment there was nothing. Then he heard a cry, followed by the crisp orders of the centurions. "*Testudo! Testudo!*" The Romans were forming their tortoise, using their shields to build a wall overhead and along their flanks.

Judah was already unwrapping the sling from his waist. Unable to carry knives in the streets, the young men of the city had improvised. Wearing the wide leather band as a belt kept the Romans from noticing it if they stopped you. And the sling was a holy weapon, the choice weapon of kings and shepherds alike.

As more Judeans clambered up to launch their spears, Judah knelt and found a rock no bigger than his palm. He nocked it into the leather sling and started the weapon spinning.

"For Jerusalem!" shouted the wild man, throwing a second spear. "For Israel!"

"For Asher," murmured Judah. Three months ago his twin had vanished in the riots at Alexandria, when a Roman legion massacred the entire Jewish district. Shaking, Judah sent his stone hurtling down into the Roman ranks. Recovering his balance, he found a film over his eyes. He blinked it away and bent down, feeling around for his next missile.

The next time he cast his sling loose, his bullet was joined by dozens more, raining down a ragged but deadly volley into the disordered Twelfth Legion below.

The Valley of Beth-Horon was a legendary place in Hebrew history, a place of revolution, of the casting off of tyranny and oppression, conjuring visions of heroic deeds and noble causes.

Judah's cause this night was avenging his brother. Blood thundering in his ears, he reached down for the next stone.

In the valley below, down among the Romans, a woman called Cleopatra screamed. Dressed in a gown more fit for feasting than flight, the Roman woman buried her head under a goose-feather pillow and spit curses at the invisible Jews above, employing the only Aramaic she had bothered to learn in her three years here. "*Raca! Adhadda kedhabhra!*"

Her husband, Gessius Florus, dismounted and dragged her out of her litter. Pushing her head down, he made her kneel down behind a dozen stout Roman shields, far better protection than goose feathers.

It was a full moon, and by the light leaking through the chinks in the upheld shields Cleopatra saw she was crouching by the foot of King

Agrippa, titular ruler of Judea. The king stood upright and unflinching under the patter of stones on the shields.

"Typical Judeans," spat Cleopatra, "assaulting their own king. And typical of a Jewish king, to be so ineffectual! Aah!" Another volley of rattling stones made her throw her hands over her head.

On her other side, Florus patted her shoulder. "Now now, Cleopatra. Just keep your head down." He shot a grin at the king, who ignored the despicable Roman couple.

All around them the Twelfth Legion struggled with an unseen foe, known only by the rattle of stones and the screams of wounded legionaries. A second shower of stones had started from the other side of the valley as well – the Judean rebels now held the high ground on both sides and were decimating the legion with their slings.

Having run out of Aramaic curses, the Roman lady switched to her native Latin. "*Cunni! Verpae! Mentulae! Fellatores!*"

"Quiet woman!" snarled King Agrippa, unable to contain himself any longer. "Florus, control your wife!"

But Gessius Florus, Roman knight and Procurator of Judea, ignored the king's order. Despite the danger, the plump governor was improbably gleeful. Under a hail of slingstones, he was thinking, *O, thank you, Jews! Thank you! You have saved me!*

Florus had spent the last three years raping this land. He'd hated the Judeans from first sight of them, having dealt with enough Hebrews in Rome. From the moment he'd arrived he had set out to enrich himself at their expense. He'd raked in taxes and bribes in unheard-of quantities. Those Jews who could not pay were tortured and crucified.

Early on, the complaints had been easy enough to ignore. But eventually even the Hebrew priests had expressed their displeasure, opening up an avalanche of complaints and accusations that had gone all the way to Rome. If it had gone on any longer, Nero Caesar would have taken notice, threatening the grand fortune Florus had stolen from these heathen Hebrews.

The only way for Florus to hide his deeds (and his gold!) was to start a war. Not that he could declare one himself – he was only a knight, not a senator. But what he could do was bait these silly Jews into starting one. For decades there had been fear of a revolution in Judea. All he had to do was fan those flames.

He began by adding more taxes. The Jews bent, but did not break. Then he demanded the gold from their great Temple. Even that insult hadn't been enough to move these dullards. So he had struck them where they were most sensitive – their lonely god. Noting their reaction to any sacrilege, he had placed the image of Nero inside their precious Temple, to be worshipped alongside their god.

Predictably, the citizens of Jerusalem had gone wild, sacking the

Roman garrison there, and burning King Agrippa's palace. Best of all, they burned all the contracts and deeds lodged in the governor's palace, thus removing all proof of his chicanery. The uprising provided Florus with a pretext to demand reinforcements. The governor of Syria had dutifully marched on the city, and now the Judeans were responding just as Florus had hoped. When news of this attack reached Rome, Nero would wage all-out war. And Florus' gold would be safe.

Noting the cold stare of the Judean king, Florus said, "Invigorating, is it not, your majesty?"

Agrippa turned away. Florus grinned until he noted the look on the face of the king's bodyguard. A thin man, taller than any Roman, he was a fearsome sight. Unlike the king, this man eschewed Western dress, and grew his beard in the old Hebrew way, long and neatly squared. But his head was shaved, and the moonlight reflected off a deep scar along one side of his scalp just above the ear. He carried an enormous sword, half as tall as himself and as wide as an outstretched hand, but crooked halfway down the blade. Not a soldier's blade. A gladiator's blade. A barbarian's blade.

This fearsome monster, so foreign and other, was staring down at him with undisguised scorn. Like any coward, Florus felt a burning resentment and consoled himself with thoughts of revenge. *I can't kill your king, but I can have you killed easily enough, my friend. In fact...* "My dear king, should not your man here be helping? Such a fierce warrior should be in the thick of things, not hiding with women and old men!"

"Levi is my bodyguard," replied Agrippa. "He does not need to be fighting his brothers, my own people."

"Even when they're calling for your royal blood?" asked Florus lightly. Beside him, Cleopatra hissed, "Cowards, all of them."

Disgusted, Agrippa stalked away to find a horse. The bodyguard Levi lingered a moment more, gazing down at Florus. Then he followed his master. Watching them go, the governor of Judea stifled a laugh. Romans bowed to no king, and especially not a client king who needed Rome's protection against his own people. Thinking of all the insults he'd heaped upon the king and his sister-queen, Florus laughed outright.

The laugh died in his throat as one of the slingstones punched through the edge of a Roman shield and struck the paved road just inches away. Florus reached out and felt the pit in the road it had made, and imagined what that would have done to his flesh. He called up to the Syrian governor, still astride his horse. "Gallus! Get us out of here!"

From his saddle, Gaius Cestius Gallus scowled at the squat, pudgy knight. A consular senator and general, it was inconceivable to him that a Roman man should cower with women and foreigners.

He had Florus' measure, to be sure. But duty to Rome had

compelled him to bring the Twelfth Legion to Judea and patch up whatever crisis Florus had caused.

However, he had misjudged the situation entirely. The resistance he had encountered in Jerusalem was fierce and bitter. This wasn't anger at a few years of abuse. This was the boiling resentment of generations.

Even this retreat was going poorly. Already he had lost dozens of men, including his entire cavalry. These damn Judean sling-stones were usually no more than a nuisance, but his men were exhausted, thirsty, and on uncertain terrain. And the Judeans had their blood up.

Gallus issued crisp orders to his senior legate. "Find five centuries to push up the slopes and guard our retreat. Four hundred men should have room to deploy. They're to drive them back, buy the rest of us time to make an orderly retreat up the valley."

Mid-note, the bugler issuing the order was struck by a hail of stones, destroying his instrument along with his life. The five centurions had to be given their task by word of mouth. Obediently they started their men up the rise to meet the enemy, with the good lady Cleopatra still spitting curses behind them.

The Twelfth Legion had a proud legacy to maintain. They had fought with Caesar against the Nervii, had made history at the siege of Alesia, and defeated Pompey the Great at Pharsalus. They would not fall to a pack of Judean rabble throwing stones.

◆   ◊   ◆

Judah was scrabbling for another stone when the whizzing sound of the slings stopped. Looking down the slope he saw legionaries climbing to meet them. "That's right, bastards," said someone nearby. "Come on."

A sword scraped from its wooden sheath, and Judah turned to stare enviously. The blade was held by an Idumean, to judge by the dark skin and long hair. The hairline was receding, making this man an incongruously comic figure. But his voice was all angry defiance. "For Israel!"

On Judah's other side, the wild priest Simon bar Giora beat his chest with his hands. "For Israel!"

"*Israel!!*" Howling and keening, the Judeans surged down to engage the Romans.

Adding his voice to the battle cry, Judah leapt down the slope, thrilling. This wasn't like the fighting he had done in the stews of Jerusalem, brawling with friends and neighbours, clouting the occasional priestly snob. This was man's work. This was the Lord's work.

A Roman soldier lunged at him, the wicked point of the blade angling up towards his bare ribs. Judah didn't even flinch. He slapped it aside with the flat of his hand and punched the Roman full in the face, knocking the man off his feet to tumble into his fellows.

A second Roman stabbed at this handsome fool of a Judean. Judah threw himself back from this blade and lost his footing. Worse, the angle of the slope was so steep that his fall had him skidding and slipping down into the Roman ranks. His feet struck a legionary's ankles and brought him crashing down on top of Judah. Suddenly the two men were rolling, careening into other men, a mass of limbs. Romans leapt out of the way, cursing in Latin as the two combatants hurtled through the ranks, down towards the road.

Judah was taking the worst of it, crushed and buffeted by the Roman's breastplate, shield, and greaves. But he ignored the pain as they continued to tumble, struggling for dominance. *The sword!* Judah stopped fighting to be on top, and instead used all his strength to grasp the legionary's wrist. As they slid, he held the hand against the rocks, knocking the weapon free.

The Roman answered by bashing at Judah with his shield and kicking with a nailed boot. The stinging pain made Judah gasp – his back was already bloody from the fall, and now his left leg was awash with blood. But the ground was evening out, slowing their descent. Judah twisted around, still kicking and elbowing. His hands grasped one of the Roman's legs at the knee. He twisted, hard. The Roman screamed, crying out in some guttural Latin dialect for some distant god. Using his hands to slither to a halt, Judah cursed at him and shoved him away.

He put a hand out to rise and discovered it wasn't earth under his hand, nor rocky outcroppings of jagged stone. This stone was flat and smooth and even. He had fallen all the way down to the road. Alone, among a whole Roman legion.

I'm a dead man.

Somewhere higher on the hill behind him the balding Judean leader released a feral shout. "Israel! Death to Rome!"

Death. The Roman's sword was lost, but his shield was still on his arm. Kneeling over the groaning man, Judah knocked the Roman flat, wrenched the shield, raised it high and drove the edge of it like a massive spade down into the gap between helmet and armour. The Roman's head parted from his body, sending spurts of blood onto the stones all around.

Judah staggered to his feet, looking frantically around him. He'd fallen clean through the ranks of one century, and was now between the horses of the vanguard and the tortoise of the legion. Weaponless, blood-ied, naked – even his kilted loincloth had ripped away – he was sure that death was coming for him at any moment. *I'm going to die a fool's death.*

But so far no one was seeing him. The soldiers to the south were huddled behind their shields, and the horsemen were galloping north for the mouth of the valley, and escape. Every heartbeat brought more

Judeans down towards the road. If Judah could survive just one minute more, he'd be among his fellows again.

There were Romans in the road, dead or dying from spears and slingstones. Clutching the bloody shield, Judah ran to the closest, a groaning man in a silver helm whose chest was spurting irregular gouts of blood through a hole in his breastplate. Judah bent low and plucked the man's sword from its hard scabbard.

"*Fellator*," gasped the dying Roman. Judah wondered if it had been his stone that had caught this man.

He heard a clatter of hooves behind him and turned. A mounted man had glanced back, seen him, and was now reining about to cut him down. The moonlight reflected off a bald pate and huge Judean sword. "No! I'm a brother!" Judah opened his arms, refusing to fight another Jew.

The horse came racing at Judah, the massive sword held high. Judah lifted his own blade to parry it—

The clang of metal on metal sounded like it was inside his head. But it came from just behind him. Judah ducked and glanced back. The horse was already past him. Lying on the ground Judah saw the injured Roman whose sword he had stolen, a long knife in his hand. He had no face. His helm had been split, and there was blood pooling all around him.

Judah glanced up at his rescuer. Much older than Judah, wiry and very tall. Deep-set eyes, bristling brow, and a neatly-squared beard. He'd killed the Roman with a huge version of the traditional Judean sword, long blade angled forward at the midpoint like a crooked finger.

It was less than fifteen seconds since he'd landed on the road. Now the Roman centuries on the slopes were falling back under the crush of the thousands of Judeans racing down from above. Boulders bounced down into the ranks of the tortoises, breaking the Roman ranks. The Romans themselves were abandoning their tortoise shell to draw their swords and attack their besiegers.

The lone horseman looked back the way he had come. A rabble of Judeans had come down onto the road, chasing the other riders. He was cut off from his companions.

"Thank you," called Judah.

The tall man gave Judah a disdainful glare. "Gratitude later. Fight now!" With a grimace that was part snarl, part grin, he leapt down from his saddle and waded into the ranks of the scattering Romans, leaving Judah behind.

Clever, thought Judah. *Cut off, his only chance now is to change sides and fight with us.*

But he was cut off because he rescued me. I owe him my life. Judah followed the bearded turncoat onto the valley floor where the forces or

Rome and Judea were meeting to become a roiling mass of men, blood, and steel.

◆   ◊   ◆

Roman legates were shouting orders. "Forget the siege engines! Leave the baggage! Kill the mules!" The stones had started again, this time from the front of the valley – some clever Judeans had climbed the crests to harass the Roman escape route.

A stone struck a glancing blow to Cestius Gallus' breastplate, rocking him back in the saddle. "*Cacat!*" The Roman general clenched his knees on the saddle's horns, but the weight of his armour threatened to topple him.

A hand shot out to steady him. King Agrippa was leaning sideways in his own saddle. "*Gratias.*"

"If the general were to fall, Caesar's wrath would be all the greater. Besides," added Agrippa with a ghost of a smile, "my sister likes you." His Latin bore no trace of foreignness or rusticality. A client king, Agrippa had been raised in Rome, and was in spirit far more Roman than Jew.

"Thanks," repeated Gallus.

Glancing back, the king scowled. "Though I confess, I might risk Nero's fury to see Florus fall." Just behind them, Florus was refusing to get back into his saddle, choosing instead to climb into a covered wagon with his wife.

Though he agreed, Gallus had no time for a chat. The emboldened Judeans were coming ever faster. If the Twelfth Legion and all its reinforcing cohorts did not escape this valley at once, they would die to the last man. He shouted to every man that could hear: "Fly fly fly!"

As Agrippa shook his reins and galloped off with the Roman officers, he realized in passing that he had lost his bodyguard.

◆   ◊   ◆

Judah chased his tall savior through the thick of the fighting. A silent challenge had been issued, and Judah had never backed away from a challenge in his life.

But if the goal was to kill more Romans than his opponent, Judah was clearly out-classed. The gaunt moonlit figure bested two legionaries with contemptuous ease, killing one and slicing out the other's eyes with a single stroke. The man was clearly well trained, a merchant of death, purchasing one life after another. Every flick of his wrist drew Roman blood.

Lacking training, Judah fought by instinct, relying on his size and strength to see him through. He was used to shifting stones, and now he employed his strong arms to haul Romans off-balance and stab them or, more often, punch them with the hard wide pommel at the sword's other end.

More and more Judeans were joining them down on the road, and it was pure confusion. Screams and shouts and the occasional sparks of steel on steel. The smell in the air was earthy and electric – blood and sweat and shit and fear.

Judah still held the shield, but it was getting in his way. It slowed him too much, and he was not interested in defense. This was the moment to attack! What did it matter if he fell here? This would be a fine place to die, and in a fine cause.

This would be a good death. Though I wish I weren't naked...

Embracing the inevitable, Judah threw his shield aside. At once a Roman seized the opening and lunged. Judah caught the man's arm in his free hand and brought his sword down hard. The Roman screamed, blood gysering out of the stump at his elbow. Judah twisted the severed arm and stabbed the Roman with his own blade. The lifeless fingers fell away from the grip, and Judah waded into the enemy ranks with a blade in each hand. *That's better*, he thought.

He wasn't aware he was laughing until a voice said, "What are you giggling at?" The question came from another Judean fighting beside him. Phannius, another mason. *Where did he come from?* Phannius was a lout, and fought like it, clubbing as many friends as foes, the idiot. His family considered itself above Judah's because it had a drop of priestly blood. Judah hoped the fool was cut down. *Would serve him right.*

Judah's bile was very personal. Last month, after almost a year of courting, Judah had asked for Phannius' sister's hand in marriage. He'd been refused. Not good enough.

Deborah. She'd smiled at him with such eyes—

Judah gasped as a Roman spear was knocked away from his nose. He hadn't seen it at all, not until the tall bald turncoat had beat it aside. "Pay attention! I didn't save you for nothing!"

Almost sheepishly, Judah redoubled his efforts. He was covered in blood, a fair amount of it his own. Despite his strong lungs he was panting now. Worse, his mind was beginning to fog. The hardest part of sword-work, he was finding, was the shock of the blows. That, and pulling the sword out of flesh – though it went in easy enough.

He saw a sword coming down to cleave his skull, and he brought up both his blades in a cross to catch it. He was about to shoulder his attacker away when a reflection of moonlight caught his eye. The lamp-like orb was shining down upon a pair of golden wings, bobbing high above the roiling swords and spears. It was a shaft of illumination just for him. The V of his swords overhead made a perfect frame for the large eagle perched high atop a pole. The Roman *Aquila*, symbol of Rome's might and majesty.

The eagle...

Binding the Roman's sword away with one blade and stabbing with the other, Judah was seized with an insane notion. To his protector he shouted, "Tell me your name!"

The fearsome turncoat was driving back three legionaries. "Levi!"

"Levi, I'm going for that eagle! You can come or not."

Levi barked out a short. "Oh, can I?"

But Judah was already moving. The thing was just a dozen paces away. *Not good enough? I'll show them how good I am. How good we both are, Asher. I'll die a hero of Israel.*

He moved without thought, without fear. He felt only an angry confidence, as if his sword strokes were being guided. *The Lord is my sword, and my sword is His. I am that I am.* "Come on, you bastards! Come on!"

Suddenly Levi was by his side, and Judah grinned in spite of himself. *I'm not the only fool.* They fought furiously, heaving, shoving, slashing, hacking, stabbing, Judah with twin Roman blades, Levi cleaving with his massive crooked one. They called out taunts and curses in every tongue they knew as they moved inexorably towards the eagle.

Sensing the danger to their standard, the Romans closed ranks, creating a solid wall around the aquilifer. Dressed in glittering silver armour and the skin of a desert lion, he was a man chosen for his absolute fearlessness. The aquilifer would give his life before he let his eagle fall.

The Roman shield wall was bristling with spears. Dodging a spear thrust to his face, Levi grabbed a nearby legionary by the chin-strap and hauled him around onto the sword of his neighbour. Hacking down with his massive sword on the other side, he created a momentary gap in the thin line. "Go!"

Judah leapt at once, diving and stabbing out with both swords. One blade drove through the leather skirts into a thigh, the other one up under a Roman's chin, exiting through the top of his skull.

Both swords were torn from Judah's grip. He let them go and roared as he shouldered through the ranks. Barking his knee on a breastplate, careening off another armoured shoulder, he touched the road with one foot and launched himself at the aquilifer.

The aquilifer's silver armour gave him an almost ghostlike presence in the moonlight. But he was quick. He lifted the staff in his hands and thrust the butt end of it at Judah's face. Judah's hands clamped down just before it struck him, diverting it to one side. He landed badly, but held on to the staff, wrestling for control of it, the eagle at the far end dancing jerkily.

This was more like the fighting Judah knew, the rough and tumble battles of Jerusalem's stews, where elbows, knees, and teeth came into play. There were swords around him, but the Romans were too busy with Levi and the others to waste precious seconds ending his life.

He yanked the staff, hard. The lion's head fell askew and Judah butted the aquilifer's nose with his forehead. Blood erupted, misting the air between them. Some entered Judah's nose and mouth as he breathed in, and for a moment he choked on Roman blood. "Bastard!"

"*Cunnus!*" snarled the Roman. "*Fellator!*" Enraged, the aquilifer tripped Judah and they tumbled together to the hard road, just missing a spear thrust aimed sidelong at Judah's back.

Landing on top, the Roman straddled Judah's chest and pressed the staff hard against Judah's throat. "*Irrumator! Mentulam caco!*"

Gripping the staff tightly, Judah ground his teeth and focused his strength. Slowly, incredibly, the hearty oak shaft began to bend. Oak was a wood beloved of Mars, Judah had heard. *Stupid foreign gods, with their stupid pagan loves and idiot superstitions!* He heaved harder, and harder, grinding his teeth so fiercely they felt like they might shatter.

It was the oak that shattered, bursting in a shower of splinters right in the aquilifer's face. Taking advantage of the Roman's surprise, Judah drove the two splintered ends of the staff upwards. One gouged a deep furrow in the Roman's cheek while the other tore away most of the man's left ear.

The aquilifer was damnably well trained. Even as he twisted away in agony, he drew his dagger and stabbed blindly down. Judah used the broken stave to block the blow and jabbed up again. This time the wooden shaft deflected harmlessly off the hard Roman breastplate.

Smearing blood from his face with one forearm, the aquilifer pinned one of Judah's wrists with his knee. He stabbed down, and Judah barely got the broken haft in his free hand between him and the dagger's wicked point.

The aquilifer put all his weight down. Slowly, inexorably, the dagger inched towards Judah's throat.

Is this how Asher died? At the end of a Roman knife? Surging with rage, Judah heaved the aquilifer sideways and clubbed the Roman hard on the side of his head with the golden eagle, cracking his skull. The aquilifer fell to the dirt under a spray of blood.

"For you, Asher! That's for you!" Shoving the limp Roman off him, Judah struggled to his feet, a nightmarish figure, naked, howling, drenched in blood. "You hear me! That's for my brother!" Swinging the broken Roman standard around his head, he dived into the Roman ranks and beat at them with their own symbol. Behind him Levi came fast, sweeping his massive blade to protect Judah's back. But Judah was past caring about safety. He had the eagle, and with it in his grip he was fearless, unstoppable.

"The eagle! The eagle!" Judean cheers spread like wildfire. The whole world knew the significance of the Roman *Aquila*. Touched by the hand of Nero himself, it was a piece of Rome. Taking it was nothing less than a miracle, a sign from the Lord!

The massed Judeans surged forward and began literally tearing the legionaries to pieces.

♦   ◊   ♦

At the mouth of the valley, governor Florus saw the eagle fall and chortled. *Now they've done it. These Judeans have doomed themselves for certain.*

Not far off, King Agrippa shared the pride of his people's great deed, yet felt sick at heart. Today his countrymen had touched off a self-immolating inferno, building their funeral pyre on a tower of bravery. The definition of a Pyrrhic victory. He saw the massive crooked blade among the Roman ranks, slicing and maiming. *O Levi – what have you done?*

General Gallus reacted practically. "Ride! Now, while they're cheering! Ride!"

The two governors, the king, and a handful of Roman nobles and officers escaped into the night, leaving behind more than four thousand Roman soldiers dead or dying. A few hundred struggled on, fighting for their personal share of honour, hoping their gods looked on them with favour.

♦   ◊   ♦

Judah was in the thick of it, a prodigious figure of death. One Roman he approached was his own age, but thin and unmartial – an officer sent from Rome, probably some scion of a famous house. The fellow dropped his sword and knelt before Judah, hands clasped and eyes streaming. *"Pax! Pax! Elision!"*

Judah didn't know the last word, but the meaning was clear – mercy. Picturing his twin brother doing the same before some Roman, Judah stabbed the young officer in the throat and moved on, looking for his next foe.

But there was no one left to kill. The Legio XII Fulminata – Wielders of the Thunderbolt, conquerors of the Nervii, victors of Alesia and Pharsalus – were no more.

II

THE CELEBRATIONS LASTED straight through the night. Word of the victory had gone back to Jerusalem, and the city's women, children, and elderly had poured out to bring their men food and water. Dead Jews were lovingly returned to the city. Pyres for the Roman dead were made from broken wagons and siege engines. Around the huge fires there was dancing and singing, and many prayers of thanksgiving.

Dawn found Judah walking aimlessly among the jubilant Judeans, the eagle still clutched in his hand. He had been carousing all night, and now exhaustion and wine made him feel muddled and stupid. But still, whether cavorting with the crowds or searching the dead for loot, every fighting man stopped to shout acclaim for the hero of the hour.

It wasn't pride that kept Judah holding the standard. The damned thing was glued to his hand by gore, and he was too tired to pry it free. Seen up close, it was a homely image. Crude, not at all magnificent. The likeness of Nero Caesar was laughable, worse even than the one on coins. The eagle's wings were lopsided – no, that was from where Judah had crushed the aquilifer's skull. The golden talons clutched the engraved Roman numerals XII.

It might not have been much to look at, but a lost eagle was a grave blow to Rome's immortality. Only a handful had ever been taken, and Rome had proved it would do anything to reclaim them. Famously, Augustus had negotiated a humiliating peace with Parthia in order to recover the eagles of Crassus, dressing it up as a Roman military victory. What would the Romans not give to get this eagle back? Judea's freedom was a small price for Roman honour.

He'd pulled a long tunic over his head at some point to cover his nakedness. Blood and offal made the garment cling to him in a most ill way. He was sticky all over, his leg was throbbing where the hobnails had torn him, and he had countless scrapes, cuts, and bruises. There was a gash along his chest where a Roman sword had nearly laid him open.

Dazed, he belatedly noticed that some men were picking through Roman corpses looking for arms and armour. *I should do that.* He attempted to pull the staff out of his grip, but his left hand became lodged in the sticky mass of gristle and hair as well. Laughing at the absurdity of it, he was shaking at his fingers when a quiet voice said, "Step on the haft."

Levi. The tall man seemed to be Judah's own shadow. Obediently, Judah bent over and used his foot to wrench the broken staff from his grip.

Hands free, Judah made a proper introduction. "Judah ben Matthais. Thanks for saving my life."

"Levi ben Patroclus. You're a young fool, and brave. Such men need protection."

"I've never seen anyone fight like you."

"*I* did not take the eagle."

"Are you a soldier..?"

"A bodyguard." Levi grimaced. "Though after last night I'll need a new employer."

Judah was wondering if he should apologize when someone shouted his name. "Judah!" The harsh voice made Levi's hand drop to his sword. But Judah knew the voice – that idiot Phannius. "I've been looking for you!"

Judah had been looking for Phannius, too. Not for the pleasure of his company, but for vindication. If anything might have earned him the right to marry Deborah...

He wondered if she had come from the city, and for a moment his heart leapt. But there was no sign of Deborah, just her loutish brother, riding awkwardly on a Roman horse beside two other men. Built wider than Judah, he was older and far less handsome. Yet the drop of priestly blood in his veins gave him a pugnacious superiority that made Judah's skin crawl. Thankfully Deborah hadn't inherited her brother's pretentions.

"They tell me you took the eagle! You! I can't believe it!" The fool was grinning, and when he dismounted he clapped Judah on the shoulder as if they were best friends. "Well done, brother! Well done!"

Brother? Your family refused me that title. Now my only brother is dead. Aloud he said, "Praise means so much when it comes from such an elevated person."

Phannius wasn't sure if it was sincere or a jab. Before he could decide, the two men riding with him introduced themselves. One was the feral priest who had thrown the first spear. He gave his name as Simon bar Giora – an odd name, as Giora meant *The Stranger*. The other was the balding Idumean who had been calling out 'Israel'. His name was Eleazar ben Simon. Like Phannius, they now rode captured horses, and had been looking for Judah.

"Where is it?" demanded Simon bar Giora, dropping from his saddle. His face was a bristle of beard, eyebrows, and crooked teeth. "Where's the eagle?"

Arms too tired to move, Judah jerked his chin at the dented and blood-stained object at his feet. Instantly both Eleazar and Simon lunged. Eleazar came up with it and leapt at once upon his horse's back, the symbol of Rome's pride in his hands. Simon cursed loudly as he flung himself back in the saddle to chase Eleazar, galloping away with the eagle high aloft.

Phannius laughed. "Serves them right – the Romans, I mean. Graven images! Hah! You know where we are?"

"Beth Horon."

"An auspicious place to start a war," observed Levi.

Phannius was scornful. "Win one you mean! A shame Asher isn't here, eh Judah?"

Judah bit back his answer. Asher had been meant for better things.

Phannius clambered back into his saddle, which took him three tries – he'd clearly been drinking. "Good show, Judah. I'll tell my sister – you're a hero." He kicked his heels until the mount trotted off after the leaders of this revolution.

The thought of Deborah warmed him. But Judah didn't feel like a hero. He'd thought killing Romans would fill the hole left by his brother's death. In the moment of battle, it had. Now, surrounded by thousands of dead men, he felt empty, spent. He recalled the man who had begged for mercy, and was ashamed.

I took the eagle. That's something. Judah glanced to where Eleazar was using the gold trophy to rally the men. A shadow passed overhead. Vultures were circling, forced to delay the feast as the Judeans cheered the tarnished eagle.

Levi said, "He's wrong, you know. This war has only just begun."

Judah said absently, "Has it?"

"The Romans lost an eagle. They *have* to come."

Ready to sleep for a month, it took Judah several moments to actually hear what Levi had said. "What? No. No – they'll negotiate."

"They won't. They'll attack."

"Augustus Caesar went crawling to the Parthians to get eagles back."

Through the crusted blood in his beard, Levi almost smiled. "Nero is no Augustus."

The truth of this statement struck Judah like a hammer between the eyes. He hadn't thought past the momentary victory over the Romans, hadn't considered what their humiliation would mean.

No, Nero was no Augustus, who had built the Pax Romana. Nero would attack, nothing surer. He would send a plague of legions down upon the Jews, raze the country from one end to the other. There would be no quarter, no forgiveness. Not for this.

Staring at the receding eagle surrounded by vultures, Judah felt his stomach drop. "What have I done?"

The older man was using sand to scrub blood from his beard. "You took an eagle. You'll be famous forever."

"I've ensured that Caesar will seek revenge."

Levi grunted. "That too. Want to give it back?"

Judah felt defiance stir at the very thought. "No!"

"Then prepare for war," advised Levi. "Or else run. There is no middle ground."

Seventeen years old, Judah could hardly fathom the cascade of consequences he had set in motion. Seeing the young man's confusion, Levi smiled. "Ignore me. Revel in your success. You're a hero. Enjoy it while you can."

◆   ◊   ◆

At that moment, on a magnificent estate not far from Jerusalem, an old priest sat with his family. His two surviving sons were present, along with their wives. That neither had yet produced grandsons was a sadness, but understandable. The elder boy had ever been fallow, of both purpose and seed. The younger and more promising son was just returned from Rome after an absence of nearly two years.

Hunched in his chair (he could no longer rest easily on cushions), the priest Matatthais sat looking at his sons. The elder, who shared his father's name, was thirty-five now. The younger, Yosef, was nearing thirty. It was he who had entered the priesthood and studied so hard. The young man was like a calculating sea-sponge, taking everything in. He flirted with ideas only so long as he saw their usefulness. The moment he was sure there was no profit in a thing, it was discarded. There was no one as ambitious as Yosef.

"You should have let us fight," said Matatthais the Younger mulishly. He was sitting upright on a cushion, while his brother lounged in the Roman style.

"Perhaps," admitted Matatthais the Elder. "In hindsight, it would have been good if you were among them. But how were we to know they would not be slaughtered? It was a miracle." His eyes narrowed. "It would also have been a miracle had you felt strongly enough to make that decision on your own, without first coming to me. A little spine would not have been amiss."

Both his sons bristled. Good. He had spent a lifetime instilling their duty to the family. If they chafed at their leashes, all the better – so long as they continued to obey.

"It is not too late. You must go out at once and join in the rejoicing. Be seen to be there. Dirty yourselves up as though you were a part of it. In the night, in the dark, who is to say you were not present? Then, when you return to Jerusalem, you must attend meetings in the Blue Hall."

His elder son stared at him. "A week ago you were counseling us to remain aloof and have nothing to do with the rabble rousers!"

The old man spread his hands. "Matters have shifted. Things are not what they were. The Zelotes have won the day. It should not have been possible, but it is so. Their next step is to seize power, and you must be thought their friends, not their foes. There is too much tradition of *sicarii* in them. They'll not exile those who stand against them, they'll do murder. Having found success in violence, I doubt they will hesitate to do more of the same."

"If I go to the Blue Hall, I'll lose my priesthood," said Yosef. It was not a protest, merely a statement of fact.

"Hmm. true. The Sanhedrin will see the Zelotes as a greater threat than ever, and anyone associated with them will be killed. Hmm."

"We could speak to Joshua ben Gamala," suggested the mother. Mariah spoke as freely as the men, which awed both her daughters-in-law. But she had always been an exceptional woman. Her father had seen that she was educated, which among some circles was heresy. But she was descended from the Makkabi, and had royal Hasmonean blood in her veins.

Matatthais the Elder considered his wife's words carefully. "A good thought, and perhaps I will. But there might be a simpler answer." He pointed to his elder son. "Let Matatthais go to the battlefield and join the revels. Let him attend the Blue Hall. Yosef, you will remain in the good graces of the Sanhedrin. A foot in each camp will see us clear. Whoever prevails, we'll be safe."

Yosef looked mulish. "Let me go to the Blue Hall, then. Let him hold himself aloof."

"No no," said Matatthais the Elder. "You're just back from a successful embassy to Rome, you actually had the ear of Nero Caesar. The Sanhedrin will try to make peace with Rome. You could be useful to them. No, this way is best."

Yosef remained impassive as he took this in. A sign of acceptance.

Matatthais considered the vagaries of fate. The elder boy should have been the priest. But he'd been born with a large birthmark on his neck that reached up to his chin. Worse, he was cross-eyed. Such obvious imperfections would have kept him from ever attaining a high rank. He would never be one of the Kohanim, never be allowed to officiate a service in the Temple, or carry the golden censer, or blow the Magrapha. So instead Matatthais had used his namesake as a shield. Priests were not supposed to own land, but like most, Matatthais winked at the restriction. He put all his (illegal) wealth into his elder son's name, and then raised the boy to manage it while he concentrated on his younger son, filling Yosef's head with all the knowledge of the Law and Scripture that he could impart.

Gifted with a fine mind and a beautiful, musical voice, Yosef made an excellent priest – or would, as soon as he learned some orthodoxy. *I should never have sent him to study with that old fool Banus. Ever since he's had queer ideas.*

"Should I keep my Latinized name, then?" In Rome, they had called him by the Latin version of Yosef.

"No! From this moment you must stop using Greek or Roman words, both of you. Patriotism will be the order of the day. In fact, Matatthais may be too Greek-sounding. Matityahu sounds more Hebrew. So I shall be called, and so shall you," he said to his elder son. "Now you get yourself out to Beth Horon and be seen!"

But it was the younger son who stood. Matatthais scowled. "Where are you going?"

"Nowhere, it seems." Bitingly polite, Yosef held out a hand to his wife, kissed his mother on the cheek, then returned to his own house in the city.

After they were alone, Mariah turned to Matatthais (now Matityahu). "He's only angry because he thought his return would elevate him. He's been eclipsed by all this trouble."

"I know. And I'm glad. That boy has no brakes inside him. He needs to be checked now and then. But have no fear, my dear. He will be a great man."

"Yes," agreed Mariah pensively. "I'm only afraid of what he'll do to get there."

◆   ◊   ◆

Judah never got his promised hero's reward. True, he had found a good Roman breastplate and helmet, and stripped some ornate silver greaves from the dead aquilifer – only fitting. But the sun had traveled barely an hour in the sky when reality returned. He was sitting beside Levi, resting and accepting passing praise, when he spied a familiar face in the crowd. Young Malachai, an apprentice at his father's yard. The boy was winded, frantically searching faces in the crowd. He could only be looking for Judah. "Boy! Here I am!"

Malachai's head snapped around, and he looked at once relieved and grim – a hard thing for a twelve year-old. Expecting praise, Judah was not at all prepared for the words that tumbled out of the boy's mouth. "Your father – we found him this morning. He wasn't moving. We sent for doctors. They say a stroke – and an attack of his heart."

Judah struggled up on his weary and stiff legs. "He's still alive?"

"He was when I left, but—"

Judah glanced around. There were plenty of horses, though all had been claimed.

Levi jumped up and shouted, "Who has a horse for the hero of Beth Horon?!"

A dozen men offered their captured mounts. Grabbing the biggest, Judah threw himself into the Roman saddle, hauled the boy up beside him, and set off racing towards home.

III

JUDAH RODE hard, ironically blessing the Romans for building a decent road. He was fighting a tide of citizens, still flooding out of the city to join the celebrations. He shouted loudly for them to move aside. "Urgent business!" They obeyed, thinking him an agent for the priests or generals.

Roman saddles were large and square, with pommels at all four corners. Judah was unused to riding. He hooked his knees around the front pommels as he'd seen the Romans do, sitting close to the horse's head. Malachai rode behind him, arms about Judah's waist. About halfway there, Judah felt the boy's grip slacken. Exhausted from his run to Beth Horon, the young apprentice was falling asleep. To prevent the boy falling off, Judah slowed long enough to sling the lad around across his lap, then continued on.

His destination taunted him, distant yet so clear, glowing white in the sunlight, like a snow-capped mountain. He seldom approached at this hour, and was blinded by the sight of his native city. The White City, it was called. Hierosolyma, Aelia Capitolina, the City of David. The Holy City, Abode of Peace. High upon the central hill was the greatest structure in the world, a golden cap to the whiteness of the walls.

Beyth HaMiqdash. The House of the Holy. The great Temple of Jerusalem.

♦   ◊   ♦

A thousand years earlier, the Hebrew king David had captured a small town on the ridge separating the Mediterranean from the Dead

Sea. Renaming it Jerusalem, he'd declared it the capitol of his new king-dom, Israel. His son Solomon had built a magnificent Temple there for the worship of the one true God.

After four hundred years the city was conquered, and Solomon's Temple was destroyed. It had taken another sixty years for the Hebrew people to return, building a second Temple on the site of the first.

Conquered again two hundred and fifty years later by the Greek Alexander, Israel had passed from hand to hand until the leader called Makkabi led a war for independence, beginning with a battle at Beth Horon. For a hundred years Jerusalem had once more been its own master, until it was captured by the Roman general Pompey, enemy of the great Caesar. Pompey fell, and so too Caesar. After Caesar's death, Mark Antony had bestowed the land around Jerusalem to one of Rome's client-kings, Herod the Great, with a new official name – Judea.

The Romans had moved the capitol to Caesaeria Maritima, closer to sea-traffic. But to Jews, Jerusalem would always be the center of the world.

This war with Rome was inevitable. Truly, it was only surprising that it had taken so long. The Sanhedrin, the Temple's council of elders, had been preaching against it for decades, warning that Rome's wrath would bring an end to Judea, the Land of the Jews.

But Judea had been created by Rome, not Jews. Four genera-tions of rebels and patriots had shouted 'Israel' in the hope of rallying others to the cause. Still the unrest between Rome and Judea had only simmered, with murders and kidnappings on one side and executions and taxation on the other, but never open revolt.

Until now.

♦　◊　♦

Approaching the walls at a gallop, Judah said a mental hello, as he always did. He knew these walls. He could walk around the city and point to the stones his family had made, identify them without even searching for the scratched sign of a pyramid of bricks that was his family's mark. To another man, they'd all look the same. But there was a care, a skill, a delicate craft in shaping and placing those four-ton blocks of stone. He could name the masons in his family who crafted each one: Yoel, who had lived in the days of the Makkabi; Gideon, whose very name meant '*hewer*'; Noam, who had seen Pompey the Great, and spit upon him; Eli, who had been sent by Herod to fortify Masada, a moun-tain stronghold to the south.

This wall, Agrippa's Wall, was more recent. It contained stones crafted by his great-grandfather Amaziah, by Judah, the grandfather for whom he was named, and by Matthais – his father.

Father. Judah slowed to a trot as he passed through the Damascus gate, the large portal in Jerusalem's outermost wall. For the first time in his memory it was entirely unguarded. The same was true within. The whole city was oddly quiet, with only small knots of revelers too timid or frail to wander into the countryside. In a city of a million souls, it was eerie to see it so deserted.

The lack of people made for swift passage. The only times he had to stop was to make way for wagons leaving the city. These wagons were heavily laden with rich, expensive goods. Noble Hebrew families were fleeing the city, certain that the wrath of Rome would soon descend, and they had best be elsewhere. Judah could not hide his scorn, and actually spit on the ground as one such wagon passed.

He spied little knots of men and women who kept off the main streets and avoided the larger gates. He realized these were Romans and Greeks trying to escape the city before they suffered reprisals. He grimaced, and wondered if he should do anything. But they were no concern of his. His cause for returning was to attend his last remaining family member.

Ever since news came from Alexandria that Asher was dead, the old mason had been sulky, downcast and beaten, hardly willing to move. Brooding and irascible and hard, Judah's father had never gotten on with Asher, who would be lost with his head in the clouds for hours at a time. A true dreamer. They had parted on bad terms, and for two years there had only been a handful of letters between them.

Then had come news of the massacre. The crusty fifty year-old had barely coped with the loss of one son. *And last night I just ran off with the mob.* The old man must have been beside himself. A heart attack and a stroke – twin ailments for his twin sons. *And he'd lain all night in his own vomit.*

Judah wended his way through the streets of the Bezetha, the New City, and slid down from the saddle at the gates of his father's workshop. He prayed he was not too late.

The workshop door was unlocked. Judah carried the sleeping Malachai inside, laid him on a slab of unhewn limestone that stood upon a wooden pallet, then ran towards their home.

Their living area was located at the far end of the yard, above the masonry workshop. A modest home with three rooms and a balcony overlooking the yard, it had served the family for five generations.

Judah pounded up the stairs, calling out, "Father? Father?" There was a stench of vomit and urine. But also something much sweeter – lemon blossoms and an earthy scent that reminded him of Spring. Knowing to whom it beonged, Judah moved faster, his breath catching.

Turning a corner, he reached the door to the old mason's bed chamber. Sunlight was creeping through the slats of the windows, and there was a single candle burning. Matthais the Mason lay unmoving in the bed, looking shrunken and grey. Beside him, holding his hand, knelt a woman with raven-dark hair.

"Deborah."

She turned and, as ever, Judah lost the ability to breathe. Looking at her, he always felt like he was falling. Most men focused on her good hips and ample bosom. But Judah's eyes never strayed from her face. Shaped like a teardrop, but with a proud chin, it was framed by a luxurious fall of thick black hair. Her full mouth was made to pout, but her eyes held an amused kindness that came only in wise old men or young girls blessed by the Lord.

The amusement was absent now, and the kindness was tempered by grief. But looking at him there was a moment of fear. "Judah – is it you?"

Had he been able to see himself, he would have asked the same question. Caked in blood and grime that had dried then been partly sweat away on the ride, he was a ghastly figure. The breastplate, the silver greaves, and the two Roman swords on either hip made him all the more menacing. "It's me."

"Thank the Lord," she sighed, in such heartfelt relief that he felt guilty. He had rushed off without thinking that anyone would grieve if he fell. Not only had his father suffered. Clearly Deborah had worried as well. He felt like a heel.

Another apprentice was in the room, little Chaim. Judah nodded at him, but felt strangely unable to cross the threshold into the room. "How is he?"

Deborah's expression and the hangdog slump of Chaim's shoulders told all. Laying Matthais' calloused hand gently down, Deborah said, "It was a blessing, at the end,"

Judah slumped in the doorframe. In a strangled voice he croaked out, "Thank you." It came out almost a whisper. Swallowing, he said more clearly, "Chaim, Malachai is downstairs. He's exhausted. Find him some water and see he's all right."

Chaim rose to obey and Judah let him past. Still he did not enter the room. "Did he say anything?"

"Nothing you want to hear."

Judah nodded. "Asher."

"Both of you. He said you were both destined for great things. That the Lord came to him when you were born and told him so in a dream. He was angry that the dream hadn't come true."

Judah thought about that for a long time. His eyes burned. Finally he crossed to his father's bedside and looked at the grizzled face, so oddly slack now. Deborah had cleaned him, washing the filth out of his beard and changing his tunic. But the marks of the stroke were all too evident. Even in death, the left side of his face was fallen and listless.

"I took a Roman eagle last night, father. Me. They're calling me the hero of Beth Horon." Deborah stared at him, and he nodded once, a hopeless half-smile on his lips. He knelt clasped his father's cold hand. "All that fighting in the streets? All the times I came home with bruises and swollen fists? It was all for something, father. You'd've been proud."

"He was always proud of you."

Judah shrugged. "It was Asher that he was focused on."

"Only because he didn't understand him."

"True. Me, I was too simple. Simple Judah." He shook his head. "Asher should have lived, not me."

After a moment, Deborah rose and crossed around the bed. She knelt beside him and took his face in her hands. "You took an eagle?"

"Yes." He wanted to nod, but she had a surprisingly strong grip.

"Could Asher have done that?"

Judah smiled outright at that. "Not without me by his side."

"Then it was the Lord's will that you were spared. And I know at least one person who would grieve for you."

"Would you?" She was close. Very close.

The moment lingered, two birds at the edge of the nest. But both knew how inappropriate it would be to take flight. She let go and leaned back, breaking the moment. "Yes. Even if you pulled my hair and trapped desert crickets in my dress."

He smiled ruefully. "I was just a boy. A stupid boy." He bit his lip, but couldn't keep it from her any longer. "A month ago I asked your family's permission to marry you."

Her eyes were shining. "I know."

"They said no."

She ducked her head. "I know."

He reached out to take her hands. They were filthy from touching his face. "Should I ask again?"

"What?"

He grinned. "They can hardly say no to me now. I took an eagle."

She said nothing and he waited, uncertain, his chest beating harder than during the battle. Finally she nodded, a light smile playing across her whole face.

"Ask."

◆   ◊   ◆

They did not speak words of love, not then. There would be time. Instead they took up the vigil over the dead man, whose passing now seemed more mercy than sorrow. They sat side by side, hands folded together, and said prayers for the passing of Judah's father.

After an hour they heard a low roar approaching. Music, drums and pipes and more voices than the city had ever heard raised up at once.

Chaim came to the door. "They're back! Did you know, they captured an eagle!"

Judah nodded. "I heard that."

"You should go," said Deborah. "They'll be looking for you."

He shook his head. "I belong here. I'm the last of the family." Hebrew tradition demanded that a family member sit with the body for a full seven days.

She insisted with a statement he could not deny. "I'll be family soon enough." So he walked outside, feeling lighter than he could have imagined. He did not join in the throng, climbing instead to the roof to watch the procession in the streets.

The celebration parade stretched for miles. He scanned for familiar faces, but saw none in the press of humanity. He was watching for Levi or Phannius – he meant to have very different conversations with those two.

The procession continued, and Judah was uncomfortably reminded of tales of the Roman Triumph, where the Caesars paraded captives and booty from their wars through the streets.

He spied Simon bar Giora and Eleazar ben Simon, still mounted on their stolen Roman horses. They held the eagle aloft between them. Placed upon a fresh pole, it had been polished so it was at least recognizable. They heaved it high in the air, and men screamed themselves hoarse while women blew kisses and wept for joy. Eventually the eagle was marched up to the Temple, where the priests of the Sanhedrin took charge it.

From the New Gate all the way up to the Tomb of David, the people of Jerusalem went wild. For so long fear of this war had been like a massive fist clenching the throat of every man, woman, and child in Judea. The coming of war came as a relief – the Roman fist was gone, leaving the Judeans with their voice for the first time in living memory.

Judah felt oddly bad for the golden eagle, captured and demeaned in this way. Then he shook his head. *That's the danger with idols – too easy to treat them as if they were more than hunks of molded metal.* But if it hadn't been a symbol, he'd never have fought to take it in the first place.

As Judah frowned and puzzled over men's need for symbols, the reveling continued. There was dancing in the streets that night. Wine flowed freely. For a whole century Judea had been in Roman hands. Today they had declared their independence in a most spectacular way. Like the Makkabite revolt, this would be to a new Golden Age for

Jerusalem. A new dawn for the Lord's Chosen People on earth.

Deborah went home at dusk, and Judah sat vigil in the small house looking over the masonry yard and tried to understand what he was feeling.

I took the eagle. I lost my father. I'm getting Deborah. All because I'm too stupid to stay home when there's a fight.

"Father, forgive me. I had to go. For Asher – for all of us. You never said so, but you fought, in your own way. I know it, consorting with men like your friend Simeon. Outlaws and heretics. You should understand. You wrote to Asher, demanding he come back and fight in the war. Then I go do just that and you drop dead. In fairness, father, you could be a right bastard when you had a mind to." He smiled to show the dead man he was joking. They'd always enjoyed rough humor.

He'd never known his older brother, dead of a fever at the age of two. Nor had he ever known his mother, buried these seventeen years. There was no pain for either of those strangers. No, for his whole lifetime it had been just his brother and father. Now only Judah was left. The last mason of a line stretching back two hundred years and more.

Asher, I wish you were here. If only to throw some Greek quote at me and make me punch you. You'd tell me all about the history of eagles, or of war, or tell me a poem about Beth Horon. Maybe even compose one...

Frowning, he recalled what Levi had said. That this was the start of something terrible. Judah shook his head, hoping the turncoat patriot would be proved wrong.

He hoped in vain. It had already started. As news of the lost eagle spread, fighting erupted throughout Judea and the neighbouring lands. In Hebrew territory, gentiles perished. In gentile towns, Jews were slain. Worse, all this fighting took place on the Shabbat, the Lord's day of rest. Such a dark holy day took on a name all its own – *Shabbat Chazon*. The Black Sabbath.

It was only the beginning.

IV

A FREEDMAN stepped into the tiring chamber. "Lucius Junius Caesennius Paetus to see you, *domine*."

"Hmph." Whoever the man at the door, this visit was a message from Nero Caesar, and there was no doubt as to what the message was. Trust the man's perverseness to send a family member to demand a general fall on his sword.

"See him entertained." Struggling with his senatorial slippers, the old general gestured to the voluminous toga on the stand beside him. "Then come back and help me with this wretched thing."

"I'll help you, father," offered Titus, stepping forward. This might prove to be his last filial act.

They looked very alike – wide, squat heads that looked as though a giant had grabbed them by the ears and pulled. In the father, the effect was of perpetual straining, a permanent frown about the eyes. Whereas Titus' face turned upwards, a visage of good cheer. Which suited his personality.

Another difference was the scars. Titus had none, whereas his father's skin was riddled with them. The old soldier could point to each one and name the battle in which he'd won it, and sometimes even name the man who'd given it him. Odd names, Gallic or Celtic, German or African. Having risen through the ranks, Vespasian was a general who led from the front. As a young man, Titus looked forward to the day he, too, could name his scars.

Father and son bore the same name – Titus Flavius Sabinus Vespasianus. The father was generally known by his cognomen, Vespasian. Whereas the son was quite unusually known by the simple prenomen, Titus.

Titus aided his father in donning the toga praetexta, white with a broad stripe of purple running along one edge. With his purple shoes bearing crescent buckles and a fat gold ring on his left hand, Vespasian appeared every inch the Roman senator. Appropriate garb for the coming interview. But Titus knew it was strange for an inveterate military man not to wear armour when going to his death.

The general had considered donning a toga of mourning. He was certainly entitled – Titus' sister had just recently died. But it was unmanly to blazon that fact in this, his ultimate hour.

Vespasian had been expecting the order for two weeks now. When he asked his father why, rather than return to Achaea or even Reate, he'd chosen to rent a house in Marathon, the old man had said, "Because my race is run."

"Funny way to honour the old oak," said Vespasian now, trying to be wry. "So much for portents."

The night of his birth, back on the old family farm in Reate, a massive and dead oak tree had been split by lightning, and a shoot of green had burst forth to take new life. Taking it as a sign that her second son would be a great man, Titus' grandmother had forever pushed her son beyond his comfort. Vespasian was happiest upon a horse, a sword in hand. He was not made for the toga, nor for the Senate.

Yet he had tried. If he was now mocking that portent, he really did expect to die. Titus cleared his throat. "Before we go in, father, do you wish to see Caenis?"

Antonia Caenis was his father's mistress, a woman far cleverer than anyone Titus knew. Youthful lovers until Vespasian had married Titus' mother. The pity was that father couldn't marry her. But how could he? Caenis had been a slave, serving Mark Antony's daughter at court. She had known Tiberius, Caligula, and Claudius as men, rather than gods, and had lived at the heart of every intrigue and scandal that Rome had endured in the last fifty-odd years. She had been freed upon Antonia's death, and the moment Titus' mother had died, Vespasian had sought Caenis out again. It was almost poetic – true love conquering all.

Vespasian surprised his son by shaking his head. "No. We've said our farewells. Besides, best not to keep your cousin waiting. Might as well try to keep you alive."

Together they entered the *tablinum*. The study was cramped but not airless, owning a fine ventilation grille that led to the brisk December air outside. For two weeks this little Greek villa had been their home. There was a bee-farm nearby, and a stud farm. The scene was pleasantly rustic, and reminded Titus of their family seat near Reate. Probably why his father had chosen it.

Paetus was waiting. Unmistakably Roman in both height and

nose, those proper features had been over-layered with what seemed several dips in tallow. Not fat, exactly. Just thick.

His immaculate clothes proclaimed he'd come by litter instead of horseback. Perusing the pigeonhole shelves of Vespasian's traveling library, Paetus exclaimed, "What a frightful bore you are, Titus Flavius! Don't you have anything other than military manuals?"

"A pity you find them boring, Lucius Junius. A few more military manuals and you might have won your little war with the Armenians."

Titus grinned. If his father had to die, at least he wasn't going meekly. For a moment his cousin's smoothness vanished. Then Paetus threw his head back and laughed. "O, how glad I am they sent me, of all people! I do like you, Titus Flavius. You have a – a *commonness* that is utterly refreshing. How it pains me that I will now be denied your company."

Vespasian stared back, expressionless. Titus knew his father prided himself on the very trait that Paetus was now deriding. Plain speaking, common sense, lack of 'sophistication' – these were excellent qualities in a soldier. A man unburdened by genius, for all that life had forced him to be a politician, Vespasian was at heart a *virs militarus* – a Military Man.

"Well, nephew, as much as it pleases you to see us, I assure you we are delighted in equal measure." Rather than retire to couches, he crossed to the far side of his desk and sat in the hard chair behind it.

It was an insult to force a guest to sit in a chair like a client. But Paetus merely smiled as he sat. He waved his hand again at the rows of scrolls. "Is it really bare of anything poetic?"

"Probably a copy of the *Aeneid* in there somewhere."

"But nothing more recent? A copy of the *Satyricon* might earn you a fortune now that Petronius is dead."

Vespasian's eyebrows twitched. "I hadn't heard. Too much high living, or an angry Greek?" There was a double meaning in that.

"Some are saying poison, but he's been poisoning himself for years. Petronis was an artist. They have large appetites. Of every kind."

"So I understood from his little book." The late Senator Petronius was rumoured to be the author of the *Satyricon*, the ribald adventures of a former gladiator and his young boy lover – based on his own relationship with young Nero. Hilarious, deliciously scandalous, yet social suicide to admit having read it.

Not that it mattered. Vespasian had already committed social suicide. Since the early Fall the nobility of Rome had been traveling Greece, a tail to the comet that was Nero as the newly-minted god bounced from one Greek city to another for chariot races, wrestling matches, and poetry competitions.

Vespasian had been among his train until two weeks ago, when, during a concert by Nero in the temple of Jupiter on Corcyra, Vespasian had fallen asleep. He had even snored. Audibly. Of all insults to give, a slur against Caesar's art was the gravest. Hence the expected order to fall upon his sword.

"May I offer you something, nephew? Our fare is plain, but my cook might be able to create some honey-wafers, or wrapped sausages."

Malice danced in Paetus' eyes. "Actually, I have a hankering for some braised turnips. Or does your cook not keep them?"

Titus bristled. While governor of Africa, his father had been so unpopular that the people had pelted him with turnips whenever he took to the streets.

But Vespasian remained impassive, his permanent frown immobile. "Son, ask the cook to dig up some turnips for our guest."

Fuming, Titus departed. He had been sent off to control his temper, he knew. The Temper of Titus was famous in their house. But it was as quick to cool as to rise. When he returned, followed by slaves from the kitchens, he was calm again.

Paetus had evidently been prattling about the frivolous scandals of Nero's court. Now it looked as if it was the old general's temper that was fraying. The father was just the opposite of the son – slow to anger, slow to cool. Titus could tell it was on the tip of his father's tongue to tell this fool to get his business over and done when suddenly they heard a commotion outside.

The steward appeared in the doorway. "Domine, forgive me. Quintus Petillius Cerialis Caesius Rufus has called."

Cerialis was Vespasian's son-in-law, husband to Titus' late sister. *What in Jupiter's name does he think he can do here?*

Paetus frowned as Cerialis entered, all in a rush. Thirty-six years of age, he was day to Paetus' night: a man of no meat whatsoever, just skin stretched across bone, giving him a grayish tinge. But like all redheaded men, he was quick to colour, hence the name Rufus.

The red flush to his cheeks spoke of a frantic ride from Athens. "Titus Flavius, you must let me come with you!"

Titus shared a look of frustration with Vespasian. *Did the rash fool not know enough to keep his head down?* "Your duty is to your little girl, my grand-daughter. Watch over her, and see that Domitian is properly raised as well."

Privately, Titus thought that the best solution to his brother Domitian was drowning. Or the sharp end of a knife.

But Cerialis looked hurt and confused. "They have tutors and relations enough. My daughter will hardly miss me. Besides, with you in command, we'll all be back before she reaches her tenth birthday!"

The glance Titus and Vespasian shared was one of pure confusion. "What? I – command?" said Vespasian, while Titus said sharply, "What command?"

The glow suffusing Cerialis' cheeks drained away, leaving his face splotchy with anger. He rounded on Paetus. "You haven't told him?"

Still in his seat, Paetus flicked imaginary lint from his sleeve. "I was coming to it. One ought not hurry grand news. It must be savoured."

There was little doubt what Paetus had been savouring. His sport forced to an early end, he rose, straightened his spine, and delivered his commission. "Titus Flavius Sabinus Vespasianus Major, I bear the greetings of Nero Claudius Caesar Drusus Augustus Germanicus, Princeps Senatus and Imperator Invictus. You are hereby ordered by the Senate and People of Rome to take command of the available legions in the region of Judea and put down the revolt there with all due haste. Do not fail, on peril of your life. Long live Rome!"

A warming glow spread through Titus. *Thank you, Mars, Bellona, and all you gods of war! The death Nero desires is not my father's.*

Instead, we are to bring death to the Judeans.

◆ ◊ ◆

Unsurprisingly, Paetus declined to remain for dinner. He was unrepentant for his little game, which told Titus the script had been written by Nero himself. Though he was granted this marvelous war, Vespasian's offense was not forgotten.

It was a small dinner, with the three men laying on couches, and Antonia Caenis sitting upright on a chair across from Vespasian. She remained silent, as was proper. But Titus knew the moment the dinner was finished, she and father would retire and have the real conversation.

Unlike his little brother, Titus did not resent the lady Caenis. He could certainly see the attraction. She was a beauty, despite her years. Perhaps there were lines at her eyes and mouth, but she had darkly silver hair and wide purple eyes that always seemed to laugh knowingly. Added to that was a grace learned from her years at Caesar's court. More, she was the one person who could make his father laugh outright.

Himself a widower, Titus had taken to discussing family matters with Caenis before mentioning them to his father – she always knew how best to move the old mule. For two weeks they had mutually fretted, fearing Nero's reprisals. Then Caenis had disappeared for a day, returning just this morning. "Visiting old friends," she had said smoothly. In the wake of the great news, Titus had his suspicions.

Naturally, Cerialis was the evening's guest of honour. Famished after his hard ride, he busily tucked in as he was pressed with questions.

"First the war, Quintus Petillius. We only heard there was a revolt, nothing more. Tell us everything."

Between mouthfuls of bread, Cerialis grinned. "Only if I may join you."

"You earned *that* right when you put Paetus in his place. Answer me now and I'll give you your choice of legions."

The old general clearly regretted the words as soon as they escaped his teeth. It was not just the ginger tint of his hair that earned Cerialis the cognomen *Rufus*. Thirty-seven years old, Titus' brother-in-law was given to rash acts of boldness and daring, few of which paid off. Like Paetus, Quintus Petillius Cerialis was in military disrepute. Six years earlier he had lost nearly half the Ninth Legion in Britannia. The city of Camulodenum had been under siege by the Briton queen Boudicca, and Cerialis had rushed to their aid. Valuing speed over sense, he took only his first cohort and a detachment of cavalry, and still he arrived too late. Rather than wave off, he attacked and was mauled, retreating as fast as he had come.

The rout cost him. When the Ninth won the war, credit had gone to other commanders, while blame clung to Cerialis like stink to excrement. He had continually failed to achieve the consulship. A man who did not know when to be adventurous and when to be prudent.

Now he clearly hoped to retrieve his wounded reputation. Beaming, Cerialis ran a hand through his thick red hair and launched into the news from Judea. "We don't know all the details yet. Lots of conflicting reports. But you know the current Prefect of Judea, Gessius Florus? The squat knight Poppaea used to fawn over?"

Vespasian said nothing, but Titus saw Caenis' lips press tighter. Nero's late wife Poppaea was the reason Vespasian had stayed out of public life for ten years. That vengeful bitch had hated him.

"Well, if there were an Olympic trial for how swiftly a man may gain the enmity of an entire people, the victor would be Florus. He openly despised the Judeans. In one case, some Jews sued the local Greeks for a religious insult. Florus accepted a massive *sponsio* – eight talents of gold, if you please. Then, after hearing the case, he dismissed the Greeks, imprisoned the Hebrews who had brought the case, and kept all eight talents for himself! Ha!"

Vespasian's natural frown deepened. "You find this atrocious business amusing?"

Cerialis shrugged. "I appreciate such monumental cupidity."

"It *is* funny, father," agreed Titus, grinning. "If only because it's so blatantly villainous."

"You're idiots, both of you. But I shouldn't complain – it's given me a war. Go on, Quintus."

"The men of Jerusalem chose to find it funny, too. They mocked his greed, passing baskets about, begging for alms for poor Florus, who was in such desperate need of money."

"A fairly measured response," observed Vespasian approvingly. "Humiliate the fool. I expected them to riot."

"The riots came when Florus flogged and crucified the leaders of this little protest. Despite their being Roman citizens. Seems he was unamused."

Titus was aghast. It was one of the cornerstones of Roman Law that no citizen could be struck with a lash, nor could he be put to death in any manner that denied him his dignity. The core of the rights Romulus had laid down was *dignitas*, the sum of a man's reputation and social standing. To a Roman man, nothing mattered more. To die a slave's death was an insult worse than mere execution. It was a *damnatio memoriae* – a declaration that the dead man owned no *dignitas* in life, and was not worth remembering. "What happened next?"

"The Jews outright refused to pay taxes or make the weekly offering on Nero's behalf to their god. When Florus tried to force them to offer a prayer for Nero – or possibly to him, that's unclear – the city rose up and sacked the garrison. A whole cohort, wiped out. Except for their commander who, I understand, was forced to make himself a Jew." Cerialis inclined his head significantly towards his groin and made a scissor-motion with his fingers. Then he inclined his head to Caenis. "Forgive my crudeness."

Having been addressed, Caenis smiled. "I have been acquainted with many Jews in my time. Including the current king's father. Their rites are familiar to me. As well as their peculiar sacrifice."

Knowing the rumours about the wild years at court, Titus wondered how well she had known the Hebrew king's father. Vespasian laughed at the look of consternation on his son's face.

Equally flustered, Cerialis continued his story. "Ah, yes, so – in a right panic, Florus called upon Cestius Gallus to bring a Syrian legion up to restore order. Gallus took the Twelfth, with vexillations from the Third, Fourth, and Sixth."

"The Fulminata, Gallica, Scythica, and Feratta," said Titus. Vespasian nodded proudly.

"Yes. So Gallus arrives at Jerusalem, and there's confusion as to what exactly happens next. We know Gallus began a siege, then retreated. The Judeans gave chase. Without shields or armour, armed with sticks and slings, they destroyed the legion. It was a disaster." Cerialis' brow darkened. "The Twelfth lost its eagle."

At these words Titus felt his blood freeze in his veins. The *Aquila* was the very essence of a Roman legion. Better every man should fall than let their eagle be taken. Any passing sympathy for the Judeans vanished. They had taken an eagle. Time to grind them into dust.

The only one who seemed unsurprised was the lady Caenis. Meaning she had already heard this news. Feeling Titus' gaze on her, she exclaimed, "How terrible!" with just the right intonation of horror and grief.

Vespasian reached across the table to pat her hand while. "Terrible? These blessed, blessed Jews have resurrected my career!"

"Pity you have to repay them by killing them all," observed Titus wryly.

"Oh, not all, surely," said Caenis.

Cerialis quickly finished his tale. "Florus and Gallus have both been stripped of their commands. You'll be pleased, father – you have the highest *imperium* of any man in Judea." He leaned back in satisfaction, having married into the right family after all.

"Which brings me to my next question," said Vespasian, his frown deepening. "How in the name of Mars and Bellona was my name even floated?"

"No one knows! Nero Caesar accepted names, and several senators offered their services. Then, out of nowhere, Nero said, 'What about Vespasian?' It was like a thunderbolt from above. But the moment he mentioned you, several people spoke in your favour. Including Paetus, of all people. I think he's trying to win back some of his reputation after that disaster with the Armenians. Since he's no general, he's angling to be the chooser of generals."

Titus was again looking at Caenis, but she was gazing adoringly at her lover. Vespasian continued to frown. "But why did Nero even suggest me? I'm fifty-six years old! And I'm hardly in his good graces."

Caenis said, "It's because he knows you're the best man for it, of course."

"Thank you, *meum mel*. But I doubt that was the reason."

Watching Caenis, Titus felt certain he knew the answer. "Someone probably reminded Nero Caesar that he needed to nominate a general who was not a threat to him. That perhaps he should get a name in before the nominations got around to the more popular generals, like Corbulo. That his choice should be someone already in Greece, not back in Rome. And maybe, just maybe, that unknown someone then reminded him of your service in Britannia, and that you allowed Claudius Caesar to take all the credit for that war."

Caenis' expression was neutral, but his father's natural frown added an extra crease. "So I'm given command of this war, not for my own merits, but to keep it out of the hands of someone who might actually eclipse Nero?"

"It helps if he believes you owe him," teased Caenis, poking her lover in the ribs across the table. "How hard is it to stay awake, Titus Flavius? Imagine it as a musical siege!"

At her touch, Vespasian rumbled with laughter. "Is it my fault that my Achilles' heel is lyre music? Like the savage beast, I'm helpless!"

"Nero did say he pities your lack of understanding of the finer things," said Cerialis with mock-gravity.

"I appreciate the form his pity takes. Now tell me, how many men have the Judeans mustered? Is it only Jerusalem, or are other cities rising as well? Who is the over-all leader? Which sects of Hebrews are the troublesome ones? Where are they now?"

All of which Cerialis answered with ignorance. It was not that he did not care. No one knew.

"So," said Vespasian, "I could be entering a war against two thousand men, or two hundred thousand."

He was not in the least put out. In fact, Vespasian looked more pleased than his son had ever seen him. The same could be said for Caenis, who appeared completely satisfied.

Titus himself was glowing with happiness. A great war. A once-in-a-lifetime war. And he would be there, right in the thick of it.

Time to start earning those scars.

V

FIVE WEEKS after Beth Horon, Judah was hard at work in his
father's yard. In his hands he held a great two-headed hammer, heaving
it up and shattering stone with thunderous blows. *Crack!* His handsome
face set a fierce grimace, glory and joy all but forgotten. *Crack!* This was
not an age of heroes. *Crack!* Men achieved greatness through birth, not
deeds. *Crack!* Having played his part, Judah was expected to return to
his role as the humble mason. *Crack!*

And bachelor.

Crack!!

He was striking with far more force than was needed. He imagined
the rocks bore the faces of Phannius and Euodias, Deborah's mother, as
he smashed them into grit and shards. *Damn! Damn! Damn!*

He'd waited a whole week after his father's funeral, then gone
to the house of Samuel the Mason. Samuel was long dead, as were
Phannius' elder siblings. But Phannius' mother was alive and well, the
old bitch. Crusty, bitter, bent by a hard life, Euodias was a survivor. One
of eleven children, she was the last standing. Sometimes Judah thought
that there was not actually blood in her veins, but bile. She thrived on
anger and resentment, and all other human emotions were foreign to
her. She was as proud of her loutish son as she was jealous of her beautiful daughter.

She'd certainly been in rare form that day. Dressed in his best
clothes, washed and with newly pared nails and hair, Judah had arrived
with a basket of gifts in his arms. Bread, wine, cheese, salt, and a gift
he'd received from the priests – a fine goblet made of crystal, of Syrian
design. His sole official reward for his great deed.

But that didn't matter. Deborah was all the reward he needed.

Entering their yard, he'd noted at once it was not as neat as his father's. Saws were left untended, and some bore broken teeth. Chisels lay disregarded. There was such wealth here that they could be careless of their tools. Phannius had seven apprentices working for him, making the House of Samuel far more productive than the House of Matthais. It didn't matter that they turned out less quality stone, or that the joins didn't quite fit. All that mattered was that one drop of noble blood.

To become a priest, one had to prove he could trace his male lineage back to Aaron, brother of Mosheh the Lawgiver, who was the first Kohen Gadol. If a man could do that, he had a leg up on the rest of the Hebrew world. If he chose not to be a priest – there were several thousand priests in Jerusalem alone, tending all sorts of business for the state – a man could carry that advantage into life, no matter his trade or profession. Hence the difference between Phannius and Judah.

Phannius had greeted him coolly. He couldn't be hostile, not after the eagle – and not after the death of Judah's father. But he knew all too well why Judah was here, and clearly didn't approve.

After they embraced, Judah offered his gifts. Phannius was bemused. "Offer them to mother, not me."

Judah frowned. Phannius was the man of the house. If he was passing the responsibility of accepting the gifts to his mother, it was a bad sign.

But Judah kept a confident smile on his face. He'd talked with Deborah at the funeral, and they had agreed that there was no way he could be refused this time. So when he entered the house and saw the widow Euodias sitting on her hard stool, hunched and crabbed as always, he made an effusive greeting and presented her with the gifts. He kept his eyes firmly off Deborah, seated beside her mother.

The woman could hardly be more than fifty-five. But she looked so old, like a grape that had soured early. Old even when she was young, an age of the soul.

Euodias examined his gifts, not noticing anything but the crystal goblet. That she ran her fingers over a few times, looking for flaws. Finding none, she set it aside. "So, boy. You're a hero, now, are you?" Euodias looked over Judah from heel to head. "They don't make heroes the way they used to."

Judah couldn't be wounded by the widow's venom, not today. "I came, lady, to ask—"

The woman cut him off with a click of her tongue. "Tch. I know why you came. Like a dog to vomit, you're here to lap up your prize. Well, we can't deny you now, can we? You're a *hero!*"

Judah didn't know how to handle her sarcasm. "I don't claim to be a hero."

"Nor should you!" Her voice had the dark edge of a blood-stained knife. "My son told me all about it! How you left him to defend himself while you leapt after the eagle! How he kept the Romans off your back as you stole the eagle, then raced to safety. A pity you were too stingy to share any of the credit with those good men who kept you alive. *They're* the real heroes!"

Judah turned to stare at Phannius. The lout didn't even have the good grace to look embarrassed by his lie. They both knew he'd been nowhere near the eagle when Judah took it. It had been Levi who had protected Judah's back. But Phannius' face was set in a mulish expression, as if daring Judah to make him look bad in front of his mother.

Judah blew air out his nose like an animal, but knew the truth wouldn't help his cause. Carefully, he said, "Lady Euodias, no one has asked me for an account of the events. I agree that the man who defended my back should have all the honour due him. And I would be happy to share the credit with your son, or whomever you please."

"Oh? Magnanimous, isn't he? Already trying to act better than his place. As if he wasn't some jumped up son of a labourer. Just like his brother, ideas above his station—"

"Mother..." said Deborah softly, her lips pinched tight.

"Quiet, girl! I suppose you think that we should pity him, having lost his brother and father. I could have told you that the brother would come to no good. As for Matthais – imagine, being felled by the loss of a son. Tch. I've lost three, including the best of them, and I'm still upright. But men are made of weaker stuff..."

The inference that Phannius was not her best son didn't seem to affect the big man, he'd heard it so often. Judah almost felt sorry for the lout. At least he understood why Phannius had told his lie. No doubt she had flayed him for not bringing back the eagle himself.

It was clear she had no intention of granting permission for Judah and Deborah to marry. Technically, of course, that refusal should have come from Phannius, the senior man in the household. But there was no doubt as to who ruled here.

Still, Judah wasn't about to slink away like a whipped cur, his tail between his legs. He would make her say it. "Lady Euodias. I have come to humbly ask your permission to take your daughter's hand in marriage."

Tears stood in Deborah's eyes. She didn't look at her mother, but tried to convey as much as possible before he was made to leave.

Euodias let the moment drag out as long as possible. Then she jerked her chin at her son. "Phannius is the man of the house. You should be asking him. Insulting! Imagine, asking an old woman's permission when he's standing right there. First you keep him from his just desserts, then you heap scorn upon him by placing a woman over him.

Or worse, acting like he doesn't even exist!" She looked to her son. "And what kind of man are you, that you let him treat you so? Are you afraid of him? He always was a bully, even as a boy. Well, Judah ben Matthais, you can't have your little prize. Stupid as she is, she is comely – almost as pretty as I was at her age. She's made for a better husband than a common mason – even a *hero*! Her maidenhead will go to a wealthy man of the Lower City, maybe even the Upper. But don't worry, hero, you won't have to see it. We won't want common folk at the wedding. Come, Deborah!" She took her daughter's hand and physically led Deborah deeper into the house. She took the goblet with her.

That left Judah alone with Phannius. Judah wanted to say something insulting, but decided that the best thing to do was to treat him just as his mother had described. Ignoring him completely, Judah left the house with his head held high.

He didn't remember the walk home, and the weeks since seemed a blur. Work, work was the answer. He pushed his body past enduring, taking up the worst physical labour he could find, straining so hard he tore open the scabs from the battle and bled afresh.

Fortunately there were many orders to fill, mostly from the priests wishing to fortify the city walls. *Priests*. But Judah swallowed his anger and worked from dawn till dusk. When he fell into his bed each night – alone – he had to be too tired to think. Because thinking made it worse. In his unworthier moments he wished he'd succumbed and bedded Deborah the night after the battle. Euodias would have had to agree, or else complain to the priests that the hero of Beth Horon had deflowered her daughter. But Judah didn't wish that kind of shame on Deborah. And on the night his father had died...? Everything conspired against them.

Among the neighbourhood, the refusal reflected poorly on everyone. Deborah's family had denied her to the hero of Beth Horon. But some said they must have had reason. People began looking at Judah as an upstart crow, a man with ideas above his station. The luster of his great victory was a little tarnished. Not that Judah cared. He threw himself into work, imagining each hammer-fall a blow against his enemies.

His other respite was his new friend, Levi. The gaunt and bearded bodyguard appeared one day in the yard, a mocking smile on his lips. "So this is where you learned to fight. Pity you didn't have that hammer at Beth Horon."

"We did well enough without it." Judah dropped the hammer to embrace the taller man. Seen in normal circumstances, not covered in dust and blood, Levi ben Patroclus looked to be in his middle thirties, though the shaved head made him seem older. His skin was weathered, too, aging him further. Judah couldn't say what the original hue had been, but the man had some northern features – a slightly wider nose that flared when he talked, a jutting chin under his neat square beard. The massive sword hung in a baldric upon his back, too long to be carried at the waist.

"Thank you," said Judah when they were sipping water and lemons in the house. It wasn't empty anymore. He'd kept his word to his dead friend and taken in Jocha's widow and son. The woman kept house for him, and the boy earned their keep as his third apprentice. It was the widow, close to Levi's age, who brought them the fruit drink, and then returned with small wafers frosted with sugar. She smiled at Levi, who thanked her, then said to Judah, "As for your thanks, hothead, I'll do without them. You thanked me once, which was more than was required. Thank me again and I'll make you eat that rock in the yard."

"I'd enjoy seeing you try. Though I suppose if I had to have just one man protecting my back, I'm glad it was a bodyguard." He paused, then said, "I feel bad. You lost your position because of me."

"No. Because of me."

"I never asked who you were guarding. Some priest?"

"No," replied Levi, swirling the cup in his hand. There was a patina of dust floating on the surface – everything in the house was inevitably covered in grit from the yard. "I was the bodyguard for King Agrippa."

Judah choked on his drink and Levi grinned. For a moment Judah didn't know whether to believe him or no. Then he started laughing and invited him to supper.

They supped together three more times in the last two weeks, and Levi kept Judah informed as to the course of the war. "Not that there's much to tell, yet. The murders have ended on all sides – no one left within reach to kill. Now everyone waits to see what Nero Caesar will say."

"Is there any doubt?"

Jocha's widow, Shalva, had made them a thick stew this time. Her cooking inexplicably improved whenever she knew Levi was coming.

Picking out a hunk of lamb meat and lifting it to his lips, Levi shrugged. "From what I heard the king say, one never can tell with Nero. He thinks he's an artist. He might just compose us a ballad and let it go."

Judah pulled a face. "You don't believe that."

"No," agreed Levi. "I don't."

◆　◊　◆

Now, chest heaving, Judah paused to wipe the sweat from his brow. He was working shirtless today, wearing just a kilted wrap about his loins. It was cold, but Judah's anger warmed him. That, and the heat from the kilns, which was good for Judah's hands. It was dangerous to work large stones with numbed fingers.

Just as he lifted his hammer he heard an ugly sound and turned to see one of his apprentices standing over a badly-chiseled piece of stone, with jagged shards littering the ground. "Damn it, Benayahu! Limestone isn't granite, you can't just hack away at it!"

Young Benayahu stepped fearfully back. His father, Jocha, would have had his hide, and Judah's mood these last three weeks had threatened as much. Everyone knew why.

But Judah was a fairer man than the boy's father. Taking a deep breath, he stepped close and merely relieved Benayahu of his hammer and chisel. "Try again. Start by pouring the water over the stone. Look for cracks. There's nothing worse than cutting into a stone only to have it shatter from some hidden flaw. That's happened to me too often. The worst damage is always inside, waiting. Which is why we need to be careful."

Once all the creases had been identified, Judah raised the chisel into place. "Remember, new-quarried limestone's soft, more likely to crumble. So you have to guide it, give it form. One bad stroke and you'll have wasted the day. Malachi, Chaim, step back."

His two older apprentices obeyed, having seen this lesson several times but still enjoying the skill and raw power that Judah brought to the work. Judah neatly struck the stone in five separate places, then five more on each side. As he worked, he talked. "I know we're in a rush. The Sanhedrin is breathing down our necks. But we're masons, not magicians. We can't rush just because they're scared."

"I'm scared, too," admitted Benayahu softly. He was only nine years old. Chaim snorted, but Malachai put a hand on the boy's shoulder. "So am I." Normally Malachai sang while he worked, but not lately. Part of it was the images of the war, still carved into his eyes. Part was Judah's mood.

"No shame in that. Only a fool doesn't feel fear." Shirtless torso caked in airbourne grit, Judah took wedges and gently tapped them into each of the holes. "But think of this – properly fitted stones make all the difference against a Roman battering ram. This stone could be here a hundred years from now. Five hundred, a thousand, even. But if we rush, if we leave cracks or weaken the stone by going against the grain, it will shatter when hit. One shattered stone leads to a breach. A breach means the city falls and the Romans win."

The three apprentices listened intently. Here was a man still bearing the marks of battle, treating this stone as gently as he would a child.

Hefting a large mallet, Judah started hitting the wedges – lightly at first, then with growing intensity. "You have to be calm – with stone. Patient. Within this slab – there's a perfect square held prisoner, yearning to be free. We must *help – it – emerge*."

His final blow was answered with a tremendous *crack!* A large chunk of limestone fell away, leaving a nearly flat surface underneath.

Grinning, Judah tossed the hammer to the ground. As always, the work made him feel better. "That's the way. When you're bigger, I'll let you use the stone-saw. But for now, get the pumice and start smoothing out that end so we can turn it and do the next side. Take your time. Forget about the war. Think of the prisoner in the stone."

A sharp rap made the apprentices jump, thinking there was indeed someone trapped within the limestone. Laughing at them, Judah crossed to the door in the yard's wall and yanked it wide. To his surprise he saw bodyguards outside, surrounding a bald stranger of middle years and rich attire. "*Shalom.* Can I help you?"

"I – I hope so." The fellow was clearly taken aback by the muscled young man in the kilted cloth. He produced a piece of slate with a chalked marking on it. "Is this the marking of this house?"

Judah looked at the insignia, the name Matthais with the letters forming a pyramid. "It is."

"Are you Matthais?"

"His son."

"Ah. I should have known." The man squinted hard out of watery eyes. "He looks just like you."

Instantly Judah's heart began to hammer against his ribs. "Who?"

"Don't know his name. We found him on the road from Aegypt."

Judah had a hundred questions, but only one mattered. "He's alive?"

"Alive? Oh yes – barely. We didn't know how to find his people, but he had a letter on him bearing this mark –"

Judah was already moving, fetching a tunic and hauling it over his sweating, grimy frame. "Boys, let the fires dim. Chaim and Malachai, fetch doctors. Benayahu, tell your mother to prepare a sickbed. Then wait here, I may need you." Returning his attention to the man at the gate, he said, "Where is he?"

"At our house in the Upper City. I'll bring you to – what's his name?"

"Asher. His name is Asher."

VI

SITUATED AROUND three hills, Jerusalem was divided into four parts. Most prominent was the Upper City, also called the Old City because it was here that David had built his walls. Sloping down from the heights of Mount Zion, the Upper City was home to the priests and wealthiest citizens, and held palaces of kings all the way from David to Herod the Usurper. The latter had made certain it contained such Roman constructions as an amphitheatre and Hippodrome.

Just east of the Upper City, yet apart from it, stood Mount Moriah. A fortress in and of itself, this was the most ancient and holy of sites, where Abraham had offered up his son Isaac to the Lord. Here David had lain the foundations for the Lord's home on earth, the heart of the city. Here David's son Solomon had completed the great Temple. Here, too, Herod had built a great Roman-style fortress called Antonia, after his patron Mark Antony.

The last hill was called Acra, so named for the fortress that had once stood here, also built by Israel's enemies. Slightly south of Mount Moriah, it was shaped like the horned moon. Built on the slopes of Acra was the Lower City, where lived the populous and prosperous middle-class. Centuries of enterprise and hard work had made this area a gleaming crossroads for traders, craftsmen, and artists of all kinds.

But in the centuries since David's reign his city had continued to sprawl. With deep gorges of Hinnon and Kidron running south and east, settlers had built homes north and west. Thus was born Bezetha, the New City. Enclosed by a wall named for Herod's son Agrippa, here lived the poor, the rough labourers, and the peasants who toiled and scraped together means to survive.

The rich Upper City to the West, the Temple to the East, the prosperous Lower City to the South, and struggling Bezetha to the North. This was Jerusalem.

Judah's masonry yard was in Bezetha, just inside Agrippa's Wall. If the trader's home was in the Upper City, they had a trek ahead. Going anywhere in Jerusalem meant a climb, which was why pilgrims always referred to 'going up to Jerusalem'.

As they set out, the wealthy man's gait was maddeningly relaxed. Judah had to resist the temptation to pick him up and carry him. Instead he pressed for information. "You said my brother was on the road from Aegypt. Where? When did you find him?"

"Nearly two weeks ago. He was sick with fever, and sunstruck. And –"

"And what?"

"He had a wound in his side. It had been doctored, but not well. I don't know how he managed to keep his feet for such a journey, all the way from Alexandria."

They were only just passing the Clothier's Bazaar. "How do you know he came from..?"

The squinting man reached into his belt and produced a dirty piece of papyrus. "The letter. I've been trying to trace the mark for the last week. I'm sorry it took so long..."

He handed the letter over, and Judah unfurled it to behold his own handwriting. As they turned right at the Potter's Square and climbed the steps through Second Wall leading to Fort Antonia, he scanned the words he knew far too well, words dictated by his father:

> *Son,*
>
> *Perhaps amidst your piles of scrolls and book-buckets you have failed to note it, but your Nation, the pride of King David and the Prophets Abraham and Mosheh, is under siege. Perhaps, tucked away in your precious Alexandrian library, you are oblivious to the shedding of your country's Blood. Perhaps, engaged in deep thoughts of gentile heroes and their deeds, you have been blind to the true Heroes that now fight to free your People from Tyranny. Already the People in their righteous wisdom have risen and sacked the enemy garrison at Fort Antonia.*
>
> *There is a time for Study. Any father would laud a son's investment in Learning, even if that Learning is not of matters properly Hebrew in nature. Education is to be valued and cherished.*
>
> *But is it valued higher than Patriotism? Than Fidelity? What would your philosophers and poets say? Do they not*

*say 'Better to die Free Men than live as Slaves'? Would they
deem him a Righteous Man who went gadding off to foreign
lands while his father, brother, and country burned? Or
would they accuse him of Neglect, Cowardice, even Treason?
Have you, in all your reading, ever come across a poet who
extolled the virtues of the Timid? Perhaps you have. Poets
can write whatever they please. But men must act!*

*There is a time for Study, and there is a time to defend
your Nation, your Family, and your G-d.*

*Perhaps this letter will miss you. Perhaps you are
already on your way home. I pray this is so. But if this letter
finds you on Yom Rishon, and you are not aboard a ship on
Yom Sheini, you are No Son of Mine.*

These were the words of Judah's father. But just below, marked
with a star, was an appendix Judah himself had added, a private message
to his twin:

*Don't listen to him. He just wants you home. But
Jerusalem is dangerous these days. Stay there, brother, and
stay safe.*

This letter had been sent three months earlier, when all the trouble with Rome was just starting. Judah had been proud of his advice. His brother did not belong in war. Asher was meant for better things.

Twins, Judah and Asher had both been raised to follow the trade of their father, grandfather, and great-grandfather. But while Judah could happily spend his whole life among pulleys, chisels, and grit (so long as there was the occasional fist-fight in the yard to liven things up), Asher had shown signs of a greater future. Where Judah loved pummeling stones, Asher pummeled ideas. Learning was his passion – and his undoing.

Blessed with an astonishing memory, at nine years old Asher could recite the whole of the Torah with word-perfect accuracy. Despite the fact that they did not come from a priestly family, he began to elicit interest from the educators at the Temple. Ability, they said, was a gift from the Lord, and never to be ignored. He had even been called before Jochanan ben Sakkai, Rector of the Temple University, to answer questions. Judah remembered that day, because Asher had suggested they switch places, for fun.

"You're an idiot. They want to take you off and teach you, make you a priest, even."

"A priest's clerk, maybe." Even at nine, they had both been aware of the deficiencies of their birth.

"So? It's a good life – especially for someone so in love with books!" Judah made it sound like a taunt. There was a small, unwelcome part of him that envied his brother. But he made sure never to show it.

At Judah's urging, Asher had gone. Whatever he had said to old Doctor Jochanan, it had impressed the white-bearded scholar. The next day Temple rabbis came to press Matthais to allow the boy to come study with them in a *beth hasefer*, a House of the Book. Matthais had reluctantly agreed – so long as the boy did not neglect his duties in the workshop. He was afraid his son would become rarified in the company of priests.

That hadn't happened. Instead, Asher gradually became a problem for the holy men. After four years of teaching, he showed he owned more than a great memory. He also had a questing mind, and no stopper to dam his thoughts – he spoke them right out. The Temple scholars found themselves facing uneasy questions of philosophy and faith, and did not enjoy having their own words thrown back at them to make Asher's points.

Judah recalled the most contentious of the battles his brother had fought, a war over the First and Second Commandments: *I am the Lord thy God. Thou shalt have no other gods before me. You shall not make for yourself an idol.* This was generally agreed to mean there was but one God, and that He was Jehovah. But Asher had argued a different meaning, using the very language of the commandment as his proof.

"'*No other gods before me*' – Yahweh is claiming pre-eminence, not exclusivity," the fourteen year-old Asher had declared. "By even using the phrase 'other gods,' He implicitly acknowledges that other gods do, in fact, exist. He's just denying us, His Chosen People, the right to worship those other gods. Or rather, the right to pray to them more than to Him. He is claiming us as His own, but He does not deny that other gods exist."

"The Lord does not peddle in semantics!" one of his teachers had argued hotly.

"The Lord is the Word," Asher had replied in earnest astonishment. "And the Word is Law. Therefore His words matter, and His choice of words are of the utmost importance."

Such exchanges led to reprimands, even threats. To please their teachers, other pupils took to assaulting Asher, forcing Judah to escort his twin to and from Temple. With Judah beside him, Asher became a better fighter, and the other boys soon learned to fear the pair.

Where once the Temple priests had ignored Asher's ignoble birth, it now became a way to discredit him. Despite his family's long roots in Jerusalem, they unjustly called him '*am ha-arez*, a peasant. They were at the point of casting out the fifteen year-old troublemaker when, to the relief of the priests and the fury of his father, Asher suddenly departed to study in Alexandria.

Judah had helped his twin slip out of the city, and secretly sent money ever since. In return, Judah received letters. There was much in them he didn't understand – references to Aegyptian authors, Greek philosophers, Roman poets. But it was clear that Asher was flourishing. So when their father dictated his scathing letter, Judah had added his own coda to keep his brother where he was both happy and safe.

It had been a cruel joke. Shortly after the letter had been sent, news came from Alexandria that the Aegyptian and Greek citizens had risen up against the Alexandrian Jews. The Jews had fought back, causing the Romans to sack the whole Jewish quarter. Instead of saving Asher, Judah had condemned him.

Or so he'd thought.

♦　◊　♦

They reached the wall to the Upper City and were forced to wait, as the Fish Gate was jammed with worshippers heading to pray at the Temple. Ever since the battle the city had been flooded with pilgrims and penitents praising the Lord for their great victory.

Even in normal circumstances, the Temple was the center of life in Jerusalem. For one day a year it was also home to Yahweh Himself. Before King David, the Lord had owned no home, traveling alongside His wandering people. Then the city had been founded, and David had lain the foundations for this monument to the Lord. But David had shed too much blood in life to be allowed to finish so glorious an edifice. That honour went to his son, Solomon, who enclosed the area around the massive unhewn stone where Abraham had bound his son for sacrifice. Ever since, generations of the faithful had emulated Abraham by leading their finest lambs to the huge rough altar.

The original Temple no longer existed. The Babylonian king Nebuchadnezzar had razed the Temple of Solomon and enslaved all the Hebrews of the city. When they'd returned from their captivity they set about building the Temple anew.

That second Temple had been a humble palace until a just hundred years before. Determined to build an undeniable legacy at any price, Herod the Usurper had doubled the size of the Temple Complex, fortifying it with new walls. The interior he entirely remade in Greek fashion, adding Corinthian columns, coloured panels, floral and geometric motifs, marble, paint, and gold – gold stolen, it was said, from David's own tomb. As Herod infamously quipped, "David can pay to finish what he started."

Herod had been no true Jew himself, of course. His mother had been an Idumean princess of Nabataea, and Hebrew blood was always traced through the mother – the half that could be proved. But the Romans had given him the throne anyway. After all, what did they care for Hebrew laws and traditions? In return he was their puppet, going so far as to place a graven image of a Roman eagle above the Temple doors. Taken down after Herod's death, it was restored by the procurator Pilatus, and taken down again by the Kohen Gadol Caiaphas.

Aware of his own people's enmity for him, Herod had become the greatest builder in Hebrew history. Palaces, fortresses, monuments, temples for Jews, temples for gentiles, theatres, arenas – he built these and more all over Judea in the hope of winning both Rome's approval and that of his own people. He succeeded in the former, but had been disastrously unable to purchase the love of the Jews.

Yet, in the greatest of ironies, Jews of all stripes had embraced Herod's Temple. The reason was simple: no Hebrew was immune to beauty. And the new Temple was undeniably beautiful.

Twenty–five thousand men toiled within the massive Temple complex daily. Not just priests, but musicians, poets, money-changers, teachers, janitors, cantors, treasurers, even shepherds. With pools for cleansing, stalls for the purchase of grain or animals, areas for teaching or debating, the Temple was like a city unto itself.

A city with a single purpose: worship.

◆   ◊   ◆

Just now a special order of priests were singing psalms. Trumpets blared and the sweet smell of spices wafted into Judah's nose. Four times a day the silver trumpets announced sacrifices on Abraham's altar. The wind caught the smoke from the special mix of flesh, herbs, ointments, and incense, dispersing the scent through the city, making Jerusalem the sweetest smelling city on earth.

Suddenly an unwelcome stench filled Judah's nose, the odor of an unwashed body. His path was blocked by a straggle-haired ancient known as Y'eshua the Prophet.

The title was mocking. For years the beggar had wandered around the city speaking only four words: "Woe! Woe unto Jerusalem!" He did not thank those who fed him, nor did he curse those who beat him. Early on, he was taken by the authorities and scourged. He never cried out, and just continued to repeat his refrain. Eventually he was declared a madman and released to stalk the streets, shouting his lamentable cry.

Judah tried to step around the old man, but Y'eshua grasped his wrist. In a crackling tone he spoke in Judah's ear. "A voice from the east, a voice from the west, a voice from the four winds, and a voice against Jerusalem and the Sanctuary, a voice against bride and bride-groom, a voice against the people!"

Judah had no time for insane rambling. The trader had kept on, and Judah was in danger of losing sight of him. "Move aside, old fool!" Y'eshua hauled Judah closer with surprising strength. "Destruction comes from within! The Iron Broom sweeps the lost into the Well of Blood – so many faces, all looking down! Do they cheer or weep? Clemency begs Caesar, but Caesar murders Clemency! The wondering faithful must be Clement, but the heretic brother dies in his place!"

The old man spat three times, then blinked and looked around as if startled to find himself there.

"Move!" Shoving past Y'eshua, Judah forced his way after his guide.

The merchant had turned right, away from the Temple, and was waiting just inside the Gate of Ephraim. Catching up, Judah remarked, "Sorry. Old Y'eshua, raving again."

The man sighed. "Poor fellow. I feed him, when he allows it."

"Kind of you." Judah suddenly registered his own rudeness. "I didn't even ask your name."

"O, forgive me! Apollion ben Zakkai. I am a spice trader."

A successful one, thought Judah, noting the neighbourhood they were entering. Between the houses there were hanging gardens, olive groves, and small orchards of various fruits and flowers. "So you travel the Aegyptian route often?"

"I used to," said Apollion darkly. "This was my last trip. I'm closing my business. Too much uncertainty."

Judah eyed the pair of bodyguards. "I see." He had a sudden thought. "Are you in the market for another bodyguard? I know a man. He was the protector of King Agrippa, until Beth Horon."

"Beth Horon," said Apollion tartly. "What madness that was. The fools! I'm half tempted to run to Caesarea and throw myself on their mercy. Otherwise my business will perish, and for what? Patriotism? What's that? Can I eat it? Will my daughters wed it?" He gave Judah a sudden, wary glance, his eyes scanning for the mark of a Zelote. But Judah wore no blue. "I am sure, my friend, that you were much too wise to partake of that insanity."

You saw my scars, friend. Did you take them for the marks of masonry? Or do you not have eyes? "I wish my brother was that wise."

"Yes, well, what happened was a shame, to be sure. He did well to get away. I'm sure he was not involved in the uprising." Apollion paused before a finely wrought gate with spikes at the top. Gilt spikes – the gate was more ornate than functional.

Ornate was also the word for the small garden that led up to the house. Brick walls enclosed a narrow walkway of flowering plants and pomegranate trees. The path itself was a mosaic of lapis tiles, making

Judah think he was walking upon a stormy sky. *How rich can one man be?*

Apollion had priestly connections. There was no other explanation. By rights he should be dwelling in the Lower City among the others of his ilk. Yet here he was, among the palaces of the priests and kings and barons of wealth. A small house here was worth half the Bezetha, and the people in it.

Stepping up to the finely carved door, Apollion didn't have to knock. A servant was waiting to open the door to a world of pleasant smells, sparkling cleanliness, and wealthy appointments. Judah might have felt bad about tracking dust with every step had he not been focused on the purpose of his visit.

Instead of leading Judah up the stairs, his host took him to a rear room. Softly he said, "He is within. Please, keep your voice low. He's often delirious."

They entered a large room with tall slatted shutters over massive windows, tall enough for a man to step through into what was probably a rear-garden. The angle of the slats could be controlled, and they were opened just enough to illuminate the room, no more. The interior held carved chairs, hanging rugs, and marvelous statues of fruits and trees. Despite the chill December air, the room was blazing hot. Beside a sumptuous bed, a brazier burned.

In the bed, skin healing from sun-blisters, was a man tightly wrapped in blankets, the better to burn the fever out of him. Despite the layers of cloth and the paleness of his face, the face was unmistakable. It was like looking in a glass.

Hardly breathing, Judah crossed to his brother's side. Asher's eyes were closed, but his mouth was moving. Remaining by the door, Apollion said, "He keeps repeating a name. Edith. Does that mean anything to you?"

"No," said Judah. Then he was struck by a vague memory. "I think – he wrote of a neighbour in Alexandria whose daughter was named Edith."

"Ah." For Apollion, it was a mystery solved.

Kneeling beside the bed, Judah leaned in close. "Asher? Asher, it's me, Judah."

Eyelids fluttered. There was an indeterminate noise as the chapped lips moved. Then, more clearly: "Judah."

A gaping hole suddenly became whole as Judah pressed his forehead against his twin's. "Yes, you idiot. It's me. You're home."

VII

THE YARD had a massive cart for hauling stone, though they didn't own a mule to pull it. Throwing aside the pulleys, wedges, and joists, Judah and his apprentices hauled the vehicle up to the spice-trader's house and loaded Asher into it. Judah offered to pay Apollion for his troubles, but the rich spice-trader adamantly refused. "Just see you make the walls strong."

It was a long journey down into Bezetha, and slow, with Judah cursing every uneven stone in the road. He was hauling the cart himself, with a boy on either side to watch and Benayahu riding with Asher to make sure he didn't roll or shift. Asher was oblivious to the world around him, moaning even when the road was smooth, living in a private fevered torment.

The moment the cart rumbled across the threshold into their father's yard, Judah called out to the doctor Chaim had fetched. The man hurried forward. Behind the doctor he saw something that made his heart lift even higher – Deborah was rushing out in his wake. "What are you—?"

"Shalva sent for me." The wooden walls of the cart were too high for her to see in. "Is he..?"

"Fevered, but alive." Judah noticed that she had a chaperone – her brother. Judah flexed his fingers, but swallowed his pride. The lout was better suited for what came next than the boys. "Phannius, can you help me get him upstairs?"

They took hold of the bed of the cart and together they lifted the whole contraption up the stairs and indoors. It was the first time he'd ever been grateful for Phannius' strength.

Once Asher was transferred into a far less ornate bed than he'd been in that morning, the doctor examined the wound. "Months old. From the angle of the stitches, I'd almost think he sewed it up himself."

"Typical." Judah could easily imagine his brother trying to replicate something he'd read. "Is it healing?"

"Very well, actually. His rescuer clearly had doctors tend it, but it would have already been too late had Asher not used maggots."

Judah, Shalva, Deborah, and Phannius all shared horrified looks. "Maggots! Why?"

The doctor laughed at them. "Disturbing, I know, and hardly kosher. But the foul little buggers do clean wounds. The Romans use them often. They eat dead flesh, but don't touch living tissue. The maggots, I mean, not the Romans – though I wouldn't be at all surprised!" He chuckled, then advised heat, water to drink, and repeated cleansing of the stitches. "And rest. Lots of rest."

Judah grimaced. "If the fool will keep to his bed. He's always been willful."

"Not at all like his brother," murmured Deborah with a smile.

Back in the Upper City, Apollion's sickroom was being swept out and thoroughly cleaned. Apollion's wife Naomi was overseeing the work, but when she saw her husband passing up the stair she couldn't resist calling out to him. "I told you we should never have gotten involved."

He paused to look down on her before continuing up the stairs. She was forced to follow. When they reached his study he closed the door. "Now, Naomi. What is it?"

"That man. His brother. You know who he is?"

"Some mason. Low-born, but decent. He was properly grateful, and clearly loves his brother."

"And his country. Some of the girls told me – he's the one who took the eagle."

The blood drained so swiftly from Appollion's face it turned a blotchy yellow. He recalled his words during the climb, damning the rebels and their folly. His voice was almost a whisper. "You're joking."

"Yes, that's very likely. A funny, funny joke. You're a fool. You saved one man who defied the Romans in Alexandria, and in so doing did a great favour to the man who doomed us to Rome's wrath. I told you and told you, leave him by the side of the road!"

Apollion thought back to the sight of that comely youth crumpled and ailing in the dust. He might have been mistaken for a corpse, but he'd moved just barely as the wagon rolled past. "No. It was a mitzvah. The Lord will look kindly upon us for it."

"The Lord may," replied the white-haired Naomi, "but the Romans won't. They'll deem us rebels. Zelotes!"

Apollion frowned. "This may be a boon. There is more danger at present from the Zelotes, half of whom are Sicarii. They'll be knifing anyone they think is a Roman collaborator. But we've now done a good turn to two of their number. Only – what a fool I was to let my tongue run away with me!"

It was Naomi's turn to pale. "What did you say?"

"I talked of the foolishness of this war. He said nothing. Perhaps he didn't hear me.... No, he did, I'm sure of it." The middle-aged man frowned. "He also mentioned a friend, one who was looking for work. A bodyguard. Perhaps if I find him employment, that may make up for my tongue's treachery. And he's a mason – I could employ him to build something..."

Naomi was exasperated. "Now we have to do more favours for this rascal?"

But Apollion wasn't listening to her as he considered his path. "I shall visit my friend Matatthais. His elder boy has been seen in the Blue Hall. His younger son is just made a priest of the First Order. His advice will see us through. Yes, I'll go see Matatthais – no, he's calling himself Matityahu now. Should I change my name, I wonder? Apollion might be too Greek in this current climate..."

"I told you! I told you, I prayed for you not to get involved!"

"Yes, my dear one, you did. But not all prayers are answered. The man who lives by the labour of his own hands is more admirable than the man who fears God. Now leave me, I must write a note requesting a visit. The man who took the eagle," he said to himself as she withdrew. "And he seemed such a nice fellow."

◆　◊　◆

Asher's was an uneasy rest. Deep in delirium, he twisted and fretted, seeing unknown images, muttering disjointed words. Sometimes he called for Judah, sometimes for his father, and sometimes for someone called Edith. In those cases he was answered by Deborah, who insisted on coming each day to nurse him. This allowed Judah to continue labouring in the yard – the walls had to be built.

On the third day the fever broke. Judah was working below, so he missed the moment his brother's eyes finally unfogged. The first thing Asher saw was a woman with dark hair pulled back to frame her teardrop face. But what made a greater impression on him were her marvelously full bosoms.

"Did I die?"

"Nearly," answered Deborah, mopping his brow with a cloth.

Asher turned his head. "Father's room."

"Yes. You're home."

Asher squinted at her. "I know you?"

She dazzled him with a smile. "You used to laugh while your brother pulled my hair. I'm Deborah."

"Phannius' sister?"

"Yes."

Aghast, Asher said, "You married father?"

Shocked, Deborah laughed. "No! Your brother…" She paused, biting her lip as her brow furrowed.

"Judah's married?!"

"Certainly not," came a tart answer from across the room. Blinking in search of the sound, he saw an old crone with a humped shoulder and frizzy white hair seated in a corner, a loom in her hands. When Deborah had insisted on helping Shalva nurse Asher to health, Euodias had grudgingly come along, refusing to let her daughter come into this house unchaperoned.

Now gazing at Asher as if he were fouling the air, she made a sour clucking noise then returned to her weaving. "Tch."

Deborah ladled some water from a bucket, and Asher drank it down eagerly. Just that much motion was exhausting. He sank back, gasping.

"I'll fetch Judah," said Deborah, rising. "He's been hovering like a mother hen."

"Or a vulture," said Asher, the image of Euodias still with him.

♦   ◊   ♦

It had taken three days for Apollion to secure an audience with Matatthais (*Matityahu! Matityahu!*). The old priest had never held the larger offices. But he was a power behind the power, a kingmaker of sorts. For the last seven years he had been the Amarkalin, the priest in charge of Temple property, and the keeper of the storehouse keys. A humble office, to hear it spoken. But in practical terms the Amarkalin wielded huge power, doling out the grain, oils, spices, and other necessaries for the daily offerings. There were so many priests working in the Temple, any given one might make the sacrifice just once in his lifetime. So to him, the elements of his sacrifice had to be perfect, both to honour the Lord, and also to advance his career. If a priest wished to wear the robes of one of their ancestors that resided in a place of honour within the bowels of the Temple vaults, then he had to petition Matityahu. Who would sometimes make excuses, demur, exclaim the impossibility of finding the garment in question. But with enough pleading, the grave man might lend his aid – in exchange for a favour sometime in the future. Matityahu was a man owed a thousand favours, and owed none himself.

One of those favours had been called in to achieve his second son's mission to Rome, which in a different world might have gained him great praise. But freeing a handful of men from Nero paled in comparison to Beth Horon. All a matter of timing. Alas.

Matityahu was an important man in more than just his office. Within the veins of his children mingled the blood of Aaron and the blood of the Makkabite kings, the Hasmoneans. His younger son, the scholar, had even written a stirring and bold account of the Makkabi uprising. Almost a call to arms. *I wonder how old Matatthais feels about that now.* But Apollion would never ask such a question.

He found the Amarkalin sipping a sweet wine that had been heated, for the days had been bitter cold. "*Shalom.*"

"*Shalom,* I hope," answered Matityahu. The greeting literally meant 'Peace.' So commonly used, it was easy to forget this simple fact. An auspicious beginning.

Sitting together, they filled the air with pleasant words and sipped pleasant drinks, Apollion working hard for the careless amiability such meetings required. Finally Matityahu said, "I am gratified to have such a genial guest. Too many of my noble friends have seen fit to absent themselves from the city – or have vanished against their will. Did you hear about old Nachum the glass-maker?"

Apollion had heard. The poor fellow's elder son had been kidnapped and ransomed by Zelotes in the city. "It's whispered that Nachum's younger son arranged it."

"I wish I could disbelieve it, but alas," the Amarkalin spread his hands, "in these dark days, human nature is fickle. As fickle as they call the Roman goddess Fortuna."

Now they were in it. "Did I tell you of a guest I had under my roof?" asked Apollion lightly, as if still making conversation. He breezily laid out all that had transpired – the injured man met on the road and nursed back to life, hunting up his twin brother, who happened to be the Hero of Beth Horon. He made rueful mention of his misstep regarding the battle. "I fear I insulted him, all in ignorance."

"I'm certain his gratitude outweighed any insult, as one of his stone blocks would a speck of dust."

"He was very grateful," agreed Apollion. "And as gracious as a baseborn man could be. I understand his brother has some learning. A scholar – not at the level of your son, of course. But he went to Alexandria in pursuit of pure learning."

"He was blessed, then. There's nothing greater to own than that which cannot be stolen." The Amarkalin touched a finger to his temples.

"Yes. Though sometimes I wonder if too much learning may lead one astray. If the young man I rescued was turned rebel by some poet's words..." He trailed off, leaving an opening for his host to fill.

"Then he acted foolishly. But if instead his learning helped him survive his ordeal, as you say it did, it was a blessing. To live, when so many others did not – that is a feat as great as his brother's, in its way. The key to Judea is the survival of the Jews. We must all, I think, carve out a means of survival."

"I am of the same mind," replied Apollion carefully. "But how? We are like a piece of metal caught between the hammer and the anvil. The hammer is Rome, and the anvil..." Again he trailed off, hoping.

"...are the Zelotes. These new Makkabites, the so-called Avengers of Israel. Yes, that is a dire predicament. But you know what happens to the metal that is so caught? It is forged into a sword. That is what is happening to us, I think. If the hammer falls, we will become a sword. If it does not, there is nothing to fear from the anvil."

"Forgive me, father," said a deeply musical voice from the door, "but I disagree."

Matityahu only raised his eyebrows. "Apollion, you remember my younger son. Yosef, what point do you dispute?"

"The roles of anvil and hammer. The anvil is Rome. It is immovable. The hammer is the rebels, the Zelotes and agitators. It is they who force us against Rome, pushing us to war. If the hammer falls, we must indeed become a sword. But it is not Rome that was urging us to war. The hammer has long beat the martial march. Makkabi, Makkabi, Makkabi."

It was a pretty point, and artfully made. In Hebrew, Makkabi meant 'Hammer'. Matityahu smiled and nodded, steepling his fingers before him. "You are clever, my son, and perspicacious. That is a more suitable metaphor. Regardless, we must befriend both the hammer and anvil to survive."

Apollion was a trifle confused. "How?"

The Amarkalin smiled. "First, tell me of this bodyguard the one brother commended to you. I should like to meet him. Then tell us more of these remarkable twins."

◆   ◊   ◆

When Deborah appeared in the yard and said that Asher was awake, Judah dropped the stone saw and entered the house at a run. But when he reached the door, Asher's eyes were closed.

Creeping in, Judah sat on the stool beside the low bed. After waiting a moment, he cleared his throat.

Without opening his eyes, Asher smiled weakly. "Impolite, waking a sick man."

Judah let out a relieved breath. "You want to talk about impolite? What about making us think you were dead?"

"Maybe I am." Asher opened his eyes, blinking them clear. "You look older."

"You age me."

"This is father's room."

"We turned yours into a storeroom. Water?"

"Yes." Wincing, Asher leaned forward and let Judah ladle some to his dry lips. "Dust on top. Tastes like home."

"The great traveler. How does Jerusalem stack up against Alexandria?"

Asher's smile faded. *Stupid! He doesn't want to talk about Alexandria.* Judah's predicament was made worse when his brother asked, "Where's father?"

Judah was saved from answering by Deborah, watching the reunion from the door. "Judah, don't tax him. He needs rest."

"Right." Judah patted Asher's shoulder and stood to go.

"Where is he?" Suspicion was creeping into Asher's voice.

Judah couldn't find the words. But he didn't have to. Old Euodias took the bull by the horns. "Dead, the old fool."

"Mother!" Deborah looked furious, and Judah felt a rush of anger – was she trying to kill Asher with such a shock? But the old crone just kept on working her little hand-loom, ignoring the angry looks aimed at her.

Asher had sunk back into the bed, his eyes pressed tight. Deborah crossed to kneel beside the bed, just the way she'd done for their father. "His heart. When he thought you were dead... Then Judah went off and fought at Beth Horon. The strain was too much."

"Beth Horon? Judah, you fought?"

"Yes." He tried to say it neutrally, but pride shone through.

"I should have been there," murmured Asher.

"You're an idiot."

Deborah turned on him. "Judah!"

"What? He is! He shouldn't be here at all! He should've gotten on a ship and gone to Greece, or Hispania! There's nothing but trouble for Jews here."

"There's nothing but trouble for Jews everywhere, now." Asher seemed suddenly stronger. "I want to fight."

"Why, when you're clearly so bad at it?" Judah pointed to Asher's wound. "And who taught you to be a doctor?"

"I did it fine! I've read everything written since Hypocrites."

Judah threw up his hands. "Reading isn't doing. Just because you know Homer doesn't make you a soldier!"

"That's father talking," retorted Asher.

Deborah laid a hand on Judah's arm. "Judah, lower your voice. Asher, he's really relieved. He thought it was his fault you were dead."

Asher snorted. "Because the whole course of human history is about him."

"I thought you stayed there because I told you to," exclaimed Judah. "Turns out you didn't listen to me, as usual."

"Why should I? You make such terrible decisions—"

"Me? I'm not the one gallivanting off to foreign lands to read poetry and get stabbed!"

"No, you're too busy chasing a whole Roman legion. Tell me, did you kill them all yourself, or leave some for the others?"

"If you must know, I took their eagle!"

Asher skeptical expression was echoed in Euodias' snort from the door. "Of *course* you did," said Asher. "*Men may say, 'He is far greater than his father,' when he returns from battle...*"

"Don't throw fancy quotes at me. I thought I was avenging my poor sweet brother. I forgot what a nattering, nagging little pest he—"

"Stop it! Stop it!" Clambering to her feet, Deborah threw her arms up in the air. "Can't you two do anything but fight?"

The twins stared at her for a moment, then burst into laughter. Asher winced at once. "Oh, that *hurts!*"

Judah held out a hand. "Happy to be home?"

Asher grasped it weakly. "Overjoyed."

Deborah stared at them. "Idiots. You're both idiots." From the doorway came a loud grunt, as Euodias finally found a statement she could agree with.

VIII

As SOON AS ASHER could walk, Judah began the work of rebuilding his brother's strength. He set his twin on a backed chair in the yard working the clay, mud, and straw for new bricks, freeing the apprentices for more vigourous work. Then, before the sun reached its zenith, Judah would hand Asher a stout stick and together they would walk about the yard, tracing a circuit again and again until Asher felt strong enough to venture into the streets.

They stayed close to the workshop at first. At the start, Asher was sweating too much to really note their surroundings. The strain was immeasurable, and he spent most of the time watching his feet. But after a few days he could focus on something other than the effort.

"Lots of people," he gasped. "Is it a holy day?"

One arm supporting his brother, Judah shook his head. "The war. Country folk are flocking to the city. Want to be well inside the walls when the Romans come."

A parcel of young men walked truculently past. All were about the same age as the twins, and each bore an arm-band of blue cloth with white stitched letters: *Makkabi*. It was more than a harkening back to an ancient hero, or the simple word *'hammer'*. The word was also made up of initials, the first letters of the ancient Hebrew prayer: "Mi Kamoka Be Elire, Jehovah?" *Who is like unto Thee among the gods, O Lord?*

Asher said, "What are those?" He meant the arm-bands.

"That's the mark of the Avengers of Israel," answered Judah. "They fashion themselves as the new Makkabi, and fight the war a hundred times a day in the Blue Hall." The Blue Hall was a gathering place of the nationalists upon the Temple Mount. "Phannius is one, I hear."

"Remind me not to join, then," said Asher, chest heaving. Hearing the tale, he had naturally sided with his brother in despising Phannius. He would have, regardless - Phannius had taunted him too often as a boy for Asher to have any friendly feeling.

One of the men made a face when he saw Asher, thinking him a cripple. Then he noticed Judah, saw the resemblance, and gave a respectful nod. So some of the fame had lingered after all.

Soon they were venturing further out into the city, traversing the steep, narrow streets around the Valley of the Cheesemongers. "Amazing."

"What?"

Asher shook his head. "The lack of statues."

"Statues?" said Judah, perplexed. There were dozens of carvings and statues – all of fruits or plants, or geometric shapes. "There are plenty—"

"In Alexandria, the streets are lined with heroes and gods, Romans and Aegyptians. Busts and phalluses fill every niche, adorn every door-way."

It was the first time Asher had mentioned Alexandria. Judah resisted the impulse to ask more. Asher would talk about it when he was ready, not before. Instead he chuckled. "Well, you know how it is. Every few weeks some Roman-lover tries to put up a bust to Nero Caesar, but it mysteriously disappears the next day. There must be a house around here somewhere filled with Caesar heads."

"Ha! Ooo. Don't make me laugh."

Each day after their walk, Judah would return to work while Asher fell into bed, exhausted. But when they got home that day there was a note from Apollion asking if he might call to check upon his former charge. Surprised, Judah sent back a welcoming message, invit-ing Apollion to call whenever he chose. Then they spent the afternoon cleaning the yard and making it presentable.

The spice-trader arrived the following morning. Greeting Judah as an old friend, he then went to shake Asher by the hand. "It is odd to think that we have traveled miles and miles together, you've shared my house and my bread, and yet we've never truly met. I am Apollion."

"I – am grateful. Not many men would have done what you did."

"We must all stand together," replied Apollion gravely. "No one knows that better than I. Well, except perhaps your brother here. Judah, you must forgive me, when we met I had no idea you were the Hero of Beth Horon, the Taker of Eagles and Scourge of Rome." And he bowed low, as he might have done to the Kohen Gadol.

Judah was visibly shocked. "Master Apollion. I – those are not names I use. I fought, like so many others. We were very lucky."

"Blessed," corrected Apollion. "Blessed. And you are humble, as befits a hero. But if it embarrasses you, I'll say no more. I just did not want you to think your great deed has gone unremarked. We are in your debt."

Judah put his hand on his brother's shoulder. "I think you have that the wrong way around. It's us in your debt."

"No no! Believe me, I am happy to have been of some small service. But your brother would certainly have survived on his own. So resourceful! Sewing up his own wounds. May I ask – I confess, I've been burning with curiosity – how did you come by your injury?"

Asher frowned, but could not refuse to answer this man. "A dagger. Fighting in the streets. I was foolish," he added, feeling Judah's eyes on him.

"Brave, more like," replied Apollion. "And blessed as well. Clearly you are a family beloved by the Lord. And for such men, it is a privilege to assist you, in every way I can. What do you require?"

"No," exclaimed Judah, then hastily added, "I mean, sir, you've done quite enough already."

"Nonsense! First, Judah, I've made inquiries for your friend, the bodyguard. There are many men in need of such services, but I'm trying to find him the choicest position. Secondly, I must ask you – you have been to my house. What do you think of its security?"

Judah's lips twisted as he framed his reply. "You are perfectly safe in the Upper City. I'm sure you need no further protection."

"Ah! Damning, damning! You are too honest to lie to me, and I thank you. But we live in dangerous times. I have a mind to raise my walls and put in a proper gate. Might I hire the services of the noblest mason in Jerusalem? I can pay a full talent of silver."

Both Judah and Asher's mouths fell open. A talent was as much as a strong man could carry. It was the income of several years of labour, an unheard-of sum for a private commission of just raising the walls. "That's too much!" protested Judah.

"Is there a price too high for security? For peace of mind? No, my wife will not rest until we are secure in our little home. And I am sure when they see the quality of your work, our neighbours will likewise wish to raise their walls."

The House of Matthais had never wanted for work, but the jobs they were hired for had always been local – new bricks for a falling-down wall, cornerstones for a new shop in the Bezetha. Sometimes, as now, they had government commissions for large stones to raise Agrippa's Wall, which their father and grandfather had helped build. But never in five generations had they done work in the Upper City. They didn't have the blood. Now it seemed they had elevated themselves.

Their genuine thanks warmed Apollion's heart, and as a down-

payment he left a purse of silver shekels – no one was using Roman dena-
rii at the moment. After sharing a cup of juice in the house ("Charming!
Charming!" their guest had declared upon viewing their spare, eternally
dusty home), Apollion departed, well satisfied.

Judah and Asher were satisfied too. "It means hiring out the work
we already have, and sub-contracting to other masons."

Asher was leaning against the wall. The effort just to take part in
the conversation had exhausted him. "But it's our name will be on the
work." He closed his eyes. "A blessing. Maybe something good came out
of me being an idiot."

"Oh no, it was *my* idiocy that brought us this. When we met, he
was prattling on about the folly of Beth Horon. Changed his tune today.
I think he's afraid I'm a Zelote, and he'll end up tried for treason. But
with us working for him—"

"—we can't speak against him. You have a devious mind."

"Or he does. You know what this means?" asked Judah suddenly.

"You can ask for Deborah's hand again."

Judah's brow darkened. "No. If they wouldn't give her to me after
Beth Horon, this won't do it. I'll not ask for her hand again. They'll ask
me." He lingered for a moment on that thought, then shook himself.
"No, what I was thinking is that, when you're strong enough, we should
host the Shabbat dinner."

It was a tradition that when a mason received a large contract, his
house would host the weekly dinner. Judah had been to many over the
years, but the House of Matthais had hosted very few – the contracts
they had were small, never sizable, never needing the goodwill of other
masons to join in and help.

There had been several such dinners since Beth Horon, and Judah
was a sought-after guest. But after the first he had declined all invi-
tations, preferring to stay at home and eat with Shalva and her son,
and now with Asher, who provided the perfect excuse. As much as
they wanted to praise him for his act of valour, there were also too
many knowing looks from his neighbours, too many sorrowful shakes of
the head. Among his fellow masons, the refusal of Deborah was more
weighty than the taking of the eagle.

But now it was time for the House of Matthais to open its doors,
and after all the kindness of their neighbours – gifts of food, help with
the wash, even some books for Asher to read – it would be churlish
to avoid being hospitable. Besides, this contract was a huge leap in
prominence, and a swelling feeling of pride to be able to provide work
to others in their field. *Perhaps I'll even hire Phannius...* That thought
made Judah grin wolfishly.

He noticed a hesitant look on Asher's face and quickly said, "If
you're not feeling up to it..."

"No no. It's just – no, it's fine."

Judah understood. Everyone would ask about Alexandria. He'd just have to shield his twin from questions.

◆　◇　◆

The call went out, and Judah used a fair portion of the silver in the purse to buy new furnishings and fill the larder. Shalva was excited to be cooking for the event – she had taken over the kitchen since Judah had invited her in, a change from a pair of bachelors who were used to cooking for themselves, or eating in the common market.

In one way it was fortunate that everyone knew about Judah's deep passion for Deborah. It prevented any rumours about him and the widow Shalva. It was instead looked upon as a great mitzvah, taking in the slain mason's widow and son. It was what a man should do, but too few did.

Besides, Shalva had her eyes on another potential husband. "Will Levi be coming?"

Technically the evening should have just been for masons and their families. But Judah had already decided to stretch a point. Asher hadn't met him yet, and there was certainly no shame in inviting a man who had saved his life. "I've asked him."

"Good," said Shalva. "Do you know if he has a favourite dish?"

Laughing, Judah confessed it had never come up.

The evening of Shabbat arrived as it did each week, honouring the day of no labour decreed by the Lord in the Fourth Commandment. From sunset to sunset, there would be only prayer, family, and friends. *Or at least*, thought Judah wryly, *neighbours*. The gate to the yard was opened, and a curtain was drawn across the door of the house, a sign that the meal had not begun and guests were welcome. In the corner of the room were the chests containing food for the next day, ready-cooked, packed round with straw to hold in warmth. The smell filled the room with a rich and welcoming aroma.

As the sun began to set the guests arrived. Most were masons, with their wives and daughters. Everyone greeted Asher as the prodigal son, asked after his health, and told him how proud his father would be that he was home. Judah wondered how Asher managed to answer them all so politely.

Suddenly there was a tall man ducking under the lintel and looking around. Judah's face broke into a huge grin. "Levi! You came."

Levi arched an eyebrow. "How could I refuse the Hero of Beth Horon?"

"Oh no," groaned Judah. "Not you, too."

"Not me what?"

"Nothing. Come here. Asher! This is Levi ben Patroclus."

The times Levi had called, Asher had still been unconscious and fevered, or else resting. Introducing them now, Judah tried to see Levi through his brother's eyes. At least twice the twins' age, Levi was an odd mixture of proportions, with long arms and small eyes, bald head and jutting beard. And so tall!

"He saved my life at Beth Horon," explained Judah.

Asher extended his hand. "Why would you do such a foolish thing?"

"I promise you, I've been asking myself that every day since." Levi's tone was so flat that it took Asher a moment to realize he was joking.

Just behind Levi came Phannius, broad and brash as ever. Euodias was on his arm, her face in much the same expression as his. Deborah came just behind them, glowing and giving Judah a beaming smile of congratulations.

Seeing Asher, Euodias looked him up and down once. "Tch." With that pronouncement, she passed to her place at the far table.

But Deborah made up her mother's lack of warmth, and more. She greeted Asher, remarking how well he looked. Judah introduced her to Levi, and when she learned that he had saved Judah's life she kissed his hand. How a sweet creature like Deborah had escaped such a sour womb was a wonder.

Deborah's presence made it easier for Judah to play the role of host. Seventeen years old, he was technically a man. But this was the first Shabbat dinner his home had hosted since his father's death, and the largest in years. Judah found himself unconsciously aping some of his father's habits and words. Fortunately there were ritual greetings and traditional phrases to fill the awkward pauses.

I feel like a child wearing his father's shoes. Too big, and every step is awkward. He wondered if Asher felt the same.

But Asher was experiencing a wholly different sensation, of having stepped back in time. He had not been to one of these neighbourhood gatherings in two years and more.

When everyone had arrived, but before the prayers, Judah formally announced the contract with Apollion. He was cheered by the assembled masons, all of whom would see new work – either hired by Judah and Asher, or else picking up the work they would be too busy now to perform. Deborah's smile was as bright as a full moon. Whereas Euodias' scowl was as dark as a new one. *Doubtless she thinks this should have been her son's contract, and I've cheated him again.*

The sun set, the curtain was pulled open, and the women and children retired to their table. The twins took their place at the head of the low table, sitting side-by-side on cushions. As the dining room was not over-big, they were all cramped, rubbing elbows, but that was nothing new – no one here was rich.

Judah invited Asher to lift the wine of Eskol and recite the Shabbat prayer of consecration. *O Lord, does Asher remember the prayer?* But Asher's phenomenal memory saved them from embarrassment. The beaker of wine went from mouth to mouth, the bread was broken, and the feast began.

Shalva had outdone herself. With money at her disposal, she had purchased the best food available in the Bezetha. There was chicken smothered in raspberries, grapefruit, oiled olives, a salad of fresh spinach, and challah fresh from the ovens – the same ovens used to bake the bricks, having been assiduously and ritually cleaned. There had been no masonry work this day, as the men and apprentices had all been pressed into service for the dinner.

Not only were there new cushions to sit upon, but also new bowls and servers, all bearing the emblem of Israel, a cluster of grapes.

Judah and Asher had both undergone a personal overhaul as well. Washed in a bath-house instead of out of a barrel, they were dressed in tunics of fine cloth with crimson and black stripes, not their usual roughspun. Judah had refused to submit to a haircut. As hosts, they cut fine figures, sitting cross-legged side by side at the head of the long low table.

As befit his birth, Phannius sat just to Judah's left. He wore the blue *Makkabi* cloth about his bicep. As the meal began, he pointedly said to Judah, "You still aren't wearing an arm-band."

"No. Pass the olives, please."

Phannius ignored the olives. "Why not?"

Judah reached for them himself. "Because I am a mason, not a joiner."

It was an old masonry joke, and all the men laughed – all save Phannius, who looked past Judah to Levi. "What about you? You were there. You should be with us!"

He was there, on the other side, thought Judah. But no one else needed to know that.

Levi's answer was bored – he had little time for fools. "I'm a professional. My sword is for hire, not for free."

Phannius was incredulous. "For hire?"

"Of course. No one values a thing given for free."

"A damned mercenary. Your country burns and you want money? What were you doing at Beth Horon at all?"

"Following my employer. Sadly, he did not partake in the fighting." Levi shot a covert look at Judah, who said, "Have you found a new one?"

Levi shook his head ruefully. "Poor references."

"I may be able to help. I know someone who is interested." Raising his cup to his lips, Judah took a sip, then set the cup down, reminding himself to set it down twice more before finishing the wine, as the Law proscribed. Judah tended to eat and drink like a wolf, hardly bothering to chew. But he was trying moderation.

"Money!" Phannius continued to be outraged. "How can you want money? We're talking about *freedom*!"

Levi shrugged, tearing some bread. "Can you eat freedom? You are a mason, that is your trade. Do you cut stones for free? Even if your country needs walls?"

Finding that question uncomfortable, Phannius rounded on Asher. "Surely *you'll* join, Asher! After what you've been through? Come to the Blue Hall and see how right we are!"

Asher shook his head. "I don't need a piece of cloth. If the Romans come, I'll fight to my last breath."

"Well said," answered several men down the table.

"They'll come," asserted Levi, passing a dish. At the women's table, Shalva was watching him, making sure he ate some of everything.

"They wouldn't dare!" declared Phannius hotly. "We destroyed their legion. They're too frightened to wage a war."

It was unseemly for the host to disagree with a guest, and the enmity between them was too well known for Judah to be impolite. So he forced himself to hold his tongue, saying only, "I pray you're right."

Asher had no such qualms. "They have to come. If they don't, other provinces will follow our example and rise up. The Romans fear that far more than they do a war with Judea."

A twenty-five year-old mason by the name of Ezekiel ben Shimri chimed in. "Which is why the priests should be forming a massive army. A national army – the army of Israel. When the Romans come, we should push them back into their sea." He looked to his father for agreement, but Shimri was far less enthusiastic about their prospects, and said nothing.

"They won't come," insisted Phannius. "They fear our Lord."

"All the more reason for them *to* come," argued Asher. "Romans have always adopted the gods of their foes – Carthage, Greece, Aegypt, even Parthia. If they believe Jehovah has power, they'll try and take Him to live in Italia, changing Him to suit their needs."

A new and particularly horrific thought for the others. Jehovah in Italia? Unthinkable!

Levi swallowed his mouthful. "If we're fortunate, they'll attribute our victory to luck. That way, they won't send an overwhelming force. No offense, Judah."

Judah grinned. "None taken. It *was* luck."

"*Luck?*" gaped Phannius. "The Lord gave us that victory. It was a miracle!"

"Rome has twenty-eight legions," observed Levi coldly. "Should we expect twenty-eight miracles?"

Phannius gripped his cup so tight it threatened to shatter. "If we are righteous, the Lord will see us through! But we must have the will to purify ourselves!"

From the far table there came an assenting noise. By custom the women could not address the men's table unless asked. But with every bold statement her son made, Euodias grunted in loud agreement.

Judah covered his frustration by trying to take another bite, only to find his dish empty. He'd done it again – scarfed down a whole meal almost unchewed.

Leery of where this war talk among the young men would lead, Shimri changed the subject. "Asher, do you plan to return to your father's business? Or will you continue your studies?"

"I – to be honest, I hadn't considered it."

Judah tried to rescue his brother. "You sound like our father, Shimri. Though his letter to Asher was more pointed."

Asher surprised his brother by saying, "That letter probably saved my life. I got it the day of the massacre, and left the Delta to walk and think. If I had stayed..." He shrugged and every man took his meaning.

Several men offered up prayers for the dead of Alexandria – a bitter hypocrisy, as Jerusalem Jews never had a kind word for their brothers in Aegypt until they became the honoured dead.

"Tell us about it," urged Ezekiel. Phannius nodded, leaning his elbows on the low table.

Judah was ready to intervene, but Asher had a deflection ready. "I'd rather hear about Beth Horon. Judah hasn't said much."

"He's just being modest," said Ezekiel.

"Funny," replied Asher, cocking his head, "that doesn't sound at all like him."

After a ripple of laughter, the young men at the table laid out the events, using the dishes and salvers to represent cohorts and bands of rebels. Judah and Levi refrained, letting the others tell the tale. "The Romans attacked during the Feast of the Tabernacles," said Ezekiel, "when the city was full. Many of the visitors were Galileans – you know the type, lots of anger, little sense."

There were knowing glances, for even the labouring men of Jerusalem viewed men from Galilee as uneducated and curiously fanatical. They were called *'am ha-arez* – 'the people of the land' – and even the great Rabban Hillel had viewed them as criminals at best, beasts at worst.

"Not to mention our friends with the arm-bands," added Judah. "The honoured *kanaim*, the Avengers of Israel."

"The Greeks call them the Zelotes," observed Levi.

Judah pulled a face. "Greeks have to rename everything."

Phannius waved this off. "Whatever you call us, you can't fault our passion. One of our leaders is called Eleazar ben Simon…" His eyes took on a far-away look.

"He's an Idumean with a way with words," explained Judah. "When he starts in on that *kanai* cant – one nation, one Lord, one rule – it's like standing on a cliff and being told that jumping is the only way down. The Kohen Gadol tried to calm things down, but no one listened."

"The Kohen Gadol is a traitor," exclaimed Phannius, repeating a common refrain from the Blue Hall. His mother let out a fierce grunt.

"He's a wise man," said Shimri.

"He's a traitor and a coward."

"And your whole band are criminals!" countered Shimri. "Zelote, Makkabi, Avengers – fancy news name for Sicariots! I remember all too well the trouble they caused! Murderers and fanatics!"

The Sicariots was a title given to the previous generation of zealous extremists. It meant *the knifemen*, a title the Sicariots earned by approaching their targets and stabbing them up close. They had murdered Roman officials, Roman citizens and, most horribly, any Jew who collaborated with the Romans. Men and even women died on the streets, in their homes, some even having their throats slit while the slept.

"We aren't murderers!" countered Phannius hotly. "We're patriots! We face the Romans in the open, not in dark alleys!" Grunt.

Shimri wagged a finger. "And the Kohen Gadol is the High Priest of the Sanhedrin, youngster! You do not casually slur him!"

Before Phannius could answer, Judah continued with the story. "Eleazar and another priest, Simon bar Giora, led us to Beth Horon. Men are already declaring Eleazar the *mahsiah*."

"He is!" declared Phannius. Grunt.

"I think," said Judah carefully, "the mahsiah needs to win more than one battle."

Phannius was undeterred "If he's not, then why did you follow him?"

"I didn't even know who he was!" He'd tried to keep his temper, he really had. But Phannius had a way of nettling him. "Jocha's blood was still cooling, the city was a shambles, people were screaming and dying. I went to bloody some Roman noses." *I thought they'd killed my brother, you ass!*

Phannius leaned close. "Yes, we all know you like to fight. But what do you believe in? What are you willing to die for?"

"My family."

"Pity, then, that there are so few left." Grunt.

Everyone tensed. Judah was ready to overturn the table, but caught himself. Breathing deeply he unballed his fists. "As you might recall, I wanted to expand my family."

He held eyes with Phannius, daring the lout to speak of the refusal. Any explanation would shame him. Any act save striking Judah would hurt his honour, but striking his host was forbidden. Swallowing his pride, Phannius returned to his meal.

Asher piped up with suspicious cheer. "I wish we could just pick two champions and let them decide the war, like in the old days."

"An excellent idea," agreed Judah.

"Achilles and Hector," said Asher.

Judah pulled a face. "David and Goliath, please."

Levi smiled and shook his head. "It never worked that way, you know. Not really. Even in the old days."

"I know," replied Judah with a crooked smile. "But wouldn't it be grand? Two men deciding the fate of the world!"

"Pfah! You're all mad!" growled Phannius.

Grunt.

IX

AT THE SAME moment Phannius was insisting they would not come, the Romans were moving with a speed only they possessed. Couriers were riding or sailing all over the eastern end of the *Mare Nostrum* with orders, requests, and requisitions. Vespasian had set off from Greece to Syria at once, stopping only to collect soldiers along the route.

There was another cache of Roman soldiers that had to be collected, one mustered for a wholly different war. Nero Caesar had been planning an invasion of Aetheopia, and had quietly gathered three legions in Aegypt. The adventure was not exactly secret, but neither had it been announced publicly. Therefore turning those legions around to quash the rebellious fires was acceptable.

These three legions had to be collected. Vespasian entrusted that task to his eldest son.

Debarking at the docks of Alexandria, Titus was exultant. At twenty-seven years of age, this was not his first war. He'd served in both Germania and Britannia (though not in his father's famous campaign there). The difference was that now he was a senior legate, in command of his choice of legions. His fingers positively itched with excitement, and his smiling features reflected his inner glow.

Stretching his stocky legs on the quay in the Royal Harbour, Titus noted a structure on an isolated spit of land – Mark Antony's famous *Timonium*. Like the misanthrope Timon of Athens, Antony had sulked inside a shack until he could bear to face his defeat at Actium.

Titus had often been told he resembled the great Antony – not necessarily a compliment. Handsome, yes, but Titus also owned Antony's hulking frame, with a face too small for his body. Or rather, a neck so wide it made his head seem small.

It never occurred to Titus that the resemblance was also spiritual. Antony was famous for his cheerful disposition, quick temper, strength, petulance, and love of excess. Most of all, he was famous for his end, here in this very city.

Mark Antony, Julius Caesar, Crassus, Cato, Achilles, Hector – why are so many great men best remembered for the way they died? Certainly I won't be! The legacy I leave behind starts here, today! With that steely thought, Titus marched ahead of his bodyguards into the Royal Palace to be introduced to the Prefect of Aegypt, Tiberius Julius Alexander.

"Greetings, Tiberius Julius," Titus said, kissing his host on the mouth.

"Welcome, Titus Flavius," replied the elderly prefect.

"Just Titus will do." His name stemmed from the Titans, divine forerunners of Jupiter and the rest, and it amused Titus to being likened to a god. He cut right to the point. "I've come to collect the Fifteenth Legion and send them north to my father. Then I'm jumping on the fastest horse you have to find the Fifth and Tenth."

This was news, yet Tiberius evidenced no surprise. He had been around a long time, and must have expected the repurposing of these armies. "Excellent, Titus Flavius. Though I would advise against the horse. A camel-train, perhaps. Or why not row up the Nile? Much faster, and more relaxing – for you, if not the rowers."

Titus knew good sense when he heard it. "*Gratias*, Tiberius Julius. That sounds splendid."

"As for the Fifteenth, would you like to review them now?"

Having dreaded hours of chit-chat, music, and dining, Titus leapt at the offer. In minutes they were riding out the Sun Gate to the Fifteenth's winter quarters.

Confident on horseback, Titus talked freely as they rode. "How ready are they? When was their last action?"

"September," answered Tiberius, equally at ease. "They had to quell an unfortunate uprising between the natives, the Greeks, and the Jews."

"Tell me."

Tiberius pulled a wry face. "The Alexandrians held a meeting to discuss an embassage to Caesar. After the sacking of the Jerusalem garrison, they intended to show their loyalty by offering to betray the Hebrews here. The fools were surprised when the Jews showed up to the meeting."

"The meeting wasn't a secret?" said Titus, chuckling.

"I know! You'd think Greeks and Aegyptians would be more skilled at backstabbing. Anyhow, they accused the Jews of spying. Three were caught and burned alive. When more Jews stormed the theatre to rescue them, I asked them to return to the Delta and leave the matter in Rome's hands." Tiberius held his hands wide for a moment before regripping his reins. "They threw my sensible request in my face. I had to unleash the legions upon the rioters in the Hebrew quarter. So much for my supposed calming effect on Jews!"

"How many?"

"One hundred fifty thousand men, women, and children. I regret it, naturally. But I can't be lenient with them, thanks to the infelicitous nature of my birth."

Titus studied his companion. "Jew-born? You don't look it."

Tiberius smiled thinly. "Thank you. Yes, despite my excellent-sounding name, I was born to an Alexandrian Jew. My father gained the Roman citizenship under Tiberius Caesar."

"Hence Tiberius Julius," mused Titus, parsing his companion's name. "Is Alexander for the city?"

"And for my father," explained Tiberius. "He served both King Agrippa and Antonia, mother of Claudius Caesar. My uncle was the philosopher Philo."

"Sorry, not much of a philosopher, myself." Truthfully, having no great ancestors of his own, Titus did not much care for those of other men.

"Perhaps this will matter more. Before his death, my elder brother Marcus was married to Queen Berenice of Judea."

That earned Titus' attention. "Oh-ho! Lucky fellow – I hear she's a beauty."

"A temptress," said Tiberius coldly. "A wanton. And an incestuous one, if rumours are to be believed."

"They never are. Still, I should like to meet the Judean queen. She sounds – interesting. But tell me more about you! Did you give up the Hebrew god?"

Tiberius nodded. "I did. As a young man I renounced Yahweh in favour of the Roman pantheon, and have prospered for it. I'll never be a senator, but I've held two of the most coveted offices a knight can – first Procurator of Judea, and now Prefect of Aegypt."

"Procurator of Judea? So you know the people. Tell me about the rebellion. How did it start?" He'd heard only what Cerialis had said. Surely Tiberius would have better information.

Sighing, the elderly Tiberius took on a teaching tone. "What is a governor's duty?"

"To preserve order," said Titus at once. "To maintain soldiers and build roads."

Smiling, Tiberius shook his head ruefully. "Alas, no. Our chief concern is to farm taxes. And Judea is a wonderful province for taxes –

as I well know! But I didn't squeeze them the way Florus has. And so blatantly! From the moment he arrived, he favoured Romans and Greeks over the Jews."

"Are there many Greeks in Judea?"

"Oh, yes! There's so much intermingling between Helens and Hebrews that no one thinks twice of a Greek named David, or a Jew named Apollo. But nevertheless there are tensions and rivalries. For example, a few Greek wits sacrificed some birds in front of a Hebrew school in Caesarea. Akin to a dog entering Jupiter's temple. Made the place—"

"—unclean." Titus shivered. To Romans, dogs were nasty creatures, useful for hunting but religiously odious. "Was that the religious lawsuit?"

"Oh, you've heard? Yes. Florus shamed the Jews badly by taking their gold and imprisoning them. Salt in the sores."

"I take it Florus didn't stop there?"

"Stop? The man went on a rampage. He taxed the living daylights out of the Judeans. He demanded precious pieces of art and literature. Finally, when every golden nail, marble table, or bronze lamp had gone, he followed the example of the greediest man in Rome's long history, Marcus Licinius Crassus."

Titus had heard that part. "He looted their Temple."

"Seventeen talents in all," confirmed Tiberius. "Gold, not silver. Imagine it."

"But is the man mad? The place is cursed! Pompey did no more than peek into their Temple and he ended up beheaded. Crassus actually stole from it, and he ended suffocating on molten gold!" While he was not particularly religious, Titus was a Roman, with a Roman's naturally superstitious nature. He regarded omens and curses with particular awe. *No wonder the legion lost their eagle! The fool angered the Hebrew god!* "Where is Florus now?"

"Hiding until the war is won, I imagine. Ah, here we are."

Approaching the camp gates, Titus was greeted with a familiar sight. From the farthest mists of Britannia to the wildest sandstorms of Aegypt, from quick marching camp to permanent quarters, every Roman military camp was built along the same plan. Longer than it was wide, its two major avenues neatly quartered the space inside. Smaller streets held barracks, camp hospital, baths, forge, stables, granary, workshops.

They rode up the *via Praetoria*, leading from the main gate to the Praetorium, where lodged the legion's commander. But Titus wanted to see the men before they got wind he was among them, so he pulled his horse left and trotted instead down a narrow avenue of barracks.

Legionaries lived eight to a room. This was a permanent camp, so the stone houses had proper roofs and chimneys. Titus was pleased to note how clean each barrack was. Then he noticed that the men were making a show of honing their weapons and polishing their armour, and sighed. So much for a surprise inspection. Nowhere was gossip spread so effectively as in the ranks.

Halfway down one of these side 'streets', Titus noticed a stone plinth nestled between two barracks. On it was an ornately carved wood block depicting a man in Eastern garb wrestling with a fierce and enormous bull. Over the block stood a makeshift cavern, that sunlight would not fall directly upon the image. "What's that?"

Tiberius reined in beside Titus, his face tight with displeasure. "That is Mithras. A Parthian god of the Sun and War."

"So that's what he looks like." Titus had heard of this god from his father.

Tiberius turned to the staff trailing after them. "Who barracks here?"

"The Second Cohort, Prefect."

"Inform their lead centurion that the whole cohort is on report. Roman soldiers worship Roman gods. Take that wretched thing down and have it destroyed."

Titus had enough experience to know that soldiers drew confidence from odd places. If this shrine made the men fight better, then Mithras served Rome, whether the god wanted to or no. Idly flicking his reins, he said, "Come, Tiberius Julius. Where's the harm? So long as they pay homage to Jupiter Best and Greatest, he won't mind them praying to a foreign god. Especially as they are fighting in foreign lands."

Tiberius inclined his head. "It's your legion now." As they rode on, he added, "In this current climate, religion is a subject to which I, of all men, must strictly adhere."

"I completely understand." No adherent like a convert. The former Hebrew could not be seen condoning any un-Roman god.

The tour finished at the *Principa*, the headquarters at the camp's center. All the centurions were summoned to witness to the transfer of command. Tiberius presented the legion's eagle to the aquilifer, who intoned the ritual prayers and presented the eagle in turn to Titus, who gripped the standard and spoke his own formal prayers.

The instant he finished, a gust of air came in from outside, flickering the flames in all the lamps. Illumination reflected off the golden wings of the eagle, dazzling every man present.

The soldiers, veterans all, were awed. Excited murmurs and admiring looks greeted the young commander, and it took all Titus' self-control not to fall to his knees in exultation. A truly magnificent omen!

After the ceremonies and usual busywork, Tiberius departed and Titus retired. But his mind was so full of the omen that he couldn't rest. So just after dusk he slipped out of his quarters and ventured alone into the camp, disguising his features under a heavy, hooded sagum cloak. He had been warned that the desert was brutally cold at night. It was no lie. He passed several fires around which roared lively games of knuckle-bones, rude dice constructed from the joints of pigs. There were also storytellers and a few gifted singers. Best of all was a boxing club, with the men testing their skills in a rough pit of sand. Face muffled, he stood and cheered with the rankers for a while.

Eventually he arrived again at the shrine to Mithras. There was a bowl of blood before the shrine, which had not been there before. Seated nearby was a lone centurion. Titus had noted him during the ceremony. The day's stubble gave his strong chin a darkish cast, and his Italian nose and thick lips made him look primitive, primal. But his tunic was neat and clean, his armour shone, and clearly his weapons were sharp. A true *vir militaris*, a Military Man through and through.

Unfooled by Titus' heavy cloak, the centurion leapt smartly to attention. "At ease, centurion. Your name?"

"Gaius Sacidius Barbarus, sir." The fellow resumed honing the edge of his dagger with a stone.

"See you don't make it too thin," Titus advised. "It's liable to break when you need it most."

"No, sir. Thank you, sir." The centurion managed to convey that he had been honing this blade's edge for as long as Titus had been wearing an adult's toga.

Smiling, Titus jerked his thumb at the shrine of Mithras. "Will he bring victory over the Judeans, do you think?"

Barbarus squinted at the shrine as though he had never seen it before. "Looks like a right good scrapper. Can't be an easy thing, wrestling with bulls. Those Greeks on Crete used to jump out of their way, didn't they? Saw pictures of that once."

Titus chuckled. "I think they were jumping over the bulls."

"Better than under them, sir."

"True." It was dark now. Their breath fogged the air. "Gets cold quick!"

"That it does, sir. Would you like a blanket? You could warm yourself at our fire."

The last thing Titus wanted was a reputation as a commander that needed coddling. "I'm fine. Just noting my new environs." He pointed to the bowl of blood. "That isn't human blood, I hope."

Barbarus smiled. "Doubtful, sir."

"So long as it's not. No human sacrifices. It's un-Roman. Except," he added with a grin, "the blood of our enemies. *That* we offer up in battle to Jupiter Best and Greatest. And any other god who might be handy."

"Might those enemies be the Jews, sir?"

Titus shook his head. "Not the Jews. The Judeans. Let's leave religion to the priests, and politics to the politicians."

"Very good, *legatus*," said Barbarus, testing his dagger's point against a finger. It drew blood at once. "Then they can leave the soldiering to us."

X

JERUSALEM

TWO DAYS AFTER hosting the Shabbat dinner, Judah was
working a large stone, the last of an old commission, while Asher loaded
a bag with awls, files, stonesaws, chisels and such, preparing for the
morrow's trek to the Upper City and the first look at the work ahead of
them at Apollion's house.

Suddenly the door to the yard swung wide and Phannius ducked
through. Judah stopped working to stare coldly. Asher fingered an awl.
Even the apprentices were grim.

Upright, face pinched, Phannius said stiffly, "Judah ben Matthias,
I apologize. I truly regret my offensive words and hope that you can find
some level of forgiveness."

Shocked, Judah managed not to bark out an acerbic reply. Clearly
this was Deborah's doing. Swallowing his impulse to shove the apology
down the lout's throat, Judah offered his hand. "It's forgotten."

It was fortunate that Phannius was also a mason. Any other man
might have shied away from the dusty, sweaty grip Judah was offering.
But they clasped arms, neither one playing grip games.

Phannius eyed the large stone that Judah was molding. "Need a
hand with that?"

"Why not?" He didn't, but the lout was making an effort. And,
to be fair, he was a competent mason. They soon had the uneven slab
squared and ready for polishing. Thus the work of a day was done by
noon.

It turned out that Phannius had an ulterior motive. When they
were finished, he said, "Judah, I know you prize your independence—"

"Isn't that what we're fighting for?" piped Asher.

Phannius ignored him. "—but I'd like you to come to the Blue Hall this afternoon. Just hear what they have to say. They ask about you all the time. At least give them a chance to applaud your deed."

"Don't you mean *our* deed?"

Phannius had the good grace to look abashed. "You know my mother…"

Judah felt churlish. Yes, he knew Euodias. If he was honest, Judah doubted if he could cope with such a force, either.

He shot a glance over to his brother, working among the brick-molds. Asher shrugged. After such a handsome apology and the free aid in the yard, what choice did they have?

"Very well," Judah said. "We'll come."

♦   ◊   ♦

The Blue Hall was in the Upper City, not far from the Temple Complex. As this marked Asher's first climb into the Upper City, Judah and Phannius helped him, ascending the hill with Asher supported between them. "I'm not a child," he protested.

"You whine like one," answered Judah.

"Remind me why Levi saved your life?"

"He didn't know Judah yet," suggested Phannius.

"Nice talk! And I was going to give you credit for the eagle when we got there." Phannius flushed and they continued to climb.

Though they had allowed an hour for the walk, they still arrived late. Asher was pale and sweating profusely. "Just – need a minute…"

"I'm expected," said Phannius tartly. He was obviously annoyed at being delayed, and he pushed his way into the chamber, leaving the twins outside while Asher caught his breath.

Judah peered inside the packed building. The Blue Hall was so called for the perfectly blue tiles that adorned the floors, a colour matched by the paint on the tall cedar columns and high roof, making the whole chamber appear to be hovering in the sky, or floating on the sea. In contrast, the dais at the far end was fashioned from pure white marble, a floating cloud or foamy wave amid all the blue.

Finally Asher's breathing eased. "All right – let's go."

They pushed in as far as the first series of columns. Taller than most the crowd, Judah nodded at Phannius, now standing near the dais. Atop the marble platform stood two men Judah remembered well – Eleazar ben Simon and Simon bar Giora. The taller of the two, Eleazar's handsome Arabic features made him look youthful and vigourous, whereas Simon radiated fury, with his wild-eyes and short bristling black beard. Both now wore the garb of minor priests, though some-how any clothes Simon bar Giora wore looked rough and disheveled.

He stalked the dais as restless as a desert lion while Eleazar smoothly addressed the assembly:

"The Kohen Gadol and his priests mean to make peace with the Romans!" There was an answering growl from the crowd. "They have no stomach for war, no pride in their nation, no faith in the Lord! One nation, one god! We are His chosen people, and this is the land He gave to us. Land our fathers, our fathers' fathers, fought for, bled for, died for! But rather than raise an army, the Kohen Gadol hides behind the city walls like a cowering child, hoping the bully doesn't come!" This was answered with boos, hisses, and shaking fists.

Eleazar took a step forward, gazing imperiously down at the crowd. "There are those here who think the Romans are not coming. That they would be fools to try, after the beating we gave them at Beth Horon. But, my countrymen, my brothers, you are deceived! Just today we've had news that Nero Caesar has appointed a general, and dispatched three legions to tame Judea. Yes, *three legions!*"

Simon bar Giora leapt forward. "And do not think, friends, that is the extent of their might! Our ancestral enemies will certainly join these bastard Romans. They'll have Syrian horsemen, Phoenician slingers, and Samaritan soldiers – for who here thinks the Samaritans will stand with us? If history is any guide, those heretics will side with Rome! They're only too proud to proclaim themselves Hebrew when we are on the rise. But in times of trouble, they're suddenly Greek, or Roman, or whatever wolf's skin they need to don to hide the fact that they are sheep!" There were more raised fists and angry shouts – to a Jew, there was no such thing as a good Samaritan. "I've heard tell, too, that the Nazarenes are fleeing the city, refusing to take part in this war. And let us not forget our 'king', Agrippa! Will that Roman puppet and his whore sister stand with us? Or will they bring their army to bear against us, forcing Jew to fight Jew, like Cain and Abel! No longer will it be the Mark of Cain! It will be the Mark of Agrippa!"

Displeased at being diverted by his partner's venting of spleen, Eleazar skillfully brought the crowd back to his main point. "Yet despite all these forces arrayed against us, the Sanhedrin of Jerusalem has not yet lifted a finger to raise an army. There are no training camps, no allotment of swords and arms. There is not even a full garrison for Fort Antonia – a fortress we ejected the Romans from! Instead of preparing, High Priest Ananus means to make peace with the Romans – crawl to them, beg for forgiveness, and no doubt hand over me, you, and all other patriots to Roman 'justice'!"

Judah listened to the roars of outrage, uncertain what to think. Eleazar was a stirring speaker, and Judah could already feel his fingers flexing for a fight. But the rational part of his brain added three legions to whatever aid Agrippa and the foreign kings would send, and came up with somewhere between fifty and a hundred thousand soldiers. Turning to Asher, he whispered, "What do you think of the numbers?"

"I think if Judea stands together the way he suggests, as a single nation, we might possibly win. *If,*" he added.

Judah understood. *When has that ever happened?* "That's the problem with idealists. No grounding."

"They have all the characteristics of popular politicians," said Asher vaguely. "Horrible voices, bad breeding, and a vulgar manner."

A nearby figure in a cloak turned curiously, and Judah's gut filled with panic. He had no idea Asher was quoting a dead Greek playwright, nor did he care. If someone took his brother's words wrong, they might end up beaten to death in this very hall. "Asher, you'd best – *are you alright?*"

"Fine..." Asher was clearly lying. He was swaying, dazed, a hand on the nearest column for support.

"Let's get you out of here." But as he took his twin's arm, Judah was interrupted by a shout from the dais. "There! There stands Judah ben Matthais, Hero of Beth Horon! The taker of the Roman eagle! Legionslayer!"

With Phannius whispering in his ear, Eleazar was pointing to the back of the chamber. The whole assembly turned to cheer, and Judah felt hands pulling him towards the dais. He struggled until the cloaked man reached out to support Asher. "Go, placate them. I'll help him." Under the heavy robe, his voice was deep and musical, and he spoke Aramaic with an aristocratic accent.

"Go," agreed Asher, staggering for the door. "I'll be fine."

Judah reluctantly let himself be dragged forward towards the dais. He looked back and saw the cloaked stranger escort his brother outside. *I hope he's in good hands. We might be here awhile.*

Arriving at the dais, he noted Phannius' smug smile, Eleazar's eager grin, and Simon's scowl. The short wild man was not at all pleased at Judah's appearance, though for the life of him Judah couldn't imagine why.

Eleazar grasped Judah's hand and hauled it into the air. All around the Blue Hall men cheered, shrieking like eagles and making chains of their fingers, symbolizing capture.

Judah's discomfort multiplied when he was told to make a speech. He had no idea what to say. He opened his mouth, but the only word that came to him was the one that had been shouted on the battlefield. "Israel!"

The assembly echoed him, screaming their answer. "Israel!"

Suddenly Judah was back on the battlefield, his blood surging through him. He felt powerful, necessary, full of life and purpose.

This is what I am made for. This is my purpose. I am that I am, says the Lord. And I am a warrior. Put a sword in my hand right now and I'll cut off the legs of Atlas and bring the whole world crashing down.

◆   ◊   ◆

Outside, the stranger helped Asher to a stone bench not far from the hall doors. Asher had pushed far too hard on the climb, his world was tilting and beginning to spin. "Thank you, I'll – I'll be alright."

"Not if you continue tossing off smart remarks so recklessly," advised the musical voice. "Few in there would see the humor."

"It's – a quote," gasped Asher. "Aristophanes."

"Be that as it may, if you can't curb your tongue you shouldn't be here. But then, neither should I."

Seated, his world slowly returning to focus, Asher noted that under the cloak the stranger wore a robe of white, with long white tunic and trousers underneath. Around his waist was a blue sash embroidered with red flowers. On his left hand shone a gold ring. "A priest?"

"Exactly," said the man, sitting down beside Asher. "Though there are priests who favour the war, few dare come to the Blue Hall." He threw back the cowl of his cloak, revealing his face. In his late twenties, the man was good-looking in a particularly Semitic way. Under his curling black hair, his dark eyes were deeply set. His upper lip was almost twice the size of the lower, and his beard was neatly squared, extending to the bottom of his neck. The only mar to the handsome face was a scythe-like nose – too sharp, it cleaved his visage in two.

"You've been ill," observed the man in his wonderful baritone.

"Don't worry. Heat-stroke isn't contagious. Neither is hunger."

"I disagree. The hunger for rebellion has swept through all Judea."

"*To the hungry soul, every bitter thing is sweet,*" replied Asher absently.

"*A crust eaten in peace is better than a banquet partaken in anxiety,*" answered the stranger with a smile.

That startled Asher. He'd quoted Scripture, and the priest had produced a phrase straight from Aesop. Brightening, Asher invoked Aristophanes. "*But who knows whether living is dying, and breathing is eating, and sleep is a wool blanket?*"

He was countered with Heraclitus. "*God is day and night, winter and summer, war and peace, surfeit – and hunger.*"

Asher chuckled slightly. "Who's to say the hunger will be ours? The Roman hunger for war may swallow them up. Scripture says, *If thine enemy be hungry, give him bread to eat, and if thirsty, give him water to drink, for thou shalt heap coals upon his head.*"

The priest looked Asher up and down. "I did not notice an armband. But if you are determined to fight, *Let us eat and drink, for*

tomorrow we shall die."
Asher extended his arm. "I am—"
"— Asher ben Matthais. I know."
Asher felt an odd shiver. "You know me?"
The stranger smiled. "For all its size, Jerusalem is a shockingly small place. My father is friend to Apollion the spice-trader. He's mentioned you – you, and your remarkable twin in there. We are a matched pair, it seems. Both our brothers are in there, while you and I are out here quoting heathen texts." Grasping Asher's half-extended forearm, he gripped it tightly. "Yosef ben Matityahu. Priest of the first rank."

Asher was impressed by both the man and the title. There were over eighteen hundred potential priests in Jerusalem, each one able to trace his lineage directly back to Aaron. Phannius, for example. But only a handful of potential priests were noblemen. Of over thirty ranks of priests, this Yosef came from the most prominent. No doubt his father was in the Sanhedrin, the religious council of aristocratic judges that ruled Jerusalem very much the same way the Patricians of old had ruled Rome.

Asher's appreciation wasn't just a result of his high rank. "It's rare to find a priest so well-read," he observed. Priests not only memorized Scripture, but also the oral tradition of interpretations that had grown over centuries. A lifetime was hardly long enough for a priest to learn it all. Outside reading was considered a waste of that precious time.

Laughing, Yosef confessed, "I write for a wider audience than priests."

Asher suddenly knew who this Yosef was. "You wrote the history of the Makkabi revolt!"

"Yes," admitted Yosef, pleased.

"It was excellently constructed."

Yosef's smile revealed handsome dimples. "Thank you for not pointing out how flawed my Greek is. Still, it was some small attempt at bringing our history to the Western world." The learned young priest studied Asher quizzically. "Your brother is a mason, and your frame and hands declare you the same. But your words would do any scholar proud. How did a mason's son come to quote both Aristophanes and Proverbs so perfectly? You enjoy learning?"

"Enjoy it? I hunger for it."

They grinned at each other, and Yosef nodded. "And you fear starving now that war has come."

This statement summed up all Asher was feeling in just nine little words. He answered one insight with another. "What about you? The priests of the Sanhedrin are said to be against this war. But the prospect of war excites you."

Yosef's brow furrowed. "Because I write of one revolt, I am in favour of another?"

"Why else risk coming to the Blue Hall?"

Yosef looked rueful. "You hunger for learning. I, for freedom."

"Freedom to do what?"

"Succeed. Advance. Grow. Prosper."

Asher nodded. "*'War brings opportunity.'* You wrote that."

"Because it's true. A man can prosper. So may a nation. A clever nation."

Asher was thinking of Alexandria. "War also brings destruction."

"Which is why there must be moderation in how we fight Rome."

"Now you sound like a priest."

"What does that mean?"

"There cannot be half-measures in war."

Yosef pointed back towards the Blue Hall. "Their talk in there is all well and good, but we must live with the Romans when this is over. Aristotle – *We make war that we might live in peace.*"

"Anacreon," countered Asher. "*War spares not the brave, but the cowardly.* If we don't plan to win, we'll lose the war before it begins. We can't have half a war. War is like a woman with child – she either is, or is not."

"Wars can be fought civilly," insisted Yosef, "with respect for both sides."

"Then it's not war, is it? It is a game, with men as the pieces. And the wager is all Judea."

Yosef again indicated the Blue Hall. "That's what *they* want. Risk it all. The priests take the more moderated view. If we fight well, we'll win Roman respect. Then we can negotiate a reasonable peace."

"I've seen the Roman legions at work."

"As have I. They are efficient, disciplined, and orderly. War is their business. Even their entertainments are a form of war."

"Which is why we either fight to win, or accept destruction!"

"I disagree. If we fight to win, we will *invite* destruction." Yosef became animated, leaning forward and using his hands. "I've been to Rome, Asher, I've lived among them. Fierce tempers, but short memories. If we endure this one year, a single season, we shall outlast their anger."

"We may not survive a single season if we don't fight," challenged Asher. "*Carthago delenda est.*"

"Yes, precisely! Carthage provoked Rome many times over! If we stop poking a stick in the she-wolf's eye, she may find other prey."

Asher sat in utter bemusement. The truth was that he wanted to fight the Romans – after Alexandria he wanted to strike a blow for Jews and Judea. But his desire to fight was visceral, not logical. Yosef's arguments were compelling. It was a strange sensation, being out-reasoned. It had not happened to Asher in a long time.

Yet there was something off about the priest's arguments. "I don't understand. You say that to survive we must not provoke Rome, but you come to the Blue Hall in secret and rub shoulders with the most eager revolutionaries."

"Perhaps I'm a spy?" mused Yosef with a smile.

But Asher was thinking. *War brings opportunity*, he mused. Aloud, he quoted Homer: "*You will certainly not be able to take the lead in all things, for to one man a god has given deeds of war, and to another the dance, to another the lyre and song, and in another wide-sounding Zeus puts a good mind.'* Or as Virgil put it, *We are not all capable of everything.*"

Yosef inclined his head quizzically. "I don't follow you."

"In the last ten minutes, you've been priest, author, soldier, patriot, and pragmatist. Someday you will have to choose."

Yosef face became grave, and Asher was suddenly reminded of the vast social gulf between them. He had gone too far. Yet the priest answered Virgil with Virgil. "*Each of us bears his own Hades.*"

Asher should have remained silent, but his lips formed a reply even before his mind had framed it. "Another way of saying that destruction comes from within."

"The very definition of sin."

Asher pressed the idea. "Does that mean that the true peril for Judea lies within, not without?"

"Certainly. To believe otherwise would mean we have no control over our destinies. And *that* I refuse to accept. There is always a way out."

There was a deafening cheer from the Blue Hall, and the eager rebels began to emerge. It was too stuffy within to hold a long meeting, men would start dropping like flies. Judah soon emerged, Phannius at his shoulder. Both were grinning. Seeing Asher safe, Judah crossed to the bench. "How are you?"

"Fine." Asher was about to introduce Yosef, but the priest had plucked his cowl up over his head. "I must be off. Gentlemen, blessings upon you. Asher ben Matthais, it has been a rare pleasure." Turning, he walked briskly away.

Judah jerked a thumb. "Who's he?"

Asher stared after the priest, already lost in the throng. "An interesting man."

And indeed, Asher stayed interested. For days after, he found himself thinking of that conversation. Asher wasn't certain if he agreed with Yosef, or even liked him. To his credit, Yosef hadn't dismissed the words of a mere mason's son. Whatever contradictions lay with him, he was fair. There was a great mind in there, a questing mind. Certainly an ambitious one. Asher spent a long time wondering which would prove victorious – reason, or ambition?

XI

JUST AS ASHER found it impossible to forget Yosef, so too the priest continued to reflect on his conversation with the learned mason's son. He was especially reminded of their talk on the occasion of Eleazar ben Simon's audience with Ananus, the High Priest of Jerusalem.

After resisting for weeks, eventually the Sanhedrin had no choice. The members of the Blue Hall had grown too powerful. Beyond their daily rabble-rousing sessions, they'd also held on to a vast supply of weapons and gold looted from the Roman baggage train. The combination of wealth, weapons, and popular support meant that a public meeting between the Avengers of Israel and the Kohen Gadol was inevitable.

At least the Avengers had the sense not to send Simon bar Giora, who in recent days had frightened even his most ardent supporters with his angry rants. Elected to be their official leader, Eleazar ben Simon came alone to face Ananus ben Ananus, holy warrior to High Priest.

The audience took place in a grand palace courtyard high atop Mount Moriah. Men clustered under the open sky to hear a fascinatingly bitter debate between two men who should have been allies, but were not.

Ananus, Kohen Gadol of the Sanhedrin, sat sipping a brew of hot water and lemon as he was harangued by Eleazar. They could not have looked more different: Ananus the classical Hebrew, with a long forehead over his deep-set eyes and neatly squared beard, and Eleazar, a roguish figure with long hair, clean-shaven Arabic face, and eager energy. Ananus had cunningly arranged for them to be seated, making the debate seem less urgent from the start.

Yet Eleazar was doing well, leaning forward and declaiming

loudly. He seemed to have taken a page from Simon's book as he said, "You must let me organize the men of Jerusalem into an army! And where is our eagle?"

"*Whose* eagle?" said Ananus archly over his cup.

"The standard we took from the Romans. And when I say we, I mean the true patriots, the common people of Jerusalem." Though too well-mannered to cheer, there was a murmur of approval from his supporters.

"Whatever do you want it for?"

"I want to display it for all to see, right on the Temple gates."

Ananus' face became pinched. "It is a graven image. Man is allowed to name the beasts, not carve them. The right to fashion creatures of the earth belongs to the Creator alone."

"I don't mean to worship it!" snapped Eleazar. "I mean to parade it, show the men it isn't to be feared!"

"That is a form of worship. I refuse to allow such acts anywhere near the Sanctuary walls. Besides, I've already had it melted down."

Amid gasps from the crowd, Eleazar turned ashen. "You had no right. We won that in battle."

"*You?*" Ananus radiated power. "The Lord won that battle. You were merely His instrument."

Sensing he was losing ground, Eleazar abandoned the subject of the eagle. "Then let me be His instrument again! I tell you, we cannot sit and wait here. We must go out and crush the Romans before they mobilize!"

From the front ranks of the crowd, a new voice spoke. "We have poked the hornet's nest enough. When the swarm comes, it will find our windows shuttered, and will buzz away in impotence. Then we may negotiate with the queen." Smiling at his metaphor, Joshua ben Gamala stepped forward to pour himself a cup of wine. A former High Priest, one of the most respected men of the age, inventor of a system of universal education in Judea, Joshua took pride in being a calming influence in any debate.

"I didn't realize we were allowed a second voice," said Eleazar coolly.

"The Sanhedrin speaks with one voice, young man," answered Ananus.

"Perhaps you feel you need someone else to do your debating for you." Eleazar turned theatrically. "And are you, Joshua ben Gamala, so naïve to think Romans will keep to any agreement they make?"

"Romans have a healthy respect for law, if not our Law. They are not unreasonable."

Eleazar snorted loudly. "Did you meet Florus?"

"Rome is made up of its best and worst. That is true of any

nation," added Joshua with a pointed smile. "We must show sense. Rome is coming. We must earn their respect."

"By lying down beneath their nailed boots?"

Son to one Kohen Gadol, brother to another, Ananus was obviously weary of this upstart. "Not at all. We will fight them. But in a measured way. We shall show them that we are not weak, that our demands are not unreasonable. Then, having earned their respect in battle, we shall treat with them. As equals."

"You're the father of all fools!" exclaimed Eleazar. "We must make the Romans fear us the way they once feared their Germans, the way they still fear the Parthians."

"Ah, the Parthians," said Ananus, as though pleased by this turn in conversation. "What if we do as you suggest, and muster every man in Judea to battle the Romans, toe to toe? What if we succeed beyond our wildest imaginings and expel them from our borders? How many of our men will have died? How many wounded? How many would still be alive to defend us from the slathering Syrian and Parthian hordes that would descend upon us like the Babylonians of old?"

"I don't have the gift of prophecy. I can only see the enemy right before us. That enemy is Rome."

"The wise man makes his enemy into his friend," observed Joshua ben Gamala.

"David did not win the world by speaking meekly to Goliath!" Eleazar paused dramatically, then rose to his feet. "I will muster every man of fighting age, and offer to lead them into the field against the Romans as soon as the campaigning season starts! I will march until we reach them in their own camps and toss them back into their sea!"

Now there was outright cheering from the Zelote-supporting priests and jeers from the moderates. The numbers were surprisingly even.

But everyone fell silent as Ananus rose from his seat and approached Eleazar. "You may try. But I am the Kohen Gadol. I am the supreme authority in all things religious, political, and sacerdotal."

"Appointed by Rome's puppet king! I have been voted the command of the war by the people of Judea."

"You may be able to rouse the disaffected rabble with rhetoric and largess from your captured Roman gold. But the men of substance, the men who *matter*, will not follow you. They know which of us hold their interests at heart."

"Their property interests, you mean! That's the truth here, isn't it? The wealthy like the Roman way, where the rich get richer, and the poor get poorer! Well, if it's a pauper's army, it will at least be rich in courage. We shall see who holds Judea's best interests at heart!"

"You speak of Judea's best interests. Is it in our interest to have our friends, our sons and daughters, parents and cousins, kidnapped?" The High Priest was referring to a recent phenomenon. After the banning of knives in the streets, the rebels had resorted to a different kind of violence. Family members of prominent Jews were kidnapped and ransomed for huge sums. Begun months before Beth Horon, the practice had only grown – the rebels had discovered a milk-cow, and were filling their war chests with the wealth of Judea. "If you wish to have a voice in the running of this land, you should not condone fleecing our own people for Sicarii coffers."

"As opposed to the Sanhedrin fleecing the poor to fill Roman coffers?"

Upper lip trembling, Ananus strove to keep his voice even. "Eleazar ben Simon. You might have been a promising priest in your native land. But your radical ways are not welcome in Jerusalem. We thank you for your services in our time of crisis – a crisis, I must add, you helped create. My advice is this: do not gainsay me. I tell you again, you are the leader of one battle. I am the Kohen Gadol."

"That appointment is only for life, old man!" With that rather naked threat, the rebellious priest departed, followed by dozens of followers.

Watching the crowd disperse, Yosef shook his head. *The mason and I did it better. The same debate, but without the resentment of class, birth, or history.*

His father appeared at his elbow. Matityahu the Amarkalin had sat closer to the heart of the exchange, in a place of prominence. Now he whispered in Yosef's ear, "Wait here, and be of service to Joshua. Do not fail."

Yosef nodded. He itched to say it was what he planned to do already – he was, after all, his father's son. But he knew that petulance would gain him nothing. So after his father moved on he waited patiently for Joshua ben Gamala. The wise old teacher was one of the men who owed favours to the Amarkalin, and had repaid his debt by acting as Yosef's patron within the Sanhedrin. It was Joshua who had recommended Yosef for the embassage to Rome, a mission to release four priests wrongly accused of treason against Rome.

As Yosef waited, he considered the state of the world, weighing not his country's prospects, but his own.

◆　◇　◆

That there was greatness in store for him, Yosef had no doubt. He'd known it all his life, and had become sure of it the night he'd almost drowned.

On his way to Rome to free the prisoner priests, the ship he was on had foundered. To this day he didn't know why – the sky had been clear and there was no jolt as from hitting a rock. Perhaps the ship was over-encumbered. Six hundred men, women, and children had been aboard.

On a sudden there was water below decks and everyone was shouting. All six hundred were cast into the chill waters of the Adriatic. As he pitched towards the edge, Yosef plucked up a large basket woven of rushes. In the sea, he turned the basket over and used it to keep his arms and face above the water. Thankfully, the tar of the basket had held the rushes together.

He remembered the moon reflecting off the water, showing the great many dark shapes bobbing in the unruly water. Many souls cried to him to share the basket, but he knew too well that even one other would sink him. So he'd hardened his heart and closed his ears, kicking further away from the other desperate swimmers. As he swam, he prayed – for forgiveness, for guidance, for salvation.

As the number of voices crying for aid slowly decreased, Yosef could hear the Lord more clearly. It was but a single word spoken to him, as if in his ear: *Live.*

That voice kept Yosef swimming all through the cold night. In the morning, a Cyrene ship found the survivors. Of the six hundred passengers tossed into the Adriatic, only eighty still had their heads above water. Most, like Yosef, had retained some device to float upon – boxes, crates, broken bits of ship wood. All were exhausted. And none could look each other in the eye – save Yosef. He arrived in Puteoli with his head held high and a renewed purpose.

To Yosef, that night spent in the Adriatic waters was a *crucibulum*, just like the earthen pot used for melting metals. Heated past endurance, the metals became stronger, turning to bronze or steel. So Yosef had been tempered by the Lord. And Yahweh would not have forged him without a purpose. *That night the Lord showed He has plans for me.*

And in Rome, he'd risen right to the top. A man of culture and learning, he'd felt right at home among the Roman Jews. But the real bequest, the greatest joy, was the two years spent outside his father's shadow.

Free to be himself, left with nothing but his own charm, cunning, and ingenuity, he had applied himself how best to present his case to the Romans. It had taken time, but with all due modesty, he had to admit his solution was brilliant. Knowing Nero Caesar's love of the theatre, Yosef had worked his way through a famous Hebrew actor to an audience with Nero himself. The Princeps had little interest in Yosef's mission, but he'd been fascinated by Yosef's voice. "It's natural talent, you say? But what do you eat? What do you drink? I must copy your diet, exactly!"

Chance had also been at his side. It so happened that Nero's wife Poppaea was just then dabbling with the Hebrew religion, the way some Roman women did with Isis. She made it fashionable to be seen with Hebrews. Suddenly Yosef had found himself dining and sporting with the highest level of Roman society. He'd even had to fend off several offers of marriage, both from Roman Jews and proper Romans as well. Not that he was unwilling to put aside his wife for one better, but rather he did not want to tie himself to any one petitioner. That way, he could enjoy all their favours.

He'd had little experience of women before Rome – just his wife, and before that a shepherdess in the wilds of Galilee. He had accepted a beating for that, not from her husband but from his master, the priest Banus. "When you lie with a woman, the Lord will not speak to you for seven times seven weeks!" the old man had hissed as he scourged his pupil's shins raw. And for years thereafter Yosef had prided himself on his chastity, even in the marriage bed, sleeping with his wife only four times a year. His purity, he thought, showed his dedication to the priesthood. *I am pure! See? Speak to me, Lord!*

But in Rome he had not needed the Lord to speak to him. Things were so clear, and he was free to be himself, indulging in pleasures he had never imagined. He was no Epicurean, but he had tasted the sweet nectar of women's lustful juices, and felt the thrill of coupling in public. His own manhood was something of a sensation – Roman men were not circumcised, and his naked head caused women to ogle and fondle it.

Several women of Nero's court were neglected by their husbands, whose tastes ran in other directions. So, under the amused eye of Nero's wife Poppaea, Yosef found himself passed among her Roman friends like chattel. Because he was ardent, flattering, learned, foreign, and most of all expected nothing, he was able to gain their good graces, and through them the support of their husbands. It was not at all difficult for him to extract the release of his poor prisoners and have them shipped back to Rome.

He'd done it just in time. The Great Fire that swept through Rome was blamed on the Jews. Many were rounded up and executed publicly. Yosef had never feared for his own safety, as the bulk of Nero's wrath had fallen upon the small sect of Jews called the Nazarenes, whom the Romans called Chrestiani. Yosef had been able to continue on with Poppaea as his personal patroness.

It was during this time that Yosef wrote his book on the Makkabi Revolution. In it, Yosef had written glowing words about King John Hyrcanus, a Makkabi ancestor. He was the ideal Jew – ruler, high priest, and prophet all in one. Gifted with visions of the future, Hyrcanus was blessed by God to lead His people. Yosef, too, had once been gifted with visions, and for a time he'd felt a similarly great future lay before him.

In Rome the visions had gone, replaced by an assurance that he was indeed destined for greatness, not just another man clawing his way up the priestly ladder.

The success of his book only brought more praise. Hailed by Hebrew scholars in Rome, he was on his way to becoming a fixture, despite the rising anti-Jew feeling in the city. Then Poppaea had died, and with her Yosef's protection. He suddenly realized that, though they had no interest in their wives themselves, no Roman enjoyed being fitted with a pair of horns. With no powerful patron to keep him safe, Yosef prudently decided to follow his rescued priests home.

After two years in Rome, Yosef had expected a hero's welcome. After all, he'd bearded Caesar in his den, gotten the favour of the court, and freed the four captive priests – a great achievement by any standard.

But instead of being a hero, Yosef arrived just in time for war.

◆   ◊   ◆

Yosef saw the elderly Joshua making for a private chamber. He did not need to be beckoned to know he was supposed to follow. Falling in step with his mentor, he remained silent and watchful as Joshua led him through a series of halls to a small, finely appointed room and shut the doors. Out of earshot of the mass of priests, Rabban Joshua cocked an eyebrow. "You are remarkably silent."

"I had no remarkable remarks to make."

Joshua made an appeal heavenwards. "Your literary bent is unneeded at the present. I would hear your thoughts."

It was on the tip of Yosef's tongue to point out that thoughts could not be expressed without words, and spoken words were literature of the air. But he restrained himself. "The Kohen Gadol handled things as well as could be expected. But Eleazar knows what was not said: the wealthy are in hiding, and they took their gold with them. We need his money as much as we need his influence. He has all the wealth that was in the Roman baggage train, which contained the combined spoils of Aphek, Lydda, and our own suburbs." Yosef spread his hands. "However long his money lasts, so will his power."

Yosef tactfully left aside all the truthful arguments Eleazar had made. Under Roman rule, rich Judeans grew richer. It was a new application of an old Roman idea, that a man of property would defend that property to the death. By extension, if Rome had granted that property, then Roman rule must be defended. It was an arrangement that had benefitted a very few Judeans. But those it had, benefitted hugely.

Joshua had an uneasy way of watching a man, as if reading his thoughts. But whatever he was perceiving, the moment was interrupted by the arrival of Ananus himself. Closing the chamber door, the High

Priest gave vent to his frustration. "The fool! He will bring destruction upon us! Him, and all these Avengers of Israel. O, the sons of Ishmael are a scourge!"

He was referring to his foe's ethnicity. Eleazar was an Idumean, an Arabic Jew descended from Abraham through his slave-girl, Hagar. It was common for the legitimate offspring of Abraham – the sons of Isaac – to look down upon the sons of Ishmael.

"Romans feel the same way about Italians," Yosef observed.

Only then did Ananus notice Yosef's presence. "And you, Yosef ben Matityahu? What do you think of our self-appointed Mahsiah?"

Yosef temporized. "You must admire his passion."

Ananus grave face tautened. "Must I?"

"What Yosef means," explained Joshua smoothly, "is that Eleazar's passion is the only way he was able to compete with you. Reason was on your side, as you displayed most magnificently."

"It's odd," mused Yosef. "Just the other day I had much the same conversation with a mason's son. He too thought that we should fight full out."

Ananus was dismissive. "A Zelote, no doubt."

"He did not wear the arm-band. And he was learned, argued well."

Ananus' expression became severe. "Did he convince you?"

"Not at all. I merely point out that Eleazar's sentiments are far from unique. He will not lack for followers."

"How then, my son, would you prevent all out war?" asked Joshua. It was a Socratic question, where the teacher posed a query in such a way as to lead the pupil to discover the correct answer. But Yosef understood Joshua's true intent. This was a council of war, disguised as a student's essay.

Allowing the question hang for a moment, Yosef collected his thoughts. If he spoke well in this moment he would go very far, very fast. "I see three immediate courses. Firstly, we must be seen as active. Show the people we are in control, afford them no time to think."

Ananus stroked his long, squared beard. "Just so. The walls. Refortifications. New towers. Infrastructure. All this is already in the works."

Joshua bowed to the Kohen Gadol. "When peace does come, Jerusalem will be the stronger."

"We are also minting new shekels that read, *The Freedom of Zion*."

"Excellent," said Yosef. "The Romans use coins for propaganda. So should we."

"And your next course of action, Yosef?" prompted Joshua.

"We must reach out to those sects that have traditionally stood apart – the Essenes, the Sadducces, even the Nazarenes." That clearly made the Kohen Gadol unhappy, so Yosef hurried to explain. "At the moment there are two camps, the Zelotes and the Sanhedrin. The Pharisees are evenly divided between the two. To show our side is in the right, we must show a great coalition. Bring in the religious sects that think themselves purer, less material and earthly, more devout. Do this and we show that Jews of all beliefs side with us." Yosef turned to his mentor. "What was it you told Eleazar? It is the wise man that makes his enemy his friend."

"The Nazarenes will never join us," observed Joshua.

"If only to spite me," added Ananus. He had executed the brother of the sect's founder.

"If not," said Yosef, "we must at least ensure they will not fight for the Zelotes."

Joshua added his voice, though in his usual sidelong manner. "We do require allies. Chanania the Miser has fled, and taken his riches with him. Secretary Liev's house is empty and collecting dust. I hear that the priests Herod and Zebulon, those who fled just after Beth Horon, have appeared at King Agrippa's court. The Nazarenes are fleeing as well, and the Essenes are saying this war has nothing to do with them. If we were to woo these disparate elements, the Zelotes must treat us with the respect we deserve."

It was unpalatable. Pharisees looked down on all the other sects as impractical, unrealistic, and uninterested in the world at hand – which was why politics was dominated by Pharisees. "What will this do, other than waste time?"

"Besides diminishing the influence of the Zelotes, it may show King Agrippa that all Jews oppose his Roman masters. If he thinks his people are united, he may keep his army at home."

The practical answer won the day. Reluctantly, Ananus nodded. "And the last course?"

"The Sanhedrin must create an army."

"What?!" roared Ananus at once. "Give in to their demands!?"

"No, sir. Take his teeth. An army is inevitable. The question stands, will it belong to him, or to the Sanhedrin? If there is an official army, sanctioned by you, Eleazar's standard will attract few followers. Even in revolt, every Hebrew wants to be legal."

Cooling, Ananus frowned in thought. "Yes. Get in first. Put our own men in command." He turned to Joshua. "Make the dispositions, that we may implement our plans at once."

"We should delay announcing the army," added Yosef, "for at least a few days. Otherwise…"

"Otherwise it appears that Eleazar won our debate. Yes, excellent. Thank you, Yosef."

This was a dismissal, and Yosef dutifully headed for the door. As he backed out, he saw the ghost of a wink from Joshua.

Oh, is it possible that I'm on my way at last?

XII

EVEN UNDER the specter of war, the rituals of the White City continued unabated. The great shell horn called the Magrapha continued to summon the faithful to prayer. Men continued to lead their lambs to the great jagged altar, ritually sacrificing the best of their flock to the Lord. Y'eshua the Prophet continued to wander the city, calling out his creed: "Woe! Woe unto Jerusalem!" And on the night of the new moon, priests of the Sanhedrin took the testimony of three witnesses and sent out messengers to declare the new month, Shevat. It was halfway through the Roman month of January.

At noon the next day, Judah sauntered back to the workshop wearing a smile and sucking skinned knuckles. Though he still did not sport a blue armband, he now frequented the Blue Hall – to hear the news, he told himself. But for a young man just turned eighteen, it was a heady thing to be hailed as a hero whenever he appeared among the Avengers of Israel.

Pushing open the gate in the workshop wall, he was glad to see things getting along fine without him. The boys were working, Malachi's voice lifted in song to fill the time. The boy had powerful lungs to heave the hammer and keep his rhythm.

Asher was still reacquainting himself with the business of masonry. Today he was leading two apprentices through the process of making new bricks: carving and pressing the straw-mixed clay, then sliding the bricks into the low oven. "Be careful!" he warned them. "My fingers still own scars from mishandling hot bricks."

Judah strolled in the yard, lowering his bleeding hand from his mouth. "Huh."

Asher glanced up at him. "What? I like teaching."

"It's not that. I'm not surprised you're a natural teacher. I just didn't know you ever paid attention in the first place!"

"Knowing how and wanting to are entirely different." Asher set aside his work. "So what happened?"

"Was there a fight?" asked Chaim eagerly.

"A disagreement." Judah leapt up onto a stone block and sat comfortably. "The Romans are definitely coming. Two legions marching from Alexandria, and one more sailing to meet the Roman forces in Syria. The Kohen Gadol announced he's forming an army."

"Then why the fighting?" asked Malachi. "It's what they've been calling for."

"He didn't put a Zelote in command," guessed Asher.

"Ex-*act*-ly," said Judah, laying a finger alongside his nose. "Though he hasn't named his generals, he's saying they'll all be men of the Sanhedrin. Anyone who's spoken at the Blue Hall is barred from command. The priests who announced it brought bodyguards because they knew it would turn into a brawl. And they were right," he added cheerfully.

"Whose side did you take?" Asher was genuinely curious.

"I'm not entirely sure." Judah grinned ruefully. "I punched Phannius, so I must've been on the side of the aristocracy."

Asher rolled his eyes. "Judah, you idiot..."

Judah raised his hands defensively. "I think I hit a couple of priests, too!"

"Oh, and that makes it better. Does it? They're not going to let her marry you if you keep hitting her brother!"

Judah frowned. He didn't want to discuss it in front of the boy. "What does it matter? At least I feel better. Besides, the way they go on, it's an honour to be punched by me."

"Did *anything* get accomplished?"

Judah shrugged. "Lots, and nothing."

"Where will the army meet the Romans?"

For the first time Judah looked well and truly disgusted. "Everywhere! They don't mean to muster one great force to face the Romans on the field. Instead, they're sending their priest-generals out to defend each region separately. Ensuring Jerusalem will receive a siege."

"What?" asked Chaim. "How?"

"The Romans will come here first," explained Judah. "If nothing else, our lack of an army clinches it."

"I'm not so sure," mused Asher. "Agamemnon's army saw Troy's unbreachable walls and turned to laying waste to the countryside for nine years."

Judah rolled his eyes. "This isn't poetry, Asher, it's real life!"

"Your imitation of father is improving. But the military sense remains. It all depends on what kind of general the Romans send. Is it Corbulo?"

"Ha! No, they've sent the Old Muleteer instead. Vespasianus the Plodder. Well, we knew Nero was mad."

"We shouldn't underestimate the Romans," warned Asher.

"And they shouldn't underestimate us!"

"You sound just like Phannius! You don't really care as long as it's a good fight."

Judah blinked. "Is there anything wrong with that?"

◆ ◇ ◆

Yosef was summoned at dawn to the Kohen Gadol's palace, only to cool his heels in the courtyard with a hundred other priests. At noon news of the announcement and the riots began to circulate among the small knots of waiting men, and they all began to wonder the same thing – if the army was to be led by priests, were they the potential generals? Eyeing each other, they waited with a mixture of hope and fear.

"Do my old eyes deceive me, or has Yosef the Traveler returned to us?"

Yosef turned to face his childhood teacher, Rabban Yochanan ben Zakkai. Irascible and undoubtedly brilliant, he had never advanced far up the priestly ladder, being far too unwilling to suffer fools. Instead he had taken to teaching the Torah, adding lessons of his own that he interpreted from the stories in the ancient text.

They embraced, and set to talking, with Yochanan quizzing Yosef to his doings these last several years in Rome. It was a pleasant diversion from the knife's-edge of waiting, and they chatted happily, Yochanan asking insightful questions and never afraid to tell Yosef when he'd been foolish.

"Ah, I do miss students of worth," sighed Yochanan. He had bleary eyes, crusted and running, and he squinted through them determinedly. "These pupils today subscribe to the Sadducee ways – literal, literal! No interpretation but literal! Even if we all agree the Torah is perfect, we must still interpret its perfections! The Lord gave us minds for a reason, and reason is that reason! Anyone who mindlessly recites without applying the gift of the Lord, the mind, is a fool. I say a fool!" Several of the men the rabbi was decrying were standing nearby. "Yes, I mean you, Rabban Benjamin! You are just the sort of fool I mean! Yes, that's right, shy away! Hide your head in the sand – and I don't mean that thing on your neck! That's completely worthless! How do I know? Because you refuse to use it! A eunuch of the intellect! A gelding of the wrong head!"

Yosef was laughing in spite of himself. "I've missed you!"

Yochanan nodded. "Of course you have. No one challenges you young men anymore. Today there are lessons without learning, recitations without reason. Let there be light, I say, light! Light – just so! Does the Torah mean light, as we do, sun or fire? Or is it a light of the spirit? We count days by the sun, but for three days there was no sun – He hadn't created it! So what was a day? The Lord doesn't need to count as we do. Fools!"

Yosef remembered hearing the very same arguments fifteen years before. Yochanan was a squabbler and quibbler by nature, but his undeniable brilliance made him impossible to dismiss entirely. He had even convinced a former Kohen Gadol from following the literal interpretation of the ritual sacrifice of the Red Heifer, in favour of a more symbolic sacrifice. Quite a feat, as that Kohen Gadol had happened to be a Sadducee, and the interpretation was therefore his own. But then, finding a Red Heifer was next to impossible.

Yochanan maintained his monologue. "I had hoped Galilee would be better, but for a land that has produced so many Zelotes and fanatics, they are surprisingly godless in their daily lives. Perhaps it is proximity to the Temple that brings forth devotion. No wonder you fell into Roman ways when in Rome – the distance is enormous. I doubt any man so far removed could remain true to his faith." He made a sputtering noise. "Not that we lack men of faith here. It's men of sense we lack. War? I ask you, war? Swords into plowshares! But Heaven forefend we actually embrace the teachings of the Torah! Even a meaning so plain that a literalist Sadducee like Benjamin there could see it. Yes, Benjamin, I'm speaking of you again! What will you do about it?" Again the sputtering noise, this time accompanied with a contemptuous wave of the hand. "And they let him teach. We're raising a crop of stunted minds. Wouldn't know how to reason if their lives depended on it. Which, as it happens, they do. You know, there was one I saw, oh, five years ago. He bore a brain and knew how to wield it like a sword. Almost as clever as you, Yosef, and much better mannered. He didn't laugh in his sleeve like you are now – don't think I don't see you. I remember he brought up the implicit acknowledgement of other gods in the Decalogue – saw it for himself! Because, of course, none of these fools were going to point it out to him. They'd rather pretend it didn't exist. But the Torah is perfect, remember! Perfect, Benjamin! So it's in there for a reason. But rather than engage in the debate, they scolded him and set the other boys to beat him. I had it half in mind to take him under my wing, but I was just off to Galilee and couldn't be bothered to take some poor mason's son with me."

That brought Yosef up short. "His name wouldn't happen to be Asher, would it?"

The wizened rabbi craned around. "It is indeed."

"I met him," said Yosef. It was on the tip of his tongue to add, *at the Blue Hall*. But the rabbi was as free with his tongue as many men were with drink. Any mention of the Blue Hall could well scuttle Yosef's chances at a decent office during the war. "He's kept up his reading, though mostly Greek, I think."

"Alas, and that's the way of it! We lose our best minds to foreign thoughts and foreign ways because we do not foster reason here at home! I tell you, boy, that I have half a mind – well, more than half, half and half again, which is three times as much as any of these—"

They were interrupted by loud cursing through the main double doors that led into the Kohen Gadol's private rooms. Yosef expected to see Eleazar come storming out, but the man who emerged had a bristling beard and wild eyes. Indeed, he looked so feral that every man present took step back.

"Have it your own way, Kohen Gadol! I'll go to Masada and take arms with some real patriots! But I'll be back, Ananus! Trust to it! I'll be back and you'll be in no position to stop me, because you'll be dead!"

Yochanan turned to Yosef. "Who on earth is that?"

"Simon bar Giora," answered Yosef. Mindful not to betray his trips to the Blue Hall, he answered with general knowledge. "A minor priest from Acrabatane. He wanted command of an army. I guess Ananus removed him from his office instead. Fool – he's the most outspoken man in the Blue Hall – or so I've heard," he added hastily.

"Oh he's definitely a fool," agreed Yochanan. "But at least he's brave."

Simon was not the only one so removed. Through the day Yosef saw many men called in, only to depart in anger or grief minutes later. Ananus was making sure of his priests in the rural areas, replacing hotheads with more reliable men.

As Yochanan prattled on, Yosef wondered if that was why he was here, to be the loyal man sent into the field. *Oh please, Lord, not Acrabatane.* It was a region close to Idumea, and thus far from where the real fighting would be. *Though it would put me in command of Jericho…*

◆   ◇   ◆

Inside the private chamber, Ananus sipped his hot lemon water and reassembled his temper. "That was the last of them, and the worst. What now?"

As usual, Joshua ben Gamala was there to assist him. "As you commanded, we have accelerated the refortification of Jerusalem's walls, and announced the formation of a national army, under the command of the priests of the Sanhedrin."

"Having announced it, I suppose we must create it."

"Indeed. In four months, five at most, the Romans will be upon us. We must make a good showing. Organized. Efficient. And if we are to recruit raw troops," observed Joshua, "it would be well to offer them ready arms."

"I shall pry loose the arms taken at Beth Horon. The so-called 'Avengers of Israel' can hardly argue with the cause."

"And Masada?"

Ananus' grave face became graver. At the same moment the Roman garrison had been ejected from Jerusalem, a band of Zelotes had stormed Herod's old fortress at Masada and executed all the Romans there. It had taken time for anyone to even learn of it, because the Zelote leaders gathered enough food, water, and weapons to last for years, then cut themselves off from the world. "Masada is closed to us at present. I've sent messengers, but the Zelotes who took it refuse to work with Jerusalem until we fully embrace their cause."

"We're preparing to battle the Romans," huffed Joshua. "What more proof do they require?"

"My removal from the leadership. By death, I believe, is their preferred method. I am too well known as a moderate, and am already being accused of accepting Roman bribes." Shrugging, Ananus produced a piece of slate marked with chalk. "On to the issue of commanders. Naturally, I will take nominations from the Sanhedrin. But I prefer to have my choices already in place."

"I applaud your foresight," said Joshua.

Ananus half-smiled. "As always, I welcome your input."

Invited, Joshua held forth. "The key will be Galilee. Its defense is vital. It's our most fruitful land, but also the birthplace of these Zelotes. The man in charge will have his hands full with both the Romans and the *'am ha-arez* – the unwashed masses. If the commander does not please them, they will be upon his neck like jackals. It requires a man of many parts – ambition, intelligence, compassion, and ruthlessness."

"I assume you have a name?"

Rabban Yochanan had wandered off, bored. His ever-questing mind needed constant stimulation, and he'd been disgusted at Yosef's reticence to speak his mind freely. But Yosef was trying to keep his own council.

Still, as he sat waiting outside the High Priest's chamber, Yosef wished he had someone to talk to – *really* talk to. If only his old friend Nicanor had been about. School-mates and rivals, Nicanor had espoused the Nazarene cult later in life. One of many poor choices, it seemed, as

Nicanor was said to have sided with King Agrippa and now served as a centurion in the Hebrew King's army – an army that soon would be marching alongside the Romans, not against them.

Yet Nicanor was someone Yosef could confide in. A reasonable man, not a fanatic, despite his chosen faith.

And what does that say about the rest of us? wondered Yosef. *Yochanan is right, no one truly believes we can win – at least, no one rational. Still we plan for war. Are eager for it. Rome has heaped coals upon Judea's head. Is it any wonder our hair is on fire?*

He thought again of his conversation with the mason's son. It was the closest to a genuine discussion of ideas he'd had since returning from Rome. *Perhaps I should seek him out...*

Joshua emerged from the Kohen Gadol's chamber. His eyes searched the crowd of men, whose numbers had thinned through the day. Yosef waited until he was beckoned, then hurried over.

"Ah, Yosef. Excellent." Joshua handed over two slate tablets covered in chalk. "The Kohen Gadol has made his dispositions for the army. They are to be copied out fair and distributed to our loyal supporters in the Sanhedrin."

Yosef felt his heart sink. *I am reduced to copyist.* "Very well."

Joshua's eyes twinkled. "Aren't you curious as to what he has decided?"

Stifling a sigh, Yosef braced himself. "Of course."

"He has designated commanders for Idumea, Peraite, Jericho, and Perea." He rattled off several names, all known to Yosef, his peers. His own name was nowhere among them. "For practicality, he has wisely combined the regions of Thamna, Lydda, Joppa, and Emmaus into a single command. He also put one man over both Gophnitica and Acrabatene."

All this made surprisingly good sense. There were only two regions yet unnamed. "What about Galilee? And Samaria?"

"Samaria." Joshua made a sour face. "They have not declared their intentions, but that is only because the Roman army is not yet here to protect them. No doubt they're still secretly kidnapping Judeans and selling them to be Roman slaves. No, we need send no general to Samaria."

"And Galilee?"

"Ah, Galilee. Apart from Jerusalem itself, the most important of our lands. Which is why we require a commander we can trust." From his belt, Joshua produced a roll of paper. "Yosef ben Matityahu, you are hereby charged to take immediate command over both Northern and Southern Galilee and guide its defense."

"What? I —" The fleeting shock was replaced by exultation. Barely thirty years old, he was being given perhaps the most prestigious and demanding post of the war. Not merely a command, a great one. Live or die, he would be famous, and his children's children would speak of him with reverence.

"I wish I had more self-restraint," admitted Joshua with a wicked grin. "I thought about letting you copy out those names, so that you could discover it for yourself. But I simply *had* to see your face."

Crowing inside, Yosef feigned modesty. "I am as shocked as I am honoured."

"Beware," warned Joshua, becoming grave. "This honour is a double-edged sword. The goal, young Yosef, will be to raise a magnificent defense for one season, then negotiate terms. Do not let the Galileans goad you into all-out warfare. We must fight just hard enough to gain peace, and no more. That is why you have been chosen. As I told Ananus, you are uniquely suited. You are of David's house, yet you spent time in the wilderness, learning the Essene way. What was the name of that old hermit?"

"Bannus." Yosef was at once transported back to his two years of self-starvation and ritual cleansing. Unlike the popular and worldly Pharisees or the vehemently traditional Sadducees, the Essenes adhered to the ancient rituals. At their most extreme they ate in silence, owned no private possessions, and considered it sacrilege to even evacuate their bowels on the Shabbat. At sixteen, such purity had appealed to Yosef – apart from that business with the shepherdess. For those two years he had felt closest to the Lord, blessed with visions and profound thoughts.

But Essenes took no part in government, no responsibility for the greater whole. They believed that everything was pre-ordained, that free will played no part in the Lord's design. Yosef had desired a role in the larger world. A role he now was to play.

Joshua continued listing Yosef's traits. "You know the Galilean ways, yet are no idealist – that's a compliment, by the way. You've been to Rome, so you know the enemy. The book you wrote on the Makkabi wars was quite popular among the Zelotes. And you have also attended meetings in the Blue Hall, so they know your face."

Yosef's blood went cold. *The cunning old wolf knows everything!* "I went only to hear their words. Forewarned is forearmed."

"If you had spoken, this appointment would not be possible – the Sanhedrin would disown you. As it is, your brother is marked as a fervent Zelote – no doubt your father wanting a foot in both camps. Your family has been very careful, my friend, walking on a gossamer strand over the Valley of Hinnom. See you do not fall in." Joshua patted Yosef on the shoulder. "Go, make me proud. And tell your father all debts are paid. Or rather, now he is in my debt."

Departing in a daze, Yosef was strangely resentful. The edge had been taken off his joy. The implication was that this was a favour to his father rather than due to Yosef himself. *If I do well, my father and Joshua will claim the credit. I will be a hollow vessel for their success.*

Unless I succeed beyond their wildest imaginings. Unless I do something no one believes we can. Unless I cover myself in glory and go down in history as one of the bravest, most cunning generals in history. David, Alexander, Makkabi, Caesar. Yosef.

Yosef suddenly recalled an unwelcome line from Virgil, the one that Asher had thrown at him: *'We are not all capable of everything.'*

I'll prove both Asher and Virgil wrong. Priest, author, soldier, patriot, pragmatist. Now, general. Like the great Hyrcanus, I could be all those things, and more.

XIII

WITH THE ANNOUNCEMENT of a formal army, Asher's recovery advanced by leaps and bounds. He was up long before dawn each day, dragging Judah down to the enclosed yard to practice combat. Judah invited Levi to join them, and was surprised when the older man agreed. Levi claimed it was to keep his skills fresh. But really he had come to teach.

Most often the trio practiced with the Judean sword, a long forward-bent blade resembling a crooked finger. Unlike the Roman gladius, it was meant for slashing, not stabbing.

Yet Levi insisted they practice with the gladius as well. Not only that, but staves, spears, long-axes – anything they might find at hand in battle.

No matter the weapon, Levi's skill was uncanny. In single combat, he always ended the victor. Only when he faced both twins together did he occasionally lose.

Rising from the ground after a throw, Judah demanded. "Who taught you to fight?"

Levi smiled. "I learned at the hands of the best teacher – the enemy." It was all he would say.

Judah and Levi were both natural fighters. But Asher had a surprising contribution to make. In Alexandria, he had studied the ancient books of fighting. With his excellent memory, he could recall every detail of the pictographs demonstrating this move or that. He recreated them in the yard, instructing Judah and Levi in the fighting styles of a half-dozen cultures, some of them forgotten.

"They couldn't have been that skilled," observed Judah wryly, "if they don't exist anymore."

In truth, Asher had expected his knowledge to make him a better fighter than his brother. But watching Judah fight was the difference between a drawing of a panther, and the thing itself. Asher was a journeyman soldier, workmanlike and solid. Judah was made for fighting, as was Levi. It took all Asher's attention to just hold his own.

Then one day, out of the blue, Levi informed the twins that this would be his last day of training with them.

"Found employment at last, eh?"

"Yes, actually. I was at the Blue Hall and heard an address by Asher's friend, the priest Yosef." They had all heard of his elevation. "Thanks to Apollion the Spicer, the young general has hired me to be his personal bodyguard. You gave Apollion my name. I thank you." Levi bowed his head.

Judah felt a warm glow – he'd repaid part of his debt. "His good fortune."

Asher was focused on something else. "Is Yosef my friend?"

"He remembered you, at least. He told me to ask you about heresy and other gods in the Decalogue."

Asher laughed and winced at once. How had Yosef heard about that?

Judah said, "Does that mean you're off to Galilee?"

"So it seems."

"Don't tell Shalva. She'll never cook a good meal again."

Judah meant it in jest. He knew that Levi rarely laughed, but still he was surprised by the angry flash in Levi's eyes. "She's better off without me. Now, come at me. Perhaps today is the day you win."

It wasn't. By the time the sun was fully up the twins' arms and thighs were aching and they had new pink bruises to compliment the purpling and green old ones. They were both eager to continue, but it was time to start the day's work. The twins bade farewell to Levi, roused the apprentices, and went to work.

Asher was well enough now to do the larger chores, sharing the heavy lifting with his brother. Today they were shaping a new sturdy gate arch for Apollion's house in the Upper City. Already their work was being praised, and demands from the spicer's neighbours were giving them more work than they could cope with. For weeks now their only respite had been Shabbat, the day of rest, contemplation, and prayer. Though welcome, Asher could not help thinking the Romans were not resting every seven days.

They worked the huge stone, shaping it, honing it, drilling the grooves that would hold the gate posts. Meanwhile the apprentices were baking bricks and doing the fine detail work on the front of the arch. To entertain them, Malachi sang. His choice for the first song was the eighty-second psalm:

> *GOD standeth in the congregation of the mighty;*
> *He judgeth among the gods.*
> *How long will ye judge unjustly, and accept the*
> *persons of the wicked? Selah.*
> *Defend the poor and fatherless: do justice to the*
> *afflicted and needy.*
> *Deliver the poor and needy: rid them out of the*
> *hand of the wicked.*
> *They know not, neither will they understand; they*
> *walk on in darkness: all the foundations of the*
> *earth are out of course.*
> *I have said, Ye are gods; and all of you are children*
> *of the most High.*
> *But ye shall die like men, and fall like one of the*
> *princes.*
> *Arise, O God, judge the earth: for Thou shalt*
> *inherit all nations.*

Asher joined in the last few lines. He'd forgotten the trouble he'd gotten in for using this psalm to defend his interpretation of the First and Second Commandment. Levi mentioning it meant that it was still remembered among the priests and rabbis. In truth, he hadn't really cared about the argument. Oh, he had fought hard, to be sure. But not because he thought he was right. Rather, he had argued because the priests had been so sure he was *wrong*.

Judah was born to fight with swords. Asher's best weapons were words.

A knock at the gate revealed a messenger with a note. "It's for you," Judah said, handing it across to his brother.

Asher undid the twist of grass binding the small papyrus roll. Reading, his brow furrowed. Judah asked, "Who's it from?"

"That priest. Yosef."

Judah was surprised. "What does he want? To debate the exact number of your heresies?"

"Be serious, please."

"Well?"

"He's inviting us to take the air on the Mount of Olives at dusk."

"Both of us?" Asher nodded. Judah looked down at his sweaty, dust-covered arms and legs. "We'd best clean up, then."

♦   ◊   ♦

Climbing the three-peaked ridge along the city's eastern side, the twins reached a grove of spindly trees. The dry, acidic scent of olives filled their noses, soaked into their skin. This was a favourite spot of theirs, as boys – which made them quite common. It was a favoured spot for anyone who could make the climb.

The Mount of Olives was a stark place. Save for the thin trees and scrub brush, there was no decoration. This was deliberate, for no ornament could compete with the view. This promontory had been created by the Lord to look down on Jerusalem and the monuments raised to His glory. There below were David's tomb and Herod's palace, fittingly at opposite ends of Mount Moriah. Far off was the palace of Solomon, and closer stood the Roman tower called Antonia, awe-inspiring in its own right.

In the midst of it all, the glittering gold and white of the Temple. The setting sun reflected off the golden rooftops of the Sanctuary, blinding Judah.

Shielding his eyes, he saw Asher turn suddenly away. "The *Panieum.*"

"What?"

Swallowing, Asher took a breath. "It's – this place. I forgot. There's a place Alexandria. Pan's Finger. A man-made spire, the only high place in the city. At least, the only one open to Jews. I used to go there, and feel like I was home…"

Judah wondered if now was the moment that Asher would open up. He'd taken to thinking of Asher's untold tale as a poison, one that would only be cured if it was drawn out. And it looked like it was on the tip of his brother's tongue to tell the tale. But just then heard the scuff of footsteps on the dusty path. *So close…damn!*

The silent priest Judah had seen repeatedly at the Blue Hall came up the path. He walked with purpose, chin held high. Yes, Yosef ben Matityahu was certainly proud of his new post. Arriving, he held out his arm. "Asher! Excellent!"

"Good evening, sir," greeted Asher, shaking it. "Or should I call you General?"

"Yosef, please. This is not a formal meeting." Turning to Judah, Yosef's mellifluous voice filled the air with warmth. "Judah ben Matthais. Good to see the Hero of Beth Horon is alive and well!"

Judah wasn't sure if he was expected to shake hands or bow. He inclined his head slightly. "General of Galilee. Congratulations."

"Thank you." Yosef turned to look out at the view. "Ahh. You know, this is my favourite spot in the city. I wanted to see it one last time. One never knows what will happen in war."

"I thought war brought opportunity," said Asher. Judah detected a slight push to his brother's tone.

Yosef smiled. "Another word for opportunity is chance, and

chance means risk. But naught ventured, naught had, yes?"

"So you don't believe in the Greek idea of Fate? That destiny is ordained?"

"That is the Essene way. But I believe in the Lord's Will, and that He gave us both reason and choice for a purpose."

"*I have found power in the mysteries of thought, exaltation in the chanting of the Muses; I have been versed in the reasonings of men; but Fate is stronger than anything I have known.*"

Judah rolled his eyes. Asher was quoting some dead poet again. But the priest seemed absurdly pleased, replying in kind.

"*The nobly born must nobly meet his Fate.*" Yosef slapped his hands together in pleasure. "This! This is why I wanted to see you! Already I'm thinking clearer! I'd actually hoped to see you before now, but I've been unimaginably busy. I suppose you masons, too, are vigourously employed at the moment."

He politely directed this question more to Judah than Asher, hoping to hear of the contract with Apollion. Judah's reply disappointed him. "True, we have work enough. But we would prefer our stones to be used to shore up Agrippa's Wall." It rankled that their state-issued contracts were all for the inner walls, not the outermost. Begun by Herod's son, Agrippa's Wall had never been completed – fear of offending Claudius Caesar had permanently suspended the work. "It will be the first line of defense when the Romans come."

"I understand," said Yosef, rather condescendingly. "But we must make certain that the Temple and the holy sites are protected above all else."

Shrugging, Judah did not waste breath pointing out the obvious flaw in that statement: reinforcing the outermost walls would render everything safe, including the Temple.

"How go the preparations?" asked Asher. "When do you leave for Galilee?"

"Tomorrow." Suddenly Yosef turned from the view. "Come with me."

Judah blinked. Asher said, "Excuse me?"

"To Galilee. I need you. Both of you. My plan is to fortify the largest cities and force the Romans to waste their resources taking them one by one. A pair of skilled masons advising me would be invaluable."

Asher smiled. "Nor would it hurt if one of them was the man who took the Roman eagle."

Yosef took it well, laughing mellifluously. "I'll accept any advantage, even if I must surround myself with reflected glory. It would also be good, my friend, to have someone learned to talk to among the rough-living Essenes."

A great offer, though clearly meant more for Asher. The fact that

Asher's twin happened to be a popular hero was just gilding. But Judah didn't begrudge being second to his brother. He was used to Asher being shown favouritism.

Yet, for all his desire to go out and fight the Romans again, something in this offer that made his fingers itch. Premonition? Or was it the smooth way Yosef had asked, as if it were spontaneous, when clearly he'd thought matters through. Yosef was not a man to act without thinking through every possible consequence.

Judah decided to push back, test the firmness. "We're not allowed. No mason may leave the city, by the Kohen Gadol's order."

"Not to sound too impressive," Yosef confided, "but I have the ear of the Kohen Gadol. A dispensation could be arranged."

To Judah's surprise, Asher showed a similar reluctance. For weeks his twin had longed for nothing more than a chance to fight Romans. Now he said, "We'd be abandoning our city. Everyone says the Romans will come here."

Yosef's smile became wry. His dark eyes twinkled. "You and I both know that everyone is wrong. But I can appreciate your devotion to our home." He reached for a slate board at his belt and chalked a few words upon it. "*Asher and Judah ben Matthais are in the service of General Yosef ben Matityahu, and have free passage to travel through Galilee,*" he read aloud. "*Whoever reads this is hereby required to give them aid on their journey.* There." He pressed the slate into Asher's hand. "If I am wrong and the Romans come here, then you must absolutely stay to defend our city. But they will come to Galilee first."

"Agamemnon's stratagem," Asher said.

"Exactly! And remember – in war, there is always opportunity. If a shepherd became a great soldier with the Lord's help, what might a mason achieve?" Yosef pressed Asher's shoulder. "Promise you will come."

Asher could not promise for them both. He looked to Judah, who said, "If the Romans do not come to Jerusalem, we will come."

♦   ◊   ♦

They descended the Mount of Olives just as the chill entered the evening air. Though he still breathed hard, it was a mark of Asher's good recovery that he could keep pace with his brother.

"You surprised me," said Judah. "I'd've thought you'd leap at the chance."

Asher gave his brother a curious look. "I would have, but you seemed set against going."

"What! I only said—"

"—we weren't allowed! You were looking for a way not to —"

"No, I was just pointing out—"

"So now you want to go? Should I go tell Yosef we're leaving with him?"

That brought Judah up short. He had misgivings. But he'd also given his word. "We'll do exactly what we said. We'll wait and see where the Romans strike. If they come here, we'll fight them here. If they go to Galilee, then so will we."

XIV

THERE WAS ONE part to Judah's daily routine that he did not share with his brother. An hour after noon each day, while everyone was still logy from dinner, he would slip out the small door in the gate and stroll up to one of the markets, a different one each day. Sometimes he would go to Baker's Circle, or the Hill of the Vines. On the third day after Shabbat he would invariably head to the Valley of the Cheesemongers, between the Upper and Lower Cities, where goats bleated and generations of experience went into each block or wheel of cheese. Not only was there cheese to be had, but all sorts of spices, cakes, and delicacies. The next day he would visit the markets near the Fish Gate, and the day after that, the Abattoir, where fresh meat was properly prepared.

He was not shopping. He and Asher could not normally afford such fare, nor would their stomachs have known what to do if they tried it. No, Judah came to keep company with Deborah. This was the only time they could be together, and in the crowd they were never alone. So he talked to her, and listened to her talk, and carried things for her, and whenever someone tried to make her a poor offer, he got stern with them until they made a better one.

She had been briefly mad at him for punching her brother. But most days she was cheerful – perhaps too cheerful. She was not a naturally chatty person, but she always made an effort while with him to engage him in conversation. It seemed to Judah that the latest refusal had blighted her nearly as much as it had him.

The day after his encounter with Yosef at the Mount of Olives, Judah met Deborah in the Bazaar of the Clothiers. Following her from stall to stall, he told her all that had happened. She listened until he was finished, but for once she did not immediately reply. Instead she busied herself with some cloth she clearly had no intention of buying. Finally, still running her fingers over the rough silk, she said, "So – if the Romans go to Galilee..."

"Asher and I will go to meet them." He thought that she'd be proud, and was curious to see her frown and bite her lower lip.

"But you *don't* think they'll go there."

"No. But Asher and the priest seem certain, and they know the Romans far better than I do." Though he'd met his share of Romans living here in Judea, they had mostly been merchants. High-handed and arrogant, but they had valued his father's product and so treated him with a measure of respect. "We'll see."

"So wherever they are," Deborah said slowly, "you'll be fighting them."

"Absolutely. Wherever they are."

She thanked the merchant for letting her view the cloth, then set off to another stall. "You took the eagle. Some would say you had done enough already."

"More would say that my taking the eagle made the Romans want revenge. Not to fight now would be cowardly. And irresponsible."

"So, not you at all," she said with a ghost of a smile. Then the frown returned.

"What?" He had that bottomless feeling in his chest that he'd made some mistake.

She seemed to be weighing something. "We should have run when we had the chance."

Judah felt an invisible hand reach into his chest and squeeze. "Run," he repeated dully.

"Yes. The moment you came back, we should have run." She sighed. "But your father had just died, and you'd never have known Asher was alive... Staying was right," she said, more to herself than him. "It was the right thing."

Judah was stunned. She'd never suggested, never even *hinted*, that running off was a possibility. "You never—"

"No, I didn't. Because I knew you wouldn't. You'd never do anything underhanded, behind anyone's back. You're made of honest stone, not clay. You can't be molded. You are what you are."

It sounded like an insult. "I would have run, if you'd just said..."

She turned to look him in the face. "And what then? When the thrill had worn off, and we needed money, and food, and a home? You would have lamented the choice. Not being with me, maybe, but the way we'd done it. Because you're a good man, Judah. The best of men." She dropped her gaze. "I don't know what you want with me."

People were turning to look at them. The last thing Deborah needed right now was for word to snake back to her mother that she'd been seen with him in public. Judah guided her off behind a stall that fronted on a walled garden with polished turquoise tiles leading up to the door. A tree stood overhead, sheltering them from the sun.

He put his hands on her shoulders. "Now, what are you talking about? You don't know what I want with you? You're mad. I don't know what you'd want with me! Asher's the smart one. I'm good with my hands, is all. That's it for me. I don't know how to talk, or recite poetry, or ride, or any of the things a decent man should. I don't have even a drop of noble blood in me. No surprise your mother hates me – to her I'm an upstart, a nobody that could never deserve you." He was angry, and bowed his head to hide the welling in his eyes. Her eyes were entirely clear, and he felt foolish. "Maybe she's right."

She clasped her hands up to his face. "O, Judah! It's not your birth! Don't you see?" She let out a bitter laugh. "No, of course you don't. You think there has to be something wrong with you. Judah, she hates you because you are so clearly a better man than the one she married. Better than her sons. She can't bear to imagine her children might be happier than she was."

Judah was truly aghast. "You're joking."

For the first time he glimpsed a sourness, a pain deep within her. "I promise, if she thought you'd beat me, she'd have us wed inside a week."

"You don't mean that." In answer she stared at him, her expression hard like he had never seen. When she just continued to stare, he began to feel a little panicked. "What?"

"Judah, why do you want to marry me?"

It was a naked question, and he felt naked answering it. "Because I love you."

It was the first time he'd said so. Perhaps he expected too much, but he was disappointed when she didn't melt or kiss him or any of the things women in poems did. If anything, her look became harder.

"But why? You don't really know me. Not the real me. You never see me when I'm not with you."

"That doesn't make sense." He tried to laugh. "Of course I don't!"

Deborah shook her head sharply. "I'm not joking. With you—with you, Judah, I'm the woman I want to be. I actually like myself when I'm with you. But thanks to my mother, I'm almost never with you. When you're not here, I'm back to being my mother's daughter. I don't –" Her voice almost vanished. "I don't have a good heart." Her head dropped down, hiding her teardrop face behind a veil of raven hair.

Judah's mouth hung open. "Deborah, I've seen you — you are the kindest person on this earth. You tended my father while he lay dying.

You make children laugh everywhere you go. People love you because of your kindness. So do I."

"It's not real."

"What do you mean, not real?"

"It's all an act. A show. An effort. I'm so afraid, Judah. So afraid that, deep down, I'm just – just like her." She bit her bottom lip, stopping herself from saying any more. She certainly looked like her mother in that moment, her face full of bitterness and dashed hopes. The tears in her eyes were angry, and Judah feared the anger was for him.

He had to say something, anything to make it better. "It seems to me that... that we are what we do." That sounded all right. He kept talking, elaborating. "If you're kind to people, that's who you are. It doesn't matter what you think you feel..."

Her head snapped up and she stared at him with what seemed loathing. He reached out a hand, but she knocked it away and fled past him, into the crowded street. Judah stood in utter confusion as Deborah disappeared into the marketplace.

The next day, when they should have seen each other at the Shabbat dinner, Phannius and Euodias arrived at the home of Ezekiel ben Shimri without her. "She's ill," said Euodias smugly when he'd politely asked after her.

And when he went to the Baker's Circle two days later, she was not there. She had changed her routine.

◆　◇　◆

Two weeks later, Judah and Asher were again engaged in their pre-dawn sparring, throwing different-sized spears at a straw target across the yard. Asher tried to joke, but Judah was grimly determined, and had been for a fortnight. As he no longer went out after the midday meal, Asher guessed what had happened. But he didn't ask. Instead he attempted to compete with his brother's skill, give him a challenge the way Levi had.

Throwing, he winced. There was still a pulling sensation in his side from his healed wound, and he still lost breath too quickly. Asher hoped that by the time the summer campaigning season began he would be fully well again. Well enough to fight. *So long as the Romans wait for better weather...*

Just as he was thinking it he heard a sound. The sun was just cresting in the East, and outside the yard voices were raised. Horns were being blown, and people were running in the streets.

"What is it?"

"Only one thing it can be." Judah looked grimly satisfied. "The Romans."

♦   ◊   ♦

The whole city of Jerusalem awoke to behold a great cloud of dust in the distance. Breathless people raced to walls, towers, precipices, any place of great height to behold the sight of an army on the march.

The rising sun reflected off the polished helmets, shields, breast-plates, greaves, and torques of thousands upon thousands of soldiers marching smartly up the road parallel to the city. Around them rode the cavalry, while behind them came miles of baggage, accompanied by hordes of engineers, servants, and slaves. Ahead of them all came the eagles, shining gold wings catching the sun and dazzling the eye.

Panic embraced the city. Women tore their hair, men beat their breasts, and little children hid. The Romans were here far sooner than anyone had expected, and up the road from Aegypt, not down from Syria.

"Woe! Woe unto Jerusalem!" cried Y'eshua the Prophet, and was beaten until he could no longer form words. But there were many men whose thoughts echoed his doleful refrain.

♦   ◊   ♦

Judah and Asher ran to the western-most part of Agrippa's wall and raced to the top of a tower, shoving their way through the heaving pack of bodies. Judah was shouting, "How many! How many!"

"Who can tell?" answered someone.

"The eagles! How many eagles?" cried Asher. Each cohort had a standard raised tall, but a legion only had one eagle. "Count the eagles!"

They all squinted. A sharp-eyed boy perched on his father's shoulders said, "I see two."

"Truly?" said Judah. "Look hard, now."

The boy did, and as the sun rose higher several others joined his count. Two eagles.

Judah laughed, rubbing his thumbs against his forefingers. "Now we're in it! Two legions. Two!"

"Why are you so pleased?" demanded a horrified stranger.

"It's not enough! Three and they might have done it. But two? Impossible! They can't take this city with twelve thousand soldiers."

"Judah," said Asher.

"What?"

"They're not getting any closer."

At first it seemed a trick of the eye. But when the marching column reached level with the city, the people began to wonder and hope. All day they stood, watching, as the rigid rows of eight men abreast marched past. Too far for attacking, too far to fear an attack. Just far enough to watch in horrified awe.

Finally, around midday, the tail end of the column disappeared into the northern horizon. At once the whole city fell about cheering, stamping, weeping with joy. Salvation! Jerusalem was not besieged!

In the Upper City, in the high towers of Herod's Palace, Ananus and Joshua watched the Romans pass them by, wondering grimly how long this reprieve would last.

But to the people, this was hope and glee, peacock bravado and weeping relief. In exultant delight, the citizens of Jerusalem convinced themselves they had won a great victory.

Judah and Asher were not at the heart of the celebrations. They were back in their rooms, already packing. Folding his few spare tunics in a neat bundle, Judah was saying, "They'll probably make a point of marching through Beth Horon. Might be through it already. So if we head northeast to Jericho, we'll miss them entirely. Then we can follow the River Jordan due north until we reach Mount Tabor, right on Galilee's doorstep—"

"Judah," said Asher. He had stopped packing. His eyes were on the doorway behind them.

Judah turned. Deborah was framed in the door, just outside it. He gazed at her, angry and relieved and hopeful and resentful all at once. He was torn between a desire to be cold and aloof and also wanting to take her in his arms. As he was eighteen years old, aloof won. "Should you be here?"

"No. But I couldn't be anywhere else. Hello, Asher."

"Hello, Deborah. Good to see you. He's really missed you."

Shooting Asher a warning look, Judah said pointedly, "I take it you're feeling better."

"No. Worse." She glanced at the small satchel containing his clothes, and the sword and sling laid out on the low bed. "So – you're going."

"I said I would." Judah carefully folded a spare tunic around his good sandals. Unlike Romans, Jews did not swear oaths, or have elaborate systems for the keeping of promises. Once given, one's word was inviolable. "Besides, Asher's going to fight, and someone has to be there to make certain he doesn't start spouting blood instead of poetry."

"I'm standing right here," said Asher.

"I know it." Judah had turned his back on Deborah again, and was hating himself for the way he was behaving, even as he continued to be churlish. He just couldn't help himself.

Asher pulled a face. "Fine. I'll walk over to Phannius and see if he can take in the apprentices while we're away. Then I'll have a talk with Shalva." To Deborah he said, "I won't tell Phannius you're here. Unless you want me to," he added.

She shook her head. "Judah's not that clever. No one would believe it of him anyway."

"Or of you, Deborah." Asher patted her arm as he disappeared through the door.

"What was that?" asked Judah.

Deborah's smile was wan. "Nothing." She bit her lip for a moment, then said, "Were you going to say goodbye?"

"I thought we had."

She entered the room, her hands folded before her. "Judah, I'm sorry."

"For what?" He asked it as if it didn't matter, as if he couldn't care less, as if his heart wasn't racing.

"For being foolish. For pushing you away. For – not being who I like being."

She was trying, dammit. Judah felt himself thaw, and hated the awkwardness that accompanied it. When he was angry with her, he knew what to say. "That's – it's fine. I like who you are. Whoever you're being. I like being with you."

She was half a head shorter than he, and their eyes were not far apart. "If I said take me with you, would you?"

He frowned. "Of course not. Take you to where the Romans will be pillaging and..." He was about to say raping. "...and enslaving? Absolutely not, no."

"I know. Sometimes I wish you were not so good a man. But if you were anything other than what you are, I would not love you."

It was the first time she had said it. He felt a shudder through him, and he wondered how he was still standing. Certainly all the strength had gone out of his arms, and his heart was like a hammer beating at the stone cage of his ribs.

She barely had to lean forward to kiss him. It was not a kiss of passion, or longing, or lust. It was the gentlest of touches, where they breathed into one another, eyes closed, lips barely parted. When it was over she didn't pull away, but turned her head and buried it in his shoulder. He put his arms about her and felt whole for the first time in two weeks. Perhaps the first time ever.

She pressed her face into his neck. "Don't die."

"I won't."

Part Two

Fortifications

XV

PTOLMAIS, SYRIA
2 MARCH AD 67

THE ROMAN ARMY passing Jerusalem was under the command of Titus, who was sorely tempted to disobey his father and besiege the great city at once. Only military discipline restrained him – that, and the knowledge that if he failed, his career was finished.

Still, he looked longingly at those distant walls. The largest fortified city Rome had ever faced – what a military coup to take it!

But instead Titus dutifully marched his two legions up the Judean coast. He passed Caesaeria Maritima, the Roman capitol of Judea, finally reaching Ptolmais, just inside the border to Syria. Here he saw an oversized camp bristling with activity, with soldiers of all hues and armours. He recognized the Syrian ensigns, but had to ask to identify the standards of Commagne and Armenia.

Proudly among them, at their very heart, was the standard of the Fifteenth Legion, sent ahead months before by ship. A scarlet flag hung below the Fifteenth's blazon, indicating the general was in residence. Titus was proud his father had disdained the comfortable nearby city and instead billeted with his men. It was the mark of a good commander. And besides, Vespasian had never been a man in need of comforts.

It was raining, one of those chill and harsh coastal rains that had plagued them through the whole journey. Leaving his armies a mile away, Titus entered the camp under a heavy cloak, riding up the camp's *via Principalis* to the Praetorium. Identifying himself, he was ushered quickly within. He was still shaking the rain off his sagum cloak when he encountered his brother-in-law, Cerialis Rufus. "Titus!? Well met! We didn't expect you before May!"

"I'm here with the Fifth and the Tenth. Is the general in?"

"He is, and thank Mars you've come to mend his mood."

"What's the matter?"

"The provincials. Your father arrived to find himself the de facto governor of Syria."

"Oh?" As slaves fetched Titus a fresh tunic, Cerialis explained how the disgraced governor of Syria, Gaius Cestius Gallus, had waited until Vespasian was near, then emulated old Catulus Caesar – sitting in an airtight chamber, he read the classics while the charcoal braziers burned away the breathable air. "He lost an eagle, so it was the only honourable way out. Saved Rome the trouble of a trial. Vespasian sent the ashes back to Gallus' widow and settled in to govern. But you know your father! He wants to focus on the war, but he's stuck talking to every wronged Latin in the region."

Titus groaned and grinned at once. "Have they started pelting him with turnips yet?"

Cerialis scratched at his ear. "They depart roughly handled, but satisfied. They say he's no politician. An Italian hayseed with no Greek, that's what they call him."

An Italian hayseed with no Greek. An old phrase, once used about the great Gaius Marius, it was another reminder that Vespasian owned no important ancestors. Though Vespasian himself had been consul, his career could hardly be said to have ennobled his family. His elder brother had done much better, and most everyone spoke of Vespasian as a dotard.

That they said so within earshot of his son rankled. So it was with some heat that Titus said, "What do they expect from a career soldier?"

"I know, I know! But with your legions he'll have an excuse to get down to planning the war – he'll be like a child with a handsome new toy. Come with me, I'll take you to him! He'll be delighted!"

"I bet you a hundred sesterces, Quintus, that his first words won't be a greeting." As they walked down the corridor of the newly-made building, Titus suddenly asked, "Tell me, how's my little girl?"

"The soul of sweetness." Family finances being what they were, Titus' daughter was being raised in Cerialis' home. "You did well naming her Julia. A true joy."

"And your own daughter?" asked Titus dutifully.

"Flavia? Growing like a weed. And she likes to hit! A few more years and you could sign her up as a cadet." Cerialis stopped beside a guarded door and rapped loudly.

"Come!" came a distracted voice from within.

The guards opened the door and Cerialis strolled in. "General, I have a surprise for you."

"Don't much care for surprises," grunted the bulk behind the desk.

"I promise this one will please you." Cerialis stepped aside, and Titus said, "*Ave*, general."

Behind the malachite-topped desk, Vespasian's brow furrowed. "What's gone wrong?"

Titus winked at Cerialis, having won his wager. "The hopes of the Judeans, that's what."

"He's brought the Fifth and Tenth," reported Cerialis. "Marched them right up the coast."

"Ah. Good then." Vespasian stood to embrace his son. The perpetual strain around his eyes was more pronounced than Titus had ever seen it. "Cerialis, gather up the junior legates, bring the Fifth and Tenth into camp. Tymon, wine here, and some hot water and food. Sit, Titus!" He waved his son towards one of the couches. "Are they in good form?"

"I've been drilling them the whole way. Life in Aegypt hasn't made them soft."

"Good. Now tell me how you're here a month before time."

"Fortuna was with me," said Titus, stretching to relieve his saddlesore arse. "Once the Fifteenth was embarked, I chased off south – on one of the old royal barges no less. Don't look at me like that, *pater*! It's the fastest way up the Nilus. I reached the legions in just two weeks."

"Just tell me you didn't sail back with them."

"You can rest easy, your son didn't ponce it up – no fans, no litters, not even a crocodile in tow. The legions had done the thing proper, building a road as they went. I simply turned them around and trotted them back up the road they'd just built."

"In winter," said Vespasian.

His father's slave Tymon returned with the food and drink, and Titus scarfed down some oil-soaked bread as he spoke. "So long as there was kindling for fires at night, there was no danger. We marched north to Lake Amanus, then east to Pelusium. There weren't enough transports, so instead we took a lovely seaside stroll past Gaza. The coast of Judea is almost entirely Greek, and therefore pro-Rome. We did pass within a stone's throw of Jerusalem. I wanted to see it."

"You didn't..."

"Oh, it was tempting! But no. I decided instead to be a different kind of hero and solve all your manpower woes." He laughed. "Though, by the look of the camp, I needn't have rushed!"

"Fortuna favours us as well," agreed Vespasian. "We have vexillations from the Third and the Fourth. With the remaining men of the Twelfth, we have eighteen cohorts. Plus all the mules we could ever need." This was said with a chuckle. After years of breeding mules for the military, he had just ordered Rome's armies to buy his entire stock. Without even taking the field, this war had turned the family a handsome profit.

Titus was doing a different kind of math. Eighty men in a century, six centuries in a cohort, ten cohorts in a legion. With three full legions and eighteen additional cohorts, his father now commanded twenty-three thousand, forty men, excluding cavalry and servants. He whistled low. "Impressive."

Vespasian's worry lines slackened slightly. "Oh, that's not the extent of the goddess' favour. Rome has just received an offer of five more cohorts from Cesarea, plus five horse troops from the Syrians. What's more, offers are pouring in from the Eastern kings. Agrippa, naturally, but also Antiochus of Commagne and the Armenian king, Sohemus. Each are contributing two thousand more men, half archers and half cavalry. The king of Arabia has sent a thousand horse and five thousand foot, most of whom are archers."

Titus was amused. "Do they perchance spy an opportunity to widen their borders at Judea's expense?"

Vespasian threw up his hands in horror. "What a shocking allegation! Until this second I was convinced they were only honouring their treaties as Friends and Allies of the Roman People." The old man chuckled to himself.

Titus quickly totted up the figures. "That's nearly fifty thousand men in all. A third more men than Marius had to defeat the Germans!"

"Marius' men were all Roman," reminded Vespasian. "In those terms, our army is about equal to his."

"However you count it," said Titus, slapping his thigh, "we'll eat these rebels!"

"Let's see that we do. With all these mouths to feed, we'd best have a smashing success in Galilee. Otherwise we'll be eating our own boots come winter."

Surprised, Titus sat up. "Galilee? Not Jerusalem?"

"No. Cities are great movers of money, but not producers of it. It's the fields and quarries where the money comes from. Secure those, and we choke off their ability to make war."

Titus was hugely disappointed. Seeing those massive walls shining white under the chill winter sun, he'd hungered to take them. That massive city, so prideful, so aloof. Like the Hebrew god himself, who kept apart from the gods of other lands.

"Besides," added Vespasian with a nasty smile, "Jerusalem is the heart of the resistance. If I strike the heart first, the malcontents will scatter in a thousand directions. But if we start in the north, we can sweep them all south until they're in a single place. Then we can quash this rebellious spirit so that it will never flare up again."

Titus leaned back, relaxing. The siege of Jerusalem was not denied. Merely delayed. In the meantime, he tried out the new word on his lips. "Galilee."

XVI

GALILEE, JUDEA

"IF JUDEA SURVIVES this war, it will be due to Divine Providence alone. Certainly the Galileans aren't helping!"

This oft-heard refrain came from the tent of the Galilean general, the handsome and musical-voiced Yosef. His doleful remark was mostly heard by his bodyguards, of whom Judah's friend Levi was one. But often he said it when entirely alone, perhaps pleading with the Lord for intervention.

The trouble began with simple geography. Galilee was bounded by Tyre and Syria to the north, Samaria to the south, Lake Gennesar to the east, and the narrow strip of Phonecian land bordering the Mediterranean Sea. Galilee contained no great cities nor central power. Instead it boasted a warren of small hamlets and medium-sized towns all in rivalry with each other.

To make matters worse, there were really two Galilees, Upper and Lower. The distinction was simple – Upper Galilee was mountainous, Lower was flat – or at least, flatter. The people of Upper Galilee were like goats, with legs grown strong from climbing and hearts grown hard from life. Their cities were on winding mountain passes, and they were wary of any stranger, be he Roman or Hebrew.

Lower Galilee was a land fertile in both crops and discontent. It contained cities like Nazareth, which had birthed countless religious hotheads. Its warlike farmers had a long tradition of defending their lands from covetous neighbours.

Unfortunately for Yosef, these Galileans were as eager to squabble amongst themselves as with foreigners. Three hundred thousand people, three hundred thousand petty grievances. Arriving at the end of the

Roman month January, he found all the cities already quibbling over resources and primacy.

"The Romans will come for Sepphoris first. We are Galilee's capitol!"

"So-named by the Romans! No, they will march straight for Garis!"

"Japha is vital to them, they will come at us!"

"Tiberias has the greatest wealth! They'll march across the land to raze us!"

"Only in Tiberian dreams! Tarichaeae is the most dangerous city to them – we'll feel the brunt of their wrath! We need funds and an army!"

It didn't help that Yosef could barely understand them. In his years away he had forgotten how crude and uncouth the Galilean dialect was. Hiding his instinctive disdain for these *'am ha-arez*, he began issuing orders. His first act as general was to levy a huge tax. Thus he succeeded in unifying the Galileans against a common foe – him.

Next, Yosef took inspiration from Mosheh the Lawgiver and deputized seventy Galilean elders as his council. Then he appointed seven judges in each city to maintain internal order. Seventy and seven, proper numbers that any Hebrew could appreciate. And the seventy elders were kept with him at all times as advisors, and as hostages. Already there were threats of violence against his person.

"I'm here to save these people!" he lamented to Levi. "Why can't they understand that?"

"They're fighting for freedom, general. They don't see how they can achieve it if they're not free from outside control."

"But that's madness! Only united do we stand a chance to overcome the Romans *fasces*. In that the enemy has it right. One stick can be broken, a bundle cannot. Why can't my countrymen see that?"

He had taken a serious liking to the gaunt, tall bodyguard. Though rough, Levi had picked up a smattering of learning in his thirty-odd years, and was clearly no dunce. More, he had a strongly practical streak that mirrored Yosef's own. He'd heard the story of Levi changing sides when he was cut off from King Agrippa, and rather than being shocked, he applauded the bodyguard's good sense. Here was a kindred spirit.

Now, as he appealed to Levi, the bodyguard could only shrug. "I understand war. Politics is beyond me."

◆   ◊   ◆

Struggling against this tide of mistrust, anger, and resentment, Yosef's first relief came the day Levi poked his head into the command tent and said, "General – Asher ben Matthais has come."

Leaping to his feet, Yosef abandoned the piles of paper and clicking abacus and marched into the courtyard. He'd forgotten they were twins. It was like having drunk too much wine – he was seeing double. "Which is...?"

One smiled. The other one stepped forward. "You were prophetic. The Romans followed Agamemnon's example."

"They're not fools." Yosef first clasped arms with Asher, then Judah. "Welcome to Galilee."

Judah gripped the priest's arm firmly. "We've come to fight."

"You've come to the right place. Though so far all the fighting has been with our own people. But come in, come in! You are more than welcome, both!" Taking Asher's arm, Yosef led the way inside.

Judah fell into step with Levi. They had already embraced and shared their greetings. "How is it?"

"As frustrating as he says."

Judah jerked his chin at Yosef's back. "How's he doing?"

Levi slowed his step, allowing Yosef to leave earshot. "Not bad, for an aristocrat. He has a natural arrogance that both helps and hurts him. So far he's made no mistakes, but many enemies. He knows what to do, but leaves no room for other men's pride."

Sitting in the tent through dinner, Judah saw exactly what Levi meant. The priest was well intentioned, and certainly smart – the conversation was soon far past Judah's comprehension, delving into foreign tongues and skipping from science and philosophy to poetry and mathematics. He was also a gracious host, funny and open, with a deeply cynical streak that Judah appreciated. But there was something in Yosef that Judah could only call *coiled*. Not evil like a snake, but with that same hidden and ready quality. Not everything about this Yosef was on display. He remembered the priest lurking in the back of the Blue Hall, cloaking his presence. The man had depths, and Judah wondered what resided in the deepest corners.

Asher seemed to share some of Judah's uneasiness. Pleased as he was to lob great ideas back and forth, Judah could see his brother holding back. Perhaps he just wanted to put the best parts of himself on display. Certainly both men were trying to impress each other.

For Yosef's part, he enjoyed himself greatly. Even as he rattled off verbal barrages with Asher, he was mentally ticking off the various uses these twins could be. They would have to be on his personal staff, not lost among the rabble. Masons both, one was a thinker, the other a famous fighter. He did not warm to Judah the way he did to Asher, which was unfortunate – Yosef thought himself the perfect blend of these two, and it wounded his sense of self to not see the familiarity reflected back from the warrior as it was from the philosopher.

He complained to them of the local situation, and asked Asher if he had an opinion why the Jews were so intractable.

"Jews are not known as joiners," opined Asher. "Too many years of oppression, perhaps. Or maybe it's the nature of our Lord. Exclusivity, independence. That's the Hebrew way."

Yosef made a show of nodding. "Then perhaps we need to find some way to use that to our advantage. Meanwhile, my friends, I have devised a task for you both. My plan is to fortify every major city in Galilee. I mean to force Vespasian to waste days, even weeks, taking a single city. Strong walls and vigourous defense will clog the Roman war engine long enough for Ananus to secure mutually agreeable terms."

"Priam's plan," nodded Asher.

"Exactly. But unlike the Trojan king, we need only survive this one summer. What I want you to do is ride from city to city and examine the various defenses, let me know where I need to concentrate my builders."

Judah pursed his lips. "We can look to see if the fortifications are sound, but we're not experienced in military placements."

"You'll do fine! In truth, the reports are secondary to having a war hero as my envoy. That Judah came to fight for me will bolster my credentials among these damned Zelotes."

Judah bristled. "I'm here to fight, not be a show-horse."

Yosef frowned at having set a foot wrong, but Asher grinned as though this were a good joke. "See? Intractable, independent, and fierce. That's a Jew."

◆　◇　◆

Despite Judah's misgivings, the twins took the work seriously, spending a month riding hither and yon, sending back surprisingly detailed reports in Asher's fine hand. The well chosen words did not, however, make the facts more palatable. The final report only increased Yosef's dismay:

> *In short, General, only two cities have embarked on fortifying their defenses. One is Sepphoris, which is fortunate. As a coastal city, they'll be the first to feel Roman might. The other is Gischala, situated on the northern border with Syria. The commander is very energetic – Yohanan ben Levi. He's eager to meet you. Perhaps a little too eager.*

Whatever Asher's warning might mean, if there was someone in this benighted land eager to meet with Yosef, Yosef was eager to meet him. Visiting Gischala in person, Yosef discovered that the youthful Yohanan was a landowner of less-than-noble birth. Despite this, the

Gischalan presented himself to Yosef at the head of four hundred ready-trained men.

"You gathered these men?"

Handsomely uncouth, Yohanan bowed his head modestly. "Gischala is not rich, but it can furnish its own defenses."

"I'm happy to hear it. Do you have sufficient masons?"

"We do, general. And manpower, as you can see. All we lack is leadership. The men you have put in charge of us are listless fools. Forgive my bluntness, but in such times as these we cannot afford niceties."

"No, we certainly cannot," agreed Yosef. "I charge you, Yohanan, with raising your city's defenses. I hope you are as capable as you are honest!"

Yohanan answered with a self-deprecating laugh. "O, more so, I hope!"

◆   ◊   ◆

Every day came word of some regional fire that required quenching. Yosef rode from town to town, freely dispensing justice and, less freely, gold. His funds were dwindling, and the tax he had levied was maddeningly slow to come in. He'd hoped that patriotism would make the Galileans cough up the necessary funds to defend their lands. But clearly this was not to be. Deploring the idea of employing Roman-style tax collectors, he nonetheless peeled off a strong force of men and appointed them to the unsavoury task.

Continuing his endless trek from city to city, he arrived in Tiberias just in time to attend a huge rally in the city's agora. Upon a podium, a silken-tongued Galilean called Justus was exhorting the crowd to go attack the enemy.

Yosef had heard of this Justus, a known favourite of Queen Berenice. Therefore his loyalty was suspect. Yet here he was, rousing the Tiberians to unite against the foe. Yosef was heartened – until he heard the enemy in need of blooding wasn't the Romans but another Hebrew city! Justus was calling for the sack of Sepphoris. His reason? Coastal Sepphoris was more Greek than Hebrew, and would therefore go over to Rome at the first sign of trouble.

Rather than put the man in chains, Yosef climbed onto the speaker's platform and engaged Justus in public argument. A mistake, as he found Justus' rhetorical skill was equal to his own. Yosef used reason like a knife, where Justus wielded passion like a mallet.

"Surely you see that Galilee's sole hope is to unite," said Yosef, employing his deep baritone to carry his words through the forum. "Like the Roman *fasces*. A single twig will surely break. A bundle of twigs will endure. Strength in unity. United, we have a chance that individual cities do not."

"Individual is the word," replied Justus, relaxed and ironic. "We Galileans value our individuality and our independence. You've taken taxes from us here and poured that wealth into the walls of Sepphoris."

"Sepphoris will be the first target of any Roman attack. Their walls needed strengthening."

"As do ours!" cried Justus. "If the Romans come, as you say they will, we will need our money to bolster our own walls. We will need our own men to defend them! Leave our cities alone, Yosef! We can take care of ourselves!"

"At the expense of your neighbours? You say, Justus, that you do not support stealing from one city and giving to another. But that is just what you propose doing – only at the end of a sword!"

"Tiberias has a right to defend itself! And it shall!"

The crowd began cheering, ignoring logical contradiction in favour of local patriotism. Inwardly admitting defeat, Yosef beat a haughty retreat and ordered Justus watched. Such a gilded tongue might lead to future problems.

◆   ◊   ◆

More than demagoguery, the greatest problem in Galilee was banditry. Small bands of robbers were springing up everywhere, beating and even murdering fellow Judeans for the smallest shekel. *War brings opportunity*, thought Yosef sourly.

His military commanders suggested mustering the recruits against the thieves. "It'll blood them, and easily."

But Yosef objected. "Against their own brethren! Hardly an auspicious beginning. No, I have a better way."

Yosef's better way was to buy the bandits off. If they refrained from making him look bad, they'd receive a monthly stipend. Surprisingly, this tactic worked. Some bandits even joined the army, expecting plunder. Thus Yosef was able to settle down and focus on training his army.

Announcing a general muster, Yosef had hoped for over a hundred thousand volunteers. Barely a quarter of that number came. The other free men of Galilee, it seemed, preferred to raid neighbouring villages to shore up their own fortifications. Nonetheless, he took his volunteers and started drilling them.

Yosef now encountered an unforeseen obstacle, one he couldn't blame on the Galileans. While living in Rome, he'd watched young Romans drilling on the Campus Martius. He'd toured the arms manufacturers' warehouses. And mostly he'd seen the games, the multiplicity of sports that were actually martial exercises made public. Many gladiators were disgraced soldiers, and even in disgrace they showed tremendous courage and skill.

It was an odd blend, Rome. The hedonism of the court against the diligent work of the people, but under it all there was a martial fervor that was almost unconscious. Living among them, the strengths and virtues of the Roman legionary had so invaded Yosef's mind that he could not imagine a Galilean soldier beating one in fair combat. Even if he had owned greater numbers, Yosef had long ago dismissed the notion of meeting the Roman army in pitched battle. His instructions from Joshua had been clear: "Don't try to win the war. Just don't lose it."

But he could not dispense with an army. Painfully aware of the irony, he based his training regimen the Roman model, dividing his men into groups of decuries and centuries, cohorts and legions. He gave the raw recruits into the hands of soldiers who knew the Roman way of fighting. Some had even served in the legions as foreign auxiliaries in such places as Syria, Germania, and as far away as Spain.

As the days advanced into weeks, it was heartening to see twenty-five thousand men drilling with wooden swords and practice spears. Walking among them as they drilled with ancient weapons collected from every corner of Galilee, Yosef urged them on, unconsciously filling his men's hearts with his own awe of Rome.

"The Romans can do this in their sleep! To them, drilling is bloodless battle, and battle is only a bloody drill! They have no anger, no fear! You may think of yourself as a cobbler, a farmer, a mason. Those are your trades. But for the Romans, *war* is their trade!"

"Your encouragement is a double-edged sword," warned Levi privately. "It pushes the men to work harder, true. But it also fills them with an image of Rome based not in a healthy respect, but in fear. By all means challenge the men, general. But don't defeat them before they've even seen the enemy."

"Isn't it proper that we respect our enemy?" demanded Yosef.

"Not if that respect is greater than our anger."

◆   ◊   ◆

Still dusty from the road, Judah found the general watching the training. "Judah ben Matthais! Welcome back! Asher with you?"

"He is, general. He's seeing the horses right."

Yosef grinned. "Still don't care for them?"

"It's them who don't care for me. I'm not made for a saddle." Judah drew a breath and said, formally, "General, we've spent the last three weeks surveying. That work is done. Request permission to join the ranks?"

Yosef cocked his head. "I'd hoped you would join my personal bodyguard. You and Asher both."

"So you can have a hero as your right arm. I understand. But I know two things – building, and fighting. I'd be a lousy guard."

Yosef's mouth twisted wryly. "I appreciate your candor. Very well, I'll have you assigned to a century. I suppose this means I'll lose Asher's company as well?"

"You'll have to ask him." But they both knew that where Judah went, Asher would follow.

Yosef was as good as his word. The next day the twins were assigned to the training unit of his First Legion. As they found their billet, Judah was frowning. "Why are we calling our army by Roman names?"

"The Romans set the standard," replied Asher.

"Makes us feel less ourselves," grumbled Judah. "Not Hebrew soldiers, just imitation Romans!"

"I know," said Asher. "But if we called ourselves by other words, we'd just be disguising the fact that we're modeled after their example. This way we can show we've learned from them."

Judah remained unconvinced. But he was glad enough to be a part of the army, preparing to fight.

They were put under the command of a hoary old soldier called Zamaris ben Jacimus. Descended from a famous horse-archer of the same name, he had grown to age in a soldier settlement at Batanaea. The town had been founded by Herod, and had a long history of collaborating with Rome, producing soldiers of all kinds to serve in the legions. Zamaris himself had seen fighting in Britannia thirty years earlier, under Vespasian of all men. Nothing would have been more natural for him than to go over to the Roman camp and enlist. Indeed, his brother had done just that. But Zamaris had instead packed up his kit, ridden to Galilee, and offered his services to Yosef.

Dressed for his first day of training in boiled leather armour (his stolen Roman armour was back in his tent), Judah felt confident and cocksure. He knew his natural skill combined with the training Levi had given him would let him far exceed the rest of his century. After all, they were farmers and labourers from rural nowhere.

In many ways, he was correct. He could out-fight, out-throw, and out-sling every member of his group of eighty men. When they dueled individually, he was invariably the victor, even with men larger than himself. But to his great surprise and deep chagrin, Asher made a better soldier.

"No no! Damn your eyes!" Zamaris ben Jacimus slapped Judah hard on the face and shoved him off the fallen man. "You fight like a drunkard – no thought, no sense, no reserve! All about landing the next blow, nothing else matters!"

Judah leapt to his feet, ready to start a brawl with his 'centurion'. "What's wrong with you? I beat him!"

"Oh yes, you beat him, hero." The sneering Zamaris helped the defeated man onto his feet. "But to do it you had to step forward and break the line." He pointed to the wall of shields behind Judah. "Creating a gap. A gap in the line means the enemy can get in. So the hero's won his duel, but he's exposed every one of his comrades to danger. Is that worth it?" The veteran pointed at Asher. "Why can't you be like your brother? He understands! And the Romans understand! There's strength in unity! Only when we break ranks do we die! As individuals, we're finished! So get back in line and *hold*!"

Pride smarting, Judah returned to the line. Asher grinned at him. Judah pulled a face. "Not a word, brother, or I'll rip off your nose."

Asher laughed. "Then at least people could tell us apart."

The horn sounded, and they returned to their drills.

XVII

MARCH WAS UNSEASONABLY cold, and Judah was glad they were training in a city – even if they were forced to sleep in tents, the nearby buildings were windbreaks.

There were eighty men in a century, which made no sense to Judah. *Shouldn't a century be a hundred?* In their little cluster of ten tents, they slept eight men to a tent. *Just like the Romans.*

Judah didn't think much of their tent-mates. Given his choice of men, Zamaris had gone through the ranks and picked an unlikely assortment of soldiers. Sometimes his reasoning was obvious, as with choosing tall muscular men who were good with a sword. But sometimes his picks were curious. One of their tent-fellows was called Pethuel, whose barrel-chest did not alter the fact that he stood almost two heads shorter than Judah. Another was a fellow called Gareb who was so lean he seemed nothing but skin stretched over bone.

The virtue of one of the tent-mates was obvious. He was a giant, nearly seven feet tall, literally head and shoulders above the rest. As he bore the common name of Eleazar, it was tempting to nickname him Goliath, but too obvious. So one night when Asher referred to him as Atlas, supporter of the world, the rest of Judah's century had adopted the name.

The awkward part of Atlas' presence – beside the fact that his head always scraped the top of the tent – was that he'd brought his pregnant wife with him. Chava by name, she was so tiny it was comical to see them together. They had come from a city called Jotapata, with him refusing to leave the mother of his child out of his sight. Due at the end of the summer, she wasn't even swollen yet. The giant was calm and steady when she was around, and she'd offered to do the mending and cooking for the tent, so the men had quickly acquiesced to her presence – despite the annoyance of their coupling each night. At least it was over quickly.

There was another set of brothers, though not twins. Philip and Netir were the jokers of the tent, always teasing and mocking, hiding Judah's sword or putting grapes in Atlas' socks. But once Judah found out they had been tax-farmers for the Romans he cut them dead, refusing to speak to them. He was not alone.

Last among them was a dour Galilean called Deuel, who refused to speak but was clearly eager to fight. He sat silently night after night, and only seemed to rouse himself when it was time to pick up a weapon and train. Asher tried several times to engage him in talk, but invariably the man stood and walked off.

An odd crew. Atlas and Judah were much alike, having trouble accommodating the rules and structure of army fighting. The rest settled in fairly well, none better than Asher.

It did not occur to Judah that while he was judging his messmates, they were also judging him. Sitting behind their tent one morning, Judah was honing his blade when he heard one of the brothers talking to Pethuel.

"Just like a Jeru," grumbled Netir, meaning a man from Jerusalem. "All airs and no sense. But he didn't really take that eagle. Just took credit from better men."

Judah sat very still, straining to hear more.

"His brother's a bit better," answered Pethuel. "Listens, at least. But he's always using fancy words, isn't he. Needs to keep us peasants in our place."

Judah wanted to storm in and bloody their noses. Instead he rose and stormed off to find Asher.

Who laughed at him. "Of course they think we're haughty! Half the nights we're being called over to the general's tent for supper. You're the best fighter among the lot of them, including Atlas."

"He's stronger than I am," protested Judah irrelevantly.

"Could you take him?"

"Of course."

"Right. So, you fight better, I talk like a poet, and we're the pets of the general. How are they not going to despise us? You've beaten each one of them in sparring matches. You know what Levi said about General Yosef? That he leaves no room for other men's pride? Well, that's you all over. You face one of them and they're on the ground with a spear at their throat before they've blinked. They're scared of you, and the only way to combat that is to hit you with words when you're not there."

Judah was shocked. "Really? Am I that – arrogant?"

Asher laughed again. "You don't have to work at it, it's very natural! I'm the same – I don't mean to put on airs when I talk about Aristotle or Cicero. I just get so excited about them, their ideas, I have no idea I'm being condescending. You and I are both single-minded when it comes to the things we love. It isn't meant as arrogance. It just is."

Judah rubbed his chin, his brow furrowed. "How come you've thought about this so much?"

Asher sighed. "Judah. I had to puzzle through all this when I was twelve. You've never been resented for your skill by your peers. As kids, when there was a brawl, you were always on their side! But I was always showing up other students without meaning to. Rather than hide my light under a bushel, I decided to accept it. But I also made an effort to teach, and be so helpful that they couldn't hate me outright. Let them have their pride. After all, we Jerus are a prideful lot!"

Judah thought hard about what Asher had said. That day he was quiet in the ranks as they drilled, careful to obey and not break the line. Then it was time of sparring. When he was paired with Netir, the other man groaned to his brother, "Why me?"

"The Lord hates you, is why," replied the other tax farmer, with a sour look at Judah.

It was tempting to bloody Netir's nose for him. Instead Judah beat him with a quick, methodical series of moves. But the moment the other man was on the ground, Judah stretched out a hand to help him up. "Want to know how not to let that happen?" He spent the next ten minutes talking Netir through what Judah had done to disarm him and send him sprawling. The man was grudging, but at least muttered a quick "Thank you" before they switched partners. It was a start.

◆　◇　◆

While Judah was learning the hard lessons of the ranks, Yosef was dealing with the headaches of a governor-general. Money was the perpetual problem, of course. Men coming to complain of money, or lack thereof, brought on a deep pain above his right eye. Men complaining of preference of one city or group over another made his jaw hurt from clenching it.

One headache arrived in the form of a letter from Yohanan of Gischala. Like the man, the missive was blessedly blunt, plainspoken and practical:

> *I'm hearing troubling reports from across the Syrian border. Many of our brethren – those who have been allowed to live – are being charged outrageous rates for their winter*

oil. Women and children are freezing in their homes. And this during a time when one amphora of good Galilean oil is selling at the piddling price of four Attic drachmas! It's an outrage.

Here's my dilemma. All of Gischala's funds are going into our fortifications. Could your coffers spare a few hundred drachmas? Not as a gift, but a loan. I'll purchase the oil here and take it across the border. The faithful in Syria have the money to buy oil at a reasonable rate, so the money will all be recouped by Passover at the latest.

It's not precisely a warlike request, I am aware. But it's the right thing to do.

Indeed it is, thought Yosef, setting down the ink of his reply.

I hope the enclosed sum is answer enough to your noble request. In truth, I can ill-afford to spare this money, but neither can I allow fellow Hebrews to die of cold.

There's another matter, one I hesitate to mention. I've heard reports of marauding thieves in the north. I'm told these are not Syrians or Tyrians, but men of Galilee, taking sore advantage of their countrymen in time of crisis. After the money just I've given you, I can't afford to buy them off. Could you peel off some of your excellent force of men, track down these impious souls, and end their evil practices?

Again, I applaud your sense of charity. Even in time of war, we must not forget the least among us.

Setting his seal to the letter, Yosef found himself wishing that there were more Jews like Yohanan.

◆　◇　◆

The next ridiculous headache began in Tarichaeae, a city on the southern coast of Lake Gennesar. The young men of nearby Dabira had decided not to enlist, preferring instead to form their own small army. This 'army' had captured and robbed the steward to King Agrippa as he traveled the road east. This deed earned them a mere six hundred drachmas, at the price of their honour – even in times of war, messengers were sacrosanct.

Deploring the deed, Yosef seized the money and deposited it with a trusted friend in Tarichaeae, one Eneas, whom Yosef knew from his days studying with the hermit Banus. Eneas would hold the money until the end of the war, then return it to King Agrippa. After all, whatever the war brought, Agrippa would still be king. Yosef had his career to think of.

Yosef decided to remain a few days in Tarichaeae, staying in the house of Eneas – another Jew with an unfortunate name, a variation of the founder of the Roman people, the Greek hero Aeneas. *How can we defeat them when they invade not only our lands, but our customs, our minds – our very names!*

But Eneas was a good man, if timid – he'd offered up gold rather than join the ranks himself. It was Eneas who brought Yosef the sealed roll of paper with Yohanan's mark, a reply to his latest letter:

> *I have heard the same complaints. Alas, every man under my command is engaged already. For myself, I am taken suddenly ill, a weakness of the belly that renders me useless in a fight. I might journey to Tiberias for the waters there. Have to be ready when the Romans come!*
>
> *Meantime, perhaps you could bring some of those men you are training north to blood them against these 'impious souls' as you call them. We would welcome the sight of you!*

A frank response, however unwelcome. These bandits had to be dealt with before the Romans left their camp. *Must I do everything myself?*

Levi entered the chamber. "Trouble."

"More like the constant nettling of gnats."

"No. I mean there's trouble coming."

Sighing, Yosef laid aside the letter. "Yes?"

Levi's long black beard bristled as if he was grinding his teeth. "The Dabirians."

"What now?"

"They've gone through the region telling everyone that you kept the money to betray us to the Romans."

Yosef dropped his head into his hands. "I want to weep."

"Weep while you run. The people are inflamed. A mob has come from the country. We must fly."

Yosef stood. "What, and be the leader who runs from his own people? I shall reason with them."

Fearless, sardonic Levi arched an eyebrow. "You cannot reason with the irrational, general."

Yosef's reply was acid in his mouth. "Then I shall shame them."

On his way out of doors he paused at a still-smoldering fireplace and rubbed soot into his hair. Lifting a sword, he waited on the steps to Eneas' house and watched as the promised mob spilled into the street in front of him.

"That's him! The traitor from Jerusalem! Tear him! Tear him!"

Before they could rush up the steps to lay hands upon him, Yosef fell to his knees and tore open his shirt, bearing his naked breast to the winter air. Visible on the top step, he pulled back his hair and raised the sword's keen edge to his neck.

"Men of Galilee! Here am I, your servant Yosef, son of Matityahu, priest of the Great Temple, general of the armies of the Two Galilees! If you decide I must die, then I will do the deed myself, that none but I might sin! For it is a sin to assault a fellow Jew. A sin! So much is my love for you, my devotion to your well being, that even betrayed by envious, impious liars, I will protect you from harm. For your cause is mine! I die to save you – even from yourselves!"

The mob faltered, lost its momentum, turned from a flood into a tide, lapping the edges of the wide steps.

Yosef pressed on. "Tell me, though, for what crimes I am to die!" Even as he threatened self-slaughter, his tone proclaimed his defiance, his contempt. "For in all truth, my brothers, I am ignorant of any transgression!"

"The money! We want the money!"

"What money?" Yosef asked in wide-eyed confusion. "Do you mean the money here in the house of my friend Eneas, leading citizen of Tarichaeae? The money taken off the servant of King Agrippa? Is that the money you want?"

The crowd swelled. "Yes!"

"Why?" He allowed the question to hang in the air, wondering what they might say.

"You were going to steal it!" There were cries of assent. "You were going to give it back! To our enemies!"

"Well, which is it?" Yosef demanded. "Was I sending the money back to Agrippa, our foe? Or was I keeping it for myself? I could not do both." Observing the crowd's confusion, he shook his head pityingly. "You see? The liars cannot even settle upon a single lie to smear me with! They call me traitor in one breath, and thief in the next! But I am neither, men of Galilee – I am neither!"

As one speaking to a troublesome child, he began his lie with the words most liars use. "In truth, I had no intention of sending this money back to Agrippa, nor of keeping it myself. I have never thought that a man who was your enemy could be my friend! Nor could anything that would disadvantage you be to my advantage! But I saw that Tarichaeae stands in greater need of fortification than any city in Galilee, and that it needs money for the building of a greater wall! I was concerned that men of other cities might lay claim to this fund, a fund that Tarichaeae so desperately needs. Cities such as Tiberias!"

Tiberias, further up the coast of Lake Gennesar, was an ancient rival of the Tarichaeans. The people responded with predictable vigour, shaking their fists at their neighbours to the north.

Yosef had to struggle not to smile. They were so simple! It was like being back in Rome, riling up the followers of the White charioteers against the Blues. Sword still at his throat, he reached out a pleading left hand. "So you see, I have thought only for the good! But I am your servant! If my plans displease you, I shall step aside and you may make whatever divisions of the spoils you desire. Or else you may, if you choose, revenge yourself upon one who meant to be your benefactor!"

He bowed his head even as the Tarichaeans roared their approval of him. The Dabirians in the crowd tried to rush him, whereupon the two groups fell upon each other in a mass of fists, clubs, and knives. Some locals, who had just moments before been howling for his blood, now rushed Yosef back into the house, guarding him against all dangers.

Levi barred the door and shortly thereafter the fearful Eneas arrived, drenched in a sweat of anxiety. "That was quite a performance."

"You forget, I'm a priest. I know how to sway a crowd."

Levi looked shrewdly at Yosef. "This is not over, you know."

Nor was it. After the contented Tarichaeans dispersed to their homes, some Dabirians and others not of the city gathered and rushed the house of Eneas in full armour, shouting, "The money! The money!"

"They are determined, you have to give them that." Yosef climbed to the top of the house and stood in full view, cupping hand to his ear. "I cannot understand you! There are too many voices! Choose leaders, men to speak for you, and I will entertain them within these walls! Once I have heard their words, I will be able to comply!"

As they descended, Levi asked, "What are you about, general?"

Yosef answered one question with another. "Do you have a stomach for distasteful things?"

"My tongue may not like it, but if they must be swallowed, I have an iron stomach."

"Excellent. Find a windowless room, preferably at the back of the house." To this, he added a few more instructions. Then he went to receive the deputation of malcontents.

The leaders were admitted just a few minutes later, eleven men in all. Yosef greeted them with courtesy, begging their pardon for searching them for weapons. Once they were comfortably disarmed, he led them to the chamber Levi had found. "Far from prying eyes or ears."

The room contained several of Eneas' servants, as well as Levi and the rest of Yosef's bodyguards. All stood in rigid formality, hands behind their backs.

The eleven men had taken seats on the cushions before they realized Yosef was still standing. They watched him turn to the huge bearded bodyguard and hold out his hand. Levi offered him a short, viciously barbed lash with a stout handle. Yosef turned, eyes hard.

The deputation began to protest, but their words were cut short by the crack of the whip. It was a signal to the servants and bodyguards, who all produced whips, crops, and canes from behind their backs. They waded into the deputation, lashing and beating them until both clothes and skin were ragged tatters. Not a whisper of their shouts, cries, or screams escaped the chamber.

"What shall we do with them?" asked Levi, bemoiled with blood.

Face a mask of disgust, Yosef dropped his whip. "I've heard their complaints. Escort them out. I must wash and pray."

The mob of Dabirians without waited, believing the long delay was due to intricate negotiations within. So when the doors opened and the eleven men were heaved unceremoniously onto the upper steps, they did not quite know what they were seeing. The doors closed quickly, leaving a twitching, moaning, weeping pile of raw and bloody flesh. None were dead, though some would certainly expire soon. Several had organs exposed. None had faces.

Instead of tending the wounded, the Dabirians fled. Yosef would have no more trouble in Tarichaeae.

"Though I would like to know," he said in savage frustration as he washed the blood and ashes from his hair, "who has been stirring them up against me!"

XVIII

AT THE START of Spring, Judah sat down to write a letter to Deborah. It wasn't his first, but he hadn't been as diligent as he had promised to be. It was just that he wasn't as good at stringing words together as Asher. And since he didn't know if Euodias was reading these as well, he couldn't be as frankly open as he wanted to be. The closest he could come was in his opening address of her:

My dearest Deborah,

> *I write to you from our camp. I can't say where it is, because this letter might fall into Roman hands. Not that they don't know where we train, or how many we are. If the general is to be believed, they have spies everywhere. He's got us seeing Romans under rocks and flying overhead. It's tempting to ridicule him, but he and Asher are still thick and I don't want to ruin that. I don't want to be whipped either.*
>
> *Please forgive these clumsy letters. I ache everywhere. It's an effort even to move this reed pen. I could have asked Asher to write this out, but then it would be his words, not mine.*

Actually, Asher was off enjoying the favours of one of the camp followers. Evidently he'd become quite the lady's man in Alexandria, and developed an appetite for feminine companionship. Ever since arriving in Galilee he'd been quietly but assiduously chasing any young skirt that would have him. The fact that he was so successful made Judah a little envious. But he didn't think he should put any of that in a letter. He continued to write.

Our 'centurion' Zamaris is a true (he almost wrote 'bastard') taskmaster. He's got us up drilling from before dawn until after sunset, with only a few breaks for water and one meal. He calls it conditioning. I call it doing the Romans' work for them. But we're all getting better at obeying orders. At least I can pick out the notes that mean turn left from the ones that mean turn right. Trust me, that's an improvement.

There's so much about being a soldier that has nothing to do with actual fighting. It's like a completely different skill-set. Asher compared it as the difference between being a mason and a sculptor. Both work with stone, but one is rude while the other is refined.

Not that the other soldiers here are refined. If there's an opposite to refined – I guess that would be unrefined, right? – these men are it. I won't go into their habits, I don't want to repulse you. Let's just say that they wouldn't be allowed into the Temple on their best day. Still, I'm beginning to see their charm. The way the Upper City looks down on Bezetha, we look down on these Galileans. But they have their own sense of honour, their own pride, and they can fight. Which is good, as the Romans have at least three legions in the field. Not that I'm worried. I took down one legion myself. The eight of us should be plenty to send Vespasian back across the sea.

I miss you. I want the war to start so it can end and I can come back. I wish we could be together.

Be well, and know that I am surviving, if not thriving. There, that's almost poetic!

Yours,
Judah ben Matthais

He laid his reed pen aside and read it over. He sounded like an idiot. But his last three tries hadn't been any better, and this was his last sheet of paper. Worse, it was cheap stuff, and if he tried to add or correct anything he'd certainly tear it. Dashing a handful of sand across it to dry the ink, he rolled it up, sealed it, and went off to find the messenger heading for Jerusalem. One benefit of having the general's ear was that Asher and Judah could make use of the official couriers to and from Jerusalem.

Letter sent, Judah returned to his tent and was about to fall into a blessed sleep when Atlas offered to play him at dice.

"Sure. What are we playing for?"

"Your greaves," said Atlas at once.

"Not a chance," answered Judah. The silver leg greaves he'd taken off the aquilifer were lucky, he knew it. "You don't have anything half as nice to put up."

"Fine. Then I'll take tomorrow's dinner."

"Done." Unlike the Roman soldiers, Judeans didn't use pig's knuckles for dice. Unclean. Instead they took the knee-joints of deer, or else the joints of wolves. But Atlas had somehow come across a real set of dice, properly weighted and cast in baked clay. Judah had studied them hard, wondering if he could make a set when he got back to his kiln.

Other men drifted over, and soon there was a good-natured rivalry. Judah lost, but didn't care – if Zamaris stayed true to form, he'd be too tired to eat tomorrow night anyway. Instead he tried to fit in with these rough, uncouth Galileans. He told a few jokes, though his couldn't compare with the winding and elaborate tales of Philip and Netir. They all sang a little, and when Asher returned he started telling the fables of Aesop, making them all laugh at the antics of foxes and grasshoppers.

At last Zamaris walked by, eyeing them all without a word. Everyone knew that he would drill their little band extra hard come morning, so they bedded down almost at once.

On his blanket, Judah whispered to his brother. "I sent a letter to Deborah."

"Nothing too indiscreet, I hope." Asher had a smile on his face that made him look ridiculous.

"I told her all about my brother the whoremonger."

Asher sat up sharply. "What? You didn't!"

"Don't be stupid. I just told her I was tired and wished we could be together. Go to sleep."

♦   ◊   ♦

Yosef's next spurt of trouble came, unsurprisingly, from the city of Tiberias. A week after he had whipped a handful of its citizens raw, Yosef received a missive from the commander he had put in charge of the city, one Silas:

> *Beware! I've heard tell of a plot against you! Several men – prominent men – have been overheard scheming to murder you and give your command to one of their own. Who the usurper is, I do not know. But he is a man within our walls, so much is clear.*

That troublemaker Justus again! Yosef left at once for Tiberias, taking only Levi and twenty others. He had no fear of allies, for he'd given Yohanan of Gischala permission to leave his wall-building duties to cure his belly ills in the famous Tiberian baths. *How fortuitous!* He sent word ahead for Yohanan to muster his men and wait in the town's theatre. There, Yosef would address the citizens and get to the bottom of this new trouble.

Yohanan's response was prompt:

> *I am confined to my bed with a great illness. But my men are at your disposal, and will await you at the amphitheatre.*

It was a newer theatre, less than seventy years old, one of Herod's many regional constructions. Instead of being built upwards, the deep bowl was dug along the slope towards the shores of the huge lake. At the bottom was a barrier made of jagged rock, against which had been built the rudiments of a theatre's back wall.

Arriving with the dust from the road still upon him, Yosef found the citizens gathered as for a show. Indeed, the stage was set with rich eastern trappings, as if for a potentate or king. Then he saw a banner bearing the name Xerxes and knew what play he had pre-empted today. *The Persians* by Aeschylus.

Ill-omened? wondered Yosef. *Or a boon?* In the play, the wealthy Persian elders await news of their king, Xerxes, who has led an overwhelming force to conquer Greece. But the news that comes back is of defeat:

> MESSENGER: O cities of all the land of Asia, O realm of Persia, and bounteous haven of wealth, at a single stroke all your plenteous prosperity has been shattered, and the flower of the Persians has fallen and perished! Ah, it is a terrible task to be the first to deliver news of disaster. And yet, Persians, I must relate the entirety of the calamity — the whole barbarian host is lost.
>
> CHORUS: Grievous, grievous disaster, strange and cruel. Alas, Persians, weep now that you hear this calamity.

Thinking of the play, Yosef was bemused. *Are we the Persians, or the Greeks?* Then he shook his head. It was too easy for a priest to look for omens and portents in every little twist of fate. More important, surely, was that Yohanan had kept his word. His men ringed the back of the stage like pretend soldiers. But unlike the actors, the swords in their scabbards were doubtless unbated.

"Levi?"

"General."

"Let's enter through the crowd. Show the people I am not afraid."

Levi escorted Yosef down the steps into the hollow bowl. Reaching the stage, Levi's handful of men spread themselves across the front.

And there, right in the midst of the crowd, was that honey-tongued Justus. Braving Yosef's withering glance, Justus interposed himself to momentarily block Yosef's path. In Yosef's ear he murmured, "I have no idea what's happening. Be wary."

Frowning, Yosef stepped down onto the stage. What did that mean? Was it a ploy? Was Justus toying with him? Or were things really so confused that even the rabble-rouser had no idea where the trouble was coming from?

Shaking himself free of pondering, Yosef began to address the crowd. "Citizens of Judea, of Israel, children of Abraham, hear me speak. I command the army of Galilee, both Upper and Lower. For those who do not know me, my name is Yosef ben—"

"Behind you!" Justus called out.

Levi was already drawing his massive sword as Yosef spun around. He saw Yohanan's men advancing on him, sunlight glinting off their naked blades. Bowels loosening in fear, Yosef leapt off the low stage into the crowd. Not bothering with aisles, he scrambled over citizens, stepping on shoulders and crawling over heads towards the exit. The crowd was as surprised as he, and as frightened. Within seconds everyone was fleeing headlong away from the swords of the advancing Gischalans, who swung them indiscriminately in their attempt to slay Yosef.

Levi appeared beside him, shoving and throwing bodies out of their path, his greatsword bloodied. Reaching the top of the theatre seats, he called, "The docks!"

Incapable of words, Yosef grunted and together they ran to one of the nearby quays. The owner of a small fishing boat took one look and tried to shove off, but Levi leapt across the divide and held his crimson-dappled sword at the man's throat. Yosef was just behind him, but he did not have the bodyguard's height and landed athwart the side, feet splashing into the water. Hauling him up, Levi threw down his sword and took one of the oars. Yosef took another, and the captain and crew joined them, for they had seen the soldiers racing towards them. Heaving and straining, they rowed themselves far out into Lake Gennesar.

Only when they lost sight of the city did they pause, chests heaving. Yosef was so winded he had to lean over the side to retch. Wiping the sick from his beard, he turned to Levi. "Your men?"

Levi shrugged. "Alive, dead, fled. We'll see."

"Could it have been a mistake?"

The bodyguard gazed back unspeaking, fingers quivering with rage.

Yosef wished he could share the fury etched into Levi's features. All he felt was a pervasive and bottomless bewilderment. "But *why*?"

◆   ◇   ◆

Soon enough the whole story came tumbling out. Yohanan of Gischala had designs on the overall command, and for months had been spreading lies about Yosef's greed, incompetence, and ties to Rome. Half the trouble with the Dabirians had begun with lying letters from Yohanan's pen. Meanwhile, Yosef's silver had indeed gone to purchasing cheap oil, but sold across the border for eight times the buying price. Still less than what the Syrians were charging, it came to a very tidy profit for the Gischalan leader.

It was now painfully clear why Yohanan's troops were too busy to chase the northern marauders – they were *themselves* the marauders! While Yohanan forced the women and children of Gischala to build the walls, his men were out ravaging the countryside, stealing everything in sight. It was difficult to say which scheme had earned him more, the oil or the thieving. In only four months, Yohanan had become a very wealthy man.

Outraged, Yosef's army demanded they march north to teach the treacherous bastard a lesson. His commanders came to him with the men's proposals, as eager as their troops to exact a measure of justice.

"No, we do not march!" snapped Yosef. His voice had recently lost some of its melody. "I cannot waste the lives of my men in killing other Judeans. The Romans are the enemy! Not our brothers – however craven." He turned to his scribe. "Have it announced that any follower of his that repents in the next five days will have a full pardon. Past that, their lives are forfeit, their property confiscate, their houses to be burned. With their families in them," he added grimly.

"And Yohanan?" asked Levi, curious.

Yosef sniffed. "He wants command of Gischala? Well, it's his. I'll be happy to watch how he fares when the Romans arrive." He turned his gaze skyward. "O Lord! How can we win if we're forced to war against ourselves?!"

XIX

PTOLMAIS, SYRIA

VESPASIAN'S JEWISH PROBLEMS were not as serious, but aggravating all the same.

"The trouble with accepting foreign levies," he groused to his son, "is that foreigners then want to have a say in the waging of the war!"

This was in response to yet another letter from Agrippa, the Hebrew king, demanding an interview with the Proconsular General Vespasian. "Tell the King I thank him for his men, and will win back his land, but I do not have time to see him!"

"Father, you cannot ignore him. If only because we may need him."

"Then you do it! Don't laugh, I'm perfectly serious. Go! Give him my regards, reassure him, award him a ceremonial sword, offer him your daughter in marriage, anything to make him stop pestering me! Scoot!"

Off scooted Titus to meet the grandson of Herod the Great.

Under Roman law, Agrippa was not a true king, merely a governor for life, with possession of several cities and the right to appoint the Kohen Gadol. His cities were scattered, ensuring he could never create a nucleus of power from which to expand.

Not that he had such plans. Educated in Rome and given a sizable Roman pension, he was a staunch supporter of Roman rule. Indeed, Agrippa's current anxiety was that, after failing to dissuade the people of Jerusalem from rebelling, he was now being ignored by the Roman commander. All he required was assurance that Rome still thought of him as a Friend and Ally.

It was a task well suited for genial Titus. Besides, this was his chance to meet the famous beauty Queen Berenice, the king's sister.

The king was in Caesarea Philippi, on the far side of Lake Gennesar. Unfamiliar with the terrain, Titus employed one of Agrippa's own soldiers as his guide. The man in question was called Nicanor, a scholarly Judean soldier who had stayed loyal to King Agrippa. The king organized his soldiers according to Roman methods, and Nicanor held the rank of tribune.

Titus and Nicanor traveled with a strong bodyguard, which kept them from moving at too brisk a pace – which suited Titus well, as he was able to experience the region for the first time. "For a country not much bigger than the isle of Sicilia, you have quite a varied landscape – fertile plains and lush forests on the one hand, dry deserts and hills only a goat could climb on the other."

"It is the land of our Lord, who provides us with all things."

"He certainly does." It was particularly gorgeous at the moment – Galilee was carpeted with late springtime flowers, the orchards full of fruit. At night they were able to stop anywhere and sample a rich local wine.

As they rode they conversed. Titus was fascinated to learn that Nicanor was of noble birth. "So you're a priest?"

"From a priestly family," corrected Nicanor, bowing his head humbly.

"From what I understand," teased Titus, "every family in Judea is priestly."

Unoffended, Nicanor laughed. "It seems that way. But there is a significant difference between the peasants who claim priestly blood and the few noble families who actually serve in the Sanhedrin. It's very like patricians and plebeians in Rome. There are plebeians who can trace their blood back hundreds of years, but are still not noble."

Interested, Titus pressed on. "So the Sanhedrin – they are like the Senate? With the High Priest as consul?"

"An apt analogy – though only if the consul were also Pontifex Maximus," added Nicanor, showing he knew the offices and divisions of Rome as well as his own. "Once our High Priests were elected, just as the consuls were. But now our High Priests are appointed by King Agrippa, just as Caesar appoints the consuls. But they are often deposed."

"For?"

"Opposing the king's interests, and Rome's."

"Just like the consuls," mused Titus wryly. "And then what happens to them?"

"They are afforded all the courtesy and honours due the Kohen Gadol. They're allowed to speak first in councils, and their opinion is polled ahead of other men."

"They become consular." The parallels to Rome were pleasing.

But then, Roman culture had spread across the world – as was only reasonable, being the best.

Still, some cultures clung to their old ways. "What about the king and queen? They're brother and sister – is Judea like Aegypt of old, where siblings marry?"

Nicanor looked repulsed. "Absolutely not! She is called queen because of her birth. Even if it were not religiously forbidden, the King and Queen were raised in Rome, and esteem Roman culture just as highly as our own."

"Glad to hear it," said Titus. "Tell me about the Queen."

Nicanor flushed, which said more than his words. "She is a noble lady, and my queen. Though when you see her," he added, "do not be surprised if her hair is quite short. Last year she did penance in Jerusalem, expunging her sins, and shaved her head as part of the ritual."

"She is religious?"

"In her way," was as far as Nicanor would go.

Arriving at last, Titus was feted all the way to the palace and ushered at once into a grand audience with the king.

King Agrippa II resembled his great-grandfather, which was unfortunate, as most men compared Herod to a bronzed toad. An Idumean, he wore the make-up and oiled hair of an Eastern potentate, appearing more Aegyptian or Syrian than Hebrew.

Fidgeting in his high-backed eastern-style throne, the king intoned, "Titus Flavius, you honour us with your presence." At least his voice was manly.

Titus remained standing – Romans bowed to no foreign potentate, especially not one bought and paid for. "It is my honour, King of the Jews."

"We have had a letter from our beloved Antonia Caenis. It speaks well of your father that he has the devotion of such an admirable, capable lady."

Titus tried to hide his surprise as he cast his mind about – *how on earth does the king know my father's mistress?* Oh, of course. Disowned by Herod, Agrippa's father had attained the Judean throne with the help of Antonia, the niece of Augustus and daughter of Mark Antony. Caenis had been Antonia's slave, and had probably known Agrippa's father well. *How well?* wondered Titus idly. He'd heard tell of Caligula's wild orgies, frequented by Agrippa's father. *Clever, clever Caenis. She's pulling every string in her loom, and all for my father's good – and mine.*

"It is for my father that I have come," said Titus. "He deeply regrets his inability to come himself, but as you may imagine he has his hands full with both the war and the provinces."

"We understand, we understand, and appreciate him sending his firstborn son. You are most welcome, Titus Flavius."

Introductions over, Titus allowed his eyes to move sideways to the throne that held the king's sister. He gasped, for Queen Berenice was breathtaking.

The oval face contained wide brown eyes that even the harsh Eastern make-up could not make squint. The short curls of her raven-dark hair perfectly framed her features. Her clothes clung to her curves in such a way as to suggest a sensual body beneath. All over her hair and neck dangled diamonds. *One for every lover*, Titus imagined.

Beautiful, proud, regal, foreign, voluptuous – nothing of the toad about her! Silent through the whole formal audience that followed, she occupied her small throne better than her brother did his large one. As Titus offered compliments and assurances to the anxious king, his eyes kept returning to her.

Finally the audience was ending, with Agrippa again offering his thanks. "Titus Flavius, your words assuage our heart. Tonight we hold a festive supper in your honour, and I hope you will convey to your noble father the general that you received all you could possibly desire at our hands."

This must have been a signal, for Berenice rose and descended from the dais. Just over five feet in height, her walk was mesmerizing, a sensuous swaying gait that would make Aphrodite blush. So graceful, so perfect, it could only be artifice. Three husbands and dozens of lovers had fallen under the seductive spell of those eyes, those lips, those hips. Now, at her brother's request, she was casting her spell on Titus.

Aware of this, Titus cared only for the result. When she reached him she held out her hand. "Titus Flavius."

"My queen." He kissed the offered wrist, having to bow to do it. Small price, when there was so much more promised.

♦ ◊ ♦

Spring did not improve Yosef's situation. There seemed no end of Galilean schemes and plots against their protector. Exposed, Yohanan of Gischala decided to wage a war of words. He wrote to the Sanhedrin in Jerusalem, complaining of Yosef's conduct, and convinced every other disaffected Galilean to do the same.

Back in Jerusalem, Joshua and Yosef's father tried to defend him as best they could. But nonetheless a commission was sent to look into the matter and, if necessary, remove Yosef from command – by whatever means required.

Yosef never gave them the chance. Forewarned by his father, he kept his movements secret, and the commission never found him. At the same time he used his army to sack the most recalcitrant cities. He was still reluctant to raise a hand against other Jews, but he was bone-weary of uprisings, having more important tasks than riding herd over his own people. Did no one realize the Romans were coming?

His men looted each of the four cities on his list with orders not to kill, rape, or torture. To lessen the sting of the sacking, he returned the plunder to each of the cities. "Think of this as a taste of what the Romans will give you. Only they won't give the spoils back!"

The sole city that did not submit to this tactic was Tiberias. No sooner had Yosef sent his army back to the front lines but the city revolted again, this time claiming that they wished to welcome Agrippa's troops and submit to the king's mercy.

"Justus!" groaned Yosef. With his army at the other end of Galilee, he desperately gathered every ship in the harbour at Tarichaeae, be it warship, fisher, or schooner – two hundred thirty in all. He could only supply four adults to each ship, so he packed every one with helmeted children carrying short spears.

When the ships arrived at Tiberias, the city saw a massive invasion fleet and raised a flag of truce at once. Yosef demanded Justus be handed over, along with the other ring-leaders. Those other men were forced to cut off their own right hands, so that they might never raise them against Yosef again.

A prisoner, Justus was brought on-board the lead ship. Seeing the massive fleet was manned by children, he just laughed. "Oh, well played! Perhaps you can win this war after all."

"If not, no doubt you'll be there to take up the high command. But until then, you can rot in a prison. Take him away." Yosef wished he could execute this rabble-rouser, but Justus was known to be a favourite of Queen Berenice – a dangerous enemy to make. And Justus had saved Yosef's life in the theatre. Having a conscience was a wretched nuisance.

When Yosef finally rejoined his army in the city of Garis near the western coast, he found them distraught. Sepphoris – capitol of Galilee, the city that Yosef had defended so vigourously – had opened their gates to the Romans in welcome.

Reaching high, Yosef clawed at the sun. "Vespasian doesn't need to stir from his camp! We're more than capable of defeating ourselves!" In his mind, he heard Justus laugh. *You should have let us sack them!*

"I am Agamemnon, King of Kings," said Yosef to Asher over supper. "Titular head of a bunch of men who all think they should be kings. I wish I could bring the Galilean leaders together to see the Romans at work. Only united do we stand a chance..." His voice trailed away as an idea formed in Yosef's mind. For the first time in weeks, he smiled.

"What is it?" asked Asher.

Yosef put a single finger to his lips. "You'll see."

♦ ◊ ♦

Titus lingered in Caesarea Philippi longer than he should have done, plying the Queen with every ounce of his attention, treating her to a siege of charm and wishing he could employ his battering ram.

But whenever he turned the topic to amorous lines, she retreated into one lament. "I cannot think of love – I am so filled with hate! Venus cannot flourish in a house of Mars. Oh, Titus, how I long to give myself over to the tender feelings of my sex. But I cannot!"

"What vexes your majesty? Is it the war? I promise, it will be over in a few months. If I have any say – and I do – this war will be almost bloodless. So long as your people have the sense to surrender," he added.

Berenice lifted his hand and kissed his knuckles. "You're sweet. But it's not the war that has me furious." Raised in Rome, her Latin was flawless. And for a woman so short, her voice was surprisingly deep and husky. "It's the thought that Gessius Florus will escape unscathed. He provoked this war, and humiliated me."

Though loath to speak ill of another Roman, the thought of her humiliation bothered Titus deeply. "In what way?"

"Last summer I was in Jerusalem, fasting and praying to cleanse myself of sin. But that was at the height of Florus' atrocities – a term I do not use lightly, Titus Flavius! I was once married to a governor of Judea, I know how hard it is for a Roman to keep our land peaceful and prosperous. But Florus was whipping and crucifying citizens – Roman citizens! – just because they were also Jews. When he stole money from the Temple, my people did not rise up. They instead mocked him."

"By passing around baskets for alms for the poor man who needed money so badly," laughed Titus. "I've heard."

Berenice nodded. "That is the patience they showed. But Florus was so enraged, he sent mercenaries into the streets to kill any Hebrew they found. I had to hide in my palace – I, the queen! When I could, I went to see him, despite my shaved head and bare feet. I got on my knees and begged him to stop the killing. Do you know what he did, Titus Flavius? He laughed in my face."

Titus felt his throat close in rage. Fellow Roman or no, Florus had to pay for treating this royal lady so. And if, in punishing Florus, he was able to gain the lady's favour... "Your majesty. This fury in your breast, tell me – will it abate if Florus is brought to account?"

"I'm afraid I would have to see the accounting with my own eyes before my heart would have room for any other feeling."

Titus kissed her hand in silence. Her price had been named, and it was small enough. A mere trifle, easily paid.

XX

IT WAS THE DEAD of night. Judah and Asher pressed themselves close to the earth, trying not to be seen. Their century was crawling on elbows and knees up a knoll across from a Roman Cavalry camp outside Sepphoris. Their commander was a Jeru called Nev, but it was Zamaris who truly led them. The centurion had them stretched out on their bellies just behind a low line of scrub, crawling as close to the fort as they could without being seen. Their armour was covered in animal hides to keep off any gleam or reflection.

Asher was restless. Judah noticed how his brother's hand kept touching the side of his breastplate, almost religiously. The same spot where he had been stabbed. "Stay on my right," whispered Judah. He meant that anyone meaning to stab Asher would have to go through Judah first.

But Asher shook his head. "I still don't understand what we're doing here."

Judah resisted the urge to sigh. "When the general attacks the city, the Romans will pour out of this camp to help, and we'll take their flank." Judah eyed the fort as an eagle does a mouse.

"I understand the plan," said Asher testily. "What I don't understand is why Yosef has us attacking at all. Fabian strategy says—"

"Stuff Fabian and his strategy. Hush now!" For an hour now his twin had prattled on about Roman commentaries on the Punic War, and how the Roman dictator Quintus Fabius Maximus had defeated Hannibal. "In Fabian-style war, you don't engage the enemy in battle. Instead you melt away, stretching the enemy supply lines and miring them deeper and deeper in your own territory. In short, it's a war of attrition, the very best way to deal with invasions."

That had been general Yosef's plan. Not daring, but tried and true. Suddenly now Yosef was on the offensive. Though puzzling to Asher, it suited Judah fine. This cavalry camp had been causing all kinds of havoc in the region, raiding inland to burn, pillage, and plunder. Time to pay them back.

But something had Asher's hackles up. "This isn't right."

"You see a sentry?"

"No, I mean the whole plan. Yosef was dead set against attacking the Romans. So why is he ordering an attack he doesn't believe in?"

"Maybe someone loaned him a pair of balls," grunted Judah.

"Quiet," hissed Netir. As always, they were grouped with their tent-mates.

Still Asher fretted, muttering, "Yosef is a thinker, a planner. Once a plan is set, he'd find it insulting to deviate. Yet here he is, abandoning Fabian tactics before the war is even engaged. Did the trouble in Galilee upset him that much..?" Asher trailed off.

In spite of himself, Judah asked, "What?"

"There it is. This attack isn't about the Romans at all! It's..."

Whatever Asher's realization, it came too late. Suddenly the night was full of trumpets and cries. A mile away the bulk of the Judean army was running screaming towards the city walls – the perfect distraction.

"Here we go!" Zamaris leapt to his feet and began to run. His entire force followed suit.

"Stay close," hissed Judah as he rose and dashed towards the darkened camp. His feet made divots in the soft earth, creating little puffs of sand behind him.

He was a swift runner, as he'd proven at Beth Horon. But the giant Atlas was somehow faster. The great mountain lumbered forward in a headlong charge, his crashing footfalls threatening to betray their approach. Judah and Asher came next, followed by the other pair of brothers, Philip and Netir. Short Pethuel was pumping his stocky legs to keep up, lean Gareb was loping lazily behind, and the silent Deuel brought up the rear.

Frustratingly, it was the men in the rear who carried the planks to use as bridges over the trenches, forcing the leaders to wait – there was no question of jumping the gap, as one slip would send a man down among the spikes and goads surrounding the camp. There was a single road leading to the camp, and they had eschewed it, hoping to maintain the element of surprise. While every eye was on the city, they would take this camp and raze it.

Judah crossed the first of these makeshift bridges and ducked low at the next trench. Still the Romans remained inside their fort. Asher knelt by his side. "Why aren't they coming out?"

Now Judah shared his brother's unease. "They should have sounded trumpets at least." He glanced north, where Yosef's army was meeting fierce resistance as they tried to scale the walls they had helped build. There were torches along the city wall. Asher was gazing in that direction, and he plucked on his brother's arm. "Judah, the Romans!"

"What about them?"

"They're not here! They're in the city!"

Judah looked to where Asher was pointing. In the torchlight, he saw the plumed helms of Roman officers on the city walls.

Zamaris had seen them as well, but there was no altering the plan. Crossing the next ditch, the centurion shouted, "Atlas, get those gates open!"

The plan had been to fall on the Roman horses as they spilled out of the camp. But that wasn't happening, so the giant put his mountainous shoulder to the swinging Roman gate and heaved it wide – unnervingly, the gate was unbarred.

Breaching the gates, the men of Zamaris' century saw for themselves that their intelligence had been wrong. The structure was empty. This wasn't the Roman camp, merely a large stable for cavalry. With the cavalry away, the fort was left unmanned. There was nothing to protect.

The whole lead century entered, then stopped impotently. "Orders, sir?" asked the stocky Pethuel.

Their leader, a legate called Nev, said nothing, instead grinding his teeth in frustration. Zamaris quickly bawled out an order. "Torch it! Torch everything!"

While the command was carried out, Judah and Asher climbed the abandoned walls to see what was happening in Sepphoris. Yosef's army was drawing off, having been repelled by the single legion within the walls. The jeering Romans mocked this pitiful Judean attempt to take back the traitorous city.

"They'll see the fire," observed Asher neutrally.

"We should wait for them," laughed Judah bitterly. "What a waste."

Zamaris led his men away, having lost half a dozen to the goads and traps that surrounded the empty fort. They left it burning behind them, a hollow act of pique.

◆　　◇　　◆

PAPHOS, CYPRUS

That same evening, Gaius Gessius Florus had gone to bed secure in the knowledge he had escaped. The former governor of Judea was living in a remote island palace with a massive personal guard. His plan was to wait until the war was over, then slowly reintroduce himself to

Rome. With Nero's mercurial moods, it would be best to arrive after the war spoils reached Rome.

Not that Florus was worried. He was a Roman knight of the Eighteen, he wore a toga and owned a Public Horse. He would be reprimanded, perhaps even forced to pay a fine. But since no one could say how much he had stolen, there was no way for anyone to take back more than a tithe of his fortune. So long as he did not incur Nero's anger, he would survive.

He was a heavy sleeper, and tonight he was aided by the copious amount of wine he'd imbibed. The singer had been good, too, lulling him into a stupor even before his head hit his feather pillow. So when the hand clamped over his mouth, he didn't register it, just tried to roll over. Only when a second hand pinched his nose and he couldn't breathe did his eyes pop open.

Strangers, in his bedchamber? *The Jews! They've found me!*

Beside him, his wife's screams were muffled by another man. And there were more, many more, in the room. Eyes bulging with fear, Florus felt a hot release along his thighs and knew he had shamed himself.

"*Cacat.* He's pissed all over."

"That's the knights, isn't it. No stomach and weak bladders." There was laughter.

"*Tace!*" The man holding Florus released his nose, but kept his other hand clamped over his mouth. "Hush, now. Your guards are dead or ours. Come quietly and we won't harm you."

Florus sucked in air, his eyes closed in relief. A Roman voice! He then felt an inner tremble. *Nero.* He would have to dance for his life. But he had the whole trip to Greece to compose himself, decide what to say. There was still life in it.

Surprisingly, both he and Cleopatra were bound. That was unusual. Marched out to a wagon, he saw his local guards had been over-awed by a detachment of troops from a real Roman legion – the Fifteenth. The Fifteenth? Weren't they fighting in Galilee? He had kept abreast of all the war news, of course.

Perhaps it's Vespasian! That brought a smile. The old, plodding mule of a general would never execute a Roman knight, not just for a little cupidity. Especially one as famously poor as Vespasian. The man raised mules! There was more life in it. He began clinking sesterces in his mind, counting out how much a proconsular general cost.

Florus endured in silence as he and Cleopatra were shipped across the water back to the land he so despised. He expected an interview upon landing, and was surprised to find himself placed in a solid carriage and driven overland instead. "Is Vespasian already in the field?" he asked his guards, but was given no answer.

As the journey grew longer and longer Cleopatra began to babble, and he had to kick her to keep her quiet. He needed his wits about him. They stopped briefly. He couldn't see out of the covered carriage – there were heavy curtains on the windows, leaving them in near darkness within – but he could hear a changing of the guard. After that they rode awhile longer, uncomfortable now with neither food nor water, and one overflowing chamber pot on the carriage floor.

Fear gave way to indignation. *Someone will pay for this. I am a Roman knight, Procurator of Judea and friend of Caesar. I am not some slave to be bound and transported to market!*

Cleopatra was weeping tears of fury when they finally came to a halt. The carriage-door opened and a rough hand laid hold of the scruff of Florus' tunic. Florus was unceremoniously dragged blinking into a marvelously ornate palace. *Odd.* He'd heard Vespasian didn't care about lavish frills.

"Greetings, Gaius Gessius. My dear Cleopatra. How very good to see you again."

Despite the heat, Florus felt his blood turn to snow. The last time he'd heard that voice, a bald woman in sackcloth had been prostrated before him, weeping and begging to save a few wretched Jews. Now he saw the same face painted in Eastern-style make-up, framed by curling black hair. Cleopatra whimpered.

Squaring his shoulders, Florus drew himself to his full height and demanded in a clear voice, "Where is the general?"

"In Syria, preparing to win the war you started. He's sent you to my care."

A frightening statement, but Florus did not back down. "I didn't start this war. You Jews did."

Queen Berenice bowed her head, acknowledging the correction. "Instigated, then. Incited. Do you find it amusing to think that so many Romans and Jews will die to salve your greed?"

"This war was inevitable," asserted Florus with conviction.

Berenice laughed. "I imagine you are correct."

That surprised Florus. "You admit I was only a spark, not the flame. Then you have no cause to be angry with me!"

"Oh, you're not here to answer for the war," answered the queen airily. "You are here to redress a most personal grievance. You insulted me, a queen, the last princess of the House of Herod."

Clutching Florus' arm, Cleopatra said, "What do you mean to do to us?"

Berenice smiled, her bared teeth brighter than the diamonds she wore. "Why, I mean to show you the full range of Judean hospitality. It's the least I can do."

Cleopatra whimpered. Florus had no doubt he would soon be joining her.

♦   ◊   ♦

Dawn saw Yosef's army safely ensconced behind the walls of Garis, the next major city inland from Sepphoris. Disappointed and frustrated, his men pitched their tents and, exhausted, fell to sleep.

All save Asher. He lingered around the general's tent until he was certain Yosef was alone. Then he asked Levi to admit him.

Dressed in a priest's robe, Yosef was relaxing upon a chair, a smile playing on his lips. "Asher ben Matthais, welcome. Some water? It's cold."

"No, thank you. So tell me, general, was your plan a success?"

The question made Yosef frown. "We did not take the city, nor did we hurt the Romans."

"But that wasn't the aim, was it?"

Yosef arched an eyebrow. "No? Pray tell me what the aim was, then."

"To provoke the Romans."

"Provoke the Romans? Why would I do that?"

"To end the bickering, the infighting, the constant squabbling and backbiting." Asher was sounding angrier than he intended. He took a breath. "No one in Galilee was taking the Roman threat seriously. But the moment the Romans start burning their towns, Galilee will unify to repel the invaders."

Yosef's thin smile was back. "That's asking a lot of the Galileans."

"Still, that was your plan."

Yosef was silent for a time. At last he began to laugh. "O, Asher ben Matthais, I'm so glad you decided to come! But you are wasted as a mere soldier! I need you here. There are no other minds." He rose and poured himself some water. "The thing you have to understand about Rome, they like legalities. Vespasian has been waiting for some excuse, some pretext to launch his attack."

"Beth Horon wasn't enough?"

"Beth Horon was far south of here. Until this moment, no Galilean had raised a hand against a Roman. The revolt could have been merely regional, confined to Jerusalem. But now that our army has attacked a Roman camp, the war is fully engaged. The Romans will come." His smile turned downwards, became bitter. "They, at least, can be counted on. A sad state of affairs when one can rely more on the constancy of one's enemies than one's friends. As you once observed, destruction comes from within. If we don't stop fighting amongst ourselves, the Romans won't need to fight at all!" Yosef quaffed his water and patted Asher on the arm. "I must go. There's a great deal to prepare."

Returning to his tent, Asher wondered if it was good to have so clever a general.

XXI

INFORMED THAT FLORUS had been safely delivered, Titus arrived at the main Roman camp to find his father on the move.

"The Judeans have attacked," exclaimed Cerialis, "so we're off!"

Cerialis' excitement was tempered by his role in the coming war. Vespasian had made him liaison to the foreign levies. In effect, Cerialis would be a quaestor, relaying orders to the foreign leaders. It was an honour, but one that removed him from direct command of any troops.

Most staff appointments were political, favours to friends whose sons or grandsons needed military experience. But a few posts required real soldiers. Thankfully Titus was just that, and had his pick of the legions. With Cerialis in charge of the foreigners, that left three other important commands – the other two legions, and the cavalry forces.

The cavalry went to a tribune called Gnaeus Tertullus Placidus. Broad-shouldered, droop-eyed, and bald as an egg, he was called Placidus out of irony. His fiery temper would keep the horsemen in line.

Marcus Ulpius Trajanus, in contrast, was the very model of cool efficiency. The Spanish-born Roman had not been on Vespasian's roster until a letter came from the disgraced general Corbulo, which he shared with his son:

> *To Titus Flavius Sabinus Vespasianus, senator, consular, and general,*
>
> *I congratulate you on your command. There is no man better suited to the siege-warfare that lies ahead of you. I wish you all success.*

To that end, I request a favour, one Military Man to another. Would you consider taking Marcus Ulpius Trajanus for a minor command? He distinguished himself in my service, but is in danger of being thought of as Corbulo's Man, a fate I would not wish on my worst enemy. He's a hungry fellow with something to prove, yet with no desire to usurp command – an ideal junior legate.

Please send my regards to the Judean king Agrippa and his sister, Queen Berenice. You may tell them you have my full confidence for the successful resolution of this war.

Long live Rome!

Gnaeus Domitius Corbulo, privatus

Despite Corbulo's insultingly patronizing tone, backhanded compliments, and intense self-pity (imagine the great general and consular calling himself a private citizen!), Vespasian dutifully summoned young Trajanus for an interview. Five minutes in Trajan's company and Vespasian understood Corbulo's recommendation. Here was the real-life citizen-soldier that was so much a part of the Roman ideal. He excelled both at combat and the more mundane side of war. If his birth had been less, he would have made an excellent clerk. But despite being born in Hispania, he was heir to a properly Roman family, and had married a patrician woman whose ancestors included one of Rome's ancient kings. His only faults, if they could be so called, were that he was not distinguished to look at, and his Spanish-tinged Latin was painful to hear. Recognizing a man who would someday matter to Rome, Vespasian drafted him on the spot to command the Tenth Legion.

The Fifth Legion's commander galled Titus' brother-in-law, as it went to another man with the cognomen Cerialis – Sextus Vettulenus Cerialis. There was no relation between the men; rather, they both came from farming families whose ancestors worshipped Ceres, goddess of growing plants. Sextus was the only legionary legate kept in place by Vespasian. He was well liked by his men and, like Trajan, had learned his craft under Corbulo.

Given his pick, Titus had chosen the Fifteenth. Created by the Divine Augustus to defeat Pompey's son, its history did not sway Titus so much as the little shrine and the bowl of blood, and the gust of wind when he touched the Fifteenth's eagle. Even a dunderhead could see that Fortuna – or Apollo, or Mithras, or all of them together – wanted Titus commanding the Fifteenth. Full of properly-Roman superstition, Titus deferred to the gods.

The bulk of the Fifteenth was already on the march with his father, and Titus rode with Cerialis to catch them up. The three legions were just deploying outside a city called Garis when he arrived. Vespasian had paraded his whole army before the walls, a time-honoured invitation to battle. So far, the Judeans had not stirred.

"They won't fight." From his saddle, Sextus Cerialis spit into the dirt.

"Any word from Placidus?" asked Trajan. With no use for horsemen, Vespasian had sent Placidus ahead to raze the countryside.

"Not since his last," replied Vespasian shortly. Placidus had sent word that he meant to take the great city of Jotapata by surprise. It was too late to do anything but wait for the result.

"I rather hope he fails." Titus was full of a good cheer he had discovered at King Agrippa's court – or rather, in Queen Berenice's company. He rubbed his hands together. "Don't want this war to be too easy!"

Vespasian wheeled about so sharply that Titus thought the old man had been bitten by a snake. "May your tongue shrivel up and wither away inside your mouth! How dare you tempt the gods so!"

Shocked by his father's sudden fury, Titus shrunk back. "*Pater*, I –"

"Not even a battle fought, and you're already riding through the streets wearing laurels! I should tear out your offending tongue by the roots! *Tcha!*" Vespasian turned back to continue his survey of the walls, leaving Titus breathless and the junior legates staring at the sky.

A rider approached with a message for the general. Vespasian took it, broke the seal, and held it to the light. Fifty-seven last November, he was beginning to complain of his eyes. Nor did it help that Latin was written in one unending squiggle of letters, with no markings to show where one word ended and another began.

The instant the general finished deciphering the message, he crumpled it and pointed an accusing finger at Titus. "See! See what divine wrath such statements incur? And so swiftly! As though Mercury was sitting at your shoulder, and darted off to whisper your foolish wish in Mars' ear!"

"What's happened?"

Vespasian pitched the offensive message at his legate-son. Catching it, Titus read:

> *Jotapata is well fortified and brimming with Judean soldiers. I tried to surprise them, but they were ware of me and came out in their numbers. My cavalry fought a creditable engagement, and withdrew having lost only seven men, these having died from Judean slings and arrows. The cowardly enemy prefers fighting at a distance.*
>
> *We are on our way to you. May I suggest we make a*

*full assault on Jotapata? Such resistance should be quashed
as soon as possible.*

– Gnaeus Tertullus Placidus, Tribunus

Titus looked up. "It's not at all bad! Seven men!"

"The butcher's bill isn't the problem!" roared Vespasian. "The rebels have now won an engagement. Placidus has just given the Judeans a reason to celebrate, where they had none before. Pfah!" Vespasian cantered away, leaving Titus genuinely at a loss to understand his father's rage, out of all proportion to the moment.

"Placidus owes you a debt," observed Trajan. "Otherwise all the general's spleen would have been for him alone."

Titus shook his head. "What's the matter? Doesn't he believe we'll win?"

"Ah, that's right. You're just back from the king – you haven't heard."

"Heard what?"

"General Corbulo is dead."

The news rocked Titus back in his saddle. "Corbulo! How?"

"Nero's jealousy finally got the better of him." Grim and downcast, Trajan rode off in the general's wake.

Titus turned to Cerialis, who filled him in. "Nero summoned Corbulo to Greece, with both his brothers. All three were met on the docks by Caesar's chief Praetorian, who ordered them to commit suicide on the spot."

Titus was aghast. "Did Corbulo fight?"

"No. He was the dutiful Roman to the last. He said only one word. Axios."

It took a moment for Titus to appreciate the irony. A Greek word, it meant *He is worthy*. Such acclaim for Nero might once have been genuine. But as Corbulo's last utterance before he took his own life, it was as succinct an exclamation of contempt as could be imagined. If Nero had indeed been worthy of such loyalty, he would not have demanded such an act.

This explained why Trajan was red-eyed and sullen. Corbulo's final act had been to salvage young Trajan's career.

"Your father is understandably jumpy," added Cerialis. "Any mistake on his part and he'll be the next to receive a friendly invitation to Greece."

"Then, brother-in-law, we had best see that if such a summons comes, the army refuses to let him go without them."

The two shared a significant look. Cerialis nodded. A pact was made.

◆　◊　◆

The Judeans did not make a stand at Garis. Instead they retreated in good order to the next city east. Rather than follow, the Romans marched north to the town of Gadara and, despite its new walls, seized it in a single day. This, after a ten mile dawn march from Garis, which they left in flames.

Titus led his men himself, riding at the head of the First Cohort. But it was his Second Cohort that faced the most organized resistance – locals with swords, shields, and the numbers to clog the streets. Women and children were raining missiles and abuse down upon Roman heads.

Legions were made of cohorts, cohorts of centuries. The first centurion of the Second Cohort was Gaius Sacidius Barbarus, the man Titus had met before the shrine of Mithras. Shield low, he led his men in, fighting in the Roman way. Engineers at heart, the Romans had long ago applied their skills to war, using the construction of the human form to best advantage. Muscles weakened and tired, joints did not. So while other armies exhausted themselves wielding long, heavy blades, the Romans used the gladius. Short, straight, and wickedly sharp, it performed best as a stabbing weapon. Stab, twist, pull. Stab, twist, pull. "At them, boys! At the bastards!"

"We're missing the loot!" groused the optio Gnaeus Thorius, second-in-command.

"The other lads'll share," barked centurion Barbarus. "But they're missing the fighting, and that we won't share. *Will we, boys?*" His men answered with a push that staggered the enemy backwards.

Amid the crackle of flame and screams of wounded, Barbarus heard trumpets commanding an orderly withdrawal. "*Cacat!*" He hated leaving fights half-fought.

Thorius grinned as he killed another Judean. "I didn't hear a bugle, did you?"

But a Roman soldier obeyed orders. "Century, prepare to withdraw!" The bugler blew the notes.

One over-eager legionary, Appius Curtus, leapt out of line to press the attack. Barbarus yanked the fool roughly back. "Curtus, you're on report! Alrighty, lads. One big push, then three steps back! Ready. *Push!*"

The Judeans were bashed back, allowing the Romans to retreat three paces. The Judeans charged, and the century's front line pushed again, then another three-step retreat while maintaining the integrity of the shield wall.

Most rioters stopping rushing the line. But one brave soul shrieked his defiance and ran right at Barbarus. The centurion didn't bother with his sword. Stepping out of line, he drove the wicked nails on the sole of his boot into the man's belly.

"Smarts, don't it?" Barbarus withdrew the hobnails from his attacker's flesh. "Better to toe the line, neh?" Kicking the man aside, Barbarus stepped forward and threw his arms wide in an invitation to single combat. No one accepted his challenge. To Judean eyes, this hairy-armed, broad-chested, grinning Roman was like something risen from She'ol, a creature from among the dead.

Barbarus knew his looks were fearsome, and he used it often to frighten foes, which was how he'd earned his third name. The word barbarian originally meant only uncultured foreigner, mocking the way their language sounded – "Bar bar bar." But as Rome had warred with the bar-bar-ians over the centuries, the word had developed a kind of rough respect. Uncultured, certainly, but fierce, raw, and strong. A name this Barbarus carried proudly.

Grinning, Barbarus led his century backwards. Joined by the other half of their maniple (centuries often fought in pairs), the soldiers waited to receive orders.

As his men pulled back, a disgusted Barbarus watched as local Greeks waded eagerly in to finish the slaughter of the Hebrews. *Well*, he thought, *civilians ain't soldiers. But there's no glory in kicking a beaten man.*

Legionary Curtus held a different opinion. "Filthy Jews."

Barbarus frowned. He rather liked the Jews. Good fighters, not at all shy. If Curtus had a personal dislike for them, that was his problem.

XXII

ARBELAS, GALILEE

ROMAN TREATMENT of Gadara was brutal. The males were put to the sword, the females insulted and enslaved, the city razed. Rome didn't lose a single soldier.

Damn! thought Yosef when he heard the news. It was not just the quick fall of the city. Yosef had hoped that by retreating and retreating, he could lure the Romans deep into Galilee and mire them there. But Vespasian was too canny to give chase.

I am not a natural military man. But surely education and cleverness can come to a solution. Something daring, yet sensible. Yosef racked his brain trying to imagine what a great commander would do. He thought of Julius Caesar, of Scipio Aemelianus, of Fabius. It was not lost on him that his examples were Roman, not Hebrew. But the strategies mentioned in the Scriptures were either vague, or relied upon the Lord.

But how do you know if it is the Lord moving you? Back when I lived the hermit's life with Bannus I thought I heard the voice of the Lord. Now I hear too many voices, all of them shouting. Did David have doubts? Did Joshua? Gideon, Samson, Omri, Ahab, Judah Makkabi? They must have. They were men, like me. They must have laid plans. They could not have simply thrown themselves to the winds and trusted the Lord to scatter their foes.

Yosef thought of another military tale steeped in religion. Troy. The most famous military engagement in history. The heroes and the gods of Troy were equally legendary. There was room in both victory and defeat for valour, honour, and fame.

A battle lasted a mere day, if that – Pharsalus had lasted an hour. A siege, on the other hand, was a prolonged affair. A siege was more monumental than a mere battle. A siege was the stuff of legends.

What's more, the siege of Troy lasted ten years. He only had to delay the Romans for a summer, just three short months. Then the Sanhedrin could negotiate a peace and Yosef would be the hero who saved his country.

Blood started racing in his temples and palms. *Yes - a defended siege. Make a stand in a single place and force the Romans to stay there, anchored to the spot, until the campaigning season is done.*

Swelling with excitement, his mind clamped down, telling him he needed to reason through this plan, poke it for flaws. But he did not trust his lesser commanders, all men of Galilee. This was too important an issue to be left to the *'am ha-arez*, these country bumpkins with their rude talk and half-savage ways. Their *emotions*.

"Levi. Bring me Asher ben Matthais."

◆   ◊   ◆

Arriving warily at the general's commandeered palace, Asher was led to a comfortable cushion and asked to partake of the juice of pomegranates. "No wine today," said Yosef, smiling. "I need your head clear. You must play Aristotle to my Socrates."

Asher savoured his drink while Yosef outlined his idea. Halfway through, though, Asher set down his cup, his jaw hanging open in dismay. He had no trouble stepping into the role that Yosef had given him. "Why risk everything on a single city? It means being trapped."

"Trapped with my army is better than free and that army disheartened."

"But your original strategy was sound. Fabian tactics. Sting the Romans and run, harass them, give up land for time."

Yosef shook his head. "They're taking cities too swiftly. Much too swiftly. Besides, it was always my intent to delay the Romans with sieges."

"But with our army on the *outside*, harassing the Romans, cutting off their supplies, whittling away at their numbers."

"That was before we discovered the Romans could breach our walls so easily. But with an army *inside* one of our cities, they would find no easy entrance. And they couldn't leave without us attacking their rear. It won't be our army that's trapped, it will be the Romans! An anchor around their necks, holding them in place."

"You forget, general – anchors are the first to sink."

"Yes, because that's what they were forged to do. Think of Troy."

"Troy fell."

"After ten years!"

"No, after a single summer. The first nine years the Greeks spent ravaging the rest of the country. They only settled on fighting in the final year. And Troy had walls lain by their gods, or so we're told. Maybe Jerusalem could hold out the way the Trojans did. But where are you going to find a properly fortified city in Galilee?"

"Somewhere with heart, strong walls, and lots of resources."

Asher saw that the general was set on this plan. He had a bad feeling about it, but had to admit it might serve. Certainly it was better than a pitched battle, though not near as sound as Fabian tactics.

But if he couldn't dissuade the general, at least he could give good advice. "A city on Lake Genessar. With water to drink and a whole coast to escape to should things turn sour."

"The only options would be Tariachae or Tiberias. I've flogged, imprisoned, and sacked their citizens, and not for love. They've rebelled too often. We can't be fighting a war within our walls and hope to keep the Romans out. No, it must be somewhere else."

A glance at the map provided his answer. Only one city had not rebelled against Yosef, and that same city had won the only victory so far over the enemy. Located in a natural bowl, meaning the Romans could only attack from one side. Best of all, there were rumoured to be caves beneath the city. If the Romans managed to breach the walls, Yosef's army could disappear, only to rise up again like figures from the Roman underworld.

"Yes, there's the place." As Yosef pressed his finger down upon the map, Asher heard the musical sound of confidence returned. "Jotapata."

♦　◊　♦

Judah was stubbornly asleep. Someone was making it hard, but he refused to wake. It had been a long week, retreating from the Roman advance. The whole army was dispirited. They'd come to fight, but their holy priest of a general kept pulling them back and back.

But sooner or later they'd run out of room to run, and then they'd have to fight. With that warm thought in mind, and knowing he'd need his rest, Judah slept.

Or tried to. Someone was pacing beside his head, letting his boots scrape the earth. But Judah slept on. The fool cleared his throat. Still Judah refused to open his eyes. Not even when he heard a sword scrape from its scabbard.

Finally a guilty voice whispered, "Judah. Judah, are you awake?"

"If that's a Roman, kill me and be done. If it's my brother, get lost. I was having a tremendous dream."

"Can't sleep," said Asher.

"I wasn't having that problem." Groaning, Judah sat up and rubbed the sleep from his face. Seeing Asher, his expression hardened.

"What's wrong?"

Asher briefly outlined Yosef's plan. Judah sat impassively. When Asher was done, he said, "You don't approve?"

"I don't know. I just – I don't know." Asher took a lingering breath. "I don't know if my objections are real, or I just don't want to be trapped in another city when the Romans storm it."

Judah was suddenly wide awake. They were to it now. Judah waited, hoping Asher would broach the topic himself. When he didn't, Judah said softly, "Asher, how did you get your wound?"

"Not the way you think." Asher touched his side, three fingers resting on the scar under the tunic. "Everyone believes I got this from a gladius. I let them think that. Much more glamorous than what actually happened." He looked away, holding a breath for several seconds. "You know why I haven't told you about Alexandria?"

"Because it was awful, I imagine."

"It was. But that's not why." Looking up into the night sky, Asher spoke with bitterness. "Shame. I ran away. *I ran away.* Old men, children, women – they fought and died. I ran and lived."

"You were injured."

Asher shook his head. "Not by the Romans. I tried to – it was stupid. There was this girl…"

"Edith." In answer to Asher's shock, Judah shrugged. "You say her name in your sleep."

"I dream of her every single night. I couldn't even save her. She was just a child."

Finally – finally! – Judah could ask the question burning in him for six long months. "What happened?"

And, finally, Asher told him.

◆   ◊   ◆

"It was the eleventh day of Elul, the same month the Romans named after Augustus Caesar. Father's letter arrived around midday. As you can imagine, I was upset. So I left the Delta and headed to my favourite place in the city, the *Panieum*. I mentioned it before. It reminds me a little of the Mount of Olives. It has lots of names – the Hill of Pan, Pan's Finger, Pan's Cock, the Phallacy of Pan, witty titles like that. The city's absolutely flat, you see. There are tall buildings, but they're all palaces built for the Ptolmeys, now owned by Romans. The only public place where you can look down at the city is Pan's Finger.

"The whole hill is man-made, shaped like the crooked finger of Pan, very like the Tower of Babel. A false creation more moving than truth. Crafted by generations of architects and gardeners, it has these trickling streams that merge to create thunderous waterfalls. Perfect rows of flowers. My favourite spot was this one short palm tree, right at a ledge. From there you can see the Moon Gate, the Sun Gate, the Palace, the Akron, and the Lighthouse all at once.

"I didn't know it at the time, but it was in the Akron that the trouble was starting. I remember noticing that the amphitheatre was full of bodies, and I had a vague recollection that the Alexandrians were meeting to discuss sending a deputation to Nero. My neighbours planned to attend. But I was too absorbed in my own troubles to bother.

"Father's letter. It was the first time he even hinted I should come back. Until then, I didn't think he wanted me to come back, ever. Which was fine with me – really! At that moment I couldn't imagine leaving. I know, but I really couldn't. Alexandria had been this marvelous, beautiful, intellectual beacon – my own Lighthouse.

"This is important, Judah. You have to understand why I wanted to stay. Everyone calls the Lighthouse a Wonder of the World, but the wonder of *my* world was just below my little palm tree. Across from the massive mausoleum to Alexander there's a huge temple faced in marble with statues of the nine Muses all around it. I know we're not supposed to worship graven images, but I tell you, Judah, these were *beautiful*. Not as women. As ideal depictions of humanity's best endeavors. I loved them all, but my favourites were Calliope, Clio, and Melpemone – Epic Poetry, History, and Tragedy. They call the temple the Museaeum. Inside it rests the fabled Library of Alexandria, with more texts than any other library in the world. Contrary to legend, only a fraction was lost during the fire caused by Caesar's ships, and Mark Antony repaired any deficiency by looting all the texts from Pergamum's library as a gift for Cleopatra. There are endless shelves holding scrolls and book-buckets, collecting nearly a thousand years of man's ideas, hopes, and dreams.

"You can't imagine how happy I was inside those walls. Two years spent wandering through plays and poems, histories and legal speeches. Homer and Hesiod, Plato and Zeno, Cicero and Caesar. I think I frightened the librarians. With my size and the scars on my hands, I think they were terrified I'd ruin the scrolls. They never knew what to think of me.

"But I didn't care. I was comfortable in there, and in the city at large. Alexandria owns a massive Hebrew population. The old joke that there are more Jews in Alexandria than Jerusalem has more than a grain of truth. When Alexander arrived, the Jews were the only ones to welcome him, and he rewarded them with rights that have lasted to modern times. He gave them the Delta, a full quarter of the city, and they've flourished there. It was Alexandrian Jews that first translated the Scriptures into Greek, giving the word of the Lord to the gentiles.

"Cosmopolitan, refined, welcoming, in love with learning and the arts, the most beautiful city in the world. Alexandria felt like home to me.

"Like I said, our people had been prosperous – too prosperous, as far as the Greeks and Aegyptians were concerned. That's what the meeting in the theatre was about. The Aegyptians and Greeks who saw themselves as the true Alexandrians wanted to ask Nero to purge the Delta of Jews. For some reason, they didn't expect their Jewish neighbours to attend the meeting. There was shouting and name-calling, then shoving and fighting. One of my neighbours was captured – a goldsmith called Bilhan. Edith's father. He and a few others were going to be executed, but more Jews rushed in to save them. That's when the governor, Tiberius Julius, told the Jews to go home. When they refused, he unleashed the Fifteenth on them.

"I knew none of this. I was sitting under my favourite tree, looking down on the Museaeum and the Delta, thinking about father's letter. I couldn't believe that the war was actually upon us. People have talked about war so long, and it never came. Why now?

"I sat in the palm tree's shade feeling sorry for myself all the way until sunset, when suddenly I felt tears in my eyes. At the same moment I realized that the light wasn't coming off the water anymore. The sun had set, but there was a growing, flickering light below. A fire. My tears weren't from grief, but from smoke on the wind.

"It was like waking from a dream – or falling into a nightmare. The moment I saw the flames, it was as if all my senses came alive. I smelled the smoke and heard the shouts. Men's voices at first, then women and children's too. I don't know how I hadn't heard them before.

"I'm ashamed to say my first thought wasn't for the Delta or the Jews, but the Museaeum. It was safe, untouched. I was relieved. Relieved! Do you believe it? I'm such...

"Sorry. I'm sorry. I just... Right. So, after making sure the Museaeum was safe, I *finally* looked to see where the fire was. At first it looked as though the smoke was coming from the Sema. But then the wind shifted, and I could clearly tell it was the Delta that was burning.

"Being on Pan's Finger saved my life, no question. But I could see others were running towards the fire. Other Jews, I mean. From where I was I watched them being cut down. Not just by Romans, by other Alexandrians. It was like some horrible, bloody festival, with the crowds cheering as the Romans slaughtered our people.

"I remember thinking, *Father gets his wish. I'm leaving Alexandria.* I hunched my shoulders and ran down to the bottom of the Panieum. I had a wild idea of going to help, but at that moment I couldn't see the point. I should have anyway. I know that now. I should have gone in and fought and died with everyone else. Father accused me of cowardice in the letter, and he was right. Better to die once as a fool than die a thousand times as a coward.

"But I didn't fight. I ran. I turned south down Royal Avenue, which was almost deserted. No one gave me a glance. Two blocks down I was safe from the mob and just beginning to relax when I heard a cry behind me. I looked back and saw four men dragging a girl. Edith. She was a sweet little thing, maybe eleven or twelve. I'd talked with her and her brother on the street, had dinner in her father's house a dozen times. A little shy, but she always had a happy smile for me.

"Now her face was like some grotesque Tragedy mask. The men dragged her down Royal Avenue until they were out of the light. My mind kept screaming *Run*, but it was like my feet had grown roots. I watched them throw Edith against a wall. Two Alexandrians pinned her arms above her head and another tore her shift open. For a second her body was lit by a passing torch up the street. There was nothing sensual about her. She wasn't even a woman yet.

"Before I knew what I was doing I was retracing my steps. All four men had their backs to me. Two were definitely Greek. The tallest was certainly Aegyptian. The fourth was of middle height and could have been anything. He and one of the Greeks held Edith's arms while the other Greek lifted his tunic and started thrusting at her. The Aegyptian watched, like an overseer.

"Her screams covered the sound of my steps. All those years of you defending me must've taught me something. I used my left forearm to hit one Greek in the nose, and my right elbow jammed the rapist face-first into the stone wall above the Edith's head. It felt good – I felt like I was you. I know. Pathetic, right? It was like I could hear you in my head shouting, '*Keep moving!*' I kneed the third man in the gut, turned fast to face the Aegyptian – and I stopped. I recognized him! His name was Panhsj, a jeweler who did a lot of business with Edith's father. I couldn't believe it! A man who had dined in Bilhan's home, violating his daughter!

"Stopping almost cost me my life. Panhsj lifted his arms and I saw a quick flash of light off his golden rings – and his dagger. I jumped to the side and collided with Edith, who was straining to get free. I hadn't kneed the one man hard enough, he was still holding on to her, and now his other hand tried to grab my hair. I ducked, thinking Panhsj's knife was after me. But then I heard Edith cry out and saw that Panhsj had her about the waist, his knife at her throat.

"I reached out a hand and said something stupid like, 'Don't.'

"He smiled at me. I can hear his voice now. 'You want her, Jew? Then have her and welcome.' He pulled the knife away and shoved her into my arms.

"I heard Edith gasp in relief as I caught her. There was this flicker of gratitude on her face. But it turned to confusion as she tried to draw breath and couldn't. Something was hot against me and I smelled copper in the air. Her hands went up to touch her throat and she held her finger-tips up between us. There was blood on them.

"She fell against me, and I watched the life pour out of her. Her eyes held so much – terror, regret, a protest of unfairness. She hardly had a chance to live.

"I should have done it better. You'd've done it better, I know. They'd all be dead and she'd be alive. I'm not a warrior. Father was right – what use is poetry in the real world? O, but I had to play at bravery! If I hadn't gotten involved they would have had their way with her and let her live, I think. Maybe. All I know is that she died looking at me.

"I remember what happened next like it wasn't real. I know hands were grabbing me. One man was still unconscious, but the other three were in a murdering mood. Then I heard a young voice say, 'You idiot! They would have let us live!' He wasn't speaking Koine, but Aramaic. I knew the voice even before I saw his face. It was Edith's brother. Her own brother! To spare their lives, he had offered up his sister!

"That's when I started fighting back. I kicked and struggled, but they threw me sideways into the wall. Edith's brother – I've forgotten his name. Isn't that strange? He was weeping, punching and kicking me. I guess that he thought if he helped kill me they might still let him live.

"Then they had me up against the wall. Someone's hands started pulling at my tunic and suddenly their intent was clear. I'd ruined their fun, and now they were going to take it however they could. I fought harder, which only invited more punishment. I remember shouting something like, 'Kill me and be done!'

"Suddenly, over my shoulder, I heard a loud bark of Latin. 'Hey! Stop that right now! Either kill him or let him be. No funny stuff!'

"Everything stopped and I was able to turn my head enough to see several Roman legionaries with torches. The man in front was clearly a centurion – his sword was on his left hip and the horsehair crest on his helmet was sideways.

"I heard Panhsj say, 'Who are you to command us?'

"The Roman's answer was impressive. 'Gaius Sacidius Barbarus, Centurion, First Century of the Second Cohort of the Fifteenth Apollonares! Hostilities are over. Leave off.'

"Panhsj wasn't about to let me go. 'You have no authority over us, Roman! We are not in the legions!'

"I saw the centurion grin. 'Absolutely true, legal-wise. But ain't in court, are we?' He patted the hilt of his sword. 'This gives me all the authority I need here. Now, the girl was one thing. But we was watching from up the road, and that man fought well enough to deserve a man's death. So be done with him and get back to your business.' The other Roman soldiers muttered their agreement – all but one, who looked rather eager for me to die.

"Panhsj snarled, 'Very well!' He turned and raised his dagger high to finish me off.

"After the beating they had just given me, they must have thought I was finished. But I've had worse. I shook off the Greek and Edith's brother and grabbed Panhsj's right forearm with both my hands. Instead of stopping the blow, I twisted sideways and guided the down-thrust of the blade right into Panhsj's own belly. I said something, but I don't remember what. I do remember working the blade, really twisting it in there.

"The Romans were all laughing as Panhsj fell screaming to the ground. Then Barbarus yelled, 'Behind you, boy!' Without that warning, I'd be dead. Just as I turned, Edith's brother drove his little knife into my side. I hit him and pulled out the knife. The Romans shouted at me to finish him off, but I couldn't bring myself to do it. He was pathetic, lying there. Kept blubbering about Edith. He was just a kid, and he'd tried to save her in the only way he thought he could. Now she was dead, and he blamed me. Maybe he was right. I don't know.

"The centurion came close to me, so close that I thought he was going to kill me. Instead he said, 'You'd best run now, lad.'

"Covered in Edith's blood and losing my own, I sprinted for the south gate. I heard one of the Romans say, 'Let me put a spear in his back!' But Barbarus said no. 'Belay that, Curtus. He's earned his life. I told you the fellow had fight in him. Now pay up, you lot!' They'd obviously been wagering on me.

"I have no idea what happened to Edith's brother. I just ran. Ignoring the pain in my side, I skirted the swampy port along the Nilus. I hoped the Nile water would wash my wound clean. I worked my way around to the northeast road heading for Judea, trying not to look back. But it seemed like the screams and smells traveled with me.

"I've heard that fifty thousand Jews died that night, some on Roman swords, some at the hands of their fellow Alexandrians. I remember wondering at the time if I was the only Jew to get away. And my escape seemed short-lived. At dawn the next day I heard a Roman legion marching up the road behind me. I was too exhausted to run or hide, so I simply stood by the side of the road and waited. But the Romans didn't spare me a glance. Must've thought I wasn't worth bothering over. And they were right."

♦   ◊   ♦

"It wasn't too far to Judea," explained Asher, "but with my wound I barely made a half-dozen miles in a day. Worse, the Aegyptians on the Judean border had begun skirmishing with their neighbours. Another shame of mine – whenever I was challenged, I pretended to be Greek.

I used my best Attic dialect to convince everyone I was Athens-born. Everything after that becomes a haze. I was badly sunburned, unable to feel my arms. Parched, delirious – I had visions. I remember one fevered dream where I was standing in a bowl filled with screaming people. Edith was with me, covered in her own blood. She handed me a scroll, but when I tried to read it the words were nonsense. 'It is not time,' she said. It was so clear..." Asher's voice trailed off.

Though he'd made hushed grunts from time to time, Judah had refrained from actually speaking until Asher was finished. Now he said, "That's hard. You owe your life to a Roman who helped kill every other Jew in Alexandria."

Asher nodded.

"Worse, he was saving you from another Jew."

Again, Asher nodded.

"You feel pity for the boy, and I guess you should. But reserve a little of that pity for yourself. You did what you could. You were right to run."

Asher ground his teeth together. "I shouldn't have lived, when so many..!"

Judah slapped his hands together. "How can someone so smart be so stupid! Asher, you had it right! There's no sense in fighting a battle that can't be won. I don't care what your beloved poets say, dying a glorious death is over-rated. It's still dying!"

"You were willing to die at Beth-Horon," protested Asher.

"But we *won*. As unlikely as it was, we won! I didn't wade in knowing it was hopeless! Just like I didn't come out to Galilee to throw myself on a pyre. I don't plan to go down in a blaze of glory. I came to fight Rome. If my death means a poke in the eye to Nero Caesar, then I'm satisfied. Just like you. When you saw you could do some good, you didn't think – you fought! I'm sorry it didn't work out, but the odds were against you. That's life, right? Life is messy, war is messier. You said I would've done it better, but I don't see how. You did exactly right, and I'm proud of you. Proud!" Judah slapped his brother on the side of his head. "I'm biased, of course. I could care less about Alexandrian Jews, as long as I've got my idiot brother back."

Asher was silent for a time. Then he said, "I'm still terrified, Judah."

"Of what? That you won't be able to fight the Fifteenth because one Roman saved your life on a bet?"

"No. Facing *him* might be a problem, but the Fifteenth slaughtered everyone I knew for two years. I don't owe them a thing."

"Then what are you worried about?"

"What if the time comes to face the Romans and I run again? Or what if I do the wrong thing and get someone else killed – like you?"

"Won't happen. If I die, it'll be my own fault. As for running, you won't." Judah grinned. "Not that I'd let you. But I know you, Asher. As much as we're different, we're chiseled from the same stone. You'll see. Given the chance, you'll stand and fight. Damn, you're a better soldier than I am. Everyone says so."

Asher waved that off. "I can follow orders in training. You'll make sure I won't run?"

"When we've completely lost, when there's no chance of doing any good, *then* I'll let you run. In fact, you can follow me, because I'll be the first to kick my heels." He thought of Deborah. "Like I said, I don't plan to die here."

"And if the Romans are going to take us prisoner?"

"Then we can do each other one last brotherly service. I'll have my sword tip for you, if you'll have yours for me."

"Done," agreed Asher. They shook hands to seal the pact.

A suicide pact.

XXIII

"GENERAL, I SWEAR by Mars, Bellona, and Jupiter himself, these Judeans have me tearing out what little hair I have left!"

The *praefectus fabrum* was the army's chief engineer and supplier. Given the task of moving the army to their next target, a city called Nazareth, he was making his report to Vespasian and the senior legates from each legion.

"Five whole days! Five! To make a proper road of, what, five miles? Six? No wonder these Judeans lock themselves in their cities! Their roads are so savage that no one can leave without first growing wings!"

"Let's hope they do not grow wings," said Vespasian. "But I'll feel better knowing that if they do, we'll be able to chase them down a properly-made road. Tomorrow?"

"By tomorrow, general, you can parade elephants without fear."

"Horses will do." Having amassed such an excellent cavalry, Vespasian was loath to lose it. "Dismissed."

Saluting, the *praefectus fabrum* stalked from the tent muttering curses upon every Hebrew back to the first, whoever he had been. Titus, Trajan, and the two Cerialii waited until the man was out of earshot, then laughed uproariously.

Placidus was scowling. "I don't see what's so bloody amusing about delays." He was still smarting – less from his defeat than the monumental tongue-lashing he had received upon his return.

"Nor do I, Gnaeus Tertullus," agreed Vespasian. "Gentlemen, if you wish to enjoy theatre, I suggest you return to Rome and allow real soldiers to take your place."

The legates quickly overcame their amusement. Five days since the news about Corbulo, Vespasian had still not mended his temper.

Returning to business, they were discussing forage and water supplies when they heard a stamp of feet outside. One of Vespasian's guards poked his head into the tent. "General, Decurion Ebutius wants to see you. Says it's urgent."

Vespasian rose from his chair – no couches for marching-camps. "Send him in."

Ebutius entered and saluted smartly. Like all decurions, he smelled of horses. "General! My decury has caught a deserter from Jotapata who claims he has information for your ears alone."

"By all means, show him in." When the man entered, Vespasian employed his rather rustic Koine, the Greek patios known to every civilized man. "Well, fellow? Out with it. My time is valuable."

The tent's lamps showed a Greek with the air of a man making a bargain. "I have information that may be of use to you. In return, I wish my freedom, and the assurance of my lands after the war."

"Both depend on the strength of your information. If I deem it useful, I'll give you those things and more."

The Greek deserter considered, then nodded. "The commander of Galilee has arrived. His army follows. He means to make a prolonged stand at Jotapata."

Vespasian's engraved frown softened. "If you've told me the truth, you will have your freedom, your lands, and the goodwill of Rome." He nodded dismissal, then raised his hand. "Wait. This commander – what's his name?"

The deserter blinked. "Yosef."

Vespasian had difficulty with Hebrew names, and had taken to creating Latin equivalencies. "Josephus. And his father's name?"

"Matityahu. He is of noble blood, a priest of the Sanhedrin. His father is the Amarkalin."

"Very well. Ebutius, this fellow is to be well-handled." As the deserter was escorted out, Vespasian spoke to his sentry. "Summon Tribune Nicanor from Agrippa's legion." He then crossed to the table that bore his maps and began poring over them. "Placidus, do you feel in need of a bit of vengeance?"

The bald tribune bolted upright. "I do indeed, sir!"

"Good. Take a thousand horsemen – Roman horse, not auxiliaries – and ring Jotapata round. Use Ebutius as your lead decurion, he's earned it. This Josephus has made a colossal blunder. We must ensure he cannot correct it. No escape. Is that clear, Gnaeus Turtullus?"

"Perfectly clear, general."

Vespasian allowed himself a slight smile. "Gentlemen, we knew it would be a summer spent in siege warfare. But to put all his forces into a single place – well, that's the mistake of an amateur. He's placed himself in a prison. However, we must assume the leaders in Jerusalem would not appoint a fool to such a post. Therefore we must capitalize on his mistake and take Jotapata quickly." He looked at Cerialis. "What are you grinning about?"

Cerialis shook his head. "I just don't want to be the one who tells the engineers we're going to Jotapata now."

Everyone laughed, and Vespasian made an appeal skyward. "I'm surrounded by imbeciles." The tent flap opened. "Ah! Here is a serious man can aid us. Nicanor, Titus tells me you're from a priestly family. The Galilean general is a priest of Jerusalem. His name is Josephus, son of—damn, what was it?"

"Matityahu," supplied Trajan.

"Yes. Do you know him?"

Nicanor gave a start of surprise. "Yosef? I know him well! We studied together at the Temple."

Vespasian smiled at the others. "Sometimes it's better to be lucky than good. He's young, then?"

"Perhaps thirty years. No more."

"Excellent!" Vespasian rubbed his hands together. "What kind of man is he?"

Nicanor considered. "There is no lion or eagle in him, but a great deal of fox. Some wolf. Perhaps some cat."

"No rabbit?" asked Placidus with a dark grin.

"None. He is a man of great intelligence and cunning. Maybe even daring. Certainly he admires daring. A few years ago he wrote a book recounting the life of the Judean hero Judah Makkabi. His teacher is a favourite of the High Priest Ananus."

"If we need to treat with him," said Vespasian, "would you be willing to speak on our behalf?"

Nicanor bowed. "Of course, general."

"Excellent. You are now posted to my personal staff. Fetch your kit and report back here for billeting." Vespasian paused. "He wrote a book, you say?"

"Yes, general."

"Find me a copy."

Nicanor saluted and departed. Vespasian turned to his Roman commanders, brows aloft. "Well?"

"A priest," said Trajan happily.

"A *noble* priest," corrected Sextus Cerialis.

"Favoured by the High Priest of Jerusalem," said Cerialis Rufus.

Vespasian was contemplative. "Gentlemen, I think we must capture this Josephus. Whatever else happens at Jotapata, I want him taken alive. No martyrdom, you understand. I want the living man. For the rest…" he pressed his thumb down on the map marked Jotapata.

The legates and tribunes shared a celebratory drink, then filed out. Vespasian yawned, scrubbed his palms over his face, and shifted his gouty foot. It was only then that he noticed his son lingering. "What?"

Titus bowed his head. "General, I have prayed at the legions' shrines, begging the pardon of Mars, Bellona, Hercules Invictus, and Jupiter Stator. I sacrificed to them and have expiated my sin. It should no longer weigh on you."

Vespasian actually smiled. "Clearly your penitence has been sufficient. The gods of war have led the Judeans to make a grave error. It is now up to us to take the best advantage of it. Well done, *mi filius*."

Titus sighed in relief. "O, thank the gods! I wish you had told me about Corbulo. I could have kept a sensible tongue in my head." He paused. "The men aren't pleased, you know. All our legions fought under Corbulo at one time or other. They're angry and sore about it, naturally. But *you* were never under him. It's not as though you were friends, or even comrades in arms. Why does his passing haunt you?"

"Isn't the death of a good man cause enough to mourn?" asked Vespasian rhetorically. Then he relented. "You are correct, son. There is more to it. Gnaeus Domitius and I are senators and generals in service to Rome. That creates a kinship as close as it is exclusive. There are a handful of men in all Rome who might command a campaign as significant as this. Corbulo. Galba. Paulinus. Me. That is all. In time, Trajan may turn into something. I hear good things of young Agricola from Gaul."

"I will be one of those men," said Titus.

"Then you should mourn as well, son. I'm reminded of the race of the October Horse, but transformed into some hideous farce. If Rome continues to sacrifice its best and brightest to serve the egos of smaller men – even if those smaller men be called Caesar – Rome shall cease to exist."

"Rome is eternal," objected Titus.

"The physical place, perhaps. But the nation we have built, from Romulus to Brutus to the Caesars – that is only as lasting as pleases the gods. They love excellence, the gods. When we cease to excel, we'll cease to please the gods, and they will look elsewhere. Then we will be in such straits as the Judeans find themselves. They have put all their faith in their One God. If He abandons them, they will cease to be."

"I never knew you espoused religion, father."

Vespasian poured himself a cup of wine, then gazed at it, considering. Drinking often inflamed his gout. "I don't. A man makes his fate." Quaffing off his drink at one pull, he set it aside. "But only a fool ignores the gods."

◆   ◊   ◆

Judah and Asher marched with Zamaris and the rest of their century into Jotapata. To look at, the city itself was unimpressive – a high wall encompassing thirteen acres. It was the geography that made their jaws drop.

The city stood upon an isolated hill in the center of a bowl, an island surrounded by lush and verdant flowers and scrubby green grass. Prickly green trees dotted the brown earth of the bowl, and goats capered carelessly up and down the slopes where men would be fools to go. The only entrance to the bowl from the north, the other sides all too high for soldiers to pass and too far away from the city for the Romans to use their siege engines.

Marching closer to the city, Judah saw that the north-facing wall was made casemate. A dozen parallel walls running north and south stood like open gates, all connected by a single solid wall behind. The effect was that of giant crooked teeth, snarling. *Like a desert dog.*

Sadly, the casemate design didn't extend around the whole city. Still, the fortifications did not look at all bad. There was an older wall and a newer pair of towers, one huge, one smaller. The casemate wall was the newest, barely sixty years old, and its smooth sides extended down the plain to the south of the city to encompass some of the plain.

The march wasn't very orderly – certainly no smart Roman stamp and crash – and there was a bottleneck at the large gate in the center of the north wall. As they waited, Judah reached out and brushed the stones with his fingertips, feeling the joins. "Good walls. No mortar, properly shaped. Not coming down anytime soon."

Asher nodded. "Whoever raised them made them strong. This might not be so bad an idea."

Their welcome went further to allay Asher's fears. The citizens cheered them as they entered, throwing their caps into the air and blowing great horns of joy and welcome. Asher couldn't help noting the young women admiring both him and his brother. He smiled and kept himself from waving back – something the rest of the army didn't bother to do.

Judah had less eye for the people than the city itself. Asher had survived Alexandria partly because he knew the place. Judah was determined to learn every inch of this city, know it better than the natives. Once they found their billet and stowed their kit, Judah dragged Asher by the arm. "Come on. We're going exploring."

They were gone several hours, milling through the streets and alleys, under awnings dyed with simple stripes of colour. They followed children, always the best at finding the secret paths and the shortest routes. There seemed no rhyme or reason to the layout of the streets, but there were three major plazas that all streets fed into. All centered on enormous wells, and one also held a dais for speakers.

This was where Yosef was making his headquarters, for they saw the impressive form of Levi standing with his arms folded, his sword loosened in its scabbard. Asher and Judah greeted him warmly, and they passed a few minutes with observations of the city.

"It's a fine place," said Levi, his eyes never straying from the crowd. "But for one thing. There's no water."

Judah glanced over to the large central well. "There seems to be plenty."

"Those are cisterns. They collect rainwater. There's no spring, no deep well. If we run out of what the cisterns contain, we'll be drinking air and dust."

"That's almost poetic," said Asher.

"Perhaps I should embark on another career."

"You should have thought of that yesterday," laughed Judah.

The twins said their farewells and continued exploring. It was after sunset when they found their way back to their billet, which was in the yard of some dyer – possibly the same man who had made the colours for the awnings all over the city. There were large copper vats that smelled of cat urine.

Hardly had they entered the yard when Gareb called out to them. "You have a visitor." The lean face proclaimed that whoever it was, he wasn't welcome.

"Who?"

"Big fellow. City lad, like you. A complete arse. Seems angry."

No, it can't be. What would he be...

Judah felt a hand clamp down on the back of his neck. "Where is she!"

Twisting, Judah flung one arm up to break the hold, shoving the bigger man back. It was like shoving a wall. "Get off! What on Earth are you doing here?"

Phannius ben Samuel snarled and raised a fist, but Asher threw himself on his bicep. Gareb and Peuthel grabbed his other side while Philip and Netir drew swords. Across the yard Atlas climbed to his feet, frowning.

It was a heartening moment. They might not have warmed to Judah and Asher to start, but when threatened, their tentmates came to the twins' aid.

Phannius didn't care about Judah's companions, nor Asher, nor even the threat of swords all around. He strained to be free, veins bulging in his neck as he shouted, "Where is she! Where is she!?!"

A frisson of panic raced through Judah. "What?"

"Deborah! You fool, you've not only disgraced her, you've risked her life! You call that love? I'll murder you!"

"What are you talking about? Where is she?"

"That's what I'm asking you, lecher! Where is she?"

Straining against Phannius' bicep, Asher said, "She didn't come with us! She's not here!"

It took several minutes for Phannius to calm down enough to realize Asher was speaking the truth. Judah's insistent demands to know what had happened helped to convince him.

"She left a month ago. Right after getting a letter from you," he added accusingly. "She didn't show anyone the letter, so mother – we all assumed you'd told her to come to you."

"Never. I just told her about training, and – well, that I missed her." Judah felt numb. Was Deborah out there somewhere? Had she gone to the training camp to look for him? Where could she be? He looked to Phannius, ashen-faced. "We have to find her."

"You're not going anywhere," said Zamaris, part of the crowd that had gathered for this scene. In the army, entertainment was where you found it. "You've mustered up. We need you – even a cock-sure brawler like yourself, hero. Besides, the general has closed the gates. The Romans will know soon enough where we are, and they'll be all over us like flies on shit."

Judah argued, Phannius protested that *he* hadn't joined any army, Asher tried to calm them both down while the rest of the century looked on in amusement. The end result was never in doubt. The gates had closed, the fortifications had begun. No one was leaving, least of all three masons who were good in a fight.

"I don't give a fat man's fart for your personal problems, boys. Like it or not, we've all come to Jotapata to stay until the Romans are beaten back, or the walls are taken. So best make sure they're not taken, eh? Now, get to work!"

Judah was ready to go over the walls that night, but Zamaris had him watched. Phannius too. Strong arms like those couldn't go to waste. They were watched the next night as well. On the third night they thought to try escaping.

But that was the day the Romans arrived.

PART THREE
THE SIEGE

XXIV

"MITHRAS, give us some real fighting," muttered centurion Barbarus as his cohort crested the rise. "Not more—" he saw their destination and sighed, "—walls."

"Balls," echoed his optio Thorius. "Balls balls *balls!*"

Riding just ahead of them was the *tribunus augusticlavus* – a stiff-rumped young knight who did not know his military arse from his military elbow. Hearing the optio's mild oath, he turned in his saddle to issue a rebuke. Barbarus beat him to it. "Enough of that cant!"

Thwarted, the tribune instead issued the order to turn. Barbarus dutifully wheeled his cohort about to face the walls of Jotapata. Unlike Garis or Gadara, these casemate walls were not some slap-dash affair they could be over before lunch. This would take effort.

The tribune was looking at the walls, too, and this caused him to neglect his duties. "We're in position, *tribunus,*" prompted Barbarus.

"What? Oh, very well. Halt!"

Barbarus halted his men and, without waiting for the order, had the column turn to create a double line. Here they would stand, inviting the enemy to come out from behind their walls and engage. Not that they would.

"Line's in order, sir," reported Gnaeus Thorius.

Barbarus grunted acknowledgement as he studied the city with a practiced eye. The Jotapatans had ringed themselves with a wall five times the height of a man, plastered over with clay and mortar to remove handholds. The city had two properly spaced towers, and bristled with men.

Worse, word had filtered down that the hill was not solid, but a warren of caves and cisterns. Barbarus had hoped this meant there was a secret entrance. But because these caves were used to gather water, none opened to the bottom of the hill. So once the walls were breached, the Romans would have to hunt through every one of those caves to smoke the defenders out.

All told, Jotapata looked half a nightmare. Barbarus expressed his feelings in a single word. "*Cacat.*"

His tribune turned. "What's that, centurion?"

"I coughed, *tribunus.*"

The tribune eyed him, then jerked his head at the fortified city. "What do you think of her?"

"I think she's a right bitch." Barbarus spoke loudly for the benefit of his men. "But we're the Fifteenth Apollinaris! No bitch can keep us out. In the end we'll get into her, and when we do, we'll fuck those *cunni* all the harder for making us wait. Sir," he added.

The men cheered and the prudish tribune turned away. Another sign of his unsoldierly nature. Real commanders appreciated salty talk. *Well, he did ask for my opinion!*

The cheer brought the Fifteenth's new commander over. "Did your men see something?"

"No, Titus Flavius." The tribune turned and pointed at Barbarus. "He spoke his vulgar mind and broke the men's order."

Titus frowned. It was a bad officer that blamed the men under his command. "Barbarus, isn't it? What was it you said?"

Barbarus did not clean it up, repeating his statement verbatim. Titus nodded thoughtfully. "I don't doubt you'll fuck them raw, centurion. After all, the men of the Fifteenth are the biggest *mentulae* in the world."

The legion roared with approval, the tribune flushed, and Titus departed with a happy wave.

"Now that's a proper commander," whispered legionary Curtus, just loud enough for the humiliated tribune to hear.

That was a step too far. "Then we should be proper soldiers for him," snarled Barbarus. "So *tace*! Shut your mouth, and pray they come out to fight."

"They won't," said Curtus. "Filthy Jews."

"*Tace, inepte!*"

◆　　◊　　◆

Yosef stood upon the larger of the two towers and watched the Roman advance. *This is it. The great moment. A moment for historians and poets. This will dwarf any other siege in modern times. I just need to keep my people's spirits up and we will survive this. We must survive this. Not just for the war. For my career. I've gambled everything on one throw. Just like the great Julius Caesar. Well, the dice are in the air. Let them fall where they may!*

Beside him was the city ethnarch, a wizened fellow called Nechum. "So many!"

"Excellent news!" answered Yosef. "If they're here, they can't be out wreaking havoc upon Galilee. All we have to do is hold out through the summer months, then the Romans will withdraw."

"All we have to..?" Nechum repeated hollowly.

Nechum's twenty year-old son Chalafta pointed to the mouth of the bowl. "General Yosef, what's that they're doing?"

"Building a camp, I expect." Already the engineers had men digging trenches and felling trees. *I should have knocked down all the trees myself,* thought Yosef. *My first mistake.*

Chalafta pointed. "And those just coming up the road?"

The boy had excellent eyes. Yosef had to squint hard to see what he was pointing at. "Siege engines, I think."

"Merciful heavens!" cried old Nechum. "We're doomed."

"Nonsense," said Yosef cheerily. "Our walls are solid, our men eager and determined. We have food enough to feed every man in our army and theirs. Our water supplies are adequate, if rationed." He patted the august Jotapatan on the shoulder. "Truly, things could not be better!"

The old man looked as though he believed the opposite. "How long must we endure?"

However long the Romans remain, thought Yosef. But the fellow needed assurances. He chose not a date, but rather a number his fellow Hebrews viewed as lucky. "Seven times seven. Forty-nine days. On the fiftieth day, the Romans will end the siege. They can't not!"

Chalafta smiled. "I'm so proud you came here, general! That you chose Jotapata. We all are!"

Chalafta's father did not look so certain.

◆   ◊   ◆

At another part of the wall, Judah's band of nine were standing together – Phannius had unofficially joined their mess.

"Lots of them," said Pethuel.

"Too many to count," said Philip.

"Fifty or sixty thousand," said Asher.

Phannius turned. "How did you do that?"

"Do what?"

"Count them so fast."

"Don't count the men, count the standards. Though isn't it interesting how the men alternate? Eight in a line, ten lines. Then ten in a line, eight lines."

Phannius made a disgusted noise, but Judah squinted. "Show me what you see."

Asher waved his hand in a chopping motion. "There's a full cohort, four-hundred eighty men in all. Ten of those make a legion. But inside the cohort are six groups of eighty. They each have their own standard." Suddenly Asher froze.

"What is it?"

Asher pointed. "That banner – that's the eagle of the Fifteenth."

Judah made a show of memorizing the banner. "I'll help you mete out a little retribution."

Eyes upon the eagle, Asher did not reply.

◆　　◊　　◆

After a full day standing before Jotapata with his men, Vespasian grunted. "That's enough. Order the men back to camp."

The front cohorts withdrawing first, the Roman army marched smartly back to where their camp had sprung up through the daylight hours like the army of the dragon's teeth. This was not a marching camp, but a true fortification, complete with walls three times as tall as any man, ditches, moats, traps, and goads. There was space within for all three Roman legions. Vespasian placed his auxiliaries in a similar camp further north, blocking the exit to the bowl.

No escape.

◆　　◊　　◆

"Maybe she went to our cousin's house," said Phannius.

Judah was hunched in a corner of their billet, Phannius beside him. "What cousin?"

"He's a mason in Tiberias."

"Why would she go there?"

"It's in Galilee. It's near *you*. It's not stupid."

"I didn't say it was." Every conversation with Phannius was defensive on some level. "Do you think she went there?"

"No. She came to you. If she's not here, then I don't have any idea where she is."

They both avoided speaking the thought that was eating at them both. If she were captured by the Romans, she was young enough and pretty enough to become some soldier's plaything. That had both of them grinding their teeth.

"Are you sure there was nothing—"

Judah slammed his fist down on the straw rushes on the floor.

"For the fiftieth time, I didn't ask her to come, I didn't tell her to come, I didn't even hint at her coming. I don't know why she left Jerusalem!" There were hot tears in his eyes and he had to blink fast to keep them from falling.

There was a pause. Then Phannius said, in an unusually soft voice, "I was just wondering if there was anything at all in the letter that might have made her think she could help."

Seated nearby, Asher said, "Was this the letter where you said you were tired and – and wished you two could be together?"

Judah frowned, thinking. "Yes. But I didn't mean…"

"Of course not. But she might have…"

Phannius shook his head. "I knew, I *knew* it was something you'd written!"

"All I said was—"

"You told her to—"

"I absolutely did not!"

"Quiet, both of you!" Asher kicked out a leg to prod the pair of them. "What's the matter with you? You'd think you were the brothers, not us. Judah, I know you like to argue and fight, but punching Phannius won't help Deborah. In fact, she probably wouldn't like it. Phannius, whatever Judah wrote, clearly he didn't ask her to come. She made up her own mind. So let's try and figure out a way to help her."

"How?" demanded Phannius angrily. "We're trapped in here, surrounded by the whole damned Roman army."

"Actually, that's good news. If they haven't found her yet, she should be safe. As long as we hold out, she won't face being taken by the Romans."

That sunk in. As advice went, it was fairly lame. But it was certainly better than anything the other two had come up with. Phannius shrugged. "I guess I'm here to fight. That's something."

"Oh yes," agreed Judah. "We'll just put you on the wall and leave the Romans to you. Maybe I'll let you take an eagle this time, and not steal the credit for myself."

"Now look, I told you..!"

"I don't want to hear it!"

As their voices rose again, Asher rolled over and closed his eyes, willing himself to sleep.

XXV

THE FIFTEENTH LEGION discovered that being commanded by the general's son had perquisites. They were billeted in a place of honour, between the front gate and the general's headquarters, on the right side of the *via Praetoria*. Close to the cooking fires, they would be the first to get meals. And whenever the army marched, the Fifteenth led. A great distinction!

That first night at supper, legionary Curtus approached Barbarus. "What are we waiting for? Why not just attack?"

The grizzled centurion bit into a hank of pork, speaking as he chewed. "The Muleteer is a crafty old warhorse, lad. He wants them to stew a bit. He wants them afraid. Not so they'll surrender, though it'd be nice. But to make them desperate enough to fight. Otherwise," he shrugged, "we're in for a long siege."

Though most of his men were veterans, few had ever been involved in a prolonged siege. So Barbarus set aside his meal and instructed them on what to expect. "A siege, lads, is a seduction. Say there's this girl – pretty, but thinks she's too good for you. You make overtures, she rebuffs 'em. But you're determined to get under her skirts, neh? So you try again. She slaps your face, tells you 'no.' But there's a 'yes' in her eyes. So you tease her a little, get sly, talk yourself up to her friends. You try gifts. She takes them, but still won't give you a poke. So you try to heat her up. Still she refuses. So you show her your equipment. She recoils, but after that she can't take her eyes off it. All the time you're talking, lying to her, telling her you love her. Suddenly she shudders and you know you've got her. A minute later you're in, and everything happens all at once. You've been so patient, so understanding, that you fuck her raw. Fuck her *raw*. And you know what? The day after, when you're marching away, you'll actually miss her a little." He leaned back, smiling. "The wait only makes getting in more satisfying."

♦ ◊ ♦

The centurion's crude analogy played out almost to the letter. The Romans sent heralds to demand the city's surrender. The Judeans shouted their defiance. Vespasian then had his foreign archers and slingers to clear the walls while he led his men to a natural rise, hoping to gain the ramparts. Sensing danger, Yosef led his men to the spot, leapt over the wall, and charged the Romans. The struggle lasted until nightfall, ending with thirteen Romans and seventeen Judeans dead, with hundreds wounded on both sides. A very solid slap.

It was in this scrum that Asher was finally blooded. To his mingled delight and chagrin, he proved his brother correct. When the time came he didn't shy from fighting, didn't cower behind the ramparts. After all the drilling with Zamaris and the private sessions with Levi before that, he stood firm and felt only the urgency of each breath. Alongside Judah, Phannius, and the rest of their unlikely cohort, Asher charged into the thick of the fighting and stabbed his first Roman, wounding him in the thigh. Absurdly, a quote from Euripides popped into his mind. *Who knows but life be that which men call death, And death what men call life?*

He fought in the cohort's front line, alongside his tentmates. Stocky little Pethuel had planted his feet and was holding the flank, allowing thin Gareb and silent Deuel to lay about them with their long Judean swords. The brothers Philip and Netir were laughing as they fought, tossing off jokes as their blades scarred Roman shields.

"Philip! What happened when the Roman put his head into a lion's mouth to count how many teeth he had?"

"The lion closed its mouth to see how many heads the Roman had!"

"Lucky for the Roman he had two, and the one on his neck the less important!"

"Unlucky for him that we Galileans have more teeth than lions!"

The giant Atlas owned the roughest accent, and could barely be understood as he laid about him with a double-headed axe. "Come on!! Come on, Romans!! Come and die!!" The Romans sheltered behind their shields and tried to stab him with their short swords, but his reach with the long-handled axe was too great. Some legionaries threw their *pila*, but Atlas was flanked by Philip's and Netir's shields, which deflected the missiles.

Phannius wasn't yet used to fighting in a shield-wall, but with his height and long reach, he was a perfect person to be behind the line, protecting the heads of the men in front of him and jabbing with a spear. He was roaring out insults and banging the helmets of his allies, but each time he thrust his spear, it came away wet with Roman blood.

But no one fought like Judah. He seemed to lose himself in the grinding, battering rhythm of it. Asher fought as he'd been taught, responding to the orders Judah was neglecting. When Judah rushed forward, pulled by the heat of combat, Asher took it upon himself to cover his twin's right side, while Zamaris of all people stepped in and covered Judah's left. He was no longer shouting insults at the 'hero'. His mouth was set in a terrible grimace as he laughed and called for more Romans to stab.

Finally Yosef's trumpet signaled the retreat. The giant Atlas backed reluctantly away, still flanked by Philip and Netir. Judah, Asher, and Zamaris were the last of their century to withdraw. Though panting for breath, Asher was grinning. The word 'coward' could now be put away.

But Judah was troubled. In the thrill of fighting, he'd forgotten his friends, his men, even his brother. He was not a good soldier. He was a warrior. He turned sheepishly to Zamaris. "Sorry."

Zamaris merely shook his head. "Either you'll fall or you'll be a great hero. There's no middle ground. Just don't get any of our boys killed and I'm happy. Besides, with you out there, the Romans are less likely to target me!"

His inability to keep to the shield-wall wasn't the only thing bothering Judah. That night he was haunted by the face of the young Roman at Beth Horon begging for mercy. Fighting in daylight, Judah had seen not Romans, but faces. Individuals. Men with hearts and minds, hopes and dreams. He could fight them, kill them – but did they deserve to die?

Snap out of it! They're not thinking of you as anything but a target for their blades!

Yet Asher had been spared by Roman mercy. Judah had been asked for mercy, and offered none. What would the Lord make of that?

◆   ◊   ◆

This heavy fighting continued for five days, with the Judeans venturing out from behind their walls to force the Romans back time and again. Cannily, Yosef kept the fighting between buildings of the suburbs, never in the open places where the Romans might deploy properly. Judean slingers kept up a steady rain of lead pellets hurtling down from the walls. The Romans called these deadly missiles *glandes* because they resembled acorns. When the Judeans ran out of *glandes*, they made use of their endless supply of polished stones.

"They're bringing up the ladders," reported Chalafta to Yosef.

"Redouble the slings! Keep them back!"

Judah's men were within the walls today, and Yosef found himself faced by a breathless Asher, who had run all the way up to the tower's top. "Fenugreek! General, use fenugreek!"

Yosef stared at him blankly.

"It's slippery!"

With sudden understanding, Yosef issued the orders. Minutes later, despite the heavy fire of slingstones from the defenders, a few Romans scaled the ladders and achieved the wall tops – only to slip and fall. The defenders had poured boiled fenugreek over the endangered ramparts. The handful of Romans who got to the top were all killed, and their comrades had to withdraw under the jeers of the Judeans.

◆   ◊   ◆

After a week, Vespasian called his legates together. "There clearly won't be a quick finish, so let's settle in for the long haul. Fire the suburbs, begin felling trees. We'll build ramps to the wall's top."

To protect the engineers from Judean slings and arrows, Vespasian used wide shields of wood and hide. But the Judeans heaved stones to break the screens and used flaming arrows to set them alight. The Romans answered with 'gifts' of stones and bolts shot from one hundred sixty siege engines. With his Arabian archers, Vespasian made the walls such a terrible place that no Judean could even draw near.

Instead of ducking behind the walls, Yosef's men ran out from the city and hacked at the engineers, setting fire to their constructions.

Vespasian shook his head. "If anything, we're making them safer. They can take cover behind the husks of the ramps and fire at us from there."

"You've heard what our friend in there says?" remarked Trajan.

"Forty-nine days," replied Vespasian with a snort. A great deal of a siege was spent in shouted insults between ranker soldiers on both sides, and everyone had heard Yosef's prediction.

"What next?" asked Titus.

"Concentrate everything on one spot. We put so many soldiers behind the screens that our wily Josephus will not dare attack our engineers."

"They'll know where we're coming."

"Oh yes. So we just have to squeeze tighter than a frog's anus and drive forward. Let's pick a spot."

◆   ◊   ◆

It was going as well as Yosef could have hoped. His defenders had lasted twelve days so far. Only a handful of his men had died, and the city's resolve strengthened with each success.

Now the Romans were clearly concentrating their efforts in a single spot. Yosef racked his brain to devise some way to counter this new assault. Directly attacking the new ramp would cost more lives than he was willing to risk. Unable to think of a bloodless solution, he humbly sought advice from all comers. After many hare-brained schemes and daring proposals, it was Judah who delivered the simple answer. "Why not just raise the wall?"

Leave it to a mason to find such a solution. Instantly Yosef ordered houses in the nearby neighbourhood torn down and used the rubble to add height to the wall across from the Roman ramp. Naturally he put his pet masons in charge of the new fortification.

Working with mortar and heaving a slab of limestone, Asher was unamused. "I came to fight, not hew stone!"

Using an old mason's trick to quick-bore a socket and fit two stones together, Judah laughed. "We *are* fighting." An arrow hurtled inches above his head. "See?"

"I'd like it better if I was shooting back!"

After two hours of labour, Asher returned to Yosef. "We're being devastated!" Eighteen men had fallen to Roman missiles, four of them dead. "Can you put more slingers on the walls?"

"Not without losing them. Let me think." Yosef's eyes had a far-off look. "Pull everyone back. We'll eat well tonight."

When Asher relayed this comment to his twin, Judah asked, "What's he got in mind?"

"No idea," confessed Asher.

That night Yosef commanded six of the city's largest oxen be slaughtered. "Take care of the skins," he told the butchers. "In fact, make sure the tanners are there to watch. I want those hides intact. And fetch me plenty of salt!"

When the animals were dead, the meat was divided first among the soldiers who had fought this day, then among the rest of the men, and finally to the women and children. Jotapata had plenty of food stored, so the evening became quite a celebration, with music and even a little dancing.

"Hey, Atlas!" called Gareb, finishing his bowl of greens and meat. "Watch out or they might mistake you for an ox and skin you too!" Other men laughed.

"Stop calling me that, beanstalk!" growled the giant. He sat with his tiny wife Chava on his knee. "My name is Eleazar."

"My fault," said Asher in mid-bite. "Sorry."

"But it fits!" protested Pethuel. "Atlas bore the world on his shoulders. You carry us!"

"You, at least," said Zamaris, digging at the little man's height.
Pethuel made a rude gesture. "See? Even your fingers are too short."

"It's why I survive," said Pethuel. "The Romans can't even see
me."

Atlas continued to fume about his title. "It's a Greek name. I
hate them Greeks almost as much as I hate Romans." The big man had
been born in Sha'b, near the coast. But his family had been driven from
their trade by an influx of Greeks, and he'd become a rude labourer in
Jotapata. It was here that he met Chava. They were an amusing pair. He
was as large as a city, while she was small like a child, barely reaching
up to his waist. Her pregnancy had progressed despite all the marching,
and she was due sometime in August. Zamaris had offered to sneak her
out before the Romans came, but she had refused. "My child will take
his first breath in Jotapata." So Atlas fought each day to protect her
and his unborn child, and looked like he could defeat the whole Roman
army himself.

Netir said to Atlas, "Eleazar is too elegant a name for you."

"True," echoed Philip. "We seem to be down a few oxen, so maybe
we should just call you Ox."

"Maybe I should call you pig," countered Atlas hotly. "For being
unclean."

Chava slapped his wrist like a naughty child. "Husband!"

The giant bowed his head. "Sorry." For such a frightening mountain of a man, he was meek as a kitten with her.

"But Chava, he speaks the truth!" exclaimed Netir with loud
bravado. "We *have* been unclean lo, these twenty-three years!"

"Yes!" exclaimed Philip. "The only answer is to wash ourselves
in Roman blood!"

Judah had developed a grudging admiration for their relentless
cheerfulness. Netir and Philip had spent the last twenty-three years as
agents of the *publicani* – tax collectors – making them reviled by every
Jew living, giving them long years of practice at deflecting insults.

"Where's Deuel?" asked Gareb. The silent soldier had slipped
away, as usual.

"Probably off talking the Romans to death," suggested Philip.
Everyone laughed.

"He's certainly missing a good meal," observed Pethuel, chewing
happily. "Judah, are you already finished? Damn, you eat like a snake,
all in one bite."

"Always has," observed Phannius.

Judah shrugged. "Comes from growing up with stone-dust covering all your food. Best to just get it down."

"Pity," said Gareb. "This is a rare treat."

"What do you think the general has in mind?" asked Netir.

"No idea," said Judah. "Asher?"

Asher shook his head. "I guess we'll see."

◆   ◊   ◆

In the morning they saw, and cheered. Inspired by the screens protecting the Roman engineers, Yosef had taken the hides of those six oxen and put the tanners to work overnight, curing the skins with salt and sand. "Let them retain some of their moisture," Yosef had instructed. Sewing the skins together three by three, he had them affixed to poles and stretched across the top of the wall where the work was to be done.

"Clever!" laughed Judah as he watched the flaming Roman arrows extinguish themselves in the damp hides. There was enough slack in the skins that ballista balls sloughed harmlessly to the ground.

Behind this screen, the Jotapatans raised their wall an extra thirty feet. Vespasian set his catapults to work, meaning to knock down the wall's additional height. But Judah knew his work. The new stones did not fall. Coming up against this heightened wall, the Romans gave up their ramp entirely. Vespasian even sent his compliments to Yosef at a job well done.

"General Yosef is rising to the occasion!" observed Gareb.

Judah nodded, impressed. He hadn't thought the ambitious young priest had it in him.

◆   ◊   ◆

However small the victory, this defiant feat was deemed a wonder by the citizens of Jotapata. They hailed Yosef almost as a king, parading him through the streets, bringing children to be kissed by him. He was offered the favours of several well-born women of the city, which he politely declined. Not for lack of desire. Yosef had remembered the words of the old Essene hermit, Bannus: "When a man lies with a woman, Jehovah does not speak out of his mouth for seven moons." Yosef had need of divine inspiration, and so practiced chastity.

This had a curious effect. The admiration of the Jotapatans turned into something like reverence. Walking briskly through the city one day, an old man bowed to him, tugging his long square beard. "Blessings upon you, *Mahsiah*."

Faltering, Yosef gazed at the man with a curious kind of awe. "You mistake me, sir. I am not the *Mahsiah*."

The ancient man bowed more deeply, but did not retract his words. Yosef hurried on, his eyes turning inward.

Mahsiah? The prophecy of the Mahsiah was from Isaiah: *For unto us a child is born, unto us a son is given; and the government shall be upon his shoulder: and his name shall be called Wonderful, Counselor, the mighty God, the everlasting Father, the Prince of Peace.* He was supposed to be the savior of Israel, a warrior descended from David who would again revive the greatness of the Lord's chosen people.

Galileans cherished Isaiah above all prophets, even Abraham or Mosheh. And it was true, Yosef could trace his lineage back to the House of David. But there had been so many false mahsiahs, with whole sects created to follow their teachings.

Yet Yosef now recalled the visions he had experienced when living in the wilderness as a youth. Had that been hunger, or divine communication? Reason said the former. But faith was beyond reason. Was the Lord attempting to speak through Yosef?

Could I be the Mahsiah?

No, he told himself at once. *The Romans have a word for such fancies – hubris.*

Nevertheless, the seed was planted.

◆　◊　◆

Invited for a private dinner, Titus stepped into the general's residence and discovered his father at his ease upon a couch, eating melted cheese with bread and reading a large scroll. "Dispatches?"

"Literature."

"Truly?"

Vespasian chuckled. "Your surprise wounds me. I'm reading Josephus' book on the Makkabi rebellion."

"Ah." Titus sat on the next couch over, bringing him head-to-head with his father. "And?"

Vespasian laid the scroll aside. "Can't make heads or tails of it." Both men laughed. Neither had intellectual pretensions. "Damn, but it's hot! Never in my life thought I would miss Britannia's rain."

"I've asked some of the engineers. They think we're closer to the sun here."

"Makes sense." They settled down to the first course. The conversation wandered a bit, then Vespasian said, "Had a letter from Caenis. She's planted herself in Rome."

Titus removed a lamb shank from his lips. "Doing what?"

"Silly cow thinks she's building me a faction. I'm too old for that sort of thing. But it might do you some good. She hints you should marry again."

"Why?" asked Titus lightly. "I've got a daughter. If I need a son, I can adopt one. What use is a wife?"

"She could do what Caenis is doing for me – work the women of Rome. Influencing the wives of senators is a strong lobby that costs you nothing."

"Then I shall follow your example and find an excellent mistress to do it for me. Hypocrite," he added with a grin.

"Hah! You have me there! Very well, son, no more pressure from me."

Titus was glad to escape talk of marriage. His eyes were on a woman that Roman society would not embrace. Thinking of her, he had an idea. Casually dipping some flaky bread into the melted cheese, he said, "Father, if you like, I can read Josephus' book."

Vespasian looked up. "Really? Why would you want to do that?"

"It can't hurt to have a better understanding of the Jews."

"You mean one Jew in particular. No, don't deny it. I hear things. Son, she's a foreign queen, and an Eastern one at that. Remember, these are her people we're fighting."

Titus was appalled he'd been so transparent. "Berenice is on our side."

"Foreign potentates are like the gods, son. They're on no side but their own."

Titus looked mulish. "Are you telling me not to see her?"

Vespasian sighed. "I'm only saying stick to your resolve – have her as a mistress, not a wife."

"So," said Titus, changing the subject. "What do we do now?"

Vespasian's natural frown turned to something like resigned disgust. "We do nothing. It won't be quick, but we're here until the end of the season, it looks like. We have to win, and victory goes to the one with more patience. They're trapped. If we can't get in, we'll have to wait for them to come out. So tell everyone to hold their ground. Don't try to advance. Lure them out. I guarantee you, inactivity will drive them mad."

XXVI

OUTSIDE the besieged city, the Second Cohort of the Fifteenth Legion had the night watch. Shortly after midnight, amid the eerie desert silence, the Judeans struck.

"Lights! Lights, and at them!" shouted Barbarus. It was ritual by now – every night the defenders snuck out to harass some part of the Roman lines. Tonight the bastards had again come to where Barbarus and his men were standing guard. Torches were lit, swords scraped from hard scabbards, and everyone raced to engage the foe.

Barbarus fixed upon a giant of a man with a huge axe, a walking wall who tossed Romans aside like children, creating a gap in the line. He whooped. "There's my fight!" Expertly, the centurion cut a path towards the giant. A stocky Judean guarded the huge man's flank. Barbarus feinted left, then stabbed the short man in the right shoulder. Pulling his blade out, he leapt past the wounded Judean to attack the giant.

Impossibly, the massive figure twisted aside. How could a man of almost seven feet and several hundred pounds move so swiftly?

The giant smashed his axe into Barbarus' shield hard enough to scar the metal. The blow sent Barbarus sprawling. Rising, he slashed his sword left and right, clearing away encroaching Judeans. Regaining his feet, he pivoted to find the giant. "Here, you bastard!"

The brute turned and was surprised to find the centurion still alive. Hefting his mighty two-handed axe, he brought it crashing down again. Barbarus angled his shield and the great blade skidded sideways, bouncing off the boss. Barbarus stabbed and the massive Judean jumped back, surprised again. Few men survived one of his blows, let alone two.

Their eyes locked and both men smiled in recognition. *Here*, each said to himself, *is a worthy foe.*

"By Jupiter, you're a prize," murmured Barbarus in Latin.

"Come get me, little man," growled Atlas in Aramaic.

Soldiers from both armies came to help. The giant yelled for his men to back away. Barbarus did the same. "I'll crucify anyone that touches him!"

Fighting in the area ceased as men turned to watch the duelists begin to circle each other. Twice they leapt, clashing and retreating. The armourless Judean had to be careful of the small Roman's expert cuts, while the Roman had to beware the Judean's near-Herculean strength.

They set to blade-work, the giant twisting away from a swipe at his hamstring even as Barbarus ducked a blow that shaved the horse-hairs from the plume of his helmet. "Do you know how hard it is to weave those damned hairs into place?"

Laughing, the giant was about to engage again when someone on the Judean side called out, "Atlas! Time to go!"

Giving Barbarus a rueful smile and a shrug, the giant turned and started back for the walls.

"No you don't!" cried Barbarus, hot in pursuit.

"These Jews are like vermin," snorted Curtus. "Spark a light, they scurry off." He hefted a pilum. "Now can I kill the coward?"

"Don't you dare!" snarled Barbarus. "He's mine!"

It was a half-mile to Jotapata's walls. Unhampered by heavy armour, the Judeans quickly widened the gap, leaving Barbarus puffing behind. In a few moments he would be within range of the slingers on the wall. Chest heaving like a bellows, he pulled up short. "Barbarus! First Century, Second Cohort of the Fifteenth Apollinaris!"

There was a startled noise from one the Judeans, but Barbarus was watching the giant, who turned, running backwards with a grin as broad as his shoulders. "Eleazar, son of Samas, of the city of Sha'b! They call me Atlas! We'll meet again, Roman!"

"I look forward to it, Atlas!" With a friendly wave, Barbarus trudged back to the lines.

◆   ◊   ◆

Not far off, Asher had heard the centurion call out a name he remembered well from Alexandria – Barbarus. His step had faltered and he'd released a surprised grunt. This was the centurion who had saved his life!

"Yes, I heard," said Judah, shoving his twin forward. "Now get inside the walls, you ninny!"

Once safely through the small gate, Zamaris ordered Asher to do a headcount. Two men were missing. "One of them is Pethuel."

Zamaris interrogated every member of his century. Everyone remembered Pethuel being injured in the shoulder, but no one knew if the stocky man had died or been taken captive. It wasn't the first loss the century had endured, but it was the first from their tent. Judah took it particularly badly.

◆   ◊   ◆

As the siege dragged on, water was fast becoming a real concern. In a city with many Essenes who practiced an intense form of ritual cleansing, it was difficult to say which was more distressing, lacking drink or forgoing the washing of hands, feet, and head.

Yosef gave up pleading with the people not to bathe, and instead made the onerous order to ration the water supplies. Guards were posted at every well, both public and private. As soldiers required more water than average citizens, resentment built on both sides.

The Romans quickly learned of Jotapata's thirst, and legionaries took to quaffing off their canteens in full view of the walls, pouring cool water over their heads, or even watering the dirt at their feet. Yosef tried deceiving the Romans by hanging sheets soaked with urine to make the enemy believe they had water enough to spare. But without drink, it was difficult to maintain strength.

"General," said Levi in his role as bodyguard, "you should eat."

"Not today." Despite an abundance of food, Yosef was denying himself all but the barest meals in an attempt to regain the clarity of his time in the wilderness. And it was working. Sight blurring and occasionally spinning, he was starting to experience the hazy sense of being part of something larger than himself.

His first vision occurred when staring at the Romans across the burnt and trampled ground. In the near-blinding sun, a reflection off a Roman's armour became a flock of doves. Yosef knew it was not real, but he smiled at it nonetheless, secretly waving to them.

What does it mean? That the Romans bring peace? Or that peace flies from Rome?

There were more visions after that, some fanciful, some disturbing. They were all more intense than during his time with Bannus in the woods, which made perfect sense – the Lord had more need now to communicate with him.

◆   ◊   ◆

Whenever the water rations were handed out, Judah noticed that Deuel took only a small sip, then disappeared with his clay cup. When not on duty, the man was never around. As he had never shirked his responsibilities, Judah had let him go, suspecting there was a woman somewhere in the city. Most of the men had women.

But the fool couldn't be allowed to give away his water, certainly not to some whore. With Pethuel lost, the whole needed Deuel at his best. So on the third night of the rationing, Judah followed Deuel to see where he was depositing his precious water.

The trail wended deep into the heart of the city, far from the fighting and out of range of falling stones – the Roman siege engines had been hurling rocks without let for days. Keeping his hand over the cup's top so as not to lose a drop, the silent Deuel finally came to an exterior stairway to a three-story building. Climbing to the highest floor, he pushed the curtain aside and entered.

The top floor of any building was the least desirable. Even without the Roman bombardment, many buildings were liable to collapse, and the threat of fire made the top floor a death trap. Whoever lived up there, they weren't wealthy.

Judah counted to ten, then climbed the stairs. If it was a woman, Judah didn't want to give the pair time to undress. Without knocking, Judah stepped through the curtain and in.

A single chamber, with a rude bed at one end and cushions around a low table at the other. Hardly a courtesan's nest. The room stank of fever and illness.

Deuel was kneeling next to the bed. In it lay an old woman, faded and withered, naked above the sheets and covered in sweat. She bore Deuel's features on her withered face. He was raising the clay cup to her cracked lips as Judah entered. Deuel's head came around, but his careful hand didn't falter as he gave his mother some of his precious water.

Dropping his gaze, Judah stepped outside again and waited, wondering what he could say. To waste precious water on a dying woman was not only foolish, it was criminal. Judeans manning the walls had far more need of it. Deuel himself needed it. Fainting while fighting would not only doom him, but endanger every man around him.

When Deuel emerged a few minutes later, he just stared at Judah. Finally Judah said, "I'll get Zamaris to give you an extra half ration. But you drink all your own. If you die, she'll lose even that half."

Deuel said nothing. He nodded once, then turned and went back to his dying mother. Judah released a long breath then threaded his way back through the city.

◆   ◊   ◆

At the large house Zamaris' century had taken for their own, Philip and Netir were telling more ridiculously low jokes. "I saw the Romans roasting a boar last night," said Philip.

"Wild?" asked Netir.

"Well, he didn't seem too happy about it!"

As the rest of the men roared with laughter, Asher shook his head. It was a very old joke. But these two had set themselves up as the clowns of this century, and laughter was certainly better than contemplating Pethuel's fate.

Zamaris nodded at the old brothers. "You two fought well today."

"Thanks!" called Netir. "We're skilled at letting blood."

"Letting blood?" asked Gareb.

"Yes," quipped Netir with a smile. "As tax collectors, the Romans even had us wringing blood from stones."

The laughter now was darker. But these two men always made a point of poking at themselves to diffuse the anger over their life-long profession.

Wherever it ruled, Rome demanded taxes. Rather than create an official tax collection agency within the Roman government, the Senate leased the rights to collect taxes to private individuals. One man might have the right to collect in Greece, or Spain, or Bithynia. Each year a sum was agreed upon, and as long as the private individual paid that sum to Rome, he was free to keep whatever else he collected.

Some of these tax-farmers were fair, collecting only a small portion for themselves. Others, like the Brutus who had murdered Julius Caesar, were rapacious, wringing every last silver drachma or shekel out of those unfortunate enough to fall into their clutches. Those who couldn't pay were sold into slavery, their lands confiscated and sold at auction. Thus the rich got richer, the poor poorer.

True, the taxes collected by the publicani were usually less than the one-tenth owed to the High Priests in Jerusalem. But the one had been set down by the Lord, the other by Caesar. After parting with a tenth of one's earnings for God, it was painful to offer up almost as much for Rome.

The Roman tax-farmers had once employed private armies to collect the money. But over time they had started to rely on hiring locals to rake in their monies. This made open rebellion less likely, and divided the locals into factions – those who collaborated with Rome, and those who did not.

Driven at first by crushing poverty to become tax collectors, Philip and Netir had quickly discovered that this work excluded them from all other kinds. No one would hire men who had worked for the Romans. Forced to continue in this work, they became wealthy, but could only associate with other men in the service of Rome. They were shunned at religious service and on the street, with men and women spitting and cursing, refusing to even look them in the eye.

It was not just the idea of taking money for Rome that made tax collecting odious. Dealing in money itself was considered unclean by the vast swathes of Hebrew society. Having money was acceptable, and earning it admirable. But making a trade entirely of money was usury, and unclean. Sadly, in foreign lands it was often the only trade permitted to Hebrews, and they were reviled for it.

To combat the insults hurled at them, Philip and Netir had become almost jesters, laughing in the face of their unhappiness. Despite the dogged nature of the publicans' banter, they had tired of living on the fringe of their native society. When the war came, they decided to throw off the yoke of their masters and join the Galilean army, donating all their wealth to the cause. Hopefully through a sacrifice of gold and blood they could expunge the sin of trading in anything as dirty as money.

"It's a pleasure, after all these years of collecting blood for them, to collect it from them," observed Philip.

"And if we're good at it, they have only themselves to thank," added Netir.

◆   ◇   ◆

"Father," said Titus, venturing into uncomfortable territory. "The men..."

"Yes, what about them?"

"They're getting bored."

Rather than rail, Vespasian smiled knowingly. "Ah. The soldier's greatest enemy – tedium."

"I've rotated the watches, and we've been drilling them silly. But the lack of real fighting is driving them mad."

"It would be better if we had some women. Round some up."

"Yes, general."

Vespasian chuckled. "In the meantime, I know what to do."

◆   ◇   ◆

Pethuel stumbled along silently cursing his injured shoulder, his captors, and his fate. The only reason the short man's mouth was not conveying his curses to the air was that he'd been beaten already for mouthing off, and his jaw now refused to work. Half of his teeth were gone, giving his left cheek a slack, hollow appearance and making his swollen face lopsided.

He expected to be crucified, the traditional punishment for angering Rome. Instead the legionaries in charge of him brought him to a rough circle of earth maybe twenty yards in diameter. There was another Judean standing in the circle, dressed like Pethuel, naked but for a loincloth. Pethuel didn't know the man, but he looked familiar – another captured defender, most like.

A whole cohort of Roman soldiers moved in, ringing the two Judeans round, the front row kneeling behind their shields, the second ring standing, with a third ring seated upon risers, a fourth tier standing behind them.

Seeing the Romans form an audience, Pethuel grasped the awful meaning. He was to dance before his death.

Two short Roman swords were tossed into the center of the ring. Slowly he crossed and picked up one. His partner picked up the other. The Romans cheered and started making bets. Pethuel was shorter and injured, but broader and well muscled. It was speed versus strength in this mock-gladiatorial game.

Pethuel wasn't interested in playing. Meeting his partner's gaze, he lifted his chin, then ran his free hand across his belly. The other man nodded. They took up a fighting stance, the way the Romans expected. Racing together, their swords didn't even touch. Pethuel gasped as his stomach was gored from side to side, but kept driving his own blade up through the soft spot under his partner's chin.

The Romans roared in anger, cheated of their sport. As he fell, Pethuel forced his jaw to move one last time. Raising his head heavenwards, he cried out, "Hear, Israel, one and eternal is our God, Jehovah!"

To Romans ears the name of the Hebrew god sounded like the braying of a mule. One witty legionary started imitating Pethuel's cry. "Juh! Juh! Juh!" Soon the whole cohort was braying, mocking the god of these defiant Jews who wouldn't even put on a good show. "Juh! Juh! Juh!"

Pethuel lay, his blood pouring from him, mixed with the offal in his intestines and the urine in his bladder. He forced his eyes shut, closed his ears to the world, and tried to hear the Lord instead.

XXVII

"YOU'RE GETTING reckless," observed Asher to Yosef.

They had taken to walking the ramparts at dusk each day, when the fighting was done but before the nighttime watch rotations began. Yosef had repeatedly said that he valued Asher's opinion. And so far there had been little for Asher to criticize. They were enduring. But for the lack of water, they showed every sign of continuing to do so.

Yet in the last couple days Asher had grown concerned as Yosef sent out larger and larger sorties to attack the Romans.

"Not reckless," countered Yosef. "It's a calculation. We're best when we're fighting. And we need to fight now, while we're strong, before thirst saps us completely. So I've been trying to sting Vespasian into mounting an assault. But the Romans merely fend us off and return to their business. If we don't give them a proper battle, they're content to wait us out." Turning to face the Roman camp, he shook a fist. "Come on, damn you! Attack us! You love to fight! You live to fight. It's in your blood. So fight!"

From behind them, Levi said, "They are fighting."

Yosef turned. "What?"

"They've organized sports," replied Levi. "You can see them from the towers. While we groan with thirst, they amuse themselves with boxing, wrestling, mock races."

"Even gladiatorial games," added Asher. "With captured Jews as combatants." How had Yosef not noticed this? Yet this was clearly news to him. The general blanched, turning a sick shade and his flesh standing on end. Asher grew frightened. "What is it?"

Yosef grasped at the wall, hiding his face against the warm stone. "Romans exist on a diet of bread and blood. Vespasian has ensured his soldiers have plenty of both. Damn. Excuse me."

Straightening, Yosef walked quickly away. Asher looked to Levi, who shrugged as he followed his charge at a discreet distance. Asher returned to his billet. Obviously the general needed time to think.

♦　◊　♦

Had Asher known the thoughts running through Yosef's mind, he would have taken a stone and hammered them away.

It's over. The city is doomed. The Romans have the resources and the skill. I was hoping to try their patience, force them to waste lives trying to get in. But now they're entertaining themselves while we waste away in here.

Yes, the city is doomed. But how is that possible? I know *the Lord has plans for me beyond this. He's shown me so time and again! He can't mean for me to be doomed!*

His fevered certainty arose not only from his many visions in the wilderness, but also from the first time he had faced certain death, three years earlier, on that endless night paddling in the Adriatic, with Yahweh whispering *live, live, live* in his ear.

I must survive. But how, if the city is doomed? Seeking assurance that he was right, he rounded suddenly on his bodyguard. "Levi, tell me – can the city hold?"

Levi made the mistake of telling the truth. "It will last some time longer. But it must fall."

Yosef nodded, looking pleased. "Just so. Just so. Please tell the city elders that I must speak with them at dawn."

When the elders met behind closed doors the next morning, they beheld a Yosef they had never seen. For weeks he had been sunburnt and hollow-cheeked, but with relentless good cheer and infectious optimism. Now he was unshaven and unkempt, and wouldn't look them in the eye. "Is there a way to leave the city undetected?"

Nechum and the rest gasped, looking stricken. "You can't leave us!"

"I've done all I can within these walls. What Jotapata needs now is reinforcements. Those will not come on their own, I must fetch them. Once the Romans learn I've escaped, they may even depart. Certainly their bombardment will end."

The elders all started gabbling at once, protesting. But Yosef remained calm – he knew what must be done.

At the back of the chamber, Nechum's son Chalafta quietly exited the chamber.

♦   ◊   ♦

Off-duty, fatigued and thirsty, Judah, Asher, Phannius, and the others were sitting in the shade. A stray Roman ballista stone achieved extra height and came crashing down not far from them.

"But may you give me back my own daughter and take the ransom," said Asher, watching the chiseled stone roll to a stop, *"giving honour to Zeus' son who strikes from afar, Apollo."*

"What?" said Gareb.

"Just saying that stone probably came from the Fifteenth – Apollo's legion."

"Was that some kind of quote?"

"The Iliad. Appropriate fare for a siege." He spied Chalafta racing towards him – they were much of an age, and had become friendly. "Ho, Chalafta! Running between the raindrops?"

"Wish they were raindrops," murmured Netir.

Chalafta wasted no time. "Asher, you need to stop him. He'll listen to you!"

"Who?"

Judah knew. He sat up. "You mean the general?"

"Another sortie," guessed Phannius.

"No," answered Chalafta, shaking his head violently. "He's convincing the council to help him escape."

"What!?" cried Asher, leaping to his feet. *No you don't!* he thought furiously. *You brought us here. You don't get to leave.*

Aloud he said, "You're wrong, Chalafta. He doesn't actually listen to me. I won't sway him – but I know what will."

♦   ◊   ♦

It took an hour, but in the end Yosef convinced the council to let him go raise reinforcements. Despite the Roman blockade, a few messengers had gotten in and out. Covered in sheepskins, they had crept away at dawn, when the Romans were the least watchful and when a wandering sheep would rouse no special interest. At dawn tomorrow Yosef would do the same.

In his heart he suspected he would fail to bring back reinforcements. Seeing what Jotapata was experiencing, no city would allow its soldiers leave. But he would try. Regardless of success, he would be free to do whatever work the Lord planned for him. His destiny did not end at Jotapata.

Satisfied, Yosef emerged triumphant from the council chamber to behold a shocking sight – an angry, desperate, fearful mob shouting:

"Don't leave us!"

"We won't surrender! We came to fight!"

"If you leave, you'll break our hope!"

Yosef addressed them, giving calm and rational reasons for his departure. They answered by pleading, cajoling, weeping, begging – and threatening. "Don't be afraid of dying at Roman hands. We'll kill you first!"

They would not listen to reason. These people looked to him as their protector. Rather than allow him to depart, they would tear him to pieces.

At the back of the mob, Yosef saw Asher and Judah. They weren't shouting, just watching. He didn't know they had organized this display. He only knew that there was more threat in their grim faces than in any of the crowd's shouts.

Live, the voice said again. But it was not the Romans that threatened him now, nor the sea. He could very easily die here, on the swords of his fellow Jews, unless he did something to prove his devotion.

Drawing his sword, he shouted, "You want me to die here with you? Very well! But I won't die cowering behind walls, waiting for my strength to fail me! I'm going out there to show the Romans what fighting an Israelite means!" He loosed a ragged, unmusical scream and ran for the city gate.

Thirty thousand voices howled behind him, charging with him to join in this impossible counter-assault.

At the back of the crowd, Asher snorted. "Well, we saved him from himself."

"Yes," said Judah. "Now it's time to save him from the Romans. If they decide to fight," he added.

♦   ◊   ♦

Barbarus heard the screaming, saw the gates open, and watched the Judeans pour out. "About damned time." Fitting his helmet on his head, he cinched the chinstrap and picked up his shield. "Come on, lads!"

"We haven't had the order," protested his optio.

"By the time the order comes, Thorius, we'll be on 'em. No more pussyfooting, lads! They're coming out for a battle, a proper slog! Come on! I want another crack at that giant!"

But already the trumpets were blaring: Fall Back. At the same moment, the Arabian archers began firing, driving the Judeans to retreat behind their walls.

♦   ◊   ♦

When the legionaries withdrew, Yosef couldn't believe his luck. *Luck? No. This is divine favour, yet another instance of the Lord's*

*love for me. I am his beloved, his David. He preserves me even in the face
of certain death. I don't need to run from Jotapata. He'll protect me right
here. Just as the Lord let a sea of men drown but spared me, so too will he
let this whole city perish, and still preserve me. I must trust Him.*

"Call the men back," he ordered. "These Roman cowards won't
fight!"

♦   ◊   ♦

"*Cacat!*" It was so very tempting to disobey the trumpets –
Barbarus had spied the giant among the Judean throng. But orders
were orders. Reluctantly retreating, Barbarus watched as the frustrated
Judeans were forced back to safety.

"What's the use of being a soldier if we're not going to do any
soldiering!"

♦   ◊   ♦

Vespasian was in the latrine when the sudden sortie issued forth
from Jotapata. Still wiping his arse, he heard his trumpets blowing the
Roman retreat. Dropping the sponge, he let his leather skirt fall and ran
outside to see what had happened.

"So many," he said, watching the Judeans retreat once more to
the safety of their walls. "That was no raid. That was an invitation
to battle!" He rounded on Titus, Trajan, Placidus, and Cerialis. "Why
didn't you fight them?"

There were disadvantages to being the general's son. The other
legates allowed Titus to answer the general's wrath. "We were obeying
our orders, sir. No engaging the enemy. Dispirit them."

Impossibly, Vespasian's face became even more pinched. "Those
orders were for petty skirmishes. This could have been a real battle!
We could have eaten them and won the siege right here!" He stretched
his hands for the skies, then slumped, fuming. "Show some initiative,
can you? A general can't be everywhere. Wars are won and lost in the
chain of command." Shaking his head, Vespasian stalked away, leaving
his legates cursing these mad Judeans who were so perverse in their
war-making.

♦   ◊   ♦

Late that night, as he sat honing his blade with a stone, Judah
suddenly said, "Tell me the Iliad."

Asher looked up from his own sword's edge. "Pardon?"

"You keep quoting from it, and I'm tired of not knowing what
you're talking about. So tell it to me."

"You already know it," objected Asher.

"I know there's a horse. And there's a man whose name means Lipless."

"Achilles," said Asher, knowing he was being goaded. "Judah, I don't have a copy."

"What," scoffed Judah loudly, "are you going to plead a poor memory? I'm not demanding a word-perfect recitation. Tell me the story."

As Judah intended, he'd gotten the attention of the other members of their unit. Philip and Netir joined in pestering Asher, and Gareb. Phannius said it would be better than listening to Judah's snores. Even Atlas' pregnant wife Chava piped up. "Please, Asher. I need something to take my mind off *this*." She waved at her swollen belly. "He's like his father, a massive brute eager to break out and fight Romans!"

"That's right," agreed Atlas, hand on her belly to feel the baby's kicks. "Maybe a story will soothe him. Go on, Asher."

Bemused, Asher began relating the story of the siege of Ilium. He told it as Homer had, starting in the tenth year with the dispute between Achilles and Agamemnon over a captured girl. Within a few minutes he'd found his stride, and ended up speaking late into the night. Other men from their century came in to listen, even Zamaris. Every time Asher tried to stop, others urged him on. When his voice began to croak, they shared their precious water with him.

Intending it as distraction for the others, Judah found himself genuinely interested. Asher quoted whole passages verbatim, and even when he wasn't certain of a phrase, his natural ability as a storyteller was evident.

Listening, Judah was particularly struck by the story of Diomedes and Glaukos, the combatants who meet on the field of battle and realize their grandfathers were friends. They refuse to fight one another because of the bond of *xenia*, hospitality – Glaukos' grandfather had been a guest in Diomedes' grandfather's house, and even two generations later, that bond was sacrosanct. He found that a very Hebrew quality.

The brothers Philip and Netir, on the other hand, showed especial interest in the Greek concepts of *Kleos* and *Timê*. "So *Kleos* is honour earned in battle," asked Netir, "while *Timê* is honour gained through achievement?"

"That's about right," agreed Asher.

"Then let's hope we earn lots of *Kleos*," said Philip, "and yet live long enough to earn *Timê* as well."

Asher did not speak his thought. *That's up to another Greek concept – Fate.*

◆　◊　◆

That same night, Nicanor was ushered into Titus' quarters. "You wished to see me, *legatus*?"

"Nicanor!" Laying aside a thick scroll, Titus rose from his couch. "How has the siege been treating you?"

"I find myself the target of my countrymen's slings."

"The cost of being loyal to Rome. Sit! I've asked you here because my father has questions about this Josephus. He wishes to see inside our enemy's mind, and he's given me the job. You shall be my guide."

"However I can help," replied Nicanor.

Titus indicated the scroll he had been reading. "This is Josephus' history of the Makkabi revolt. Fascinating stuff. I'm no connoisseur, but there are several good turns of phrase. Still, much of it is beyond me. For instance, he references three sects, but does not name them."

Nicanor sipped some wine. "Likely he referred to the current philosophical favourites. On the one hand are the Zadokim, whom the Greeks call Sadducees. They believe only in the written word of our God. They are fiercely nationalist, tied to the land, and do not believe in the immortality of the spirit."

Titus drank in the information. "Go on."

"Contrast with them the other extreme, Essenes, who are hermits entirely by choice. They adhere to the rituals of our people, both written and spoken, and lead a life of austerity. They take no part in government, and accept no responsibility for the greater whole. This, and their diets, grant them long lives – I have known Essenes who lived well past their hundredth year! But they eat in silence, own no private possessions, and refuse to engage in the sexual act." Nicanor paused. "I fear I am not entirely clear."

"No no," said Titus, fascinated. "I've followed you. The Sadducees are temporal, material, and rigidly backwards-looking. The Essenes are devout, joyless, and impractical."

"I envy the Roman way of cutting a thousand words to ten," said Nicanor agreeably.

"And the third sect?"

"The Pharisees. They are the middle ground, reasonable yet devout. They balance the spiritual with the temporal. Intellectually lenient, yet religiously rigorous. They're rather like the Roman Stoics – self-disciplined, fatalistic, yet pragmatic."

"Sadducees, Pharisees, and Essenes," mused Titus. "And which is this Josephus?"

"Yosef trained as an Essene for three years, but ended up choosing the Pharisees."

Slowly Titus' smile widened. "Started out with pure faith, but became a moderate."

"I believe," observed Nicanor in neutral tones, "he was interested in politics."

"That will please my father. He prefers practical foes to fanatics. Speaking of fanatics, what about the Zelotes? Are they Sadducees?"

Nicanor's brow furrowed. "Hmm. Perhaps they are best termed a fourth sect. They first appeared here in Galilee, and refuse to acknowledge any ruler except our God. They are opposed not only to Roman occupation of these lands, but to the presence of any gentile – meaning, any non-Hebrew."

"But then how will they prosper? Without trade, there is no culture, no growth! Surely they mean to except tradesmen and merchants?"

"None but men of our faith," declared Nicanor. "In their minds, Judea is a land for the Hebrews alone. It is not even Judea, but Israel, the land our Lord promised us. To them that means it belongs to Hebrews solely. The most extreme of these are the *Sicarii*, the knifemen who do murder to gain their end. I apologize," he added, seeing a glaze across Titus' eyes. "I drone on."

"What? No no! I was just noting the similarity between our peoples. Not the exclusivity, which is ridiculous, but the emphasis on land. Greeks believe that ideas are paramount, but we Romans understand the importance of the physical place."

"As do we Hebrews. Ideas and beliefs grow from the place where they were born. Without a place to flourish, ideas wither and perish. As does faith."

"So Zelotes fight for the land your god gave them. Damn. That's a strong motivator."

Nicanor was almost apologetic. "Yes. In Hebrew a Zelote is called a *kanai*, meaning 'devout'. The Zelotes claim that there can be no ruler of Israel that is not descended from King David."

"King David?"

"Our greatest king, the ideal leader and founder of our nation."

"Romulus," said Titus at once.

"In a way. Certainly he built our capitol, just as Romulus did yours." The corners of Nicanor's mouth curled into a slight smile. "Which would make Mosheh into Aeneas, wandering the wilderness in search of a new home. Ha!"

Titus rubbed at his head. "Clearly I am ignorant of the important names of your history. Start at the beginning – broad strokes only, please."

"Titus Flavius, I'm no scholar..."

"Good, then you won't bore me. That's an order, by the way."

"Very well." Nicanor paused to frame his thoughts. "In the beginning, Yahweh created the world..."

Titus interrupted. "Yahweh is the name of your god?"

Nicanor shook his head emphatically. "Yahweh, Jehovah, Elohim

– these are what we call Him in place of His name, which we do not speak but one day a year."

Just like Rome's secret name, thought Titus. Known to all citizens, if the name were ever spoken aloud, it would bring disaster and ruin to Rome. Names had power. *For every difference, a similarity.*

Nicanor continued. "Yahweh created this world in a state of perfection. But Man was dissatisfied with his status of subject to Yahweh's Will, and so rebelled. The Lord punished Man by removing the perfection, which is why we all now suffer, wither, and die."

Prometheus, punished for stealing fire.

"It was actually Woman who tempted Man, bringing about his fall from grace. But Woman was created from a part of Man, which again symbolizes that the fault lies within."

Interesting! Pandora, the first woman, was man's punishment for stealing fire, not the cause! But with her little jar she brought destruction. For every difference, a similarity.

"But our Lord is merciful and offered Man a chance for redemption. He chose one good man, Abraham, who is the patriarch of all the Jews. After testing Abraham's fidelity, the Lord laid down the Law for our people to follow. It forever marks Abraham's descendants as the Chosen of the Lord. We are the vehicle through which this world will be redeemed."

A special people, thought Titus. *With a special destiny. Every nation believes it of themselves. But only Rome has proved it.*

"Abraham's grandson, Jacob, was given a second name by the Lord Himself – Israel. The Zelotes take the land's name from him. He had twelve children, from whom were born the Twelve Tribes of Israel."

Much like the famous families, the Patricians, the founding 'fathers' of Rome. They ruled Roma for hundreds of years because their blood was the best.

"The Twelve Tribes were eventually conquered, and enslaved in Aegypt. They were delivered from their bondage by another of Yahweh's anointed, called Mosheh. Through him, Yahweh bound us further with a Covenant, a set of laws and prohibitions called the Mosaic Law."

"Mosaic, as in the tiles?" laughed Titus.

"As in Mosheh, the Lawgiver," Nicanor corrected gently. "The Lord guided the Twelve Tribes to this land and chose a king – David. From that time on, the King of the Jews has been the divine representative, anointed by the Lord to lead us. Until Herod," he added.

Isn't that always the way? mused Titus cynically. *From Alexander to Mithradates, kings claim divine sanction to all their deeds. Whereas we Romans did away with kings. But how clever, to wrap it in an exclusivity, at the same time ennobling the Jews by claiming they will be the salvation of the world.*

Nicanor added, "It might interest you to know, Titus Flavius, that Yosef can trace his line back to the house of David. It adds to his claim of leadership."

Ancestors, thought Titus with the anguish of a man who had none. Rome exalted ancestry, and woe to any man whose forebears did not distinguish themselves.

Suddenly another name came to Titus' lips. "What of the Chrestiani?"

Nicanor grew still. "You've heard of them?"

"Heard of them? They're infamous! Nero blamed them for the Great Fire. Which are they, Pharissian, Sadduccean, Essene, or Zelote?"

Nicanor chose his words carefully. "Originally Essene in nature, they take their name from the Greek word *christos*, meaning anointed one. In the Hebrew tongue, the word is *Mahsiah*, the man anointed by the Lord to lead our people."

Titus said, "Does this mean that the patriarch you speak of, Abraham, was the first *christos*? And Mosheh and David, they were *christosi* as well?"

This was a new thought for Nicanor. "Strictly speaking, I suppose so."

"If *christos* is a title, not a name, who do the Chrestiani worship?"

Nicanor affected the tone of a skeptic. "A man. Very little is known of him, actually. Nothing was written down. His name was Y'eshua, from Nazareth – not far from here. A carpenter, midway through life he began to preach. When he came to Jerusalem, he caused a scene at the Temple, was accused of inciting riot, and was crucified by the Roman procurator."

"Clearly not everyone felt he was the *christos*," observed Titus wryly.

"The priests maintain it is impossible he was the *Mahsiah*. The scriptures are quite clear – the *Mahsiah* will be born from the house of David, not some carpenter from Galilee."

Titus grasped the problem instantly. "Noble blood, once royal. Like the Julians, who were anointed by Venus. Your *christos* must be a Caesar for the Jews."

Nicanor nodded vigourously. "Indeed! It's amazing the power that names take on. Four or five generations past, Caesar was just one of many names – respected, but just a name. Today it adorns the greatest men in the world. What is Caesar, if not another word for *christos*?"

They talked on, Titus finding more parallels than he expected between Roman and Hebrew history. This pleased him enormously – besides looking into the mind of his foe, he could surprise Queen Berenice in their next encounter with some learned conversation.

They parted in the small hours of the morning, Titus thanking

Nicanor profusely. Nicanor promised to return, then walked through the camp in a state of relief. Titus' question about the Chrestiani had been innocent and genuine, but it had been difficult for Nicanor to answer dispassionately about them.

Which was only natural, as Nicanor himself was one.

XXVIII

IT WAS THE BIRTHDAY of the Divine Caesar, and the siege engines were burning once more. Not a thought to make a career soldier proud.

"This is growing tedious," complained Vespasian.

"Reminds me of the Britons." Cerialis shivered, recalling his losses as commander of the Ninth Legion.

"The Britons wore less clothes and more paint," observed Vespasian idly. "Remarkable, considering the climate."

"Britons are mad."

"And these Judeans are not." Vespasian pressed his lips together. "How many days?"

"Thirty-eight."

Vespasian nodded. He was in a cleft stick. His tactics were sound, yet his men were growing restless while the Judeans became emboldened with each sortie. The so-called prophecy of Josephus was looming. If Jotapata survived the full forty-nine days, it would be a tremendous spiritual victory for all of Judea.

There is an indefinable art to generaling. A plan can be sound and sure, but if it didn't have the support of the men, it was doomed. Vespasian could feel his legions growing restless. If the Judeans had only remained behind their walls to suffer, they might have gotten through. But by persisting in midnight raids, Josephus was humiliating them. More, he'd stolen away the initiative. Vespasian had to gain it back.

"Start crucifying prisoners. And bring up Big Julius."

The engineers set to work, raising crosses and affixing Judean captives placed upon them – tied, not nailed, that they might last longer.

These rebels went to their deaths praying, all repeating the same words over and over: "Hear, Israel, one and eternal is our God, Jehovah!"

"Juh juh juh!" taunted the Romans. They brought a mule to the crosses and asked the condemned men to pray to it. "Is that what hides in your great Temple? It is a mule? Is your lonely god nothing more than an ass? Lucky for us the Old Muleteer knows how to handle a bunch of stubborn asses!"

While the first batch of prisoners were being crucified, Vespasian said, "Has anyone seen my son?"

Trajan answered. "He volunteered to make the trip to Sogane to fetch the reserves from King Agrippa."

Vespasian snorted. "Of course he did."

◆　◊　◆

SOGANE, GALILEE

Queen Berenice screamed her pleasure and Titus rolled her off him, laughing and panting.

Not bothering to cover her nakedness, she struck his chest with her fist. "Why do you laugh?"

He grinned at her. "I love that you enjoy yourself."

She frowned playfully. "And you don't?"

"That's not what I mean. I'm just not used to a highborn woman so openly enjoying lovemaking. I wish more did!"

"I don't," said Berenice, curling into him and toying with the hair on his chest. "I would cease to be unique."

"That, love, is impossible." Breath returning, Titus stroked the beads of sweat on her back. He wondered if all Eastern women perspired so heavily, or just the nobility. It was a sign of balanced humors. A Greek doctor had once explained to Titus that men were superior to women because of their larger pores, which allowed them to sweat more and release foul humours. Most women were incapable of perspiration, which led to their monthly need to purge their bodies.

Perhaps it was a balance of her humours that made her such an excellent lover. Titus delighted to hear her pleasure at climax. That she did not always make those sounds only made Titus more determined to work harder next time. Like her gait, he knew this was probably craft. But he did not care.

They lay for a time in blissful languor. Then Titus said, "I take it that Mars is no longer lodged in your breast."

Berenice smiled thinly, her eyes narrowed. "I have purged all unworthy emotion." Titus understood her to mean that she had purged Florus from the earth. "Now tell me about Jotapata."

"What's to tell? They're clever, but they can't last. Their water is running short. The city has no spring, just collects rainfall. The rains were light this year, and the cisterns below the city are nearly dry. But I'm sure Josephus will think of something – he's a clever one."

"Is he?" asked Berenice. "I never thought so."

"You know him?"

Berenice smiled thinly. "More than know him. We're related."

Titus sat up. "You didn't tell me that."

She waved away his concern. "Distant cousins, no more. We share a common ancestor – a great-great grandmother, I believe – who was able to trace her line back to the House of David." She reached out to smooth his frown with her hands. "Does it trouble you? It is not as though we were ever close."

Titus said nothing. Sleeping with a foreign queen was forgivable in a Roman soldier – look at both Caesar and Antony. But if it became known that she was also a cousin to the enemy general, Titus' father would demand this affair end immediately. Which Titus could not allow. "Just promise me not to mention this to anyone until Jotapata is taken."

"Of course," she said at once, perplexed but willing to appease him. She liked this Roman, and saw in him great potential – both for his own career, and hers.

They lay together again, but not as comfortably as before. Suddenly Titus said, "The House of David. Nicanor told me about it. He also said something about a savior – Christos."

"The Greek word for Mahsiah."

"Nicanor said that this Mahsiah had to be from the House of David. Is it possible that Josephus is –"

Berenice was already laughing, a wonderful rumble that shook her breasts. "Absolutely not! Yosef has a great mind, but everything he knows is learned! There is nothing genuine in him – it is all stolen, borrowed from others. Others may be impressed, but trust me, at his core he is not a leader of men."

"So far he's done well. Nicanor tells me his people have begun to call him the Mahsiah."

"He may let them, to give them hope. But if he believes it himself, he is a fool." Smiling, she began to kiss Titus' neck. "Trust me, I know a great man when I see one."

◆   ◇   ◆

Outside the palace, Nicanor waited, tracing little lines in the dirt with the heel of his sandal. As the liaison between the Judean royal family and the Romans, he'd come with Titus. Though boring and more than a shade humiliating, it was still better than watching his country-men get pummeled by catapults, even at a distance. So far the siege had been relatively bloodless. He hoped it would remain so, though he knew he hoped in vain.

The yard outside the palace in Sogane was busy – servants were scuttling in and out with water and food for the visiting Roman delegation, who was having a very different feast at present, if Berenice's shouts were anything to judge by. Nicanor wished he'd brought something to read. Perhaps there was a library in the palace?

"Ho, Nicanor," said one of Berenice's guards, recognizing him.

"Ho, Dror," said Nicanor. They fell to talking of the siege, both shaking their heads. This war was a fool's notion, and both had strong things to say about the leadership of the priests in Jerusalem, who couldn't control the hotheaded Zelotes in their ranks.

As they talked, Nicanor felt the tingling awareness of being watched. Glancing around, he saw several of the serving girls drawing water from the well or shuttling to and fro on their various errands. One of them was watching him, and Nicanor had the idea that she was deliberately stalling, waiting for a time when she could catch him alone. Either that, or she was interested in Dror.

Eventually Dror was called back to duty, giving the handsome young woman her chance. Nicanor smiled as she approached, trying to think of something clever to say, then deciding it was best to let her start the conversation.

"Pardon me, my lord," she said. "Your name is Nicanor – is that correct?"

"It is, lady," replied Nicanor, trying not to study the magnificent breasts under her homespun dress.

"You serve the King?"

"I do."

"Then do you by chance remember a bodyguard by the name of Levi ben Patroclus?"

That startled him, but he answered truthfully. "I do. I remember him well. A fierce warrior, if something of a pragmatist. He's fighting on the other side now."

"Have you seen him?"

"At a distance, yes. He's in Jotapata now."

She nodded at him, her large brown eyes filled with hope and fear in equal measure. "Then perhaps you are the man to help me."

"It would be my honour. How could I help you…?"

"Deborah," she told him. "My name is Deborah."

♦   ◊   ♦

13 JULIUS - 39TH DAY OF SIEGE

At dawn the engineers lovingly hefted a giant battering ram upon its guy-ropes. As soon it was wheeled forth from the camp, the whole Roman army began to cheer. "*Ju*-lius! *Ju*-lius! *Ju*-lius!"

Siege technology had hardly changed since the heyday of the Greeks. Any of the engineers employed by Demetrius Poliorcetes at the siege of Rhodes would have been quite capable of managing the mechanism Vespasian's men now employed. The ram was a single massive beam of wood, very like the mast of a ship. It was slung on a web of ropes attached to a square frame on wheels, two stories high and covered with an iron roof. The men who worked the ram were inside the frame, guiding it to its destination. One end was fitted with an iron head shaped like a snarling beast. Tradition said that the first such device had carried a ram's head, from whence it took its name. The battering ram of Vespasian, however, was deliberately shaped like a snarling, sneering mule. "Juh-juh-juh-Julius!"

Cerialis gave the Arabian archers and Syrian slingers a single command. "Clear those walls!" Under the merciless bombardment that followed, any Judean who lifted his head above the crest of the wall lost that head in a moment. Beneath this covering fire, Big Julius rolled forward.

"Thank the gods, the general's lost patience!" cried Barbarus in delight. "Now the bitch will see what sizable *mentulae* we really are!"

"Move the ballistae and scorpions forward," Vespasian told the artillery commander. "Send out the siege towers." They would commit everything at once and overwhelm the Judeans.

While the artillery devices were hauled forward, tossing stones and shooting thick bolts into the city, legionaries took their places inside the siege towers. Constructed long before, these towers were like monstrous rearing caterpillars. Four stories tall, they were armoured on three sides, with a ziggurat of stairs and ladders within to allow Roman troops to swarm up in safety, then spill out over the Judean walls.

"We'll lose men," observed Titus. He didn't sound perturbed at the idea – in fact, he'd been in a splendid mood since returning the previous evening.

"Your father's got it right," answered Trajan. "Better a few lose their lives than they all lose heart."

Thirty men guided the ram to a perceived weak-spot in Jotapata's walls – they had been throwing catapult stones at it for weeks. In place, each grabbed hold of his strap that hung from the ram. Upon the order, they heaved backwards, then released. The ugly mule's head swung forward to strike Jotapata's walls at just above head-height.

The first blow of the ram shook the city to its very foundations, making every man, woman, and child in Jotapata shudder in unison.

But Yosef had not been idle. Having plenty of both grain and corn, he filled large sacks with both, then attached them to the ends of ropes.

The moment the ramming began, crews heaved the sacks over the wall to create a buffer between the ram and the wall.

Again Yosef's ingenuity brought cheers. Among the crowd, Judah said, "Where did he get the idea?"

"I don't know," shrugged Asher. "The Mahsiah doesn't talk to me anymore."

Yosef waved in acknowledgement of his genius. So thin now that one could see the definition of each rib, his mind felt clearer than ever. He was hearing the Lord, he was sure – who else could give him such clever ideas? As Asher noted, Yosef no longer demurred when people called him Mahsiah.

The Romans tried another spot, but the defenders simply hauled up their sacks, moved a few yards, and lowered them again. This farce continued until Vespasian sent forward a hastily-built scythe on a long pole to cut down the sacks of grain. The ramming continued until dusk, when Big Julius was wheeled back to camp.

To combat both the ram and the siege towers, Yosef instructed several brave men to sneak out at night and bury themselves just below the dirt. In the morning when the siege towers rolled past, they leapt up and used their slings from behind. The little stones ricocheted around inside the towers, each one slaying or wounding several men. Naturally these brave slingers died. But they were so effective that Vespasian was forced to order the backs of the siege towers armoured as well, enclosing his men to swelter in an airless coffin. "These damn Hebrews."

Yosef next employed boiling oil. Despite the ram's protecting roof, the liquid sloughed over the sides, scalding several Romans in their own armour. Their screams angered the Romans so badly they ran forward, determined to swarm over the walls out of pure rage. Barbarus was at their head, Curtus and Thorius beside him.

What stalled them was a feat of daring so heroic that both armies were forced to lay down their arms and cheer.

♦　◊　♦

Judah's century was stationed just above the ram. He watched other men dragging away the giant vats of oil, empty now, and shuddered – it was a horrible death they were delivering.

Asher saw the shudder. "Awful."

Judah nodded. "Give me a sword any day." Looking down, he saw angry Romans racing for the walls. "Brace yourselves! They're coming!"

"I hope the wall crumbles under them!" answered Netir, staggering as the ram continued to hammer the wall below. "It feels ready to shake apart! See?" he added, pointed to a nearby stone that had been dislodged by the pounding below.

"I'll stop it." Kneeling, Atlas wrapped his arms around the huge stone.

"Atlas!" shouted Zamaris. "What are you doing?"

"I'll stop it," repeated Atlas as, with a mighty effort, he rose to stand with the massive stone held over his head.

◆   ◊   ◆

For weeks Centurion Barbarus had been eager to catch another glimpse of his giant. Racing now towards Jotapata, intent on scaling the walls by hand and delivering these Jews up to their precious donkey god, he caught sight of the behemoth. Atlas stood upon the wall above the ram, holding a stone large enough to impress Hercules himself.

"Yes!" cried Barbarus, running harder. "That's right! Look for me, you big bastard. Come on!"

But the giant wasn't searching for Barbarus. He was looking down at the ram below him. Squatting low on the wall's edge, he watched the swing of the ram, finding its rhythm. Then with a grimace of effort, he pitched the stone down just as the ram swung forward.

There was a resounding crack. A moment's pause. Then the steady rhythm of the ram began again.

"Ha! Nice try, Jew!" crowed Curtus.

◆   ◊   ◆

On the wall, Judah peeked down at the ram. The stone had ricocheted off the metal roof, only nicking the ram. "Damn. It was a good try, Atlas."

Zamaris grunted. "Good tries are consolation for losers! We're not going to lose, are we, boys? They're coming! Everyone, get ready!"

"No!!" Atlas began shaking his head, swinging it from side to side like an angry ox being annoyed by flies. "No!!" He began beating his chest with his massive fists. "They do not enter these walls today!!"

Everyone stepped back from this ferocious display, and Philip said, "Atlas, what are you—?"

"Atlas?!?" The look he turned on those near him was terrifying. Judah had heard of red-eyed rage, but never imagined it was real. The man's eyes seemed to be coals. "You want Atlas! I'll upend the world!!" Bending down, the giant lifted his great two-headed axe. Swinging it once, twice over his head, he stepped up onto the parapet and jumped.

Judah, Asher, and the rest lurched forward, watching the massive wall of a man drop two stories to land on the tall roof of the battering ram.

On the ground, the running legionaries shouted warnings to the men inside the machine. But Atlas didn't bother with the engineers. Instead he walked calmly towards the front of the siege engine, heaved his massive axe over his head, and dropped into the gap between the roof and the wall, chopping down hard.

His blade passed through the massive beam as though cutting water, neatly separating the ugly iron head from the wood. The rhythmic pounding of the ram ceased at once, replaced by a pathetic *clunk!*

On the top of the wall Judah screamed with joy, joining hundreds of his fellow defenders in lifting his tunic to flash his genitals at the advancing Romans. Atlas had just circumcised the Roman ram.

Amid the cheers, the giant lashed out at the men in the siege engine, who all fled before him. He then dropped his axe, bent over, and grasped the ram's head in his arms. Using a rope still dangling from the ploy with the sacks, he began to scale the wall. It was a slow business, one-handed. He grasped the rope, hauled up his legs, let his toes find purchase, then leapt up higher.

"Come on!" urged every Jew along the wall. "Come on!"

Below, Barbarus watched in mingled joy and regret – joy for the impossible feat, regret because he would never get his rematch. Already the giant's back was riddled with arrows. Blood gushed forth from those amazing muscles. Already dead, he was just too stubborn to admit it. It was impossible he should reach the top, but still he tried.

"Come on, you big bastard!" cried Barbarus, cheering the giant on. "Come on! You can make it!"

The archers and slingers ceased casting missiles and combat stopped as every man – Roman, Judean, Syrian, and Arab – turned to watch Atlas' final act.

He was slowing now, sapped of his great strength. Judah, Asher, Philip and Netir hauled on the rope, trying to drag the great man to the top. They could hear his laboured breath.

"You're almost there!" shouted Judah! "Come on!" Only three more leaps and he would reach the top. Two more! One!

Atlas paused. Then, with a massive effort, he heaved himself up onto the wall's edge and hauled himself over.

Both armies, Roman and Judean, cheered themselves hoarse. Bravery was a gift to be treasured, whichever god bestowed it.

Struggling to stand, Atlas shook off the hoards of helping hands and turned to face the Romans. Lifting the iron ram's head above his own, he cried, "Hear, O Israel, one and eternal is our God, Jeh–!"

A lone *pilum* struck him in the heart and the giant Atlas keeled over stone dead, the ram's head still clutched in his hands. There was a gasp from ten thousand throats, a sigh of sadness that such a man should die in so churlish a way.

One voice was not lamenting. Barbarus heard Curtus say, "Got him." The centurion was tempted to strike the man. But instead he began beating his sword rhythmically against his shield-boss. Thorius picked it up, then the rest of his century. In moments the whole Roman army was doing the same, a ringing acclaim for the bravery of their fallen foe.

Tomorrow there would be more battle. But for the waning hours of this day the fighting ceased as soldiers from both armies honoured such an heroic act.

"Now *that*," said Barbarus, chest swelling in pride, "is an enemy Mithras would be proud to own! Never seen a finer!" He glowered at Curtus. "Shouldn't've done that, boy. Disrespectful."

"Sir!" answered Curtus.

It was the oldest trick in the military handbook – when you disagree with a superior, just clam up and say 'sir'. Curtus had not cheered with the rest of the army, nor would he repent. Mithras, he felt sure, had no love for the Jews.

♦　◊　♦

Inside the walls, no one was allowed to carry Atlas' body except the men from his century. Judah, Asher, Zamaris, Gareb, Deuel, Philip, and Netir bore the giant's corpse down from the ramparts in a throng of citizens desperate to touch their hero.

There was a howl as little Chava came running as fast as her swollen belly allowed. Seeing her husband held aloft, she pitched to her knees and wailed. "*Nooooo!*"

Judah let other hands bear the body away as he knelt to wrap his arms around the little widow. Tears were streaming from his eyes. A crowd formed around them. No longer cheering, they stood in silent appreciation of this little woman's loss, and of the great sacrifice her husband had performed. The body was laid on a table covered in cloth, blood still flowing freely.

Philip sank down nearby with his back against a wall. "He's earned more than his share of *Kleos*."

Sliding down to sit beside him, Asher cuffed at his eyes. "I've never heard of a finer death."

"Because no matter how skillful a poet is," answered Judah over Chava's head, "he cannot bring such a moment to life."

Asher proved him wrong. "'*As long as rivers shall run down to the sea, or shadows touch the mountain slopes, or stars graze in the vault of heaven, so long shall your honour, your name, your praises endure.*'"

Chava lifted her head and through gasps of breath asked, "Who..?"

"A Roman," answered Asher, embarrassed. "Virgil."

But she was not insulted. "Good." It was all she could get out before the spasms of breathless weeping overtook her again.

"It's true," said Judah, holding her tight. "He died a great death. He died so that we all might live another day."

"It's a blessing," said Deuel softly.

◆   ◊   ◆

There was an undeclared truce that evening. Vespasian even sent five barrels of wine to the city, a mark of how impressed he was with the giant's feat. Nicanor was allowed to go with it, to translate. While he was at the gate, he asked for a man by name. The defender looked suspicious, but Nicanor was a Hebrew, and gave his word this was no trick. "Purely a personal matter."

◆   ◊   ◆

Yosef arrived where Atlas had been laid out to find a silent crowd. Worried that the moment might turn their thoughts to defeat, he declared a celebration. "Better we celebrate his great victory than mourn his loss!" The widow was escorted away, the body removed. The ram's head was placed upon the bloody table and torches were lit. Still the evening threatened to be grim until Yosef declared an extra ration of water for every man, woman, and child present. That raised spirits, and soon there was music and dancing.

For the first time in days, Yosef sought out Asher and Judah. "A great loss."

"Yes," agreed Judah, unconsciously flexing his hands still covered in the giant's blood. "Forgive me. Don't feel much like celebrating."

"Let's head back to the billet," said Asher.

"I'll walk with you," said Yosef, surprising both twins.

They left the square and headed towards the large house near the city's heart. For a time they walked in silence. Then Asher said, "Who steps into his place tomorrow? Who follows his example?"

"Funny," said Judah, "I was thinking exactly that."

"Really?" asked Yosef, frowning in puzzlement. "I was wondering if your friend's great deed even matters." Both twins stopped and stared at him. "Don't mistake me! I honour his bravery, to be sure! I admire him – Lord, my admiration is boundless. But tomorrow there will be another head attached to Big Julius. His sacrifice earned us a reprieve of a few hours, nothing more. For that he gave up his life?"

Asher shook his head. "You don't understand. That was the stuff of legends!"

"He showed the Romans true bravery," agreed Judah. "They respect us more because of him. He died a good death."

"What is a good death?" countered Yosef. "If his death meant his country survives, I grant that's a good death. But if he sacrificed himself for a delay of mere hours, what does it matter? Isn't it better that he were alive, fighting off the Romans the way he always did, than to throw his life away in an empty gesture?"

"Empty..! Single-handed he stopped the Romans from making an all-out assault on the walls!"

Knowing Yosef, Asher tried a different tack. "You keep using the word sacrifice. Think about what it means – in Latin, it means 'to make sacred.' The Hebrew word is Korban, from *karov*, meaning..."

"Yes, I know. It means *'To come close to God'*. As a priest I make sacrifices every day."

"And when you sacrifice a lamb or a bird, the animal had to be clean, right? Unblemished, whole – perfect? That's because to sacrifice less than the best is an insult to the Lord."

"But when is sacrifice a wrong act?" demanded Yosef. "Can sacrifice ever be a sin? What if we sacrifice something we need, truly need!"

"If we sacrifice a thing without worth," said Asher, exasperated, "then the act has no meaning!"

Listening, Judah saw what Asher did not. Yosef was not lamenting the death of Atlas. He was wondering what purpose his own death might serve. "The only sin would be sacrificing something – or someone – unworthy."

Yosef looked like he'd been slapped. "Tell the widow I'm sorry for her loss." With that he turned on his heel and stalked away.

Asher watched the general's retreating back. "I don't understand. Most men in his position would be obsessed with glory, with dying a legendary death."

"Oh, he is," said Judah. "But he's too afraid."

"Of death?"

"Of a meaningless death. He doesn't understand that no death is meaningless." He paused, then said, "So."

"So," agreed Asher. "We'll likely die, you know."

"As long as you're dying with me," said Judah, smiling. "After all, you got me into this."

"*With you I should love to live, with you be ready to die.*"

Judah banged his head repeatedly with his fists. "Asher, this is no time for poetry!"

Grinning, Asher countered with another line from Horace. "*Many brave men lived before Agamemnon; but all are overwhelmed in eternal night, unwept, unknown, because they lack a sacred poet.*"

"Better that than remembered in bad verse."

They were silent for a time. Then Asher said, "We shouldn't go back tonight. They might divine our intent."

"Agreed. And we need to discuss what exactly it is we hope to achieve. If we're to live in poems, we have to do something noteworthy. Otherwise it'll be Phannius telling everyone how stupidly we died."

They both laughed at that. Then Asher pursed his lips. "I do hope some writer eulogizes Eleazar, son of Samas, called Atlas, the giant of Jotapata."

In answer, Judah stopped walking. Standing still, he looked skyward and began reciting *e-l malei rachamim*, a prayer for the dead, adding the three lines that signified that Eleazar sacrificed his life for his country.

> *"O God, full of mercy, Who dwells on high,*
> *Grant proper rest on the wings of the Divine Presence,*
> *In the lofty levels of the Holy and the Pure ones,*
> *Who shine like the glow of the Firmament,*
> *For the soul of Eleazar, son of Samas,*
> *Who gave up his life*
> *For the Sanctification of the Name*
> *And the Conquest of the Land,*
> *Because, without making a vow,*
> *I will contribute to charity in remembrance of his soul.*
> *May his resting place be in the Garden of Eden.*
> *Therefore may the Master of Mercy*
> *Shelter him in the shelter of His wings for Eternity,*
> *And may He bind his soul in the Bond of Life.*
> *Hashem is his heritage,*
> *And may he repose in Peace on his resting place.*
> *Amen."*

"Amen," echoed Asher.

"See?" said Judah. "He'll be remembered without a poet."

◆   ◊   ◆

Levi came into the billet for Zamaris' century. He found Phannius and drew him aside. "Where's Judah?"

"Likely at the celebrations. Did I hear the Romans sent wine?"

"They're tasting it now. Quick, come with me."

"Where are we going?"

"To find Judah. I have news for you both."

But try as they might, they could not find either twin that night.

XXIX

TELLING NO ONE their intent, Asher and Judah spent
the whole night preparing. They collected what they needed, discussing what would be most useful in the few moments they would have.
Judah's final act was to pen a note to Phannius, asking him when he
found Deborah to give her Judah's love. "Not that he will."

"It's the last request of a dead man," said Asher. "He has to."

Judah nodded. Dead men. That's what they were. But every man
owed the Lord a death, and it was up to each man to make it a good one.

Sending the note off with a guard just finishing his patrol, the
twins made sure they were unobserved, then dropped from the wall. It
was the small hours of the night, and they used the dangling ropes from
the sacks to slither down from the battlements. Judah paused a moment
before dropping. Letting go was the point of no return.

Asher hadn't let go either. "Changing your mind?"

"No." Judah released his grip and dropped ten feet to the dirt
below.

Asher followed, and moments later they were crouched in a
wrecked building between the walls and the Roman camp. Naked but
for loincloths and firm sandals, they carried unlit torches and little clay
pitchers of oil, with bandoliers of more oil across their chests.

"Should've brought a blanket," said Judah, shivering.

"Not long now." Asher grinned. "They'll certainly see us coming."

"The key is speed," advised Judah. "Close the gap to the archers
before they can shoot."

"Wish I wasn't so thirsty."

"Maybe we should ask the Romans for a drink before we start."

"Ha! Can you imagine that? 'Pardon us, we're here to burn your camp. May we have some water, please?'"

"Quiet. If they hear us, our blaze of glory will be very short."

Falling silent, they waited for the dawn.

♦   ◊   ♦

As Yosef predicted, sunrise found a new head attached to Big Julius. The ram again departed the Roman camp, rolling slowly towards Jotapata to offer its punishing rhythm of blows.

Vespasian watched the advance of the ram from the height of a knoll. In this damnable heat, his gout was acting up. Seated in a straight-backed chair, his swollen right foot up on a stool, he sorted the latest post from Rome. Among the letters was a missive from Caenis, which Vespasian chose to read before the official dispatches. Knowing her, it would have more reliable information.

Aware he might have to show this letter to other men, Caenis had refrained from loving superlatives. Still, she would have betrayed her sex had she not started with the most scandalous of her news:

> *Caesar is still in Greece, celebrating the games at Olympia. But it is not his athletic aspirations that have brought a smile to every Roman face. No, rather the city is atwitter with what is quickly becoming known as the Scandal of Nero's Wives. While on his honeymoon, Nero has married again! Without divorcing his poor young Statilia Messalina, I might add. But bigamy is the least of it. Nero Caesar's new wife is really his dead wife, reincarnated in the person of a rather lovely Greek boy. The details are only just arriving, but all of Rome is already weeping with laughter.*

Vespasian choked. *Jupiter! What would Nero do next?* "Titus! Listen to this!"

♦   ◊   ♦

Judah stood. "It's time. Asher, if you live, tell Deborah…"

Asher held up a hand. "If I'm alive, you will be too." Both knew how unlikely that was. "Ready?"

"Right. Let's go. Remember – speed."

Lighting their torches, they exited the hovel and began to run.

Due to the uneventful night, the Arabian and Syrian archers had begun to doze. The twins' lit torches were hardly noticeable against the rising sun. Sandaled feet silent on the trampled earth, Judah and Asher were among the archers before the first bowstring could be drawn.

They'd decided their goal was not Roman deaths – they would never slay enough legionaries to make a difference. But if they could burn the catapults, rams, and larger weapons they could delay the Romans, lift a little of the siege, and spare some lives within the walls.

Swinging his torch to ward off defenders, Judah tossed his first clay pitcher of oil against a Roman scorpion, launcher of huge bolts. Waving his torch over the spot, he felt the heat as the fire leapt from his weapon to the machine.

Beside him, Asher threw his vessel of oil onto a second scorpion and set it alight with his torch. Judah was already plucking another oil-filled pot from the bandolier on his chest and running to the next siege weapon down the line. Engineers rushed forward to defend their precious machines, but Judah doused those in front with oil and waved his torch, and they retreated, screaming.

"The Dioscouri!" To the superstitious engineers not on fire, these two fearsome warriors looked like the Greek gods Castor and Pollux. "The Dioscouri! The Dioscouri are fighting for the Jews!"

Asher heard their cries with astonishment. Romans believed that the twins Castor and Pollux always came to turn the tide of a war, usually in Rome's favour. *If the Romans think their gods are abandoning them...* Calling out in Latin, Asher bellowed, "Castor, remember when we stole the cattle of Idas and Lynceus! They tried to kill us, too! But Jupiter Best and Greatest gave us immortal life!"

Judah scowled. "What are you..?"

"We fought with the Argonauts! We rescued Helen from Theseus! We saved Rome at Lake Regillus! Now these foolish Romans repay us with steel?"

Already an entire row of catapults and scorpions was ablaze. The first legionaries were warily approaching. Were these gods, or just clever Jews?

Pitching his last pot of oil, Judah called out in their native tongue, "Stop spouting poetry and get a sword!" Judah transferred his torch to his off hand and snatched a sword from a burned, writhing engineer. It scalded his hand, but he ignored the pain. He'd just spied a particularly large catapult in the next row of siege machines. Fending legionaries off with torch and sword, he raced for it. "Come on!"

◆   ◊   ◆

"Who's that?" demanded Netir, pushing his way to the rampart for a better view of the burning Roman siege machines.

"It's Judah and Asher!" squeaked Philip. "Those bastards are going it alone!"

"Didn't they think we'd come?" said Deuel.

"It's not too late!" shouted Gareb. "Come on!"

◆   ◊   ◆

"More heroics," observed Vespasian atop his command hill.

"Looks like they caught the Tenth napping," observed Titus, still grinning over the story of Nero's new wife.

"Get down there and sort them out. Then have the Tenth's centurions disciplined and the optios flogged."

"Yes, general." Titus leapt onto his horse and galloped off, leaving the general to continue perusing the latest news from Rome, relayed as only Caenis could:

> *Hispania and Britannia are both quiet – a shock, I know. There were some minor rumblings among the Germanic tribe called Chatti, but it came to nothing. Thus you need not fear the Judean war being eclipsed. Provided Jotapata falls before the season ends, there is little doubt that your command will be prorogued into next year.*
>
> *That is not to say the Senate is entirely pleased. They all want the job for themselves. Your decision to avoid Jerusalem this year is alternately hailed and reviled, with the worst words coming from the professional couch-generals.*
>
> *These rumblings will come to nothing. As you know, I have renewed old acquaintances, and can now boast of being hostess to all the wives of the most important men in Rome – save, of course, Nero's wives. (Though I would love to meet the reborn Poppaea!) Having the ears of so many senatorial wives, I am filling them with praise for the family Flavius. While you are a trifle old for a second consulship, my machinations will certainly assist your sons, as well as your nephew, Sabinus. He is nothing like his father, and calls on me frequently. And he is beloved of Apollo. He traveled to Delphi last fall after escorting your young Domitian to Nero. Rumour is he was summoned by the Pythia herself. He has been tight-lipped about what she told him. But she did say that Jerusalem would fall, and to his family. But not – brace yourself my love – for three years. I know, Titus Flavius. But she predicts incredible honour for the whole family.*
>
> *As the Pythian prophecy shows her favour, I have promised Sabinus that he will be a legate in three years, when Jerusalem falls.*

Three more years? What on earth did that mean? How could this war drag on so long? And how could Nero possibly leave him in command if he dragged his feet taking Jerusalem? It made no sense!

Yet every Roman carried a kind of nameless dread and awe of such prophecies. At least this one wasn't dire. In fact it was almost heartening, if galling. Jerusalem would fall, but not for three years. Caenis was correct, the promise of a legateship was small price to pay for such knowledge. It allowed Vespasian to make plans accordingly.

He returned to the letter:

> *Most important between then and now is the advancement of your sons. I have several eligible young women interested in marriage. Could you arrange for Titus to fight in some grand-sounding engagements? Truly, Titus Flavius, I do not tell you how to conduct your war! I mean only that a military reputation for Titus would go a long way to assuring he is elected quaestor in his year. And the right wife would help as well.*

Vespasian snorted. *I would love to arrange another match for Titus, if he could tear himself away from his Hebrew enchantress!*

Glancing down at the field below, Vespasian saw the two Judeans were still alive, and his favourite catapult was burning. "Damn these Judeans, one and all!"

◆　◇　◆

"Damn Asher!" exclaimed Yosef breathlessly, having run to the top of the watchtower. "What's the fool doing?"

Levi said, "He and Judah are being heroes."

Phannius shook his head in mingled anger and admiration. "The fool. You didn't tell him—?"

"I never found him. Clearly because he was preparing for this."

"Damn damn damn!" Exasperated, Yosef struck the air. "If everyone plays hero, there will be no one left to defend the walls! See!" He pointed below, where dozens more men were leaping to rush to the aid of the twins. Their entire century led the way, and even young Chalafta was venturing out to fight. "Battle in daylight? They're bent on self-destruction, Levi, a meaningless sacrifice!"

But the bodyguard had gone, leaping from the wall below, Phannius right behind him.

Yosef fumed. *I am the leader! These fools are following the wrong men!*

Realizing he would soon be alone upon the ramparts, Yosef himself dropped down and ran into the fray.

◆　◇　◆

Running out of the camp in the company of his legate, Barbarus viewed the naked twins with grim pleasure. Someone had taken up the giant's standard! Fitting that it was two men – Atlas was worth at least that many.

But what men these were! Armourless, they looked like Olympian athletes. Their naked muscles were those of Hercules. Taller than the average Roman, they looked like Greek sculptures come to life. One of them was particularly skilled, skipping through the swords of engineers and foreigners with strength, guile, and speed.

Let me at him, thought Barbarus. *Let him try his skill against a real Roman soldier, one on one.* "Permission to engage the enemy, sir?"

Titus rode with one leg curled about the pommel for balance. "Denied, centurion! Wheel right!"

What? Why? Bitterly disappointed, Barbarus glanced over his shoulder. *Ah!* Defenders were rushing from the city, clearly inspired. Casting a wistful eye on the twins, he ordered, *"Ad dextram rotate!"* At once his maniple turned to engage the new threat.

Close by, Titus was tingling with excitement. Initiative, his father had said. All he had to do was hold his men back long enough to lure more Judeans out. Then these troublesome rebels would feel the full weight of Rome on their necks. *We can win the siege here today!*

Glancing left, he saw the two Judeans were still alive. *Good. The longer they live, the more their fellows will try to save them. In fact...* "Barbarus! Slow! Slow down! Let their rescuers in!"

I hate it when commanders get clever. The legate wanted the Judeans funneled between the Fifteenth and the Tenth. But Barbarus knew better than to question an order. *"Tardate! Tardate!"* he called, hoping the young pup knew what he was doing.

Meanwhile the Tenth Legion had formed a loose crescent around the twins. Trajan was shouting, "Don't kill them! We want prisoners, not martyrs!"

Damn, thought Barbarus sorrowfully. *That was a fight worth dying for.*

♦   ◊   ♦

Judah and Asher fought side by side against an angry Tenth Legion, protected by growing flames behind them and piles of dead before them. The pyre meant the twins were almost encircled, and the soldiers were funneled into narrow gap where the twins held them off. Hissing spits of oil jumped out to scald them, but better that than the tip of a Roman gladius.

There was only one route for the Romans to come at them. A sword in each hand, Judah kept the blades in constant motion, the circular motions of his swords acting as both attack and defense. Spinning, cutting, keening his rage, he felt almost as though he was dancing.

Asher was more methodical. Even in the midst of desperate fighting, he found himself able to think. He traded his torch for a shield, and his sword for one of the long sickles the Romans had made to cut down the wheat barriers. *Close protection, and a long reach – an excellent defense.*

Asher's own mind bested him. He was thinking ahead, plotting his next moves when a Roman suddenly leapt through the flames to cut low at Asher's naked legs. Desperate, he brought down both sickle and shield, trapping the sword against the ground. The sickle chopped clean through the legionary's arm, the blade burying itself in the dirt.

Another legionary from the Tenth stabbed and Asher used the haft of the sickle to block the blow. But his sickle refused to leave the dirt. Abandoning it, he backed away with only his shield, warding off attacks from both sides. It was only a matter of time. Blocking right, he was stabbed in his left shoulder. It wasn't bad, but he winced as the legionary twisted the blade, raking it across his pectoral. Asher hammered his attacker with the shield boss, staggering him.

Another sword point came at him, and Asher used the flat of his free hand to slap it away. More swords as the knot of the Tenth Legion's first cohort drew tighter.

He ducked a swing, but the enemy brought the pommel back to strike his cheek. Asher's nose erupted in blood. Against his will he shouted, "Judah!"

◆   ◊   ◆

Titus watched the growing broyle with excitement. Judeans were pouring out of Jotapata. It wasn't a battle, not yet. But if he tended it like a weak fire, fanning the embers, it could erupt into a conflagration. "Barbarus, have the men step back. Make it look like we're faltering. Draw them in!" The siege might end here and now, in a proper battle after all.

Looks like he knows what he's about. Blessing Mithras for his legate's canny strategy, Barbarus led his century backwards, as if afraid. "*Redite! Redite!*"

◆   ◊   ◆

Hearing Asher's cry, Judah spun around. Face and arm covered in blood, Asher had only a shield, swinging it wildly at the Romans closing in for the kill.

"*Asher!!*" Possessed with a fury, Judah rushed towards his twin, raking his blades in wild upwards swings, scattering the Romans between him and his brother. "Run! Get out of it! I'll –"

Asher blocked a cut with his shield. "Judah, look out!"

It was as though a string had been cut in his leg. Falling, Judah cut wildly behind him, catching his attacker at the knee, slicing clean through the leather pyteriges and into the kneecap. The shrieking Roman fell sideways and Judah dispatched him with a contemptuous flick of his wrist.

Another Roman was driving in for the kill. On one knee, Judah trapped the incoming blade by making a V with both his swords. One sword sent the thrust to aside while the other stabbed the Roman's groin.

Judah felt flesh against his back. Asher had stayed, kneeling just behind him and using the shield to protect them both for a few moments more. He heard Asher's dry voice croak, *"With you I should love to live, with you be ready to die."*

"No fucking poetry!" Judah was laughing and crying as eager Romans came at them from both sides. "Come on then! Finish it..!"

"Judah! Asher! Roll north!"

They both obeyed, rolling sideways and bumping into each other. Looking back they saw Levi leap through the flames to stab one Roman in the throat while clubbing another with his shield. The bodyguard tore into the Roman ranks, again showing his terrible skill as he massacred four Romans single-handed.

Phannius, Philip, and Netir were right behind him, while Zamaris, Gareb, Deuel, Chalafta and a dozen more defenders lifted Judah and Asher clear from the ground and carried them to safety.

Shielded from Roman fury, the twins gasped for breath. Asher's teeth were bright against his bloodied face. "I guess neither of us die today!"

"Better to be lucky than good." Judah glanced up at the Roman command hill, where the general's personal standard remained. "Bastard couldn't even be bothered to come and fight." He bent low and retrieved a bow from a dead Syrian. "Let's give the old man a fright."

Wincing against the pain in his thigh, Judah was pleased to find he could still stand. Planting his feet wide, he nocked an arrow and let it fly in a high arc over the heads of all the combatants.

◆   ◊   ◆

Unmindful of the growing skirmish below, Vespasian was still reading:

I have news, which I've heard only just this minute,
that affects you nearly. Caesar has at last found a governor

of Syria to replace the disgraced Cestius. None other than Gaius Licinius Mucianus. Do you know him at all? As his name suggests, he is a Licinius only by adoption. He was born a Mucian, and looks just like them – short, dark, and pouty. An appreciator of games and the arts – of all things Greek, in fact – his promotion was inevitable. He'll arrive in September.

He'll take credit for anything, so make certain he cannot—

A shooting pain in Vespasian's right foot made him gasp. Looking over the letter's top, he saw an arrow sticking out of his heel.

"Jupiter!" he exclaimed, more incredulous than injured. "I've just been made into Achilles!"

At once his aides began yelling for help. Hearing his mix of profanity and laughter, they knew the matter was none too serious.

But as the cry passed down the ranks, the message altered:

"The general's been shot in the foot!"

"The general's been shot!"

"The general's been shot dead!"

"The general's dead! *The general's dead!!*"

◆ ◊ ◆

Fighting close to Titus, Nicanor suddenly pointed. "There, legatus! That's him – Josephus!"

Titus spied the handsome long face with the scythe of a nose. The enemy general was in the field! "Now, Barbarus, now! Wrap them up!"

"Yes, sir!" The centurion signaled the bugler. "*Porro! Porro!*"

But just as the bugler was about to blow the order, a tribune came up at the gallop. "Titus Flavius! The general, sir! The general is dead!"

Barbarus looked to Titus. *Press the attack, young legate. Forget the news! Press on! You'll never have another chance!*

But in the struggle between son and soldier, the soldier lost. "Fall back! Fall back!"

◆ ◊ ◆

"How's the shoulder?" asked Judah, kneeling and rubbing dirt into his thigh to stop the bleeding.

Sitting beside him, Asher flexed and winced. "If I'm alive tomorrow, it's going to hurt. Your leg?"

"The same." Both were covered in blood, dirt, and small burns. Judah looked around at the Judean soldiers protecting them. "I think I love them."

Asher laughed. Then they heard a cheer. Standing, it took both twins a moment to comprehend what they saw. "They're pulling back? They're pulling back!" Asher pumped his fist into the air.

Judah was about to do the same when he saw Philip and Netir laying side-by-side, their eyes open, the ghost of laughter still on their faces. The tax collectors had finally expiated their sin with the best coin they could offer – their own blood.

◆   ◊   ◆

"What in Hades is Titus doing?" asked Vespasian, seeing the Fifteenth retreating. "He has them! All he has to do is bring his flank around and block their retreat!"

"I imagine he's heard you're hurt, sir," replied an orderly, using a blade to cut the arrowhead from the general's foot.

Vespasian groaned, not at the pain but the stupidity. "Is the foot bad? Can I ride?"

In answer, the man removed the arrowhead intact from the flesh of Vespasian's heel. "Most of its strength was spent, sir. It's amazing it made it this far. Hardly deep at all."

"Then hurry and wrap it, man!" Vespasian cried. "I've got to get out there and show them I'm not dead."

"You really should soak it for poisons, sir —"

"Pah! Just get it wrapped and put me on a horse!"

Five minutes later Vespasian was galloping down from the crest, waving and exhorting his men on. This lasted until he reached Titus, who embraced him unashamedly while the legionaries formed a protective square about them.

"*Pater!* They said you were dead!"

"Let this serve as a reminder," said Vespasian, wincing. "Always lead from the front! Now let's see if we can salvage this battle! Placidus! Get that cavalry around their flank!"

Yosef had fought his way to the front ranks, determined to be seen as brave. That it was actually brave did not occur to him. He was in the thick of it when suddenly a miracle occurred – the Romans pulled back! The Judeans swelled, pressing their attack against a disorganized foe. Could they repeat their feat at Beth Horon? Was God giving the Judeans another victory? *Is this my reward?*

But then something changed. There came a palpable shift as the Romans settled down. The retreating shields began to advance again. When Yosef heard the thunder of horses, he knew that the moment had passed. "Back! Back to the walls!"

They listened. He had not lost their love. By fighting in the front ranks, he had retained their respect, and the Lord's favour.

◆   ◊   ◆

Literally carried back to safety, the twins' feet didn't touch the ground. Hugged and blessed by crowds of women and children, Asher and Judah were finally allowed to rest in the yard to General Yosef's own palace. Asher's left arm hung limp, and Judah was sitting sideways to relieve the pressure on his thigh.

Their joy at being alive was tempered by the deaths they had caused. It was hard not to think that the joking brothers had died in their stead.

The gates to Yosef's home opened and the deafening cheers began again. Amid the cheering, Asher heard a familiarly musical voice. "Asher ben Matthais! Judah ben Matthais! Your bravery has given this entire city hope. Hear their acclaim! And hear too the Roman reply!" He cupped a hand to his ear theatrically. "Silence! The siege works have lost their voices. Come what may, your bravery will be remembered forever!"

Even as he congratulated them, there was a glower in Yosef's eye. But he played the perfect host, arranging a feast and declaring that the twins might drink all the water they desired – a great gift.

"Please, we must say this was not our plan," declared Judah. Asher looked at him curiously, but Judah pressed on. "Philip and Netir, the publicans, were the real architects of this scheme. They died today protecting us. Give the credit to them."

Asher nodded. A prayer was said. As the revels began, they were taken aside to have a doctor look at their wounds. "Nicely done," said Asher softly.

"Thanks," grunted Judah, wincing.

"Having trouble sitting?"

From his tilted angle, Judah grimaced. "Thigh wound, you hear me? It's a thigh wound."

The doctor working on Asher raised an eyebrow. "As you say. Though, in point of fact, you were stabbed in the arse."

Judah raised a warning fist at his chortling brother. "If you tell Phannius, I'll murder you myself."

Asher clutched his own wound. "Dammit, don't make me laugh!"

Grinning, Judah held out his hand. Asher took it. They had survived. It was a miracle.

Seeing Levi approach, Judah called to him. "You should be celebrating!"

"I am," answered Levi, stopping beside him. "I celebrate my liberation. I am no longer bodyguard to Yosef."

"Good for you!" Judah could admire the way Yosef had led them, and he certainly appreciated the general's inventiveness. But Judah couldn't forgive the attempt at escape, nor shake the certainty that Yosef was not here for the people, but thought the people were here for him.

"Yosef is a fool." Asher's feelings were more complex, his anger deeper. "Did you resign?"

Levi shook his head. "I was released. By chasing after you two, I failed to honour my contract."

"That would do it," chuckled Judah.

"Well I, for one, thank you," said Asher.

"Yes," said Judah, a little light-headedly. "That's the second time you've saved my life. I'm grateful, sure. But it begs the question 'why?'"

Levi spoke in his normal, affectless tone. "I had promised to deliver a message to you. I am a man of my word."

Still smiling, Judah looked puzzled. "Message?"

"From Deborah. She is alive, and close at hand."

◆　◊　◆

While the Judah heard this news, while the defenders celebrated, while Jotapata rejoiced, the Romans laboured. At dawn the next day, the engineers rolled out new catapults. The siege continued.

XXX

"WHERE IS SHE? Where?" Judah looked about, half expecting to see her magically appear within the walls.

"She's in Sogane, in the palace of Queen Berenice," said Levi. "She sent word through someone I knew when I was in the king's employ. He says she —"

"Judah! Judah, you bastard!" Phannius barreled over to where they were being treated and started smacking Judah about the head. Unable to stand, Judah had balled his fists before he realized the huge idiot was being playful.

"You incredible, monstrous fool! Do you expect me to go rescue Deborah, only to tell her you've gotten yourself killed before you even knew she was alive? What kind of bastard does that?"

"My kind," said Judah, smiling ruefully. "Is she truly safe?"

"She told Levi's friend that she was safe until she reached Mount Tabor, then she ran into ruffians – those same fools who robbed the king's courier." Phannius' face darkened. "She might have been killed – or worse. You know whose fault that is, right?"

Judah nodded. "I know."

"But she wasn't," said Levi.

"No," agreed Phannius. "By pure chance, the Queen was on her way here from Gamala, crossing the River Jordan south of Lake Gennesar. Running from the band of scoundrels, Deborah fled right into the Queen's arms. She's been there all summer."

"Thank the Lord," sighed Judah. Asher reached out a hand, and Judah clasped it, uttering a quiet prayer of thankfulness. Then he looked to Phannius. "You have to get out of here."

The large chinless mason was visibly startled. "What?"

"We have to get you out. You didn't come here to fight. You came to save your sister. We'll get a message to her through Levi's friend, then somehow sneak you up into the mountains. Get you both away from here."

For some reason, Phannius looked absolutely furious. "Why don't you go?"

Judah pointed to his wound. "I'm not sneaking off anywhere. And I'm not going to tell her I left her brother to die. It has to be you."

Phannius ground his teeth together. "You bastard." Turning, he stalked away.

Judah looked to Asher, who shrugged. It was left to Levi to explain. "He came by accident. But he's been here for the whole siege."

"All the more reason to want to escape."

"He thinks you view him as a coward. You'll stay here to die, while he creeps away and tells his sister how brave you were, and he wasn't."

"O for the love of...! I'm trying to get him to save the woman we both love!"

"Deborah is safe for the moment. The city needs him more than she does. He wants you to see that."

Judah rolled his eyes incredulously. "Since when did it matter to that great lummox what I think?"

"Since you became a hero," said Asher.

♦   ◊   ♦

The prophesized forty-nine days were nearly up, and Vespasian's honour demanded he not allow Yosef that symbolic victory. These things mattered, if only to the spirit of the people of Judea. If Vespasian was to win this war, he had to break that spirit.

Every day of the following week he sent Big Julius rolling out to bash the walls from dawn until dusk, when fighting devolved to minor skirmishes through the night.

But Vespasian did not place all his hopes on the ram, which seemed to have no effect on the thick city walls. Daily he inched his legions nearer behind fortified banks. Others tried to emulate Asher and Judah, but there was now a wall of shields around every siege engine, and plenty of sand and water to put out any fire.

As the Romans drew nearer, their catapult stones reached deeper into the city. At any moment sudden death could fall upon any place in the city.

For days Judah and Asher's wounds kept them from joining in any fighting. But Judah was soon walking, and Asher had full, if painful, use of his arm. Phannius was part of the raids every night, whether it was Zamaris leading the men or not.

"What's he trying to prove?" demanded Judah. If the idiot got himself murdered, Deborah would never forgive him. Or herself.

But he wished he could be out there fighting, too. Life in the city was a nightmare. Stones were falling with terrifying rapidity, crushing homes and palaces and taverns and men.

Worse, thirst was turning the people against each other, as throats closed and fathers saw their children suffer. There were attacks on the wells, and even attempts to dig down to the warren of tunnels beneath the city – not to escape, but just to find something to drink.

At midday on the forty-fifth day of the siege, Judah was in a plaza at the heart of the city, standing guard over a well with Gareb. It was necessary, and also a blessing to have something to do.

"We have a bet, you know," said Gareb.

"Oh? A lottery? When the Romans will run out of stones?"

"This is Judea. They'll never run out." As if in counterpoint they heard a crack, followed by the rumble of a building wall collapsing. They were deep enough in the city that stones couldn't reach. "No, we have a pool as to which of you slips away to rescue your woman first."

Judah was silent. He'd thought of little else for five days. His eagerness to heal was spurred by the thought that Deborah was close. Every night he argued with Phannius, telling him to surrender to Levi's friend Nicanor and go be with his sister, take her back to Jerusalem where it was safe. But Phannius refused. "You go! You're no use to anyone else right now. I'm here and I'm going to fight!"

Now Judah and Gareb were standing with a dozen other men, some wounded, some needing rest, all encircling one of the city's main wells. Suddenly they heard a voice shout, "Judah! Gareb!"

Turning, they saw Chava waddling across the square towards them. The short woman looked nearly as wide as she was tall, her swollen belly threatening to topple her.

"Look at you!" said Judah smiling. He winced as he waved her over. "Ready to burst."

"Any day!" she called, making slow progress towards them.

"Let's hope he waits another week or so," said the lean Gareb. "If he's born on the fiftieth day, he'll make his daddy proud. Defiant with his first breath!" Chava smiled at that, perhaps the first real smile since her husband's death.

She was still approaching them slowly when they heard a loud crack. Chava seemed to disappear, replaced by a red cloud as blood misted the air in front of her. Judah heard her gasp even over the crash of the round stone striking on the paving stone. He stared, but it was a long moment before his mind comprehended what he was seeing.

Chava's swollen belly was suddenly concave. Tracing the trail of blood from her to the ground beside her, Judah saw a pulped, bloody mass smeared across the ground. Among the smear there was a tiny, perfectly shaped hand. Judah gagged, and several of the other men turned to vomit or weep outright.

Achieving extra height, the Roman catapult stone had arced over the city and torn Chava's womb clean away, smashing the contents into the cobblestones.

Retching, Judah dragged his gaze back to the tiny woman. She was still on her feet, groping horribly at her vanished belly. Rushing to her, he turned her away from her dead child. She was about to die, and Judah didn't want that image in her mind during her final moments.

"Judah? Judah, the baby…"

"Yes, the baby."

"His name is Atlas. Tell them, his name is Atlas ben Eleazar."

"I'll tell them."

"Good." Her knees buckled and she collapsed, convulsing on the ground. It took several minutes for her to die.

Asher reached them just as the light faded from her eyes. Letting Chava down gently, Judah rounded on his brother. "Where were you?" As if his twin could have prevented this.

Asher stared at Chava's lifeless form. "With Deuel."

The flatness of his brother's tone brought Judah up short. He noticed that Asher's clothes were covered in blood. "Deuel?"

"We were walking the wall. A scorpion bolt. Punched right through him, pinned him to a wall across the yard. He yelled. Can you imagine? Deuel screamed and screamed. Worst sound I ever heard."

Judah had no tears for either Chava or Deuel. It might have been lack of water, but it felt like all his tears had been shed. Standing, he turned to his twin. "Can you take care of this?"

Looking down on the ruined body that had once been such a sweet and funny girl, Asher nodded. "Where are you going?"

Judah lifted a precious cup of water from the well. "I'm going to see an old woman and pass along her son's last gift."

But when Judah got to the single room on the third floor, the woman was beyond thirst. A stone had collapsed the ceiling. She had died just about the same time as her son. Which Judah considered a blessing.

◆   ◊   ◆

The random slaughter raining down upon Jotapata was like water upon a stone, hollowing out the city's spirit. Desertion was inevitable. Each night men, women, whole families tried to slip over the wall.

Vespasian caught them all, torturing the men for information before crucifying them. The women and children he sent to the slave markets at Ptolmais.

Yet somehow the city continued to resist. No one knew exactly what would happen if Jotapata survived the allotted time, but they saw the fiftieth day as salvation. Yosef had said so – and hadn't he kept his promise so far?

Everyone waited to see what the forty-ninth day would bring.

◆   ◊   ◆

22 JULIUS - 48TH DAY OF SIEGE

Titus was dining with his father and the other legates. "Two more days."

"Don't remind me – Nicanor, you're late. Come, join us."

Nicanor remained standing at the entrance to Vespasian's tent. "Forgive me, General. I've information from inside."

"Oh?"

"A way in."

Titus and Trajan spun about, and Cerialis nearly leapt from the couch. Vespasian wiped his lips, then said, "Out with it, man."

"My informant says the defenders are exhausted. To give them rest, some places on the walls are under-manned in the hours just before dawn. Tonight it's the south-west corner."

Vespasian blinked. "That simple? No passage? No hidden entrance?"

Nicanor shook his head. "No, that's it. General, if this proves true, my informant has a request." He explained what it was.

Considering, Vespasian shook his head. "These Judeans. Yes. If the city is taken, I'll grant the request happily. Though part of it..." He looked to his son.

"I'll talk to the Queen," said Titus. "But father, what do you think? Can it be a trick?"

"Can it not be a trick?" Cerialis retorted.

"If it is," observed Trajan, "it's a poor one. Is your man reliable?"

Nicanor shook his head. "I have no way to answer that. But I'm inclined to believe it."

"As am I," agreed the general. "The risk is minimal, and well worth taking. Titus, get the ladders. The Fifteenth attacks an hour before dawn. And make sure those *cunni* stay quiet!"

◆   ◊   ◆

More and more men were sleeping in the day to avoid the pain in their stomach and the dryness in their mouths – and to escape the horror all around them. There was a constant droning of flies as the corpses piled up – they couldn't bury them outside the walls, nor drop them into the cisterns below the city without fouling what little water was left.

Judah was just waking from a nap when he saw his twin coming in the door of their billet. The place had been hit by a dozen stones, yet still remained standing. It was becoming a badge of pride to sleep here – though there were fewer and fewer men alive to do so. More than half their tent-mates were dead.

Judah tried swallowing several times before he worked up enough spit to speak. "Where have you been?"

Asher shrugged. "Walking. Just – walking."

Judah nodded. "One more day."

"And then what?"

Judah shrugged. "Who knows?"

Their centurion Zamaris was sitting upright, his eyes closed. "Then the Lord decides." Suddenly he looked at Judah. "Are you healed?"

"No. But I can fight."

Zamaris gazed at him for a long moment. "Then tomorrow night we put you over the wall and you go get your girl. You and the big fellow both." He looked at Asher. "You too."

Incredulous, the twins stared at him. Asher said, "What in the name of all that's holy are you talking about?"

"It's the heat," said Judah. "He's delirious."

Zamaris closed his eyes again. "You have something to live for. And you've done enough."

"I owe the Lord a death," said Judah stubbornly.

"We all do. He only takes us when He wants us. You've fought well. You two gave us the hope to get through this last week. But it's going to end, and only a fool counts on divine intervention. The Lord helps those who help themselves. So help yourself. Get your girl out."

Asher said, "I'll stay. Maybe we can divert them so you can get into the mountains and sneak off to the Queen's camp."

"Shut it, the pair of you. I'm not leaving until this is over. And I'll strangle the next man who suggests I run away."

Asher opened his mouth, but luckily Phannius chose that moment to enter the through the door, Gareb by his side. "Levi's asked us to billet with him tonight. Claims he's got some wine."

"Praise the Lord," said Zamaris.

"Amen," said Asher.

Judah clambered up. "I could use a damn drink. Let's go."

♦   ◊   ♦

Since leaving Yosef, Levi had taken rooms at one corner of the city, just inside the guard tower. When the twins arrived they found a meal awaiting them, complete with a bottle of wine and, more impressively, a clay jug of water.

"I took some of the general's personal supply as payment," confessed the former bodyguard.

Grinning, the five guests took off their swords and sat down to pass a pleasant evening telling stories and recalling lost friends.

"Asher's been telling me of Castor and Pollux," said Judah, quaffing deeply from the clay jug before passing it on. Having been thirsty for so long, it was a wonder to drink well.

"Kástōr and Polydeúkēs," said Levi, using their Greek names. "The divine twins. Brothers to Helen of Troy. One mortal, one deathless."

Judah stared. "How did you know that?"

Levi shrugged. "No man is just one thing. What about them?"

Asher explained. "During our flight of fancy we were mistaken for them. Might've saved our lives."

Zamaris was resisting the water, sipping wine instead. "They remind me of Esau and Yacob."

"Or the twins who called on Abraham," said Gareb. "More mysterious."

"It's all the same story," answered Levi, working hard not to spill into his beard. "Asher, surely you've noticed it. The history of our people shares the same base story with a dozen others. Even Rome."

"I see common elements," said Zamaris dubiously. "After all, there are only so many stories under the sun. But we have one god. The Romans have dozens, maybe hundreds."

"All their gods are aspects of Jupiter Best and Greatest. In Parthia, the great god Ahura-Mazda is part of the greater entity of Zurvan, he who is Time Incarnate and the Creator of All Things. Every religion believes there is one supreme being. For us, we replace demi-gods and minor gods with prophets and angels – all of whom are a part of Yahweh."

Slack-jawed, Asher marveled. "Parthian gods? Where did you – I would kill to learn about them. No one knows them."

"The Parthians do," replied Levi simply.

"Once they shared their learning with the rabbis," continued Asher doggedly. "But not for hundreds of years. Where did get your education?"

"Same place he learned to fight," growled Phannius, a little drunk. "It's no use asking – he likes to play the sphinx."

"In Parthia." All five men stared as Levi set down his bowl and folded his hands in his lap. "I was born in Tamdor. It's a caravan stop in Syria, and controls the silk routes from Parthia." His face twisted.

"Though now that it's Roman, it's called Palmyra. We made the mistake of getting comfortable, you see – we once were nomads, and could disappear across the Euphrates at an hour's notice. But when you build, you create an anchor. Buildings have to be defended. When Corbulo came, we tried to defend when we should have run."

"You learned to fight against Corbulo?"

"No. That's just when I ceased to have a home. Tamdor has always been a contested point between Rome and Parthia. We have – *had*, great wealth. Both nations made raids against us. In one of those Parthian raids, I was taken prisoner. I was five years old." Under his beard, his jaw rippled with disgust. "At first I was just a slave. But one day my master tried to take me as his own. When I refused, he took a whip to me. I fought back, which amused him. 'You wish to be a warrior?' he said to me. 'So be it.' From that moment, he raised me to be his pet soldier. He took great amusement in seeing a boy performing with a sword. First he sent me into battle with only a sword and shield, no armour. When I came back alive, he fed me, and gave me better arms. By the time I reached manhood I had become so skilled, he adopted me for his own. That's when I slit his throat and ran. I've been running ever since," added Levi, his eyes turned inwards.

Phannius said, "You picked an odd profession, then."

"I did not choose it. Violence is what I'm good at. I don't know how to do anything else. It's why I envy you, and the twins here – you three know how to build as well as destroy."

Judah frowned. "What's made your tongue so loose tonight?"

Levi shrugged. "The wine? Or perhaps because it's the forty-ninth day. One way or another, the siege ends tomorrow. If I die, I want to be remembered. And outside this room, there is no one who will remember me."

They were all quiet after that, thinking of who would remember them after the morrow. Most had only the men in this room. Phannius had his mother, of course – though likely he would be happier forgotten than living in her memory. Asher had only Judah.

But Judah would live in Deborah's memory. That was a kind of immortality. Castor, and Pollux. One immortal, the other always forgotten. So much truth in these myths.

XXXI

TWO HOURS before dawn, Barbarus led his men to the appointed place. They had removed their pteryges and nailed boots, breastplates and helmets. Shields covered in dark wool, wearing soft leather armour and covered in sagum cloaks, the cohort was nearly invisible. They had to hold a rope for guidance.

At Titus' command, the Fifteenth hustled over to Jotapata's walls and raised their ladders. Barbarus was among the first to climb. Up and over, his bare feet landed without a sound. Moving right, he heard his optio Thorius drop down and begin moving left.

Barbarus almost tripped over a sleeping Jotapatan. *Poor lads – escaping the thirst and fatigue in the only way they can. Best put them out of their misery.* Drawing his dagger, Barbarus paused at each sleeping Hebrew long enough to slash the man's throat.

Having gained control of this corner of the walls, the Romans quickly spread out. Titus himself was among them, busily cutting throats with the rest. As dawn approached, the task grew easier – they could see their targets, thus speeding up the slaughter.

Covered in blood, Barbarus was about to descend into the city when a Judean woman, sneaking to steal precious water from a well, saw him and let out a piercing scream.

Abandoning stealth, the soldiers of the Fifteenth cheered as they taught these Judeans the final price of obstinacy.

♦　　◊　　♦

"No!" shouted Asher, bolting awake.

Judah was beside him in a moment. "Are you all right?"

"Yes. No. Just a dream." His heart was pounding.

"Edith?"

Asher frowned. "I used to be sure it was her. But she's changing. There's something about her face – it's like her cheek is weak on one side…"

Asher was interrupted by a scream. This was immediately followed by the blaring notes of Roman bugles. It came from inside the city!

Judah limped to the window and saw the Fifth and Tenth legions marching for Jotapata's gates. "They're advancing!"

"No, they're in!" Zamaris was at the window that looked down into the city behind them.

Levi appeared, already dressed in his armour. "The city is lost."

Judah refused to believe it. "There must be something we can do!"

"What about the general?" asked Asher. Despite all the ill-will, there was a bond. Asher did not wish to see Yosef dead.

But rescue was clearly impossible. The city was swarming with plumed helmets and crimson banners. If Yosef was still in there, there was no helping him.

"Jotapata has fallen," said Levi. "We must run."

"No," said Judah.

Phannius blocked the door. "We can't fight them all!"

"You heard my brother," said Asher. "He said no."

Phannius rounded on Judah. "Use your eyes! The city has fallen!"

"Not until the Romans open the gate," said Zamaris suddenly.

"What?"

"The gate!" echoed Judah, excitement rising. "If we hold the gate, the other legions can't get in. Then we hunt down the Romans inside – and we win!"

Already Zamaris had barreled past Phannius, shouting, "Judeans! To me! To me!"

Following, Judah, Asher, Phannius, Gareb, and Levi gathered every soldier manning the nearest tower, nearly thirty in all. Well armed and unencumbered by armour, together they carved passage up onto the wall and along the western ramparts, towards the main gate.

Yosef woke to hear fighting close at hand. Before he could gather any semblance of wit, a Judean covered in blood burst into the chamber and thrust a sword into his hand. "General! They're upon us! Save your honour – slay yourself!"

"What?"

"You must!" gasped the man, bubbles of blood issuing from his

lips. "Otherwise they'll ship you to Rome – to die in their games!" The
man expired on the spot, the word *games* rattling in his throat. Yosef
did not even know the man's name.

Yosef exited his chamber at a run. In the courtyard beyond the
noise was louder and more identifiable – screams, oaths, prayers, and
the Latin shouts of triumphant Romans.

*O Lord, speak to me in this moment of extremis! Provide me victory
from the jaws of defeat!*

There was no answer.

When Yosef had allowed himself to imagine dying, it had been a
glorious fall in battle, not alone, half-dressed, unprepared and unclean.

Unclean. Though he espoused the Pharisees, he had trained as an
Essene. Purification by water. He had to die clean. In the center of the
courtyard stood a well. Sword still in hand, he ran to it. Behind him the
horrible sounds grew ever nearer.

Somehow, between his first step and his last, words came to him,
words he would reflect upon for however long he might live. For all his
prayers, his soul-searching, his questions regarding the nature of sacrifice, the words expressed a single, simple thought:

I don't want to die.

And again the single word of answer came to him: *Live.*

Reaching the well, he did not haul up the bucket. Grasping the
rope in one hand, he instead shimmied down into the well to hide.

◆   ◊   ◆

Zamaris stopped short. Judah and the others skidded to a halt
beside him, their hopes and dreams of snatching victory from defeat
dashed before their eyes.

A full Roman cohort was already at the gates, bristling with
spears and shields and swords. Engineers were working the mechanism.
In moments the portal would be open.

"There's nothing we can do," said Levi. "We must escape."

Phannius nodded. "Maybe if we drop off the north wall..."

Gareb was nodding, and even Zamaris looked ready to flee. Still
Judah protested. "We can't run—!"

Asher grabbed his brother by the arm. "You promised me we'd
only run if there was no other choice. Is there? Because I'll fight to the
death if there's a use. Just tell me what to do!" Tears were in his eyes,
and Judah knew his brother was reliving Alexandria.

Looking back at the gate, Judah saw legionaries climbing the
rampart steps. In moments he and the others would be facing the short
Roman swords behind a wall of shields.

"The north wall," said Judah.

Asher looked his brother in the face. "Are you sure?"

Judah nodded, and Levi said, "We're the only witnesses."

"Again," snarled Asher. But he turned with the others and ran along the western ramparts back the way they had come, to the northeast corner of the city.

Judah lingered. It is a strange phenomenon that overcomes a man in battle. Not every man feels it, but the true warriors do. When self no longer matters. When he feels a part of something larger than just his petty existence. In a horrible way, it is enlightenment, divinity, freedom.

But like all such connections, it fades over time, leaving only the memory. Having experienced it once, a man will throw himself into the worst situations to feel it again. It gives a man that thing he longs for most in life – purpose.

Judah had felt such a connection to the divine twice before. Once at Beth Horon, and once a week earlier, fighting beside his twin. It was so tempting to let them go, to sacrifice himself to cover their retreat. Even wounded, he could hold his narrow rampart for precious minutes.

Then Judah thought of Deborah.

With a final look back, he followed the others towards escape.

Below, the main gates of Jotapata were thrown open and Vespasian entered the city on horseback, flanked by Trajan, Sextus, and Cerialis. "Well done! Well done, Fifteenth! You've broken the back of this war and no mistake!" The general looked truly cheerful for the first time in months. "Now go find Josephus. Alive! The rest are yours. Only remember – alive, they can be sold. By Bellona I swear here and now that I shall donate half the slave sales from Jotapata to my marvelous legions!"

They cheered him, for by rights the sale of slaves went directly into the general's private purse. Knowing how tight-fisted the old man was, it was an incredible gesture of largesse.

Streaming into the city, the soldiers of the Fifth and Tenth tried to use their swords sparingly. But the Jotapatans were determined to fight to the death. Everywhere there was heavy fighting. Despite Roman restraint, Jotapata was a bloodbath. Because, as ever, the Judeans refused to submit.

Judah, Asher, and the rest raced along the wall's inner parapet. They were joined by more survivors – soldiers, mostly, with a handful of women and children fleeing the city's center.

"This is the spot!" called Levi, looking down. The wall here was low, broken by a catapult. It was a fair drop – twenty feet or more – but the ground below was soft, and the lee of the wall hid them from the circling cavalry. "As good as it will get."

"Over the wall! Over the wall!" shouted Judah, running in an awkward skipping step due to the pain in his thigh.

"Ware right!" cried Gareb, spying Romans racing for them.

Zamaris threw himself forward, and the last remnants of his century's best squad stood beside him, dealing out death to defend the narrow walkway while others made the leap.

Judah fought the way he liked, with a sword in each hand. He worked his way to the center of the rampart, allowing Asher and Zamaris to defend his sides while Phannius and Levi used their longer reach to attack overhead. Behind them, Gareb was helping women and children drop to the soft earth.

Suddenly one a lucky blow struck Levi on the helmet. The tall, thin bodyguard fell like a puppet whose strings had been cut, collapsing on Judah's back, who thought for a moment he was being attacked. Then he felt Levi slide and hit the stone walkway, exposed. "No!" Asher blocked the blow that would have taken his life while Judah killed the man who had felled him.

Judah pushed deeper into the Roman ranks, creating space behind him. "Pick him up and jump!"

Phannius obeyed, throwing the bodyguard over his shoulder like a sack of wheat and dropping off the wall down to the earth below. Gareb shouted, "Come on!"

Judah was in close, using pommels and elbows and his own weight to drive the Roman shields back. "Asher, go!"

"We go together!" shouted Asher.

Zamaris leapt in front of Judah, knocking two legionaries into each other. "Go, both of you!"

"Not without you!"

"Damn your eyes, you disobedient wretch! Go! That's an order!"

Feeling the need to disobey, Judah stabbed hard at one last Roman, severing his chin from the rest of his mouth. Then he turned and, together with his twin, leapt from the battlements.

They landed rolling, dispersing the impact. Judah cursed as enormous pain shot through his thigh.

"You all right?" asked Asher, rushing to his brother.

"Fine." With an effort of will, Judah forced himself upright and turned to look upward where Zamaris was now alone. "Jump!"

Zamaris shook his head as if he were troubled by a persistent and annoying fly. Then he disappeared in a wall of shields. Yet still he shouted orders. "Go go go!"

There was nothing to be done for him. At least they could obey the hoary old soldier's last command. Judah tried to take a step, but his leg went out under him. *I should have stayed up there! I can't run, but I can fight.*

Asher was already beside him, taking some of his weight. With Levi over his shoulder, Phannius was moving of towards the nearest incline of the mountainous bowl. It was at least a mile away. Men, woman, and children ran with him, Gareb shepherding them along.

Asher helped his brother walk. "Stay together!" he called to the rest. "Cavalry won't charge into a tight mass!"

"You read that somewhere?" said Judah, his arm over Asher's shoulder.

Asher shook his head. "I think I made it up." Which made Judah laugh.

Forming up tight, Judah and Asher brought up the rear as over a hundred survivors ran towards the hills and safety.

◆   ◊   ◆

Decurion Ebutius kicked his hot-blooded mount up to where Placidus sat atop his dappled stallion. "Tribune! There's a large band of Judeans just dropped from the wall and running for the hills!"

"Where did they drop?" asked Placidus sourly.

"The Northeast corner. Permission to engage?"

Placidus grunted, then spat. "Permission denied."

"Sir?"

"Orders from the general himself. That band is to be let free. The rest are fair game. Tell your men."

"Sir!" Ebutius saluted and rode quickly away. Whatever was going on, Placidus was unhappy, and as likely to take it out on a subordinate as the enemy.

◆   ◊   ◆

Reaching the safety of the mountains, the parcel of escapees collapsed, waiting for their breath to return. Judah and Asher finally had time to inspect Levi's injury. It was a bad clout on his head. As Asher bandaged it, Judah asked, "How are we still alive?"

"More to the purpose," replied Phannius gruffly, "where are we going?"

The answer was obvious. "Deborah."

"Good." Tearing Levi's shirt to wrap his bloodied head, Asher clenched his teeth. "One thing's certain. I'm never running away again."

XXXII

THE CITY was completely under Roman control before noon. Receiving reports from his legates and centurions, Vespasian said, "And Josephus? Do we have him?"

Their silence spoke for them.

"Do you mean we've taken the city by complete surprise and still managed to lose their commander? One lone man, eluding twenty-thousand – what a credit to the efficiency of Rome!"

"We'll find him, sir!" cried Trajan.

Vespasian looked feral. "If you don't, I'm taking your share of the spoils and giving it back to the Jews! *Cacat!*"

◆　◊　◆

From above, the well looked narrow. But as Yosef discovered, fifteen feet down the space opened wide to one side, hiding him from view. The water in the cavern was ankle high.

The moment his feet touched the watery floor, Yosef was seized by several hands and dragged into the shadows. Someone hissed in his ear, "Your name?"

"Yosef ben Matityahu."

He was answered with a gasp, and a second voice said, "General – it's me, Chalafta. Nechum's son."

Released, Yosef tried to see faces in the rippling light reflected from above. "Is your father here?"

"No." The young man was hangdog. "I left him."

Yosef said nothing – there was no balm to cowardice. His own presence likely branded Yosef a coward as well.

Eyes adjusting, Yosef saw the face of the man who grabbed him, a brave old warrior called Yaron. "What will we do, general?"

"First, we drink. No need to ration water now. Drink deeply." He joined them, cupping water to his lips and having his fill for the first time in a month. It was an odd sensation, to be guilty and grateful at once.

Above them, the sounds of death ceased. As day turned to night their bellies began to betray them. He encouraged them to drink plenty of water, but by midnight they were prepared to dare anything to find food.

Under cover of darkness, Yosef and four chosen men swarmed up the rope. Most Romans were back in their camp, leaving only a skeleton force within the city. More fortunate still, they had not touched Jotapata's quantities of bread and vegetables. Yosef and his companions returned with enough to last two, perhaps three days. They also brought arms – every man now had a sword.

What they forgot were chamber pots. While hungry, they had not needed to relieve themselves. With full bellies came the press for evacuation, but they couldn't risk fouling their drinking water.

The next night a second party set out. Deciding Yosef was too valuable to risk, the four men climbed the rope, taking with them a menstruating woman who required certain necessities that no man felt comfortable fetching.

Three of the men returned almost at once, bearing the coveted commodes. They waited, but neither the woman nor the man assigned to accompany her returned. "We must hope they took refuge in some other hiding place."

That hope was dashed at dawn when a polite voice echoed down from the top of the well. "General Josephus? General Vespasian sends his compliments."

♦   ◊   ♦

"He's down there," reported Gallicanus, one of the two tribunes alerted to Josephus' whereabouts.

"We could go down," offered the other, Paulinus. "But you know what happened to Antonius." A tribune of the Tenth had been negotiating with rebels in another of the many caves under the city. Offering his hand as surety of their lives, they had run a knife under his ribs.

Vespasian snapped his fingers. "Send for Nicanor. He knows this Josephus. Perhaps he can talk sense to him."

♦   ◊   ♦

So far, this war had been a quiet nightmare for Nicanor. Fighting his own people was against the Mosaic Law, and like all Chrestiani he disliked violence.

Nor did he like his part in the taking of the city. He'd hoped the defenders would see sense and give up. Instead they'd fought hard, preferring slaughter to slavery. He hoped that the bargain he'd made had been honoured – he'd been too busy to check. Besides, he wanted nothing more to do with that traitor.

Here at last was a task to his tastes – convincing a defeated scholar and priest that he should surrender, forgoing more bloodshed. An honourable mission. Leaning down over the lip of the well, he called out, "Yosef? Yosef. It's Nicanor."

After a pause, he heard the familiar musical voice. "Nicanor?"

"Yes, Yosef. If you step into the light I can show you my face."

He heard a brief argument below. Yosef appeared. "Nicanor. I'm pleased to see you well. A blessing upon you."

"And upon you, my friend." Had he not known to whom he was speaking, Nicanor would never have recognized this unshaven, wild-eyed skeleton gazing up at him. "I am here, as you can guess, at the behest of General Vespasian."

Yosef's wry smile cracked his lips. "I surmised as much."

"But first, is there anything you require? Is anyone injured? Do you need food? I imagine you have enough water."

"All we lack, Nicanor, is a candle and a flint."

"I shall see to it. Then, if it pleases you, we may discuss how matters stand."

◆   ◊   ◆

As Yosef stepped out of the light, Yaron demanded, "What are you doing?"

"They know we are here. There is no need to sit in the darkness."

Nicanor returned, and candles were duly lowered. "Thank you, Nicanor."

"It is my pleasure. Now let us illuminate your situation."

"I confess," said Yosef, "I am surprised to find a Nazarene in service with the Romans."

Nicanor hoped none of the Romans could follow their verbal mixture of Koine Greek, Hebrew, and Aramaic – he did not want it generally known that he was a Chrestiani. Yet his answer was sincere: "We prize independence."

"Then should you not fight for it?" Yosef paused. "Forgive me. That was unworthy."

"Understandable. I would be bitter too, having fought so hard and so well. But you must see that this is a part of the Lord's plan. Judea may be in Israel, but it is not *of* Israel. The Judeans have betrayed their faith. If Judea as a whole were still faithful, the Romans could not have won. This defeat is the Lord's punishment for not heeding His words. Thus there is no sin in admitting you've lost."

"We might not have lost if we had been united. That is observation, not accusation."

"You mean the Nazarenes? But we knew this war was lost from the start. We recall the words of the prophet Daniel – the Seventy Weeks. In three more years, the Temple will cease to exist. Yahweh has decreed it."

This prediction left Yosef thunderstruck. "Yahweh spared the Temple! Florus and Gallus brought their armies right to the Temple gates, but they retreated. Disaster was averted."

"Momentarily. It was a warning. Our nation's path ensures its eventual destruction. It has been foretold." Nicanor closed his eyes and recited: "'*Seventy weeks are determined for thy people and for thy holy city, to shut up the transgression, to seal up sins, and to cover iniquity.*' We Hebrews had this time to reform, to purge, and embrace the Lord once more. We failed. The Temple will fall."

Amazed, Yosef shook his head. "I read the words of the prophet Daniel differently. He speaks of weeks, but means decades. Dating from the destruction of the Temple, our second Temple was built in seventy years. The prophecy was fulfilled centuries ago."

"Daniel speaks in weeks," agreed Nicanor, "but means weeks of years. You say centuries, but to be precise, it has been exactly four hundred eighty-seven years since the death of Ezra, who was appointed by Nehemiah to be the scribe of the refounded Temple."

Yosef could not help laughing at such a back-bending interpretation to the prophecy. Yet Nicanor carried on, again quoting from Daniel: "'*And after the sixty and two weeks, cut off is Mahsiah, and the city and the holy place are not his, the Leader who hath come doth destroy the people; and its end is with a flood, and till the end there is war...*'"

"'*...desolations are determined,*'" finished Yosef. It was the old prophecy of a Redeemer. Different from the Mahsiah, who would come to lead Israel, the Redeemer would sweep Israel with an iron broom, purging the unholy elements of society. "I could always quote as well as you. And interpret better," he added.

"Oh? Seven weeks of years, then sixty-two, and then one more. In that sixty-second year, the *Mahsiah* is cut off. By our counting, that event happened four years past. Who was executed four years ago that carried the *Mahsiah*'s message?"

Yosef grew stony. The reference was to the execution of Yacob, the brother of this troublesome sect's founder. "Yacob was sentenced to death by stoning."

"Yes, for the crime of breaking the Law. Wonderfully vague. But at least this time the priests did the deed themselves, didn't get the Romans to do it for them." Disguised for so long, Nicanor's true faith began to show. "Yacob's death marked the beginning of the final week of years. We are in the fourth year. In three more years, the end will come. Wrack and ruin. Desolation. The Redeemer shall arrive, and sweep all away. You know the portents support us."

For the last five years, Sanhedrin priests were witness to bizarre astrological signs and unnatural phenomena, usually around the great holy days. One year war chariots were seen surrounding the sun, and legions in the clouds. Another year a star shaped like a gladius had hung over the great Sanctuary, an astrological Sword of Damocles. During Passover the next year, a sacrificial cow gave birth to a lamb before the holy altar. Two weeks later, the great bronze doors, so massive that twenty men could hardly move them, had opened of their own accord during the night. Priests Yosef knew and respected swore they had heard a voice say four words: *We are departing hence.*

"But there are always portents," protested Yosef. "Eagles and doves in the air, shaking of the earth, soured milk inside a woman's breast – the world is never in a state of perfection. How can it be, when we are imperfect reflections of the Lord?" He smiled wanly. "I've missed these talks of ours."

"I hope to have them for many years to come." Returning to his purpose, Nicanor praised Yosef's valor, and told how it had birthed respect in the Romans. Vespasian merely desired to meet a man of such courage. Nor, Nicanor said, would the general have sent a known friend to lure Yosef out on false terms – Nicanor's honour would not allow it.

What a pleasure to speak to an educated man! A man whose dialect was pleasingly urban, not rustic. A man who talked sense as well as patriotism. Yosef felt a stab of guilt over Asher, who must surely be dead.

That Nicanor's aim was Yosef's willing surrender was never in doubt. But in the hours of talk, he allowed the idea to come about of its own accord. In fact, it was Yosef that first mentioned the word. "Put in your terms, it seems that surrender is the only sensible option." There was a barely human growl from behind him. "I am not entirely alone down here."

"I surmised," said Nicanor. "I promise them their lives as well."

"Thank you. I must now discuss matters with my colleagues. Will you allow us privacy? And give me your word that, until we make up our minds, we are not to be molested? I do not wish to set a guard."

"I give you my word, insofar as it is mine to give," said Nicanor. "I promise that this day and night, you will be left alone. But Romans are an impatient race. Past tomorrow, I cannot say."

"More than fair. I thank you, Nicanor."

"Persuade them, Yosef. Make them see sense."

Yosef withdrew from the light coming from above. Carefully keeping the wick dry, he carried the candle to the side chamber, wedged it onto a rocky outcropping, and struck a spark. "Let there be light."

The objections came in a flood. "We cannot surrender!"

"They've killed so many already!"

"If we swarm up, we might take them by surprise!"

Such protests grew steadily louder, and several implausible courses of action were proposed. When they had spent their energy, Yosef addressed them. "For fifty days you've tasted Roman strength at arms. Do you honestly believe that thirty-nine people, three of them women, can rise up and over-master them? You may call it bravery, but others would call it suicide."

The instant it passed his lips, Yosef regretted the word.

"Then we shall kill ourselves!" cried Yaron, rapidly becoming the spokesmen for the group. "If it's a choice of death by my own hand or on a Roman cross, I know which I prefer!" Again, the muted growl of concurrence.

"But that is not the choice," answered Yosef. "Nicanor swears the Romans will spare us. It's me they're after. If I promise to submit to them, they have no reason to take reprisals out upon you."

"To do that is to tarnish the glory of our ancestors!"

"And the alternative you propose is to tarnish our souls in the eyes of the Lord? For that is what suicide is – a direct insult to Jehovah."

"That," said Yaron, "is the excuse of a coward!"

"Coward?" said Yosef angrily. "You've seen me these last two months. You did not deem me cowardly then! If I run from death at the end of a Roman sword, then yes, I would be worthy to die on my own sword, by my own hand. For that is a coward's death. But if the Romans offer mercy, and would spare us, we must have mercy on ourselves as well. What do we gain by dying? Nothing! What do the Romans gain? Their goal! It's ridiculous to do their work for them! If we survive, we win!"

Yaron stepped forward. "If you fear self-slaughter, Yosef, I offer you my right hand, and the sword it holds. I will take upon me the sin of your death. If you die willingly, you shall die as a priest, and general of the Jews. Unwilling, you'll die a traitor."

Every man present drew his sword, even young Chalafta, ready to hack Yosef to pieces rather than allow him to surrender.

Yosef looked not at the blade, but into Yaron's eyes. "It is a brave thing to die for liberty. A man is certainly a coward if he refuses to die when necessity calls for it. But he is also a coward that chooses to die when nothing calls for it but false pride." Yosef shook his head, tears in his eyes. "What are we afraid of? Death? And to prevent that, we mean to kill ourselves? Excellent wisdom! Any other man who tried to take our lives we call our enemy. But you wish us to be enemies to our selves!"

"They mean to make us slaves!"

"And if they do?" retorted Yosef. "Is that worse than our present state? How much liberty do we enjoy down here?"

"It is a man's act," said Yaron gravely.

"A most unmanly act. If a captain at sea, seeing dark skies ahead, chooses to sink his own ship rather than risk the storm, he's not only a coward but a fool!" Yosef closed his eyes, as might a man weary of conversing with obdurate fools. "Self-murder is a crime against nature. No other animal in all the world even dreams of giving away our Lord's most precious gift. That is because it is impiety, sacrilege."

He used every argument he could imagine, from a banker entrusted with another man's money to the slave who flees his master's house – all examples of a man taking what did not belong to him. Such men, Yosef argued, were punished. So would they be, if they took what belonged to God alone – their lives. "We received our lives, our very selves, from Yahweh. And do you think that He will be pleased if you destroy what He has granted? Every man owes the Lord a death – and He will claim it in His own time! Until then, we owe Him our lives!"

But reason failed. They rushed upon him, swords ready to strike, with even the women prepared to rend him. Pulling his shoulders back, Yosef shouted at them in his best general's voice. "Very well! If you are determined to die, we shall die. But not until morning. Every one of you, spend this night praying for forgiveness for what we are about to do. Yaron, choose three men and stand guard over the exit. Let no man leave – myself included. I shall sit in the farthest corner of the cave, unarmed, and lead the prayers. If you think it necessary to bind me, I understand."

Grateful that he had finally come around to their way of thinking, they did not bind him, and though they did remove his sword, they left him his knife.

He led the prayers, beseeching the Lord to forgive, to understand, to avenge. Then the candle was blown out, and they all went to sleep.

All, save Yosef.

◆   ◊   ◆

"Well, Nicanor? Will he come up?"

"I believe he would like to, general. But the choice may be out of his hands."

Vespasian shrugged. "If he can't come up with a way to convince them, he's not the same man I've been fighting for the last two months."

◆   ◊   ◆

It had taken two days to get the other refugees to a place of safety, far from any likely Roman patrols. Guarded by Gareb, some women were taking care of wounded Levi.

Of course, many had not wanted to stop and hide. Most were running to the homes of relatives, or heading straight for the safety of Jerusalem. Of the hundred thirteen survivors of Jotapata, less than a third stayed. Of the ones that went off on their own, nearly all were caught and sold into slavery.

Assured that the remaining band of thirty were safe, Judah, Asher, and Phannius went off in the direction of Queen Berenice's borrowed palace in Sogane.

"Do you have a plan?" asked Phannius.

Judah laughed darkly. "Ask Asher. He's the brains."

"Parroting words in a book doesn't make you smart," said Phannius.

"True," said Asher. "But not reading them doesn't make you smart, either."

"Shut up, both of you," said Judah. "Let me think."

But the only word that came to his mind was *sacrifice*. To make holy.

XXXIII

I DON'T WANT TO DIE.

Fighting delirium, mind bounding from one thought to another, that lone truth kept Yosef focused. He was determined to survive.

Socratic training kicked in. Without Asher, Yosef was forced to play both student and teacher:

When is sacrifice a sin? he asked himself.

When the thing being sacrificed still has value.

That means all sacrifices should be of valueless things. But that would offend the Lord.

What if the Lord has plans for the sacrificial victim?

Yes, then it would be sinful to cut off the life before He was done with it.

Not only is self-slaughter a sin, but my untimely death would be an offence against God Himself. I feel it! I have more to offer the world than a failed defense of one minor city.

But I am not the Mahsiah. Yosef had allowed himself to believe, even hope. But he knew now he was not the promised leader of the Jews. Not even another Hyrcanus.

Odd that Nicanor, of all men, should be present to negotiate. Nicanor believed the Mahsiah had already come: his rabbi Y'eshua, consorting with the unclean. Y'eshua the troublemaker. Y'eshua the defiant. But the Mahsiah was supposed to be as much warrior as priest, would never submit tamely to death as Y'eshua had. Besides, Y'eshua had been a carpenter's son, not a descendant of David.

His thoughts turned to his conversation with Nicanor about the Redeemer, come to sweep Israel with an iron broom, purging it until only the faithful remained. Clearly Vespasian was the Redeemer, his legions the broom. But where was the Mahsiah? If ever Israel needed the Mahsiah, this was the moment.

Nicanor was correct. The only reasonable explanation for the Mahsiah's non-appearance was that he had already come. And been put to death.

But there were so many objections! Besides his birth, there was the fact that Y'eshua had not departed Judea. One prophecy stated that the Mahsiah would come out of the East, and rule the world. How could a dead man rule?

Dizzy with exhaustion, the phrase resonated in Yosef's mind. *Come out of the East. Come out of the East* – did that mean leave Israel? And where did one go, to rule the world? Who ruled the world today?

Rome. Travel to Rome, and rule the world. Like a lighting strike from above, inspiration struck. *The Mahsiah must to go to Rome!*

Or, if not the Mahsiah himself, then his message, the story of his people. God's chosen people. The message had to be carried to Rome. And who else to do it but Yosef himself?

It fit so perfectly! The Lord had sent Nicanor, a Nazarene believer, to treat with him. Why else, but to set him on this new path? *The Lord has put this glorious task in my mind. I must take Judaism to Rome.*

Reassured that his survival was required, Yosef set aside any qualms. The problem that faced him now was mathematical, not moral. How could he stay alive?

The others would not trust him to kill himself, except under their eyes. There was no way to fake his death. So he had to see the rest of them dead first. Which meant they had to kill each other.

There was a sound argument to make for it. Killing another was less offensive to the Lord than killing one's self. If they agreed, only the last man standing would have to commit self-slaughter. Yosef had to be that man. But how?

They could draw lots. But that would require rigging the lots, and he would certainly be caught. An unfixed lottery was out of the question, for Yosef would not leave his life up to anything as capricious as Chance. No, he had to engineer matters so that he seemed to take part, and was yet invulnerable.

He sat in the near absolute dark, scratching numbers and figures into the rock wall. It had to be simple, and seem random. Every man would kill some other until all but two were slain. No matter how they did the deed, there would always be two men remaining. Then it would be either a fight, or a conversation.

The number of souls with him was the key. Thirty-nine, himself included.

It was a simple matter of arithmetic. If everyone stood in a circle, and every man killed the man next to him, the survivors were in the sixteenth and thirty-first places. Could he position himself in either of those without drawing suspicion? Possibly. But it was hardly certain.

He tried again, this time killing every third man. In that case, the survivors were the men placed at the fifth and twenty-third positions. No better.

His mind kept turning the numbers over. Methodically working his way through the permutations, he discovered that with just thirty-six standing in the circle, killing every third man, the first and sixteenth men survived. He could easily be the first man – they would look to him to start the count.

He checked his math, then checked it again. Yes. Thirty-six was the magic number. *Thirty-six?* There were thirty-six men here in the cave. The other three were women. Thus Yosef had to remove the women from the suicide pact.

He could insist they be let live. But already he knew they would not consent. They had been among the most vocal of the suicide faction. He could also insist that they die first, by the hands of their lovers. They might object to that as well, demand to draw lots with everyone else.

There was only one way to obtain thirty-six with certainty. Hands trembling, Yosef rose.

◆   ◊   ◆

In the end, no plan was necessary. Climbing through the rough, dry earth of the hills outside Sogane, they were surrounded by Berenice's royal guard a mile from the city. Disarmed, Judah, Asher, and Phannius were marched down to the Roman road and directly to the palace. For once they didn't argue, just went silently. Like willing sacrifices.

◆   ◊   ◆

In the cave, young Chalafta slept poorly. He dreamed of his father being tortured by the Romans while he hid and watched. The terrible part was that whatever the Romans did to the old man, he couldn't die. He begged for death, wept for it, called out for his son to come and kill him. But Chalafta was too frightened, and so the suffering continued.

At some point in the dream his father's voice was replaced by a woman's, which only made the nightmare more horrific and grotesque. He fought to wake up, and was relieved when at last he did.

It did not seem that anyone else was awake yet. There was barely any light reflecting on the water from the opening above. Entrusted with the flint and the candle, Chalafta struck sparks until the wick was lit. To his bedazzled eyes, the water he had been sleeping in seemed very dark. He expected this effect to pass, and was disturbed when it did not.

Instead he saw clouds of crimson swirls passing by.

Chalafta peered into the corner where Yosef sat, head in his hands. "General, something is wrong with the water."

"It hardly matters," came the reply. "We won't be thirsty again."

Others were waking now, and Chalafta noted the women were not rising with the rest. Their bodies lay limply in the water at odd angles. Upon investigation, it was discovered their throats had been cut.

Yaron and the others began shouting about Roman treachery, but Chalafta looked at Yosef and knew. "General – what happened to the women?"

Yosef lifted his head, revealing eyes red from weeping. "I could not allow them to stain their souls by committing self-slaughter. Instead I took three more sins upon myself." He struggled to his feet, cuffing the last of his tears away. "Besides, they had not the strength to kill a man surely. Better they should die at peace. What we do now is man's work."

Strangely, the murder of the three women calmed any lingering suspicion of the general. It also made real the act they were about to commit.

"We shall stand in a circle," Yosef told them. "Every second man cuts the throat of the man beside him. The last man standing will slay himself, and only he will commit that particular sin in Yahweh's eyes. I will start the count myself. Are we all agreed?"

Trying to control his trembling fear, Chalafta joined the others as they gathered in a circle. He took up place beside Yosef, hoping to draw strength from the general's bravery.

"Very well," said Yosef. "All that remains is to choose which direction we should count. To the right? Or to the left?"

It was Yaron who answered. "The direction of a sundial. Right to left."

Nodding, Yosef's face was grave. "A quick prayer, and we shall begin."

They asked forgiveness of the Almighty for what they were about to do. As Yosef spoke, Chalafta was counting around the circle, counting which of his friends would be putting an end to his life. Even the general was doing it. Chalafta felt a start of surprise from beside him – Yosef's eyes were on Yaron, who stood at the sixteenth place in the circle. Chalafta wondered if the general would be required to kill Yaron, or the other way around.

Yosef was cursing himself. He had been so clever, lulling their suspicions by allowing them the appearance of a choice – what did the direction matter? But it had, for Yaron occupied the sixteenth place in that direction. If there was one man who might insist upon completing the mass-suicide, it was Yaron. Why had he not stood beside Yaron himself, to be certain? Why had he left anything to chance?

Chalafta had just realized that he would be the first to commit murder, killing the man to his left. *Thou shalt not commit murder.* Was it murder, if the victim consents?

The prayers ended, and the general suddenly turned to him. "One more thing before we begin. Chalafta, please go stand over there beside Yaron. I have killed enough tender souls this day." Yosef looked to Yaron. "You can do it, can you not?"

Yaron answered with great dignity. "If I am not already dead, I promise I will make it swift."

Chalafta embraced the general, then crossed to stand on Yaron's left. In the candlelight that reflected off the dark water, Yosef looked relieved. But then, every man was oddly cheered by this move, as it mixed up the count, changing who would kill whom. Leaving no time to count again, the general said, "Let us begin."

Moved from the first victim to the first killer, the man on Yosef's left raised his sword. The next man over bravely lifted his chin and bared his neck. Chalafta watched the mercifully brutal cut – blood spilled forth, and the man lived only seconds.

From that initial spilling of blood, matters went swiftly. One, two, kill. One, two, kill. One, two, kill. Instead of surviving, Yaron was among the first to fall. Someone else's hand would have to end Chalafta's life.

The first circuit complete, the survivors stepped in, closing ranks. Now it was Chalafta's turn to slay the man next to him. He forced himself to pull hard, but his shaking hand made an uneven cut, and the man to his left had to suffer a longer death than the others. "I'm sorry," the weeping Chalafta said to the dying man.

Everyone shared the same goal, now – build a rhythm that allowed no one to continue to count. But when there were only four left, Chalafta noticed that the other men were starting to eye Yosef suspiciously.

"Quickly now," said the general.

The next man died, leaving only Yosef, Chalafta, and one other. Yosef said, "One."

"Two," said Chalafta, with an apology in his voice.

"Three," said the third man, baring his neck. "Boy – be sure to finish this. And for my sake, strike hard."

Chalafta did better this time, severing the neck in half. The body fell, leaving only himself and the general.

Yosef took a single step back, out of reach of Chalafta's sword.

Chalafta looked down at the dead bodies all around them and shivered. "Did you know?"

"Yahweh knew," answered Yosef. "He spoke to me last night, told me that if I were preserved, it was because He is not yet through with my life. He has more in store for me. And clearly for you as well."

"Is that true?"

"It may have only been a dream. But here we are."

Tearfully, Chalafta looked at his sword. By the rules, it was his turn to kill. "If I try to finish this you'll kill me."

"No. I am in the hands of the Lord. Let Him speak through you."

Chalafta did not know what to do. Had Yosef deceived them? Had the others died so that Yosef might live? Did it even matter? They had wanted to die – but Yosef had not. Nor, in truth, had Chalafta.

"If the Lord spoke to you, I can't – I mean, I'm not the one to decide. But if you're lying, general –"

"If I am lying, He will punish me."

"Yes," said Chalafta. "He will." His sword splashed loudly as it hit the water.

Yosef sheathed his own and crossed close, holding out his hand. "Come. Let us call for Nicanor."

◆   ◊   ◆

Judah and the others were brought into the main chamber of Berenice's palace. "Stand here, traitors," said the captain of her guard. His contempt was palpable, and it was echoed on the faces of the other men. Judah felt his anger rising. They weren't the traitors here. They weren't the ones collaborating with Romans. They were the patriots in the room. He decided that before he died, he would tell them so.

Then all at once his rage vanished as two women walked into the tall polished chamber. In the lead was Queen Berenice. She was dressed plainly today, in the Hebrew garb of mourning. But nothing could hide the sensuousness of her gait.

Beside her was — "Deborah!"

"Judah! Phannius! What's happening?" She was wide-eyed with surprise, joy, and fear.

"So these are the men," said Berenice coldly. "Your names?"

"Asher ben Matthias."

"Phannius ben Samuel."

"Judah ben Matthias." His eyes were only on Deborah, his breath coming short. He wondered how quickly he could murder everyone in this room. Because if that was what it took to set her free…

"Very well," said Berenice. "Rest assured, your names I will remember. Now take your prize." With that, the queen shoved Deborah towards them.

Unable to hear anything for the pounding in his ears, Judah rushed forward and clutched her in his arms. "Deborah! Thank the Lord!"

Phannius was the same, coming forward to stroke his sister's hair. But Asher heard the queen's words and frowned. "What do you mean, our prize?"

"Watch how you address her majesty, traitor!" snarled her captain.

But Berenice was happy to talk. "What do I mean? I mean this is your blood price. A foolish girl rescued from a fate worse than death. I hope that you treasure her, for all that she has cost this nation."

Judah had been whispering endearments back and forth with Deborah. But now he looked up, his face a mirror of his brother's. "What are you talking about?"

She gazed at them scornfully. "Do not pretend. You bargained with Nicanor – her life and your freedom for an entrance to Jotapata. So instead of surrender, there was a bloodbath. The Romans are pleased. We are not. But the bargain was made in our name, so we will honour it. We didn't know whom to expect. Only that someone would call for her. And here you are. I hope she is worth it. Myself, I doubt it."

◆　◇　◆

As Josephus was a blood-soaked horror after the ordeal in the well, Vespasian allowed his captive to bathe and dress before their interview. The Roman general was in good spirits for the first time in weeks. The capture of both Jotapata and Josephus was vindication that he was the right man for this war.

Expecting Josephus, he frowned when Titus entered his quarters. "What are you doing here? You should be on your way to join Marcus Ulpius." Ordered to reduce another nearby city, Trajan had sent word that his target was about to fall, but he required another troop of horsemen. Would Titus be available to lead this force? A blatant and admirable attempt to curry favour.

But here was Titus, slipping into an out-of-the-way seat. "The cavalry is still assembling," he said preemptively. "I'll go as soon as they're ready. Just wanted to see him."

Vespasian huffed. "Fancy all of them killing themselves."

"Killing each other," corrected Titus. "They view suicide as a grave offence against their god."

"Do they?"

"So Nicanor tells me."

Vespasian was genuinely surprised. To a Roman, suicide was proper, even desirable. There was no greater control in life than choosing the time and means of ending it. Baffled, the general latched onto something else. "You've been talking to Nicanor nearly every night. I don't recall you studying so hard with your tutors."

Titus grinned. "If my tutors had dangled Berenice before me, I might have become a scholar."

Vespasian scowled. "The general's son consorting with a Judean queen. I can just hear the senators. They'll accuse you of being the next Mark Antony."

Titus looked smug. "I can think of worse fates."

He was spared his father's cutting reply by Nicanor's arrival. "General Josephus is here, sir."

"Show him in."

Yosef entered dressed in a Roman tunic and sandals. Nicanor moved to another corner of the tent, sitting as unobtrusively as Titus to watch this meeting. Cerialis, too, slipped in to listen.

Until this moment, the two generals had only seen each other from afar. Face-to-face, each paused to evaluate the other. The Roman with the straining, worrying face and placid eyes. The Jew, with the hawkish nose and haughty chin.

Vespasian was the first to extend his hand. "Well fought, sir! If we are truly judged by the strength of our enemies, I have nothing to be ashamed of."

"Thank you, Titus Flavius," answered Yosef. "Allow me to congratulate you on a most thorough victory."

"What a remarkable voice you have. Nero Caesar would kill to have one like it."

"Then perhaps you should not send me to him just yet." A plea couched as a jest.

Vespasian offered his guest some wine. "I have that horrible sweet stuff you people drink."

"Thank you, no. In my present state, I would lose my head."

"Can't have that! Now sit, Josephus, and let us talk." They sat in the Roman style, on couches. "Forty-nine days. You are quite the prophet. But then, I have heard that you Hebrew priests are gifted with the Sight."

The prisoner's brows knit, but he said nothing.

"And an author, as well," continued Vespasian, gesturing to a book-bucket across the room. "Your history of the Makkabi. No wonder the people looked to you for inspiration. You made their heroes come to life."

From across the room, Titus hid a smile. *The old man makes it sound as though he's actually read it through.*

"All this makes me look upon you as a most unique visitor."

Yosef was not crass enough to point out that a thing could not be 'most unique'. It was either unique, or not. Instead he took issue with another word. "I am a prisoner."

"Pardon?"

"I am not a visitor. I'm a prisoner."

"Let us say, guest. You understand, Josephus, Rome will win this war. Jotapata has assured it. But I don't want to leave the place a desolate, simmering cauldron of hate waiting to boil over again. I want to pacify the Judeans. There are two ways – the fur glove, or the hammer. I can either convince your people to submit without further violence, or I can do to you what we did to Carthage – salt the earth so nothing will ever grow there."

"That last would be a tragedy. For Rome as well as Judea."

"I agree. Therefore you must help me prevent it. I mean to harness your skill with words and ideas. To start with, please tell me – what does Judea want?"

"Freedom."

"That's rather vague. Certainly Judea will not be allowed to exist as an autonomous state, not after slaughtering Roman soldiers and citizens. Let's be reasonable here."

Yosef said, "Judea is a Roman construct. When my people die, they do not praise Judea. They praise Israel."

"Yes," said Vespasian, having heard Titus' reports on the Hebrew faith. "The land of your people, given to you by your god. But if your god has entrusted you with the well-being of this land, does it matter who rules it?"

"Yes, Titus Flavius, it matters a great deal." Prepared to hear taunts and crowing, this meeting was not at all what Yosef had expected. "Our people are not allowed to worship freely. This all began, as you recall, with the profaning of one of our temples."

Vespasian's head bobbed. "Yes, I see that. So Judea must have more respectful government."

Yosef bowed his head. "Perhaps a better class of governors. Senators, not rapacious knights."

Vespasian grimaced. "Senators are more rapacious, not less. But your point is well taken. What else?"

"The freedom of our religion is vital to us, paramount both as a nation and as a people." Yosef went on in great earnestness. "Rome and Judea are similar in many ways. Like you, our religion is integral to running our state. The difference lies only in the, ah, elasticity of that religion. It is vital that our religion remain pure and untampered with. Otherwise our government descends into chaos."

"Very reasonably put," said Vespasian. "What else?"

They continued talking for some time, with Yosef making specific demands as though he were the victor of Jotapata, not the vanquished.

Finally a silence descended, broken when Yosef suddenly said, "Would you like to know, Titus Flavius, why I surrendered? Why I did not join the others?"

Vespasian raised his brows. "Only, Josephus, if you would like to tell me."

"I know the duty of a defeated general. I assure you, I am here at the behest of the Almighty. He sent me a vision," said Yosef carefully. He would tell the truth, but in a way that might please the Roman. "Or rather, a divine inspiration. I knew the Lord would ensure my preservation, so that I might carry a message."

"To whom?"

"He did not say."

"And what is this message from your god?"

"Only to repeat what several of our prophets have foretold." He summoned all the musicality of his voice, using it to frame one single sentence. "A great man will come out of the East, and rule the world."

Vespasian's eyes slid momentarily out of focus as he pictured himself wearing the *corona civica*, the laurel wreath that was far better than any crown in existence. Then he laughed aloud. "Am I to believe that I am this prophesized hero?"

"I do not know," answered Yosef. "The message was clear. The meaning was not."

"But I am a Roman. I am not of the East."

"You are in the East." The corners of Yosef's cracked mouth twitched. "You know the careless nature of prophecies."

"Indeed I do. Especially their ability to be twisted by clever men. *Credat Judaes Apella, non ego!*" Horace had written in his *Satires* a reference to the credulity of Jews, coining a phrase popular among Romans protesting their lack of gullibility: *'Let the Jew Apella believe it, not I!'*

Yosef was unoffended. "Tied up with that prophecy is another, that of the Redeemer who wields an iron broom to sweep Israel clean again."

"Now that sounds more like me, doesn't it?" Vespasian turned to Nicanor. "Do you know of these prophecies?"

Nicanor was scratching his chin, his brow furrowed. "I do, general. Both are very old, and have been interpreted many ways. The man out of the East was once taken to mean Caesar Augustus, after his victory in Aegypt." Knowing how Romans viewed the Chrestiani, he did not add that his own belief about the meaning of that prophecy. Instead he shot an angry glance at Yosef, who was playing a dangerous game.

"I've heard of it, too," said Titus. "Some said that Josephus here was the Mahsiah."

"Clearly not," answered Yosef with genuine humility. "I make no claim on the title, nor do I know to whom it belongs. I merely state its existence."

"Well, thank you for delivering this divine message," said Vespasian briskly. "Time alone will tell if I was the intended recipient. For the moment, you shall travel with us."

Yosef blinked. "You're not sending me to Rome?"

"I think you might be of more use to us here. But have no fear, you will eventually be sent to Rome. The people will want to look upon so formidable a foe."

Yosef rose and bowed. "As you say, Titus Flavius."

"One more question – Cestius Gallus and the Twelfth. Where is their eagle?"

"Ananus claimed to have melted it down. But he said that to an enemy. To Rome, he may have a different answer."

"Thank you." As Yosef was led away Vespasian pulled aside Titus, Cerialis, and Nicanor. "Not a word of this prophecy business to anyone. The last thing I need after a summer of success is to let this kind of talk reach Nero. Besides, I'm sure that if it were you in command, Titus, or a Tingitanian ape, our clever Josephus would have seen the laurel there as well."

But Titus wanted it to be true. "*Pater*, what if the prophecy does refer to you?"

"Far too convenient. A more blatant currying of favour than Trajan's offer to you!"

Still Titus was loathe to let it go. "Who's to say how a god – any god – works? *A Man out of the East, who will Rule the World.*"

Vespasian shook his head. "There is only one ruler of the world. His name is Caesar."

◆　◇　◆

It was a dreadful scene in Berenice's palace. Judah had almost gotten them all killed as he launched himself at Phannius, fists flying. "You bastard! *You bastard!*"

"Me?" roared the larger man, swelling with contempt and indignation. "This was you! I would never betray our people! I am a Zelote, an Avenger of Israel! But you, you have no cause, no belief, you just love to fight—!"

Deborah was shouting, Asher too, as the guards separated them. Berenice looked on, her face a mask of contempt. "I do not believe either of you. You are both here to claim this woman. That makes you equal in guilt. This man, too," she said, pointing to Asher. "But I have given my word that you will be spared and set free, with a letter of safe conduct. So speak quickly, where do you wish to go? I want you out of my sight."

Holding Deborah in his arms, Judah stared at Phannius. The large oaf seemed genuinely befuddled and surprised. He wasn't smart enough to be that good a performer. A horrible feeling creeping up his spine, Judah turned to his twin. He didn't want to, but the accusation in his eyes spoke for him.

Asher saw it and went pale. "Judah – no! No! I never – how can you..?" His face displayed everything it should have – shocked realization, horror, hurt, indignation, betrayal. But then he was smarter than Phannius...

"Speak up!" snapped Berenice. "Where shall you go?"

There was only one answer. "To Jerusalem."

♦   ◊   ♦

Exiting the general's quarters, Nicanor hurried to catch up to Yosef. That their words might be kept private, he spoke in Aramaic. "What are you doing? Making him think he's the Mahsiah – are you mad?"

"Everything I said was true," answered Yosef. "I know in my bones that I am meant to go to Rome, and bring our faith with me. Rome is the center of the world, and our faith must go there to grow."

Nicanor's question had been hyperbole, he had not thought Yosef to be truly mad. But hearing him speak with such passion, Nicanor wondered – was Yosef's mellifluous voice disguising the loss of his wits?

Well, who can blame him? A year ago he was a promising young priest. Six months ago he was the general of a great army. A day ago he was a refugee, surrounded by men determined to make him take his own life. So many ups and downs – it's no wonder if he's gone mad.

But Yosef felt far from mad. He was thinking of himself as a scholar once more. He was not built to fight with soldiers and tactics. His battlefield was the mind, and his skill was with a stylus, not a sword. He would write another book, and in it he would win this war for the Jews. A word written lasts forever. Jotapata would not be forgotten.

"I am glad of your company in this moment," said Yosef. "As I told the general, my mind has been filled with the *Mahsiah*. I would like to hear your thoughts on the subject."

Nicanor studied Yosef carefully. "You're serious?"

"The Lord has seen fit to refuse us His aid. There must be a reason, and perhaps it is the one that you claim – that we ignored your Y'eshua. I'm not claiming to be a convert. But I am interested in learning more."

Nicanor pressed his lips tight. "We must be careful. The Romans despise the Chrestiani. They were blamed for Nero's fire."

"I remember," said Yosef. "I was there. Now, tell me everything."

EPILOGUE

JUDAH'S LITTLE BAND was traveling faster now.
They'd built a rough litter to bear Levi's unconscious form, and bought
an ass to drag it. For money, they had traded news and their armour.
But they'd kept their swords, returned to them contemptuously by
Berenice's men. Their attitude was now clear. They thought the trio was
responsible for the slaughter in Jotapata.

Worse, Judah thought it, too. He could hardly bring himself to
look at his twin. Who was avoiding him just as assiduously, angry that
his own brother thought him capable of such base betrayal.

It doesn't make sense! He didn't want to leave. He wanted to fight!

An unworthy voice said, *But he ran away from Alexandria, too.
And he was out in the hours when the betrayal must have occurred.
Walking, he'd said.*

*No. I can't believe it. It has to be Phannius. Who looked as surprised
as I was...*

The sole comfort was Deborah. She walked with him in silence,
holding his hand and squeezing it back when he needed reassurance.
She'd already been full of apologies.

"I'm such a fool! I should never have come! But I didn't want you
to die without me. I was sure I'd keep you safe, or else die with you. I
never thought—"

"You didn't do this," Judah had told her. "Of anyone, you are
blameless." He'd stroked her hair. "I'm so happy. That's the worst part.
Everyone is dead, and I don't care. I half wish I had been the one. Then
I could have died, and let Phannius take you home."

"You are my home," said Deborah. "If you die, I die with you, whether I stop breathing or no."

After a time he'd chuckled softly. "I suppose they have to let us marry now."

She'd smiled back at him. "Yes. I'm a ruined woman. There's no value to me anymore."

"There is to me."

Now they walked, protected by the shield of Queen Berenice's safe conduct. A few other survivors traveled with them, but most had scattered to friends and relations in Galilee. Only a handful saw the sense of fleeing to Jerusalem, where a real stand might be made. Of those few, they had been forced to abandon three after they became ill from drinking too much water. It was a grave temptation, now that water was plentiful and readily available. Judah himself carried two skins, and every five hundred paces he allowed himself a mouthful to savour.

They walked along in the late summer sun under the bluest of blue skies. All around they could hear birdsong. For a month the only ones they had seen were carrion birds like the black-shouldered kite, whose song was a croak of impatience as he waited for men to die. Now Judah could hear the whistled *vit* of the hooded wheatear, a bird he knew well. It made its home in rocky crevices, and often he had startled them from their nests as he searched quarries for material. Their song wasn't pretty, more like a harsh chattering, but it was music to Judah's ear. He breathed deep, tasting the air of freedom.

Deborah saw his expression. "What are you smiling at?"

"Life," answered Judah simply. "Just life."

They walked on for a time without speaking, and Judah knew that Asher was listening now too. There were thrushes calling, and a group of bulbuls flying in loops off to the right, singing their nasal song. The hum of insects was pleasant and low, not the roaring buzz of flies massed on a dead man. Fluffy white clouds floated across the perfect sun, casting fleeting shadows across their path.

"Nice day," observed Asher.

"Yes," agreed Judah. "It's fine."

Forgetting what they left behind them, ignoring whatever awaited them in Jerusalem, they walked the southbound road with their hearts open. If Jotapata had taught them anything at all, it was to enjoy God's greatest gift, life.

For it was all too brief.

AFTERWORD
HISTORICAL APOLOGIES AND ADDENDUMS

A few words about the story you've read, and the story to come.

As seems to be my wont, this series was conceived as a single book. But almost at once I found I was suffering an over-abundance of good material. The Great Fire of Rome, the Judean War, the Year of the Four Emperors, the fall of the Temple in Jerusalem. I tried, then tried again. Finally I have carved the larger tale into discrete episodes, trusting you to put the mosaic together yourself. It spans decades, weaves in and out of many events, and affects the whole of world history in dozens of ways. And yet in many ways it's a simple story.

Which leads me to a word about the brothers, Judah and Asher. They are entirely fictional, created for dramatic purposes – except that they will merge with historical personages later on. Judah's was the first voice I heard in this tale, and he and Asher shaped it for me. In fact, there are only a handful of fictional figures – Asher, Judah, Curtus, Thorius, and a few minor players. The rest were real enough, though sometimes I created names where none were before.

I found conflicting data as to who was Kohen Gadol when the war began. Several sources list Mattathias ben Theophilus as the High Priest at this time, stating that Ananus ben Ananus was already dead. But Josephus, who was there, clearly puts Ananus in the High Priest's robes. I chose to listen to the man on the ground. Much of Josephus' writings were biased, especially elements in his Jewish War, because he was writing for a Roman audience. I take any motivation he gives anyone (including himself) with several boulders of salt. But for raw facts, like who was where when, there is no reason to doubt him.

That does leave gaps to fill in. There is no mention of Cerialis Rufus being a part of the Jewish War, though another Cerialis served.

Nor is it certain the Flavia he was married to was close kin to Vespasian – many believe she was a cousin, not his daughter. But with the vast confusion these relationships create, it was better to assume the simpler explanation. It is also easier to follow one man than two or five. As Vespasian's son-in-law, it is not a stretch to bring him along to Judea, then send him back in time for the fireworks of 69. Which comes next.

Another problem: Josephus mentions Placidus, but gives us no other name for him. As Placidus is a common cognomen, not a family name, there was nothing to do but choose a family tree and graft him onto it. Trajan, thankfully, went on to sire a famous son, so he at least is decently documented.

This series was conceived in a physical place, one that hasn't even appeared in the story yet, so I will leave off inspiration for a later date.

◆   ◊   ◆

One author to whom I owe the world is Isaac Asimov. If there were only two volumes of research I were allowed to reference, one would be his guide to Shakespeare, which I use in my life as an actor. The other would be his guide to the Bible. Massive, painstakingly researched, methodical, and informative, I simply could not have written this book without it. He makes connections between verses, references history and tradition as well as pure scripture, distinguishing one from another. For a rather agnostic Christian who had never before sat down to read the Bible through, this was an invaluable aid.

I could say as much about Will Durant's Caesar And Christ. Marvelous, complete, meticulous, and at times quite poetic. He made me appreciate Seneca, a poet I have professionally reviled (his plays are atrocious, but at least now I understand why).

Antique authors I owe: Suetonius, Livy, Tacitus, Martial, Cassius Dio, and, naturally, Titus Flavius Josephus himself.

I've read many modern authors while researching this series, but most of them affect later parts of the story. There are only two whose work shapes every corner of this novel. Appropriately, one is an historian, the other a novelist himself.

Desmond Seward's Jerusalem's Traitor: Josephus, Masada, and the Fall of Judea is a gripping read. He is quite clear about so many aspects, and his details, the lifeblood of the novelist, are incredible.

Writing on this topic, I will forever be in the shadow of Lion Feuchtwanger. He wrote the Josephus Trilogy in 1932, and it's still the definitive take on the man. Sometimes I wonder if I depart from his version of Josephus just to prove my independence. But for him, Josephus was the central pivot of the story. Here he is a vital part, but only a part. Still, those books have an incredible wealth of detail, both about the man and about first century Hebrew life. I borrowed often and ferociously.

A final note on sources. When looking at Hebrew prayers for the dead, I chose the *E-l Malei Rachamim* over the more traditional *Kaddish*, despite some sources asserting that the former was a medieval invention. I chose it for the three lines added for martyrs to Israel, which seems especially important in this time and place. That the prayer is used today for soldiers in the IDF also swayed my choice.

◆ ◊ ◆

This book would not have happened without a literary agent by the name of Dan Conaway. As we discussed ideas for my next novel, he asked a simple question: was there a place I wanted to write about? I quietly scoffed at the idea, but felt compelled nonetheless to answer him. So in the pack of four story concepts I sent him, I unenthusiastically dropped in a line about a church. He wrote back telling me to look at that one harder. Dutifully, I did, and just a little bit of scraping revealed this novel. Proving, I suppose, that so-called inspiration can come from skilful manipulation. Thank you, Dan.

If this novel has one father, it has many aunts and uncles, those friends, mentors, and colleagues who gently ripped it to shreds to watch it rise again, stronger than before. Firstly, doctors Steve Pickering, Kevin Theis, and Alice Austen. These three and I are known collectively as Shanghai Low Theatricals, a collaborative writing endeavor focused mostly on theatre. They graciously took time from their various projects to read and critique early drafts, much to the novel's benefit. Also Nona Bennett and Sherry Murphy, who each have more religious knowledge than I could ever claim. And Stephanie Heller and Mike Nussbaum were other early, enthusiastic readers.

Huge thanks to Rick Sordelet. Not Epic enough yet? Just you wait, you bastard. I'll make this thing impossible to stage.

I always say the best question to ask authors is, 'Who do you read?' I usually point to my friends MJ Rose, CW Gortner, and Michelle Moran, as well as Dorothy Dunnett, Bernard Cornwell, and Raphael Sabatini. Here let me add Colleen McCullough. My understanding of Rome began with her Masters Of Rome series, and hers is still the voice in my head when I write Roman characters.

Dan Slater and Katy Ardans at Amazon have been a tremendous help in everything, and I am grateful for their cheerful patience, however badly I tried it.

Rob McLean designed the cover, which I love (no, Erin, not because it looks like me!). The image is of Bernini's *David*. Unlike Michelangelo's *David*, who is pausing before the famous throw, or Donatello's *David*, who is cheekily standing victorious after, Bernini's depiction of the young shepherd catches him mid-throw. It's a statue I admire, and it came to me again and again when I was writing about Judah.

Many thanks to John Lobur. In 7th grade we took the same Latin 1 class. He got it, I didn't, and he's gone on to become a professor of Latin. He helped me with a couple of lines in THE MASTER OF VERONA, but here his help has naturally been much greater. Clearly he is the expert, I the layman, and any mistakes within these covers are mine, never his. *Gratias*, John!

Many thanks to Constace Cedras for her 11th hour edits.

Another friend in need of thanks is Tara Sullivan. The godmother to our children, she has been the outside reader for four novels now, and continues to be a voice of enthusiasm. Also, she takes the kids out to play when Mommy is away and Daddy needs to jot something down.

Thanks to my parents, Al & Jill. I'm curious to know what my mother thinks of the series as a whole. And I'd have no appreciation of Rome at all if not for a car-trip with my father when I was eighteen. If only we'd known it was that simple...

I embarked on this series just before the birth of my daughter, Evelyn. Again, babies bring good things. And then there's Dash, who has been the soul of patience. This book was finished on his sixth birthday.

Which brings us to my wife. Jan stood with me in the place where this series was inspired, and she has continued to inspire it since. She laments that I've carved it up, so I have promised her that one day I will put all the pieces together, if only for her. Like Judah, I don't need to make an oath. For Jan, my word will always be true.

The next novel is entitled COLOSSUS: THE FOUR EMPERORS.

AVE,
DB

Appendix
Rome's Legions

For those interested in (or confused about) Roman legions, here are a few definitions.

A Roman Legion was made up of about 5,500 men. The core unit of a legion is the century. Originally a century, as its name suggests, was made up of 100 men. But by the late Republic and early Empire it was actually 80 soldiers and their support staff. Eighty men make a CENTURY. Six centuries make a COHORT. Ten cohorts make a LEGION, with the lead cohort being double-sized. That's 5,280 men. Add 120 cavalry men and around 100 noncombatants – engineers, cooks, etc. – and you reach 5,500.

Each legion had a golden eagle, the *aquila*, carried by the *aquilifer*. They also had a flag with their symbol on it. The flag was called a *signum*, or a *vexillum*, and was carried by the vexillifer. Sometimes a legion would detach a smaller unit. When this happened, the main legion would keep the eagle, while the detachment marched out under the *vexillum*. Thus the name for the detachment became a *vexillation*.

Legionaries were supposed to be citizens, but by this time recruiting standards were winked at. Many locals were recruited with the promise that if they served Rome well for between sixteen and twenty-five years, they would retire as full Roman citizens.

Some common terms to do with legions:

LEGATE (*legatus*) – Either the legion's commander-in-chief, or else senior commanders under a specific general. For example, Titus is senior legate of the Fifteenth Legion, under the command of his father Vespasian, who oversees several legions. A legate was usually a senator or from a senatorial family, as leading a legion was often a large part of climbing the cursus honorum.

TRIBUNE OF THE SOLDIERS (*tribunus militum*) – Not to be confused with Tribune of the Plebs, whose veto power had by this point been absorbed by the Princeps. A military tribune was a staff officer, often in his twenties. The term originates from Rome's earliest days, when each of Rome's tribes would send a representative to be a junior officer in the army. Usually 6 tribunes to a legion, the most senior of whom was second in command to the legate.

TRIBUNUS AUGUSTICLAVIUS – Like the military tribune, this was a staff officer, but from an Equestrian family. Usually 5 to a legion.

CENTURION (*centurio*) – Professional, career officer, the backbone of the Roman army. He could be elected, appointed, or promoted from the ranks. Caesar promoted men of valour, and many historians record centurions as being the first over a wall. The most wounded, most decorated, most valuable element in a legion. A general would think nothing of losing all his tribunes, but weep outright if he lost a centurion. 60-66 centurions in any legion (depending on the breakdown of the extra men in the first cohort).

OPTIO - A centurion's right-hand, carrying out orders and enforcing discipline. Basically a centurion in training. 60-66 optios to a legion.

DECURIAN - Cavalry commanders. A legion's cavalry was divided into four units of 40 horsemen, so 4 decurians to every legion.

MORE DAVID BLIXT NOVELS
FROM SORDELET INK

The Star-Cross'd Series

THE MASTER OF VERONA
VOICE OF THE FALCONER
FORTUNE'S FOOL
THE PRINCE'S DOOM
VARNISHED FACES & OTHER STAR-CROSS'D STORIES

The Colossus Series

COLOSSUS: STONE & STEEL
COLOSSUS: THE FOUR EMPERORS

and coming soon

COLOSSUS: WAIL OF THE FALLEN
COLOSSUS: TRIUMPH OF THE JEWS

HER MAJESTY'S WILL

Visit
WWW.DAVIDBLIXT.COM
for more information.

EXPLICIT, DEO GRATIAS!

Printed in Great Britain
by Amazon